D0888641

THREAD OF GOLD

A Novel

By

ANNE DA VIGO

Published by Quill Driver Press, P.O. Box 5272 Sacramento, CA 95817

ISBN 978-0-9745722-1-5

Printed in USA

Cover design by Karen Phillips
Interior design by Vanessa Perez

Author Photo by Joan Seitz

For Tony

1

Cora
April 2000

The murder-suicide on Sutter Street was the beginning of a lousy day that got worse. The beep on Cora's police department pager awoke her from an uncomfortable slumber on the couch. Light was beginning to creep through the fog, and the early morning news rattled out of the television. Her thin, leopard-print bathrobe was open, exposing her thighs to the cold.

It had already been a terrible week. On Monday, she'd covered the deaths of three people, including a child, in a domestic homicide. Another two had died in a separate domestic on Tuesday.

Her editor at the *San Francisco Standard* called domestic homicides "misdemeanor murders." Less important, he meant, than a murder-for-hire, an Asian gang killing, or a gay hate crime. In his opinion, domestics were simply family squabbles gone bad.

By the time Cora and her photographer, Scott Hewett, left the scene, it was half past eight. Fog still hung thick and cottony over the pavement and penetrated the narrow spaces between houses. Damp, oily condensate, tinted pink from the bloody sidewalk, ran sluggishly into the storm drain. Cora found herself speaking in a low voice as if normal volume might heap some further pain or indignity on the deceased mother, whose dead lover lay beside her on the concrete. They were covered by matching blue tarps.

Over Cora's head, the snarl of utility lines was as dense as a hunter's net, and her nerves were flicking like hot wires. Facts, names, and interviews were recorded on mini-cassette and scribbled in her narrow reporter's notebook. The grandmother of the surviving child had taken the little girl away, tucked under the flap of her coat; television satellite trucks had left, but Cora ached, her hands trembling and her breath seeming trapped in her chest.

She sat in the passenger seat of Scott's Explorer with the heater turned up and her coat collar in a stranglehold around her neck. Things would be better, she told herself, once she switched on the computer, as soon as her fingers began moving on the keys.

"That was a fucking waste of time," Scott said. "They won't use art with a ten-inch story." He jerked the wheel to avoid a double-parked UPS truck. They were passing the Burger King where the Winterland Ballroom had once stood. In the 1970s, Cora had watched a Grateful Dead concert there when she was dating her adulterous ex-husband, Stephen.

"Ten inches again? Who told you?"

"When has Manion ever given play to a domestic?"

For Monday's domestic murder, she'd been given a ten-inch hole on an inside page; for Tuesday, nine. Today a young mother had been shot to death by her lover, who then committed suicide, all in front of their two-year-old daughter. The woman was thirty-three, her lover thirty-eight. They had parents, schools, careers, successes, and huge, shattering failures. Ten inches of type.

Scott dropped her downtown in front of the *Standard* and she watched him nose back into traffic on his way to another assignment. The newsroom was mostly empty; reporters were attending meetings and covering their beats. Editors didn't arrive until later, when there were completed stories to work on.

Five clocks frowned down from the wall: Beijing, Tehran, London, New York, San Francisco.

She tossed her knapsack on the desk in her nine-by-nine cubicle. Twenty years ago, when she'd first begun reporting at a little weekly on the Peninsula, newsrooms had all had side-by-side desks where the reporters traded gossip and half-listened to each others' telephone conversations. Now she worked on a plastic surface in a square box, separated from her colleagues on either side by six-foot-high fabric-covered panels.

Heat bloomed on her chest and crept up her neck. Her heart beat against her ribs. A hot flash. Her cheeks felt as though they would burst into flame. She sank into her chair, bent over her desk, and rested her forehead on her arm.

When her pager had beeped at 5:30 a.m., she'd fished a pair of jeans and a long-sleeved pullover from the bedroom's pile of dirty clothes. She smelled her stale shirt now, enhanced by her body heat and the cubicle's enclosed space. Around her, voices were muffled and footsteps whispered on the carpet. As her heart slowed, she grew sleepy. The evening before, she'd worked late, writing an updated take on the double homicide for the final edition, arriving home after ten. Instead of cooking dinner, she'd drunk some Lodi red. She wished she had a glass now. Her breathing deepened, and in a few minutes, she was asleep.

The telephone interrupted a dream about her mother, one she hadn't dreamed for many years, a disturbing one where she tried to plug a hole in her mother's chest with a towel. It was a struggle to open her heavy eyelids, and her mouth was so dry she could barely swallow. Her computer cursor blinked, sticky notes demanded her attention, and she was encircled by piles of reports, press releases, old notebooks, and yellowed newspapers. She rubbed the throbbing spot on her forehead where it had rested on the wire binding of a notebook. The phone buzzed again. Her nails scrabbled against the handset. This could be Nathan calling from Boston College. Her voice cracked as she tried to say hello.

"Cora, it's me." Christopher Myerling, the newsroom assistant. His breathy whisper sent static into her ear. "Manion is on his way. Look sharp."

Cora opened her eyes wide enough, she hoped, to feign alertness. Over the top of the partition, the San Francisco clock read 5 p.m.

"Brooks. What the hell's the matter with you? I open the damn *Chronicle* this morning and read about the police chief's private party detail run by officers on overtime. A story you didn't have. Then the copy desk tells me you've missed deadline again."

She swiveled to face him. Metro Editor Stu Manion wore his upper-management wannabe uniform: tasseled shoes, charcoal slacks, red tie, and long-sleeved white shirt with cruelly starched cuffs and collar.

"Almost done," she said.

"Bullshit. You've been sleeping on your notebook. There's a mark on your face."

She cupped her hand over it as if it might tell her something. The dream was centered there, a beating lump of feeling. If she pressed it, she might cry.

"I worked overtime last night, then got called out early on the Sutter Street murder-suicide. Scott has photos."

"I know. I've seen the art. It's in the computer. Your story isn't."

Her legs trembled, and she pressed her knees together. Strange, how murder scene photos are called *art* in the news business. Maybe it was the color that made it art, the blue tarps, the clots of red...She pressed her temples with her fingers.

Manion picked at the knot on his red tie. "I've got Clinton in town for a Gore fundraiser, and a multi-million-dollar coke bust on the 280. I don't need this grief—chasing a lazy reporter over a misdemeanor murder."

She repressed the desire to scream. Domestics were the real stories. The important ones. Over her years on the police beat, she had been drawn to these everyday tragedies with the fascination of a jumper looking at the Bay from the Golden Gate. Readers needed to know the victims of domestics could so easily be them. Their hearts could be sweetly and achingly exercised by love, only to be torn apart by disappointment, mental illness, and bad history.

"This one's different," she said, looking for an angle to get more space. "It was a Lesbian couple, fairly unusual for a domestic." She felt ashamed to use the couple's sexuality to sell the story, but it cried to be told. They all did.

"Seven inches," he said.

The red in Manion's tie expanded to fill her vision until she saw nothing but the blood on the sidewalk: fine red spatters, trickles, even congealed lumps. The tremors in her legs moved upward to her gut. She'd felt this way during the '89 Loma Prieta quake, as if she'd taken a misstep and tumbled into space. She fought a wave of nausea. When was the last time she'd eaten? Garlic fries at lunch yesterday.

She turned her back on him. "The story will be done in thirty minutes."

His tassels clicked against his shoes as he walked away.

She flipped open her notebook and set her fingers on the keys. She'd typed a couple of words before Myerling stopped by her cubicle and flung himself into her visitor chair. She guessed the newsroom eavesdroppers already had filled him in on the dustup. The only gossips worse than journalists were cops.

"Don't feel too bad. The Great Stu is in a stew." He bit into a tuna sandwich partially wrapped in white deli paper, the fish smell making her queasy. "The judge has given the go-ahead for the merger, and I've been hearing layoff rumors all day. Liz Jonas from KABC called for comment."

"And the Rolex crew gave a statement that circulation is holding steady. The *San Francisco Standard* is well positioned in the market."

Christopher stopped chewing. "Very good."

Employees had gone through two rounds of layoffs last year, and fear hovered in the newsroom like white noise.

On his way out, Myerling tossed the remains of his sandwich in her wastebasket. "If you hear anything, let me know."

She flipped through her notebook to the details she'd jotted down that morning at the scene. Her handwriting looked unfamiliar. The pages were rippled as if tears, not morning fog, had touched the paper. She tapped the keys, her typing filled with errors. She backspaced, made typos in the corrections. Her usual flow, notes to brain to computer—a transition that always had come easily—was disrupted. Her fingers seemed swollen as she set down, word by word, the lives of a woman and a child, and the lover who had killed the mother and then herself. Everything and nothing in seven paragraphs. She clicked Save, added the slug—Sutter Street Murder—to identify the story, and sent it to the copy editor's file.

She rang Nathan. His cell phone went directly to his mailbox. She hadn't been able to connect with him for two weeks, and the messages he'd left on her phone about midterm exams and a ski trip to Stowe were curt and distant. She dreaded going home, where signs of him were everywhere. She couldn't bring herself to move his muddy running shoes from the back door to his closet or toss out the flabby toothbrush in his bathroom.

She'd clicked off her computer and zipped her jacket when Manion rang her extension. "See me before you leave."

The newsroom cubicles, which had been empty when she arrived this morning, were full of reporters at this hour; deadline for the second edition was close. Under her feet, the floor vibrated with the rotation of the huge presses in the basement as they churned out the first edition. She passed Myerling and three or four reporters talking in low voices near the fax machine. When they spotted her, they fell silent.

A hot flash started in her chest and crept upward until her neck burned. Sweat dampened her shirt and made it smell worse. The indignities of being forty-five: an ungrateful son, a husband who'd found a younger woman, a body run amok.

Manion was polishing his loafers, one foot propped on the lip of an open desk drawer. "Brooks, I'm taking you off police and putting you on special assignment."

"Hey, I apologize for falling asleep. I swear it won't happen again."

He stopped rubbing his shoe and picked up a brown file folder. "D'Arcy sent down a story idea."

She groaned. A DFS, newsroom acronym for a D'Arcy Fucking Special. The publisher's assignments never had a scrap of news value: shameless promotions for Stanford, his alma mater; puff pieces about his wife, DeDe's, charity gala for the disease du jour; crushingly boring stuff about his prize-winning cattle herd. The bovines were located on D'Arcy's showplace farm in the San Joaquin Valley, and any reporter assigned a cow story was subjected to weeks of mooing sounds and manure jokes.

"I can't," she said promptly. "George Chan and I are only halfway through the data on the SFPD's handling of domestic homicides: how many incident reports they receive on the same family, how they're handled, how many result in fatalities."

"George will have to finish it on his own."

"George is a computer and numbers guy. He needs someone who can write."

"I'm putting Traci Knapp on your beat. She'll be able to step in and help him out."

"Traci doesn't have any background on the issue. She'll let it drop." She looked into his face to see if groveling would help, but he gazed over her head.

"Traci is a fine reporter. Bring her up to date and introduce her to your law enforcement contacts by Friday."

An acid taste rose in her mouth. "She doesn't need much in the way of introductions. She's sleeping with the captain from Bayside Station."

"That's just a rumor, and Traci denies it." Finished with his shoes, Manion wadded up the polish rag and tossed it in the wastebasket. He handed her a clipping from the folder. "D'Arcy wants an investigative piece to follow on this *New York Times* story."

Cora ignored the clip. "I can't believe you're giving me the velvet kiss-off. I've worked ten hours of overtime and it's only Wednesday. Is this shit assignment because I took a nap?"

What was the matter with her, mouthing off to an editor? She wanted the old days before corporate journalism, when being aggressive was an admirable trait.

Manion massaged the leather arms of his chair. "You're always whining we don't give you enough time and space. Here's your chance."

Her eyes widened, and crusts from her recent sleep scratched her lids. "I get it. You think I'll screw up so you can fire me. Save one layoff."

His face was as smooth as whole milk, and she knew she was right.

"Have Christopher make flight reservations and get you a travel advance," he said.

"Where am I going?"

"New York State. The Finger Lakes."

Cora scanned the clipping. She saw a man posing with a large black-and-white cow. Two ribbons fluttered from her halter.

"D'Arcy's gone mental."

"He owns the paper. He can assign any damn thing he wants."

"An investigation about cows?"

"There's a murder or two. That should make you happy."

"Cows or humans?"

"Possibly both," Manion said.

———

Cora rode the bus home. It swayed on the turns and jounced over the potholes. She braced her knee against the seat in front of her to prevent sliding into the aisle. She'd been off base with Manion, but she hadn't been able to stop herself. Although her emotions had always come to the surface quickly, this was something more. She was sleeping badly, and bothered by dreams.

The bus arrived at her stop. When she stepped onto the sidewalk, a shroud of fog settled around her. The bus pulled away and farted exhaust in her face. She crossed Judah Street and plodded up the hill on Thirty-first. Her jogging shoes felt like lead galoshes. As she walked, she counted the sidewalk's uneven slabs and pieces of broken concrete.

Thirty-first was empty, suspended in the hush of dusk, when life moves indoors. When Nathan was a baby, she'd knelt beside the bathtub at this hour, rubbing lather over his soft skin. While she bathed her son, Stephen had rinsed the dishes. The clink of the plates as he wedged them in the dishwasher was a comforting song, the theme of their married life. They had been so close, so related then.

They'd met when she was a reporter for a San Mateo daily, and he was a law student at Santa Clara University. While he was crossing an intersection on his rebuilt Norton motorcycle, she'd hit him with her VW bug. She'd leaped out of the car, panicked that he was dead. He'd broken his foot, and after it was set in the emergency room, she took him home with her, mostly because she didn't have insurance and wanted to avoid a lawsuit. She cooked meals for him and drove him to school while his foot healed, and during that time they'd fallen in love. At least that was what she'd thought at the time.

The unoiled hinges on her gate groaned. When she looked up the front staircase to her bay window, a ripple of blue and green flashed between the curtains. She'd forgotten to turn off the TV.

Her knees gave way, and she sat down heavily on the bottom step. God, she couldn't take another night with the television: endless advertisements, dirty couch cushions, her leopard-print bathrobe worn thin in the elbows. Clammy moisture from the stair tread soaked into the seat of her pants. She tucked the tail of her jacket under her thighs.

Her new assignment might well be the end of her career. Only a handful of San Francisco readers cared about a story set in the Finger Lakes of New York State. D'Arcy was pushing the investigation because one of the dead men, Sean O'Brien, had been his friend. Even fewer readers were interested in the world of prize-winning dairy cattle. On the off chance she was able to write the story with a human angle that attracted readers, the *Standard*'s editors would suck all the juice out of it with their nitpicking corrections.

Not only that, it was a bad time to be away from the newsroom. Unless the company's lawyers could convince the court to block the merger, layoffs were coming. The most vulnerable staffers in the last round had been those away on assignment or working in satellite offices. They were outsiders, unable to look the managers in the eye day after day and make them feel guilty. Her replacement, Traci Knapp, worked in the South Bay satellite office, so she was seizing the initiative to edge Cora out.

D'Arcy's folder containing the *NYT* cow story was stashed in her knapsack. While she sat, hands tucked up into the cuffs of her jacket, the folder seemed to double her over with its weight. She'd given the clipping a brief glance. It involved O'Brien and a second man, who also raised prize-winning dairy cattle. They died within days of each other, supposedly suicides, but several strange twists threw doubt on the official ruling. She had research to do before she arrived in New York.

Gulls screamed in the west, nearer the ocean. A car stereo thumped close by. Wires hummed overhead with electrical power and telephone pulses. The horror of this afternoon's dream returned. Her throat still ached with the stifled cry that had lodged there, looking over her mother's wound.

Why was she dreaming about her now? Alice Macpherson Brooks had abandoned Cora when she was six, run off with another man, moved to Maryland, and died a year later giving birth to his child.

Cora's clearest memory of her mother was watching her at the kitchen table, writing. Whether it was a poem or a letter, Cora didn't know, but something she did know: Alice didn't write a single page to Cora in the year before she died. What kind of woman, what kind of mother, leaves her daughter without a word?

Rather than enter the house, Cora opened the side door to the garage and switched on the single hanging bulb. The chill air smelled of the gasoline that had spilled down the side of her Toyota the last time she'd filled it up. She edged around the hood to reach a bank of shelves. Above her loomed stacks of battered cardboard cartons stuffed with old bank statements, Nathan's moldy baby clothes, Stephen's yellowed law school notes. She scrambled up onto the lowest shelf and shoved the boxes this way and that.

A misstep nearly sent her tumbling to the concrete floor, but she managed to cling to the upper shelf. Her breath sounded loud in the cramped, dusky space. She found them, four boxes she'd shoved up here twenty-five years ago after her father died. She pushed the cartons to the floor and jumped down.

The brown tape that secured the box flaps was curled with age, and the flaps popped open, sending dust flying around her head. She knelt on the oil-spotted floor and scrabbled through the dirty leavings from her childhood home: a pair of Roy Brooks's run-over work boots, a tarnished high school baseball trophy, U.S. Merchant Marine discharge papers, overdue bills long ago settled in probate. Her father's stink still saturated his belongings: coarse Lava soap, which had cleansed his hands of printer's ink after a shift, and Jack Daniel's, which had anesthetized him for the rest of the night. She scrubbed her sleeve across her nose.

She dumped the contents of the boxes on the floor. A stealthy wind from outside crept under the car and fingered the pages.

There it was. When she was eight or nine, she'd been looking for a postage stamp in the desk, and had found the only remaining photo of her mother. It was wedged in the side of a drawer, hiding under the pencil tray. Cora had felt ashamed to look at it, as if she'd opened the bathroom door on a stranger. In later years, she had returned to the drawer, brushed off the crumbs of pencil eraser, and held the picture in her cupped hands.

The black and white was smaller than she remembered, the size of a postcard. Its edges were stained the yellow of old teeth. Her mother was very young, probably sixteen. She sat on the porch of a two-story building with peeling paint. The ground floor housed Macpherson's General Store, the name written in curved, rotund lettering on the window, a pretentious font that suggested unfulfilled expectations.

Her mother's knees touched each other primly under the light fabric of her skirt, and her hair—Cora remembered it, a vivid red-gold—was rolled up on the sides and secured with combs. Alice didn't look directly at the camera but off to the left, as if she searched for a glimpse of someone over the photographer's shoulder. Cora studied the photo for a resemblance. Not in the straight, smooth hair. Cora's was tangled like her father's, and thick as underbrush. Not in height or build. Alice's breasts and hips created dark, curvaceous shadows in the photo. Cora was tall and skinny.

She tipped it to catch more light from the low-wattage bulb. Alice's worst feature was her long nose with a slight bump in the middle. Cora rubbed the thickened cartilage of her own sizable nose.

A hot flash began on her chest and crept upward. Her mother had grown up in the same area where she was headed for the story. Outside, she heard the thump of wheels as her next-door neighbor rolled his trash container to the curb for tomorrow's pickup. She stuffed the picture in her jacket pocket, intending to drop it in her own can in the morning.

Inside the house, she unwound the rubber band she'd used from this morning's *Standard* to corral her hair. Her scalp was sore. She lay down on her unmade bed and caught the smell of her dirty clothes. Before she closed her eyes, she noticed the message light blinking on her bedside phone. She pushed Replay. It was Nathan. She'd missed his call.

2

—

Abby
November 1916

Abby stood on the porch and watched Seamus O'Brien's wagon bounce along the frozen road. He was driving pell-mell, the horse's iron shoes ringing against the stones. Crows cawed as they fluttered through the air like old leaves. Abby opened her eyes wide, but it was too dark to see Seamus's face. She shoved her hands deeper into the pockets of her woolen overcoat and danced on her toes to warm them.

Her heart pressed against her ribs as if it wanted to fly from her chest. Seamus was almost twenty-five, and she was only thirteen, but she knew. The wagon creaked when it pulled up in front of the store. Seamus wrapped the reins around the brake handle. The wooden porch planks sank a little as he stepped out. The smell of tobacco and manure clung to his coat. She felt dizzy, and the horizon tipped.

"Ah. There's my Tiger Stripes," he said.

"Why do you always call me that?"

Seamus slid his hand across the top of her head. "The sun streaks your hair yellow. Like an African tiger." A strand caught in a callus on his palm, and she felt a sharp tug on her scalp.

The store's bell tinkled. Her father, Jack Macpherson, came outside and propped the screen open with a cast-iron boot scraper. Seamus moved a step away from her.

"I've got your order ready, all except the kerosene," her father said. "Next week for certain."

He went back inside. Through the window Abby saw the men huddled around the pot-bellied stove look toward the porch. They turned back to the heat, and in a minute her father emerged from the storeroom, bending under a sack of flour he carried over one shoulder. He grunted as he lowered the flour into the back of the wagon. He was as tall as Seamus, but thin and ropy.

A furrow appeared between Jack's shaggy eyebrows as he studied Seamus and Abby. "Run upstairs, Missy. Your dinner's waiting."

Abby backed slowly inside but lingered near the window. Standing on one leg, she rubbed the back of her stocking with her high-top shoe. Store odors mingled like the ingredients in a pot of stew: coffee and tea, onions, cinnamon, pickles, kerosene, and coal. Tonight there were other smells—wet wool socks and the dark, smoky tang of Scotch whiskey. She knew to button her lip about the whiskey. It came from her father's secret distillery in the hills. When he sold it in the evenings after store hours, Mama refused to work at the counter.

While the men around the stove argued about Kaiser Wilhelm's chances of conquering France, Abby traced the letters painted on the window. Macpherson's General Store. She pressed her mouth against the cool glass. How would it feel to kiss Seamus?

Outside, Seamus and Jack talked, bodies tense like two dogs with their hair stiff on their necks. Abby's Papa folded his arms across his chest. "... any damn guns," he was saying. Oil lamps inside the store cast a weak glow onto the porch, lighting his cheekbones but leaving his eyes in shadow.

Seamus slapped his gloves against his leg. "You could take them from the armory in Cortland. You're high up in the Guard. No one would know."

"Thievery! Not me."

Abby's breath fogged an oval on the window.

"I've promised my uncles. The time has come for freedom in Ireland, and I'll not disappoint them," Seamus said.

"You'll get no weapons from me to help a gang of thieves and traitors." The bell jangled and the door slammed. "Abby, go upstairs and eat your dinner." Instead of obeying, she crawled behind the counter along the plank floor until she touched a hundred-pound sack of potatoes, then propped her back against it. Her sanctuary was dark and cozy; she liked the smell of dirt and burlap. Saturday mornings she scooped exactly five pounds of flour and sugar from the bins into paper sacks and tied them with string. That was the busiest day in the store. Families drove their wagons from miles around to lay in staples for the week. On weekday afternoons Mama let her walk to Grandma Macpherson's or play at the creek with her twin cousins, Emily and Edna Spellman.

She heard Jack load more boxes onto the dolly for Seamus and trundle them over the threshold. Beside the stove, George Wright recounted a story in his high, staccato voice. Abby knew it was obscene by his oily tone, about a salesman who rapped on the door of a farmhouse during a rainstorm. When George finished, the men's laughter rumbled, deep and coarse.

She pressed her eye to a crack in the counter. The stove glowed red. She imagined she was in the wilds of Scotland among a clan of Highlanders, like in her father's stories.

During a lull in the talk, Abby heard Jack and Seamus again. She tiptoed out the back door, forgetting to close it, and ran around the side of the store, under the bare, twisted vines covering the grape arbor. Her shoe caught on a rock, and she scrambled to save herself from falling. Panting, she peered around the corner. Her father had gone inside.

"Seamus," she whispered. The horse stamped its hooves and jangled its harness.

"Why are you ghosting about in the dark?" he said.

Up close, she felt out of breath. The fingers of his gloves protruded from the pocket of his heavy wool coat, as if reaching out to her. "Are you and my father mortal enemies?"

"You heard something?" He pinched her shoulder. When she winced, he stepped back. His voice softened. "A wee disagreement about business. Nothing to worry about."

"Are you trying to help the Germans get guns?" Abby shivered, her body tight as one of her father's violin strings.

Seamus leaned over, so near she saw the icy gleam in his eyes. "Will you grant me a very large favor, Tiger Stripes?" Her childish nickname sounded like hard candy on his tongue.

Her cheeks burned. She wanted him to need her.

"I'm helping some very brave people, not Germans, but people who love freedom, like us. It's our secret, all right?" He ran his forefinger gently across her lower lip.

3

Cora

April 2000

Cora had slept only a few minutes on the red-eye from San Francisco to JFK. During the four-hour drive to Cortland, she passed through a landscape as stark as a black-and-white newspaper photo, all gray hills and sullen sky and clumps of dirty snow. It was a noncommittal landscape, waiting for spring.

She kept the heater on as she drove, so when she got out of the car in Cortland, she was surprised at the chill. Almost May, and the temperature was still close to freezing. She huddled in her jacket as she wheeled her suitcase up the steps of the inn's wide porch.

In her state of sleep-deprived hyperawareness, Seneca House bed and breakfast seemed a Victorian nightmare. The legs on the claw-foot table in the lobby looked as though they could take off running into the jungle. The gold tassels that tied back the velvet drapes were worthy of a stripper's nipples.

Upstairs in Cora's room, Debbie Landesdowne, the B and B owner, whipped away a cobweb on the cherry armoire with her feather duster. She was as round as two balls of yeast dough and smelled of cinnamon.

"Are you here on business?" Debbie asked.

Cora hesitated. Cortland County's population was only fifty thousand. She wanted to chat with people and get a feel for the place before word got out she was investigating the death of a prominent citizen and his business partner.

Debbie's husband knocked on the half-open bedroom door. With a practiced motion, he swung Cora's suitcase onto the luggage rack. "Name's Paul," he said. "She's Bed; I'm Breakfast. Wait 'til you eat my French toast. You're in for a treat."

"I don't eat breakfast," Cora said.

"No coffee refills unless you try it." He grinned. "See you tomorrow between seven and nine."

Cora unzipped her suitcase, a hint to her hostess to get lost.

"I hope your business in Cortland goes well," Debbie said. "You're here on business, I think you said."

"I didn't say." Cora pawed through her rucksack for a bottle of eye drops.

Debbie's gaze flicked over Cora's tape recorder and laptop, visible in her open rucksack. "What is it you're going to be doing here?"

"Researching my family history." It was a strange answer, and Cora was surprised when it jumped out of her mouth. She didn't give a damn about her family history. Roy Brooks was a drunk and Alice Brooks—who knew? Maybe someday she'd find her grave site. Here, she intended to spend two days, maybe three, confirming that the dead guys actually did kill themselves, then fly back to California to see if she could save her job.

"My family's lived in this area for a hundred and fifty years," Debbie said. "I'm the immediate past president of the county historical society, so if you need any help, I'd be happy to assist."

Cora closed the velvet drapes that Debbie had just opened. The half-light was an empty, soothing gray that made her ache to lie down on the bed's puffy duvet.

"We serve New York State sherry in the parlor at 4:30 every evening," Debbie said.

After she left, Cora considered unpacking, but instead left her clothes in the suitcase. The trip had drained her. She emptied her jacket pockets of her itinerary, her cell phone, and various scraps of paper. Among them, falling on the marble dresser as carelessly as a crumpled receipt, was her mother's photograph.

She'd forgotten the photo. The two days since that night in the garage had been a tumble of last-minute details: calling all her usual beat contacts, finishing up a couple of weekend thumb-suckers, and updating her list of sources for Traci. Saturday, she'd packed a suitcase and hopped on the midnight flight.

She smoothed the photo on the desktop, bits of old paper flaking off the edges. It showed Alice sitting on the porch, one hand propped on the weathered planks. In the background, light reflecting off the front window, hung with a sign advertising Daniel Webster Flour.

Her cell phone buzzed.

"Mom, it's me."

At last. She sank down on the bed. "Nathan, I've been so worried."

Nathan snickered. "Right, Mom. You've been waiting by the phone."

Cora pressed her thumb and forefinger against her eyelids to keep from crying. It had been their game during his senior year in high school. Who is your date, she'd say, pretending to be the controlling mother. Is she a Presbyterian? How much does her father make? What is her grade point average? And Nathan would respond, She's a devil-worshipping slut whose father is a drug kingpin. But then he'd laugh, and tell her about this girl, or friend, or party.

She struggled to sound casual. "I've come East to make sure you're doing your laundry and wearing pajamas."

"Really? You're on the Right Coast?"

"For a few days. How about Saturday in New York? Ten a.m. at the Metropolitan Museum. We can get a hotel somewhere and stay the night."

"Deal," he said.

Cora wanted to talk longer, but she couldn't keep her eyes open. She sank into the duvet and slept through the night, oblivious

to Debbie's knock at the door to alert her that sherry hour was about
to begin.

4

Cora

April 2000

The next morning, she rose early and pulled on her ratty leopard robe. A stack of news clippings and Internet printouts sat on the desk, material she'd gathered to prepare her for the 8:30 interview with State Police Major Del Somer. His investigative unit, headquartered in the department's cluster of Southern Tier counties, had handled the O'Brien case.

Details were remarkably few: Sean O'Brien, a prominent Holstein breeder and dairyman in the Otisco Valley, north of Cortland, had created a profitable sideline judging cattle shows. Organizers of prestigious livestock exhibitions around the world paid O'Brien to serve on their judging panels, and Cora's publisher, Trevor D'Arcy, had first met him at a show in the Bay Area.

Over a four-month period the prior fall, O'Brien had purchased three prize-winning cows from Franklin Santerra, another dairyman who lived in Seneca County, an hour's drive to the west along Cayuga Lake. The cows, insured for $50,000, $85,000 and $250,000 respectively, had each died within weeks of the sale.

The death of the third cow, with the fancy name of Holland's Queen Beatrice, top winner at a national show the previous year, had sparked a fraud investigation by Great American Fidelity. The inquiry dragged on throughout February and into March. On March 23, O'Brien committed suicide by swallowing strychnine. Four days later, Santerra had blown his head off with a shotgun.

After she finished reading the background, her stomach was queasy, so she skipped coffee and got dressed. Outside, the chill air slapped her cheeks. The sidewalk in front of Seneca House was glassy with spring melt that had frozen overnight. In town, a few remnants of dirt-caked snow still crouched under the trees.

The weather matched her reception at the state police. After she'd shivered in the poorly heated lobby for forty-five minutes, Major Del Somer appeared behind the bulletproof glass and signaled the duty officer to buzz her in.

"Sorry I'm late." He didn't offer his hand. Rather than escorting her to the elevator, he loped ahead of her up a back staircase littered with cigarette butts ground out by the heels of closet smokers.

In his third-floor office, Cora stamped her feet to jump-start her circulation. "You need to weatherproof your lobby. I could've waited in the morgue and been warmer."

"We New Yorkers are used to the cold." Somer removed his Stetson by pinching the front of the crown. The hat, which she assumed was against the state police's uniform policy, seemed an odd attempt to brand himself a Western-style lawman more than a thousand miles east of the Mississippi.

The hatband had rumpled his gray hair, and he smoothed it down. He stood six feet two, looked about fifty-five, and packed his weapon in an underarm holster beneath his suit jacket. Despite some extra weight around his midriff, he moved quickly.

His desk was large, but constructed of some cheap dark wood. A battered leather desk chair looked as though it had survived a number of management backsides. The remaining space was occupied by a conference table and eight chairs. The bookshelves held only penal and civil code books and departmental operations manuals, and the walls were bare of the usual wooden plaques, paperweights, and other tokens of public and private esteem.

The depression that had dragged her down all morning lifted. Questions popped in her mind like small explosions. Didn't he want to impress visitors to his office? Why would a man whose profession was grounded in detail—hairs, footprints, drug residues, blood-alcohol levels, car models, tire tracks, bullet casings—choose to reveal so little of himself? Or, was his profession precisely why he chose to reveal so few personal details?

The only clue to his character was one fourteen-by-twenty-inch color photo of the Finger Lakes on the wall facing his desk. It was a sunset shot from an airplane. The rich, low light painted five of the lakes with gold and gave them the appearance of an ancient, molten hand.

He moved aside the single stack of papers on his desktop. Cora drew a sharp breath. The three middle fingers of his left hand were stumps covered in gray, twisted skin. A hot flash started on her chest and crept up her neck. Why would he hang the photo in his office? Why would he want to look at that shining golden hand a hundred times a day and compare it to his own ruined one?

She took a deep breath to keep her thoughts from scattering in all directions. Perspiration dampened her spine.

Somer looked at her oddly, his hand open on the desk. "Make yourself comfortable." Somer motioned her into one of two straight-backed visitor chairs in front of his desk, where she couldn't possibly get comfortable.

Cora cleared her throat. "When I talked to your secretary on the phone, I explained I wanted to ask you about Sean O'Brien. I'm working on a story on the O'Brien-Santerra suicides."

"I'll help you any way I can, Miss Brooks, but I'm puzzled," he said. "You work for a newspaper in a major city nearly three thousand miles away—and in California, where strange things happen every minute. Why would your paper be interested in obscure suicides in rural New York?"

"It's an interesting case," she lied. "Two friends die four days apart. One is an international cattle judge known from England to Argentina. The other is a prominent breeder and dairyman. Their deaths come in the midst of an insurance fraud inquiry involving prize-winning Holsteins."

She flipped open her laptop and snapped on her tape recorder as backup.

"There's no physical evidence that links the two. One of them was seventy-five miles away in Seneca County," he said.

"But they're related."

"You folks don't have any suicides or insurance frauds in San Francisco to write about?"

"The *Standard* prides itself on being a paper with national scope." She modestly lowered her eyes.

"We aren't interested in national publicity."

She debated which interview style to use: pitching him softballs, then gradually leading up to the tough questions, or giving him the hammer early on, and easing up as the interview progressed.

"Especially if there's a cover-up involving this so-called double suicide." She didn't often use sympathetic opening questions with law enforcement, because they almost always had something to hide. Besides, her feet were still rigid with cold, and she felt off-balance and cranky.

Somer made a pincer motion with the thumb and pinkie of his maimed hand. "The only problem with my department's investigation of the O'Brien suicide was an inquisitive reporter from the *New York Times* who did a story—mostly by telephone—about this area, 'Where cows outnumber people.'"

Briefly, his gaze shifted out the window. Wind whipped the leafless branches of a walnut tree against the glass. "I grew up in Cortland, Miss Brooks, and I own a house there, so I'll help you out by giving you a little local color."

"Oh, good. Local color."

He drilled her with a sharp look, then crossed his arms on his desktop. "The Otisco Valley was settled by veterans of the Revolutionary War, many of whom served without pay. In recognition of their contribution, the government gave them grants of land."

Cora tapped the arm of her chair. She'd give him two minutes to wrap up his diversionary maneuver.

"For two hundred years, this area has stayed pretty much the same. The same families plow their fields, milk their dairy cows, and pray at the Protestant church on Sunday."

The telephone buzzed, and he picked it up. "Neville, that reporter is here. Pull your report on the O'Brien suicide and come up, ASAP." He disconnected and frowned at the console.

"Around 1880, the O'Brien family immigrated to New York from Ireland and bought the old Malden farm near Preble."

"What a minute. The same O'Brien family?"

He ignored her interruption. "They were Irish-Catholic, and uppity. Before long, a Catholic priest was stopping by the Valley to say mass in Latin a couple of times a month. Our 'Rock of Ages' preachers declaimed from the pulpit that the Pope would be dropping down on them, fang and claw.

"Local people didn't accept the O'Briens, and from what I hear, the O'Briens didn't try to fit in. Old man O'Brien did a lot of business with Irish merchants in Syracuse, married a girl from the old country, and refused to join the Grange. But he and his sons worked seven days a week and ate potatoes at every meal. Within a dozen years, their farm had more dairy cows than any other in the county."

A knock sounded at the door and a short man with thinning blond hair and a generous paunch sidled in. He was in plain clothes, but the odor of shoe polish clung to him; he'd given his shoes a quick shine before he hustled up to see the boss.

Somer scowled.

"Sorry sir." Neville took a seat, pulling up his pant legs slightly to preserve the creases.

"This is Arnold Neville from our Bureau of Criminal Investigation."

"I need to ask a question first," she said. "Why is the State Police on this case? Why not the local authorities?"

"It's a complicated investigation, and they asked us to step in, especially since we were initial responders. Now where was I?" Somer said. Neville opened his mouth, but Somer returned to his story, leaving Neville looking uncertain. "Oh, yes. About 1914, the Irish back home began their fight for independence against the British. They launched a guerrilla war and called on the Irish immigrants in the U.S. for help."

Somer clasped his hands behind his head.

"Go on," Cora said.

"Rumors circulated around the valley that the young, up-and-coming O'Brien heir, Seamus O'Brien, was buying weapons and shipping them back to the old country. Locals got wind of it and threats were exchanged. Then in 1918, he disappeared. No trace of him was ever found."

Cora shifted restlessly. "A fascinating bit of local folklore. The moral is—let me guess—one man's fight for independence is another man's insurrection?"

"No, Miss Brooks. I'll put it this way: there's no welcome mat in Cortland County for outsiders."

The story was getting interesting. "I think I just received a threat."

"Nonsense." Somer slapped his palm on the desktop. "Neville, give Miss Brooks a rundown on the O'Brien suicide."

Neville hitched his chair closer to the desk and shuffled the pages in a file folder. "The dispatch center received a call at 3:12 a.m. on March 23 reporting a death, possibly from poisoning, at Maple Leaf Farm on Plato Crossroad. Emergency responders were sent to the scene and determined the subject, Sean O'Brien, was deceased. Rigor had already commenced."

Cora stopped typing, her hands suspended over the keyboard. "Then he'd been dead for as long as twelve hours."

"There was ..." Neville began.

Somer interrupted. "In the case of strychnine poisoning, the victim's convulsions speed up the process. Rigor is almost instantaneous."

"So the coroner ruled strychnine was the cause?"

"The medical examiner found a decreased level of oxygen in the tissue and burst small capillaries consistent with strychnine poisoning," Neville said. "The victim essentially is asphyxiated because convulsions keep him from catching his breath."

"Was there strychnine in the victim's blood and tissue?"

He riffled through the papers. "The toxicology report's not back. I'll let you know when I get it."

"Do that," Cora said. She made a note on the screen. "Where did the strychnine come from?"

Neville consulted his papers. "There was a half-full container in the barn."

Somer cut in again. "Strychnine is commonly found on farms. It's used to kill rats that infest cattle feed. Years ago, it was an ingredient in all kinds of home remedies, but now it's used in pesticides."

"And to cut heroin and cocaine," Cora added.

Somer raised his eyebrows. "You've been reading up."

"There aren't that many dairy farms in San Francisco, but lots of ODs from adulterated drugs." She adjusted the tilt of her laptop screen. "Who found him?"

Neville slid his finger between his tie and his shirt. "His wife, Judith."

"She called 911?"

"Actually, no ..."

"I did." Somer rose suddenly, and moved to the empty conference table, where he sat in the captain's armchair at the far end.

"You responded to the scene of Sean O'Brien's death?" She swiveled her head between the two men. Was this a strategy on Somer's part, to divert her attention?

"Judith O'Brien called me on my cell phone, hysterical, saying Sean was dead. I called dispatch before I left the house."

"Why didn't the *Times* story have this?" She picked up her tape recorder and set it on the conference table, halfway between Somer and Neville. She didn't want to miss a word.

"The reporter never asked," Somer said.

"I've never heard of upper management going to a late-night suicide. They leave it to the coroner." She summoned in her voice all the phony sweetness she could muster. "But maybe priorities are different here in rural New York."

Somer considered her with an unwavering stare and pursed lips, a look she assumed he used to intimidate his troops. "We had no reason to believe this was a crime. Besides, Judith and Sean are—were—long-time friends of mine," he said.

"So, let me get this straight. Instead of calling paramedics for her dying husband, Judith O'Brien telephoned her old friend?"

"She would've had no doubt the victim was dead, Ms. Brooks," Somer said.

"How long did it take you to get to the O'Brien farm?"

"Thirty-three minutes, from the time my cell rang. It's a little over twenty miles, but it was snowing hard."

"Then there's no way to confirm you were actually at home when you called dispatch," Cora said.

"What? You're implying I was at the scene, or something?" He rocked forward as if he might leap at her.

"Just asking," she said.

"No, I can't prove I was at home," he said, giving her a venomous look.

"Okay, what did you see when you arrived?"

"I'm going to let Neville respond to any additional questions. He's the most familiar with the case," Somer said.

"Wait a minute. You were the first officer at the scene."

A muscle in Somer's jaw twitched. "Neville."

The investigator looked at Cora, then his boss. "When I arrived, an ambulance was already there. EMTs couldn't do anything, since O'Brien was dead, so they stood by at the scene waiting for the medical examiner and me. The victim lay on the floor in the den." Neville cleared his throat. "His eyes were open, and his lips were pulled back from his teeth.."

Cora didn't want to hear any more. Her eyelids ached to close, and she lusted for sleep, just as she had last week after the Sutter Street murders. What was happening to her? This drained feeling, this lust for sleep was not like her. She gave the soft flesh on the inside of her arm a painful pinch.

"… told her he had two requests before he died. One, he wanted his Premier Exhibitor banner buried with him," Neville said.

Cora blinked. "What?"

"The banner was his top show trophy. Won at some international cattle exhibition," Neville said. His eyes slid over toward Somer, but the major's face was impassive.

"While he was convulsing and thrashing on the floor, in death throes, he told his wife he wanted a cattle flag in his coffin?" Cora said.

"According to his wife's statement, yes." Neville's eyebrows drew together in a frown.

"And you believed her?"

"I had no reason not to."

"Other than normal common sense and professional skepticism." Cora said.

"It was a suicide, Ma'am."

"So you keep telling me. What was Sean O'Brien's second request?"

"I don't know. He died before he got around to saying."

5

Abby
January 1917

Abby blew on her fingers. She wore her wool coat and a muffler knitted by Grandmother Miller around her neck, but the cold seeped up her legs past her wool stockings to her drawers. This morning the thermometer, hung on a nail near the back door of the store, had read two degrees.

In the schoolroom, the windows were painted with frost. The primary children's smaller desks clustered nearest the stove, while the eighth graders' desks—hers, her cousins Emily's and Edna's, and John Goins's—were the farthest away. Abby scribbled a note to Emily in her copybook, shielding the page with her hand. *John is passionately in love with Edna.* Edna was Emily's twin sister, prettier, but not as quick as Emily. Abby tore the paper slowly to prevent a ripping sound and folded it into a tiny packet.

While she pretended to read, she kept her eye on Aunt Flo—Miss Miller, as she insisted on being called at school. She was her mother's sister, who had taken over the school from Ruth fifteen years ago when Ruth married Jack Macpherson. Miss Miller sat at her desk grading papers, her back as straight as a yardstick. The collar of her serge coat was turned up to keep the cold away from her neck, and she wore fingerless knitted gloves.

Every minute or so, she lifted her head to see if the children were misbehaving. Finally, Miss Miller went to the blackboard. The chalk tapped as she posted a set of multiplication problems. Abby tossed the note into Emily's lap. Her cousin hissed to hold back giggles.

"Abigail Macpherson, come to my desk and bring that note with you." Miss Miller spoke without turning around. Abby placed the note on Miss Miller's scarred desk, the same desk her mother, Ruth, had used when she was the teacher at PS 12.

Miss Miller turned, and all at once, Abby was ashamed. The skin around her aunt's eyes was tinged with purple, and deep lines furrowed the space between her brows. Seamus was the school board president, and after the argument between him and Jack Macpherson, he'd led a move to fire Aunt Flo. Everyone in the Valley knew Aunt Flo, Mama, and her family had changed their name from Mueller to Miller when they moved from Germany, but now people were whispering the Millers could be sympathetic to the Huns. The trustees spent two meetings debating whether to break her contract. Both times, her papa and his brother Will had appeared before the trustees in their Sunday suits, and they'd beat back the opposition.

Abby stared at the floor and tried to look as sorry as possible. Miss Miller's problems with the trustees weren't over. Her pay for the last month had been late. Two desks were broken, but the trustees had sent no one to repair them. And Miss Miller had nailed a board over a hole in the porch herself.

"Go to the shed and bring back some wood," Miss Miller told Abby. Her fingers worried the brooch at her throat.

Abby groaned. The older students hated the job of hauling split logs across the play yard through the snow. Abby sat on the cloakroom bench trying to force her high-top shoes into rubber galoshes that were too small, but had to last the winter. Frustrated, she tossed the galoshes on the floor. She wiggled her fingers into her gloves and settled a wool cap over her ears. When she stepped off the porch, wind-driven snow sliced at her face like broken glass. She blinked furiously. Snowbanks rose as high as her waist on either side of the path, and grainy pellets snatched at the bottom of her skirt.

The shed was dark inside and smelled of bark and pitch. Wind squealed through the cracks. Abby lifted her hand to wipe her dripping nose but stopped with her glove in midair. Only five split pieces of wood remained—enough to heat the schoolroom for less than an hour.

She stacked the wood in her arms and careened like a dog on ice back to the schoolhouse. When she mounted the porch step, her numbed feet sailed out from under her and she fell, hitting her ribs. Wood went flying. She lay there for a few seconds before the door banged open, and Miss Miller clattered down the steps. "Abby! Are you hurt?"

Abby gasped for breath, her eyes level with the dirty hem of her aunt's skirt. Abby felt Miss Miller's arms slide under her shoulders, and finally she managed to inhale a lungful of air. "I tore a hole in my stocking." Her voice trembled.

"No harm done, thank goodness." Miss Miller helped Abby to her feet and brushed the snow off her legs.

"It's all gone." Abby stamped her feet but couldn't feel her toes.

"What?" Miss Miller grabbed a chunk of wood in each hand and nudged Abby inside.

"There's no more wood."

Miss Miller used a padded glove to open the stove's loading door as she shoved the wood in. It clunked against the metal sides. Sparks crackled and disappeared up the flue.

Under Miss Miller's rapid-fire orders, students rearranged the room, with Abby's desk pushed close to the heat. Her boots felt as though they were stuffed with blocks of wood. She propped her numb feet on the stove's ash lip.

A thump on the porch rattled the window glass, followed by a series of rhythmic thuds. Emily dashed to the front, rubbed the condensation off the pane, and peered out. "It's Mr. O'Brien. Hauling wood. He's throwing it on the porch."

Miss Miller stood as still as a stone. After a moment or two, she walked quickly through the cloakroom to the porch, slamming the door behind her. Two voices peppered the air as the students fell silent, straining to hear.

The burning wood snapped; the smell of damp hair floated around Abby's head. Slowly, wisps of steam coiled upward from her boots. She stared at the stove's red-hot door, and for an odd, clear moment, she felt no pain, only a detached interest. Then the soles of her feet began to sting. She jerked them away. Pain exploded inside the leather. Screaming, she shook her boots and tore at the soles. She tried to kick them, yank them off. Her feet were cooking, and she couldn't escape.

Slow at first to realize what had happened, students began to cluster around her. They shouted advice. Emily knelt before her and scrabbled at the shoelaces. They were damp and swollen tight. Abby kicked and screamed in pain and terror. Emily cried out in frustration. Then Seamus was there, sweeping the onlookers aside. He pulled a folding knife from his pants pocket. "Abby, stop it. Damn it, hold still." He grasped her ankles tightly. In an instant, the steel blade sliced both sets of laces down the front. He peeled off her boots and cut a slit in her stockings, exposing feet that were the gruesome pink of rare meat. The air hit her skin. Abby writhed.

"Get some snow! We'll pack her feet."

"You numbskull! That will damage them. We should rub them with butter," Miss Miller said.

"Holy Mother Mary, you want to lard her like a roast? Her flesh needs to be cooled." Seamus handed a bucket to John. "Get along now. Quickly." The boy dashed outside. Seamus lifted Abby and carried her to the cutter he'd used to haul wood over the snow. Miss Miller followed.

"I'm taking her to Doc Cuthbert in Tully," Seamus said.

"That sot? He drinks enough to be Irish."

Seamus' mouth worked as if he were preparing to spit. "I'll not leave her here untreated." He wrapped Abby in a buffalo robe. She cried out as he plunged her bare feet into the snow-filled wooden bucket.

Miss Miller unwound the wool scarf from around her neck and tied it over Abby's ears. "I'll tell Jack and Ruth."

With snow swirling around them, he whipped the horses and the cutter lurched over the snowy ruts. Abby began the longest ten miles of her life.

6

Cora
April 2000

After she left the state police office, Cora drove to a fast-food outlet and sat in her car while she stuffed herself on a Philly cheesesteak. The morning hadn't been a total waste, though Somer and Neville had fed her the sanitized version of Sean O'Brien's death. She could have eaten off it, which showed they were hiding something. But O'Brien's widow might let something slip if she could be convinced to talk.

Cora blotted the sandwich drips off her shirt with a napkin as she studied a map spread on the steering wheel. The O'Brien farm sat on the southern tip of Otisco Lake, the easternmost of the eleven Finger Lakes.

On the plane from California, Cora had seen below her this strange series of thin, parallel lakes. Their waters filled deep, granite-walled valleys gouged out by glaciers as they had melted and retreated northward during the last ice age. She imagined the valleys as scars inflicted by frozen rivers of ice and felt a momentary piercing pain in her chest, as if a glacial river moved along her breastbone.

She rubbed her chest for a moment, then tossed the refuse from her lunch in the back seat and headed north. When she reached the nineteenth-century village of Preble, she turned left. She caught herself scanning the countryside. Her mother had grown up around here. Would Cora see something—that white Congregational church at the crossroad, the two-story brick house with the white columns and rotting porch, the blacksmith shop beside the road—that her mother had touched? Cora passed the Owego Hotel, which looked old enough that Abe Lincoln might have slept there. Had her mother ever parked her car out front? Sipped a beer in the bar there or danced to swing music?

Cora stepped on the Neon's accelerator. Alice had been gone from this area for decades It would be naïve to think any of her mother's DNA still inhabited this tiny part of the world. Since she left, local rocks had sloughed off millions of tons of debris. A billion people around the world had died and turned to dust. A trillion leaves had fallen. There would be no banners flying outside that read, "Alice Macpherson drank here."

Further on, neatly plowed fields dotted with brown stubble stretched alongside the two-lane road. A sign nailed to a farm entrance gate read, "Goat meat for sale." The surrounding hills were blanketed with trees, and beneath them the last mounds of snow were blue-white in the shade. Through a gap in the trees, the lake's surface reflected a pale sky.

Cora parked her car on the road at the entrance to Sean O'Brien's farm, which marched along the undulating valley's bottom land. At the gate, a sign displaying a black and white Holstein and the words Maple Leaf Farm squeaked a tune on its post.

The O'Brien's two-story white clapboard house reigned among pine, maple, and larch. It held itself aloof on a slight rise above the red-painted barns and cattle sheds. She saw four blue silos that she'd learned from her research cost a hundred thousand dollars each. Sean O'Brien must have been making money.

Gravel rattled under her boots as she walked up the driveway. She hunched her shoulders to shield her neck against the cold wind.

A cardinal darted from one maple branch to another in a blood-red blink. It landed on a bare twig and whistled a three-note call, *what, what, what.*

"Hello? Anyone home?" Off to her right, a loose piece of metal rattled. Three trucks sat in the farmyard: a new black Ford F-150, a rusty Chevy Suburban, and a red Dodge Ram 4x4 with the driver's window open. A dozen pieces of farm equipment had been left in the open—dump trucks, green John Deere tractors, a harrower, four grain carts, a wheeled feed chute, and a jumble of rusted equipment of uncertain function. There appeared to be not a single cow at Maple Leaf Farm.

"Hello?" Her voice echoed among the silent barns. All at once, a chocolate Labrador raced from a milking shed, barking. It stopped three feet from her, its paws spread and muzzle raised. She held her breath, nerves leaping. Was the dog trained to rip intruders to shreds? She calculated whether she could thumb the animal in the eyes if he attacked. After a minute, the dog yapped one final bark of dutiful aggression, trotted up, and licked her hand. She scratched its head, sending tufts of shedding winter hair drifting in the wind.

A soft thud sounded off to her right. She called again and walked boldly toward the noise. It came from a decrepit white shed, dark and windowless inside, reeking of rotting animal manure and urine. Cora drew nearer and heard the thump of a heavy body. From the black interior came the deep, moist grunts of a pig. Cora shuddered. She'd read somewhere that hungry boars ate humans.

"How can I help you?" A voice at her elbow made Cora leap.

She swung around to see a tall woman with a body thin as an auto antenna and a face sculpted to the bone. She wore a crisp white shirt, shiny brown lace-up boots, and a pair of tailored jeans tight enough to show off her trim butt.

"I'm looking for Judith O'Brien. I assume that's you." The woman's silent approach had made Cora's heart jog quickly in her chest and her voice slightly breathless.

"You're the journalist I heard about," Judith O'Brien spoke through taut lips.

Somer had moved quickly. "I'm Cora Brooks from the *San Francisco Standard*. You probably already know I'm writing a story about the suicides of your husband and Franklin Santerra."

"I don't want to talk to you."

"I think you should, Mrs. O'Brien. The *Times* story left out a lot about the deaths. I'd like to get your viewpoint in print."

"What did the *Times* leave out?" Judith's clothes and grooming shouted perfection, but the truth of her mental and physical state was in her eyes, whites threaded with red lines, like whip cuts.

"For one thing, the state police, as the lead investigative agency, had a conflict of interest. Major Somer should have disqualified his troop from investigating."

"Even less reason to waste my time. It would only make me look bad."

"Wouldn't it be better to print your side than have the reader get the impression you were somehow involved in your husband's death?" Cora tried to guess Judith's age. She would have said a well-maintained forty, except for a hint of tiny wrinkles in the corners of her eyes. Closer to her own age, Cora decided.

"What do you mean, 'involved?' If you mean I saw him convulse horribly until he died in my arms with no one there to help me, then yes. Yes, I was involved." Judith's eyes darkened as if the curtain had risen on a macabre replay of Sean O'Brien's death.

The breath left Cora's lungs. She struggled to inhale, but her chest was full of something, not air, but a tumorous dread. Her vision darkened.

A door slammed, and two farm hands diverted Judith's attention from Cora. They strode quickly to the turnaround from a rusty double-wide mobile home at the rear of the farm buildings. One, who sported a Pancho Villa mustache, touched the bill of his New York Yankees cap. "Señora," he said to Judith.

She ignored him at first; then, when he moved closer and repeated his greeting, she said reluctantly, "Hola, Rico."

Cora managed a few shallow breaths. What was wrong with her? She had to pull herself together.

Rico tossed two shovels into the bed of the 4x4 and pulled on a pair of leather gloves, all the while staring intently at Cora. Climbing inside the truck, he kicked the engine into a smooth rumble and backed up to a grain cart. His coworker, a small man with a hatchet nose, attached the cart to the truck's silver hitch. Once it was secure, the pair drove off toward the silos.

Judith turned back to Cora. "Please leave or I'll call Major Somer. I have no interest in talking to you."

"You have a son, I think. Where was he when his father died?"

"Stepfather. Sean was his stepfather. And that's no business of yours."

Cora walked a few paces down the driveway. The wind had died, and the sinuous voices of the hired hands speaking Spanish wove through the still air. She turned back to Judith, who seemed to have forgotten her and was watching the two milkers move the grain chute over the truck.

"Were your hired hands here that night?"

"I don't remember," Judith said absently over her shoulder.

"Is your dairy farm still in operation? I don't see any cows," Cora said.

"Just enough to eat me into the poorhouse."

Cora couldn't imagine Nathan living in such a remote place. No young people living close by, miles from the school, and parents buying him off with a new truck. "How old is your son?" she asked.

Judith turned back to Cora, and her mouth slackened with worry. "He's sixteen, and looks twenty."

"I have a twenty-year-old. He's in college in Boston." She smiled.

Judith pressed her knuckles against her lower lip. "Tyler may never go to college. Sean's death has hit him hard. He's cutting school and lying to me."

Cora nodded. "I thought that about my son after my divorce. I'm not telling you divorce is in any way as serious as a death, but Nathan got better. It gets better." She remembered her conversation with Nathan last night, remembered lying propped against the feather pillows.

Judith regarded her sharply. "Oh, well, come along to the house. I've got several rush jobs to get out; we can talk for a few minutes while I work."

They walked across the farmyard and up a flagstone path that meandered between beds of daffodils, violets, and purple crocus. Cora had planted bulbs in her tiny yard for a few years. That was before that adulterous bastard, Stephen, had bailed out of their marriage.

"What sort of work do you do?" Cora said.

"I'm a livestock photographer—a servant for rich people who want photos of themselves with their prize bulls and heifers at big shows. Not that they ever feed them or move a shovel of manure." Her voice was infused with loathing, though whether for herself or her subjects, Cora couldn't tell.

They crossed a wide verandah at the rear of the house. Beside the French doors waited a line of rubber boots caked with dried mud. Some were men's sizes, pollen covering them with a yellow dust. Judith didn't leave her boots, but continued through the door and tracked mud across a bare wood floor. Cora noticed tack strips around the perimeter of the room. Carpeting recently had been torn out.

They were in a spacious study furnished with a large sectional sofa upholstered in a dark green-and-white plaid, a wide pedestal desk, and two high-backed leather armchairs. Hundreds of plaques and ribbons encrusted the walls, and one entire side of the room was lined with bookcases crammed with gold and silver trophies.

Cora clasped her hands behind her back as if she were a connoisseur and scanned the photos. Black and white cows, big black and white cows, and a few fawn and white cows.

"You shot all of these?"

"Many of them. I've been doing this work on and off for twenty years. That's how I met Sean." She lifted one picture off its hook. "This is Holland's Queen Beatrice. She was the third one to die."

The cow looked at the lens with a haughty air of bovine nobility; it was a sleek animal, its coat shiny and shoulders, well, beefy. Holding the animal's halter was a tall man with reddish-blond hair. Sean O'Brien was wearing—Cora could hardly believe it—an ascot, like someone's stereotype of an English squire.

Cora gave herself a mental shake. As a journalist, she should know better than to make assumptions, but she'd stereotyped Sean in advance as a big man with chapped hands, fond of Western-cut sport jackets and plaid shirts.

Judith rubbed a film of dust carefully off the picture's glass with her thumb, then re-hung it. When she turned back toward Cora, a nail from the tack strip along the baseboard snagged the sole of her boot, and she cursed under her breath.

Cora could almost see stains on the missing carpet—body fluids, blood. Outside, the sun emerged from behind a cloud. The room brightened with a flash of light. The hairs on Cora's arms prickled. The red and blue in the ribbons seemed to glow. She caught a brief, sickening whiff of air freshener.

"I'll never forget the sound," Judith said. "He howled, deep in his throat, as if something was tearing at him." Her voice was oddly calm.

Cora's thoughts, which had been neat and categorized a few moments ago, exploded into bits. She was dizzy, as if she'd been concussed. What was happening? She wanted to make sense of it, tell herself she was used to hearing about crime and death, but she couldn't put the pieces of an idea together.

"Are you all right?" Judith said.

Cora lowered herself into one of the leather chairs.

"You look ill."

Cora put a hand over her trembling mouth.

"It's probably better if you go back to your hotel and rest," Judith said, too quickly.

Cora took a deep breath that brought air to the very bottom of her lungs. With a supreme effort, she reassembled herself. "Forgot to eat breakfast. Got a little lightheaded. Better now."

Judith looked skeptical, but Cora rose shakily to her feet and straightened her shoulders.

"Why don't we go upstairs to my studio?" Judith said. She led the way through a stark white kitchen with no sticky notes or photos on the refrigerator, up the back stairs, and into a long wing on the north side of the house. In her office, Judith switched on one of three computers on her worktable, pulled up a wheeled chair and began scrolling through a long string of thumbnail images. "Sit here," she said, indicating a second chair.

Cora's legs were still shaky, so she sat with her legs spread like an old woman. She pulled out a notebook and propped it on her knee. Her laptop and tape recorder were still in the car, in case Judith might be the sort of woman intimidated by journalistic trappings. Cora needn't have bothered. Judith was fully able to handle herself. Rather than confront Judith head-on, however, Cora decided to approach her obliquely. "What kind of man was your husband?"

Judith clicked on four photos and leaned forward to get a better look at them on the screen. The subject appeared to be the same monstrous Angus bull, with different people holding its halter. "He was handsome," she said over her shoulder. "Sean had those Irish good looks, red hair with some gold in it, fair skin, cleft chin."

"I imagine he stood out in a crowd." Especially with the ascot, Cora thought. Stephen had stood out in a crowd, too, not because of his good looks, but because he was tall. Cora remembered he'd worn his hair in a '70s-style ponytail on the day she hit him with her VW.

"People remembered him," Judith said. "He could go anywhere, any major country in the world, and people at the shows knew Sean O'Brien. And not just people with a few acres. He knew land barons in Australia and South America. Very wealthy people in Switzerland and England." Judith's skin glowed, as though she were going on a date and anticipating a night of great sex.

"How long were you married?"

"Five years." Judith turned back to the photos, squinted at one, and marked it with dotted lines to crop it. Cora guessed Judith was far-sighted but refused to wear glasses.

"And ... would you say those were good years?"

"Three," Judith said. "We had three before things went south."

"What happened?"

She sighed. "At first, marriage to Sean was everything I'd dreamed of. He insisted I give up my livestock photography business and develop my artistic side. I had two New York gallery exhibits of my landscape images. Mostly travel shots."

Shelves mounted on the office walls displayed a few of Judith's art images, among them a burka-clad woman at a desert well and a lone horseman in a sea of soft, long grass. The dramatic clarity of the light in the photos tickled a memory.

"Then, the Mexican government devalued the peso," Judith continued. "Sean belonged to an international investment group that lost everything. He'd borrowed his share of the money and couldn't cover the notes. He was finally reduced to selling some land and dancing the credit-card shuffle. The mailbox was stuffed with dun notices. Still is."

"Is that why Sean got involved with Franklin Santerra? To raise money?" Cora said.

"Sean and Franklin had been friends since Cornell. I don't know anything about their business dealings," Judith said.

The mouse clicked as Judith edited, saved, and printed another photo. Finished color pictures emerged from the printer in short jerks.

"I understand that in the week before he died, Sean was gone for several days. That he met Santerra. Do you know what that meeting was about?" Cora said.

Judith snorted. "It would be an understatement to say that Sean hadn't been confiding in me much during the last year. He didn't tell me where he going, but I assumed it was about the insurance company investigation. That was Monday. He returned Thursday afternoon, and he was elated, almost manic."

"Did he say why?"

"No. I asked, but he wouldn't say. I assumed the fraud investigation had been dropped."

"Yet, twelve hours later, he was dead," Cora said.

Judith's fingers hammered the computer keys. "We ate dinner—pizza that Tyler had brought home. Then Tyler left for his buddy's house, and Sean went out again. I stayed up late working, and when I went down to the kitchen to get some coffee, I heard his breathing, very loud and hoarse. I went in and he lay on the floor, his head jerking.

"I tried to make him vomit, tried to force him to drink water, but he refused. He said, 'I've done myself in.'"

"Why didn't you call 911?"

"I did, but with the big storm, they were busy, and I got put on hold. Sean was getting so bad, I couldn't wait."

"And yet he had a last request ..." Cora said.

"Oh, yes. His Premiere Exhibitor banner." Judith removed a disk from the computer and scribbled a label on it with a red pen. "Not, I love you, Judith. Or, I'm sorry."

"Maybe he was getting to that."

"I'll never know, will I?" Judith fixed Cora with an accusatory stare.

Cora chewed her lip. When Alice left, she hadn't said, I love you, Cora, or I'm sorry.

"Meanwhile," said Judith, her voice rising, "he's left me with a mountain of debt, more than the farm is worth, and a son to raise. Tyler needs a car, and clothes, and a college fund. I'm traveling the show circuit again, living in a cramped RV with a smelly toilet. I spend twelve hours a day shooting and downloading photos. The owners treat me like dirt."

How did her son manage, with his stepfather dead, left alone by his mother to fend for himself?

"Why don't you earn your living doing landscapes?"

Judith looked at her art photos as if they were lost children. "My exhibits got terrific reviews. They sold out immediately, but it takes time to develop a portfolio. I might take a thousand shots before I have one good enough for a show." She turned back to Cora, and there were tears in her eyes.

"Doesn't the state police major have this one in his office?"

"That one's not mine. It was shot by my mentor, a terrific photo artist from Skaneateles. Del said he bought it because it reminded him of me. I guess he forgave me for the divorce."

"Divorce?"

"Yes. I thought you knew." A smile touched Judith's lips. "I was married to Del for awhile."

Cora's cheeks burned. Never mind that the *Times* reporter hadn't caught it, either. She'd better sharpen up. "I gather the marriage was a short-term one."

"Not that short. Six years. Longer than I was married to Sean. Del and I remain friendly, mostly because of Tyler. He and Del bonded for some reason."

"Del referred to you and Sean as his old friends," Cora said.

"That's a rosy way of saying it," Judith said. "There wasn't any competition between the two of them, but I don't think Sean liked Del all that much."

"What about Del?"

Judith shrugged. "Who knows? That's one thing about Del. He keeps his thoughts to himself."

7

Del

1967-1988

During Del's years at Cornell, he was crazy to get away from rural New York. His father had died, and, looking back, he realized his mother, who'd married his father at sixteen, was terrified of being alone. She'd invited Del home to Cortland for pot roast and tuna-and-noodle suppers. After dinner, she'd maneuver him into watching television in the Naugahyde chair that still smelled of his father's Right Guard. She tried to fix him up with Betsy Streeter, the neighbor's daughter. Every time he saw his mother, he imagined himself trapped forever on Euclid Street in the little house where he grew up.

He was callous, he admitted to himself later, but for years his home town had felt like prison. The collapse of the steel industry in Pennsylvania had created high unemployment in New York State's satellite businesses; farmers struggled with low farm prices. Del could look forward to earning a doctorate in agriculture and teaching at SUNY in Cortland or working six days a week like his father at his one-man house-painting business, which barely made a dime during the winter. During his college years, Del had opted not to start a drug-trafficking operation like a couple of his high school classmates.

By spring of his senior year, he'd dated Judith for eight months. She was a lean, nervous photography student with hardly any tits but straight dark hair that captured his eye when it brushed her butt. What drew them together back then was their desire to get away.

"New York, Boston, San Francisco, Syracuse," she said, kidding about Syracuse. "We don't need a diploma, baby. Let's just leave."

But Del was a freight-train kind of guy; once he got between the rails, he kept going down the track. He took his finals, paid the deposit on his cap and gown. During grad week, he dropped by the shabby house Judith shared with five other students. She wasn't there. After a strained conversation, her roommate confessed that Judith had moved to Boston with an anatomy major who'd been accepted to Harvard med school.

Del ached as though he'd been beaten with a board. He broke out in hives and a kidney infection that left him barely able to pee. What was it about Judith? It wasn't as if he'd been about to buy her a diamond. Marriage was considered quaint during those years of campus unrest and sexual freedom. Rather, he'd pressed upon her all his half-acknowledged longing not to be alone. He was an only child with no extended family. There had always been a part of him, like a discolored spot at the center of an apple, that felt injured and alone. Not that he admitted it, not then and not later, when he encountered Judith again.

In the aftermath of her defection, Del was easy pickings for a U.S. Army recruiter at a campus job fair. The Vietnam War was going strong and protesters demonstrated weekly at Cornell, but he was so desperate to escape that even the armed forces looked good. He spent three years with the military police, including two in Germany, and when he mustered out he joined the New York State Police.

The physical demands of the academy were nothing compared to the army's basic training, and he aced his classes in traffic control, surveillance, investigation, crime-scene processing, forensics, and dignitary protection. He amazed himself by staying up until two or three in the morning to study and not grumbling about it the next day.

His future shimmered in front of him: postings at some of the rural troops; then promotion to captain or major at Troop NYC. He'd make New York a safer place, root out child molesters, white collar criminals, kidnappers, terrorists.

And, oh yes, impress women. In his fantasies, they all had Judith's long straight hair and racehorse body. As soon as they saw his gun and badge, plus his other impressive equipment, they'd be out of their clothes and on their backs.

At first, life galloped along the way he'd planned. He received a couple of commendations, including one for a major drug bust while he was trooper on road patrol, and quickly moved to plain-clothes detail in the Bureau of Criminal Investigation. He was promoted to sergeant in the shortest possible time. Then he was sent to Troop B in the Adirondack Mountains, arrested Roy Don Turner, and things turned to shit.

The complaint from an Oklahoma couple landed on Del's desk. Their sixteen-year-old daughter had been kidnapped by a Roy Don Turner, a motorcycle-riding hippie bigamist they heard was headed for New York State. The couple had their heads up their asses, of course. The girl had run away with the scumbag, and the two fugitives were probably fucking their brains out somewhere in the thousands of square miles of mountains, forests, and lakes in the north state.

He tossed the inquiry in his basket, but a few days later ran across a report on a drug bust near Saranac Lake. In exchange for a charge of possession rather than sale, the informant offered information that a subject named Turner was living at the site of an abandoned summer camp. He ruled as the patriarch over eight welfare-scamming "wives" and thirty-three children.

Del led a team of troopers and investigators, plus two FBI agents and a county sheriff's deputy. If this assignment was a winner, he could see a transfer to Troop NYC in his future. Turner was almost certainly armed, Del told the team during briefing. Del issued handi-talkies, assigned channels, and handed out photos of Roy Don Turner and the girl.

The camp was hidden down ten miles of dirt road in thick forest of pine, maple, and birch. The team's two vehicles skidded out of the parking lot at dusk from the town of Saranac Lake. The temperature on the digital thermometer in front of the bank read 90 and humidity 89 percent. The AC in Del's Chevy Suburban conked out five miles out of town. Stink from the six men in Del's vehicle was so bad it clogged his nostrils.

Two miles from the camp, Del instructed the trooper who was driving to pull off the road, and the two vehicles reconnoitered in a grove of maples and shaggy oaks. The team donned bulletproof vests with State Police stenciled on the back, and checked their weapons and handi-talkies. Duct tape secured their pants cuffs to their boots as protection from poison ivy and snakes. They shouldered their packs and weapons.

The moon was full, but even its light didn't penetrate the tangle of trees that snatched at their clothes and slashed their faces. They stepped into unseen ponds clogged with black mud from rotting vegetation.

As they neared Turner's camp, they climbed a hilltop to keep the area in view. Spread in front of them were three wooden plank cabins. Porches sagged and windows gaped with jagged glass. The fourth building was a twenty-by-thirty concrete block structure identified by the informant as private quarters for Turner upstairs and cookhouse downstairs. Canvas covered a hole in the roof. The hollow smelled of wood smoke and untreated sewage.

On the camp's south side, a fire burned in a stone circle. Children darted in and out of the light, imps silhouetted against the leaping flames. A gust of wind slapped a loose shingle against a roof. Dogs howled. From the cookhouse, a man screamed at the dogs and called them inside.

Del's team squatted behind a screen of twisted branches. Mosquitoes and black flies, lured by the smells of sweat and anxiety, bit them behind their ears and on the backs of their necks. Twigs snapped as the watchers moved a few feet to pee in the undergrowth. At two-thirty, dogs barked again. Five pairs of infrared binoculars snapped up to catch a woman, clad only in her shoes, emerge from a cabin. She stood on the steps for a few moments, her skin glowing in the moonlight, then walked to the outhouse.

Finally, the sky lightened. "Listen up." Del's whisper drew them into a huddle. "Turner and the girl are our priority, but we've got to protect the children. Don't get distracted." His vest was heavy and sweat ran down his arms.

"As soon as your team is in place, give me the 'ready.' I'll announce the search." They moved quickly, humpbacked shadows against the gray dawn. Del crept close to the cookhouse. Muted static crackled on his handi-talkie as the teams reported. "One ready … Two ready …"

He snapped the switch on his battery-powered megaphone. "This is the state police. Open up. We have a search warrant."

A shiver in the air made the cabins swim in his vision. Suddenly, frenzied barking erupted from inside the cookhouse. On the count of ten, the officers swarmed the cabins with a barrage of hoarse yells. Flimsy doors splintered.

"Down. Down on the floor. Hands behind your head." A child wailed, and women screamed in an octave of terrified pitches. Ten minutes later, a voice came over the handi-talkie. "Three here … we have the female. No sign of the male subject."

Shots erupted from the cookhouse. Del leaped across the porch and peered around the door frame. In the smoky half-light he spotted Trooper Jimmy Wells crouched behind an overturned table, and an FBI agent on the floor flailing at two pit bulls that ripped at his legs. Del plunged inside, clubbing the dogs' skulls and vertebrae with the stock of his shotgun. They backed away, snarling. He had knelt to help the bleeding agent when a cadaver of a man with a dark mouth of missing teeth appeared from behind the dining room's cafeteria counter.

"Fucking pigs, you fucking pigs!" Roy Don Turner. He snapped open a connecting gate. A mastiff burst from the opening; its claws scrabbled eagerly on the scarred wooden floor. It smacked Del like a battering ram and knocked him onto his butt. The shotgun flew from his grip. Del didn't remember the pain, he remembered the sounds. The dog's snarls. Its grinding teeth. Finger bones crunching like chicken wings. Screams he didn't recognize as his own. The moment stretched second by second until it became his life.

Trooper Wells, afraid a bullet might hit Del, used the butt of his weapon to force the mastiff away and crush its skull. He gathered the pieces of Del's fingers and stowed them on ice in a picnic cooler he found behind the counter. Despite a helicopter flight to an Albany hospital, doctors were unable to reattach them.

There was no infection in the stumps; doctors labeled the repair operation a success. Roy Don was captured as he thumbed a ride on the highway. The girl was returned to her family, where she ran away again within a year. The judge in Oklahoma gave Roy Don twenty-five years for kidnapping. He was never prosecuted for inciting the dog's assault on a peace officer.

When the department began disability retirement proceedings, Del waged a years-long struggle to keep his job. He claimed his injury didn't bar him from performing his duties, but the case lingered in the appeals process. He finally went to court and successfully made his case. Bucking management hadn't made him friends in high places, and he had almost given up on his dream assignment.

Then an investigation unearthed a scandal in Troop C. For the previous five years, a group of rogue investigators in the division that included Cortland had manufactured evidence and sent several innocent people to prison.

The superintendent summoned Del to Albany. "I'm throwing a grenade into Troop C management. You grew up there. I want you to take over as major. Fix things. Repair relationships with the locals."

"I don't know. I hear the legislature is beginning an investigation." Del wasn't beyond cutting a piece of the superintendent's scalp.

"The department can take the heat if those assholes at the capitol think I'm on top of it. Got it handled."

"I'm putting in for NYC," Del said. "I think I have a good chance."

"Listen, Del." The superintendent folded his hands prayerfully. "Clean up the situation down there, and you can name your assignment."

As soon as he returned to Cortland, he'd run into Judith again. The medical student was long gone, and she had a six-year-old son. That had been twelve years ago.

8

Cora
April 2000

It was after dark when Cora returned to Seneca House. She wiped her boots quietly on the oriental carpet; on tiptoe, she started up the stairs.

To her left, sherry hour rollicked along in the Victorian parlor. Laughter broke out in the alcove formed by the Queen Anne window. Someone played "Moonlight Bay" on the piano. Judging from the racket, Debbie had rounded up a bigger crowd than just the paying guests.

Cora's foot had touched the third tread when a voice nailed her between the shoulder blades. "Ms. Brooks, you're not going upstairs without joining us, are you?" Debbie said it as a question, but it wasn't.

"I'm late. I'd be intruding."

"Nonsense. You put your coat away and come right down. We've been expecting you." Debbie's cheeks and the tip of her nose were pink.

Upstairs, Cora stashed her rucksack and laptop on the desk. It had been a productive day for the story—Somer's conflict of interest was even stronger than she'd first thought. She flopped on the bed and pressed her face into the duvet. Maybe the darkness would banish the memory of the tack strips and bare floor at the farm, so much worse, somehow, than the damaged carpet that had been ripped out. The terror she'd experienced and the threat of a recurrence stalked the edge of her thoughts. What was the matter with her? She'd never been thin-skinned about crime scene details. Her fingers trembled and saliva pooled in the corner of her mouth. She abandoned her effort to stay awake. A dream crept in; she crouched in a shadowed room with a dresser looming over her. A white blade of light came from a hallway. Footsteps. From somewhere close, the sounds of blows, solid smacks against flesh. Her throat strained, and a scream struggled to burst out, but she had no voice. She protected her head with her arms, willing herself to disappear.

A knock on the bedroom door. *Don't open.* She covered her eyes with her hands, a floating embryo.

"Cora, are you there?" Debbie. The room was dark except for a thin strip of light that crept under the door.

"Oh, right." Cora stumbled as she slid off the bed. Her feet seemed unfamiliar with the floor's flat, normal surface. "Five minutes." She rubbed her face with a washcloth, untied her boots, and jammed her feet into a pair of loafers.

Debbie clapped her hands when Cora entered the parlor. "Everyone, this is Cora from San Francisco. She's researching her family history." Noise continued to crowd the room.

Paul Landesdowne loomed over the food and drink table, playing the genial host among the wine glasses and onion dip. "Here's a little something to warm your California bones." He scooped three cubes from a silver ice bucket, tossed them into an etched glass, and splashed them with sherry.

"I'm not really …" Cora said. She looked down to see the glass in her hand.

He rearranged the cluster of bottles on the marble surface. "It's on the house. Part of the breakfast." He'd been breakfasting for some time, she noticed.

A song ended with a roll of bass notes from the woman at the keyboard. Her cigarette sat in an ashtray on the piano top, and smoke curled over the four singers clustered around her. "'Far Above Cayuga's Waters,'" shouted someone. The alma mater of Cornell University, where Del Somer, Sean O'Brien, and Franklin Santerra had gone to school.

"I'm sick of that one," the pianist said. Instead, she launched into "Let Me Call You Sweetheart."

Cora downed her glass of sherry in a hurry so the taste didn't linger. Sherry had never appealed to her; she was more of a hearty burgundy person.

"My dear, I must introduce you to someone." Debbie tipped the bottle to refill Cora's glass before she could protest. She steered Cora toward a settee placed at a right angle to the fireplace. "You may remember that I'm the past president of the county historical society."

"I recall your mentioning it."

"I have a treat for you." Debbie had the delighted look of someone who'd given Cora a surprise birthday gift. "Cora Brooks, this is Mimi Shafter. Mimi took over as president after my term expired. She'll be a mine of information about your genealogy."

Cora felt a twinge. Debbie had gone out of her way to corral an expert to assist with her bogus search. "What an amazing opportunity," she said.

Debbie collected the empty hors d'oeuvre trays and carried them to the kitchen. Cora intended to be polite, but brush off Mimi Shafter. The cow story was gaining traction and she didn't have time to slog through dusty records and badly written local histories on a genealogical search she didn't care about.

Mimi Shafter was a middle-aged porcupine, her black hair gelled into spikes. Rather than surrendering to the cushions, she sat boldly upright with the air of someone who permitted the couch to hold her.

"Sit right here and tell me everything." She patted the seat beside her, but Cora wasn't about to play the game. Instead she sat nearby on a hassock in front of the fire.

Cora forced down more sherry. "I know practically nothing, except that my mother, Alice Macpherson, probably came from this area. She moved to San Francisco and married my father in the mid-1940s or early 1950s."

"And you live in San Francisco now?" Mimi's bright eyes focused intently on Cora.

"Yes. I had a break at work, and it seemed like a good time to scratch around in my past a bit." Cora's shirt was hot against her back. She gulped sherry to moisten her throat, and scooted the hassock away from the fire.

"You're a newspaper reporter?" Mimi said.

Damn. "Where did you hear that?"

"Word gets around. You were interviewing Del Somer this morning about Sean O'Brien."

"There's a telephone tree?"

"I know all the dirt."

"Too bad you don't work for Del Somer," Cora said.

"Did someone murder Sean?" Mimi's voice wasn't loud, but conversation in the rest of the room skittered to a halt.

Cora scanned the circle of expectant faces and decided on evasion. "The major says no. His investigator says no. Sean's wife was at the scene, and she says no. Who am I to argue?" She felt everyone's eyes follow her as she grabbed the bottle of sherry from Paul's tray and carried it back to the hassock.

"There are a ton of suspects," Mimi said.

The piano stool squeaked. The bottle clinked against Cora's glass as she poured. "And you, as the new president of the historical society, are keeping a list?"

"Judith has to be at the top," Mimi said. "Disillusioned, facing foreclosure and possible poverty."

Cora waggled her glass at Mimi. "And ..."

"There's Del, who might still be in love with her, even though she divorced him for a guy she thought was rich," Mimi said.

Cora was enjoying a buzz. Guests snapped their eyes back and forth between the two of them. "A law enforcement official?"

"Then there's Judith's son, Tyler, who's still very attached to Del and hated Sean. And here's another one for your list, Franklin Santerra. Sells three cows to Sean, offspring guaranteed to earn him millions. They all die before birthing a single calf."

"That doesn't sound like a motive for Santerra. Maybe for Sean, who got a raw deal," Cora said.

Mimi shrugged. "Santerra and Sean went way back. Partners in a failed investment scheme in Latin America. I hear Sean was threatening to sue his old buddy for fraud."

"So Sean dies before he can file suit, rises from the grave, and retaliates with a shotgun?" Cora topped off Mimi's glass.

"That's one possibility I hadn't considered," Mimi said.

The kitchen door swung open, and Debbie edged her considerable backside into the room, carrying two trays of tiny sausages wrapped in bacon. She blinked at the collapse of the convivial atmosphere and the expectant silence of the guests.

She sent her husband around the room with the tray. "Corrine, do you know the 'Wreck of the Edmund Fitzgerald'?" The pianist fingered a fanfare and eyed the two women by the fireplace.

Debbie plumped down on the settee next to Mimi. "Now, did you get any clues on where to start your genealogical search?"

"I've been given a lot of theories, but no clues," Cora said.

"No clues? Oh, dear. Mimi, have you lost your touch?"

"What did you say your family name was?" Mimi seemed to have run out of murder suspects.

"Macpherson."

"The picture," Debbie flapped her hands at Cora. "Show it to her."

"No." Cora said.

"On your dresser. The one of the girl in front of the old store."

The stairs seemed like an alpine trek, and Cora was dizzy when she reached her room. She returned with the picture, wishing she'd thrown it out.

Mimi gave Cora a speculative look before focusing on the image. "This is the store on Otisco Valley Road, just south of my grandparents' place. The family that owned it sold the place in the 1940s. Anyway, the store's been abandoned ever since. It's falling down now."

"How can you be sure what the structure is from this small image?" Cora asked.

"See the advertising sign under the front window? Daniel Webster Flour. That sign is still there in the rubble. It's rusty, but readable."

"Otisco Valley Road. Sean O'Brien's farm is on Plato Crossroad, just off Otisco Valley Road. I was there today," Cora said.

"The old store is north of the farm. About half a mile."

Very carefully, Cora placed her glass on the rug. It teetered and overturned. The piano pounded. Mimi leaned close, suffocating her. Cora used her fists to push herself off the hassock. "I'm going outside." She bumped her thigh on the marble-topped table, rattling the bottles.

On the porch, the cold air hurt her face. She skidded on an icy remnant of snow as she picked her way down the sidewalk. She stood in the center of the street and tipped her head back. The stars were small bursts of pain against the black sky. She lost her balance and fell.

She scrambled up and rubbed her butt. Over her shoulder, she heard Debbie calling her back inside. She walked away from the voice, keeping her head down. Her vision was distorted and her feet looked small, like a child's, barely able to support her adult muscle and bone.

For a year after Alice left, Cora had felt her mother's absence in every nerve. The empty space throbbed with one memory: her mother at the kitchen table on the last day. Light pouring through the open window ignited her mother's red-blonde hair. A plastic wall clock clicked away the seconds. Her mother with one leg tucked up under her as if she wanted to protect her bare skin. She wrote, the paper resting on top of the closed stationery box. Her fingers pumped a coral fountain pen. Cora touched her mother's arm, feeling the light hairs. The rhythm of her mother's fingers and the scratch of the pen continued. Cora tucked her head under her mother's arm. The weight of her mother's breast was firm against Cora's cheek, the spice of her mother's perspiration sweet in her nostrils.

Her mother slid another chair close. Come up. Cora knelt on the sticky plastic seat and planted her elbows on the table. I'll write a letter, too, Cora said. Her mother took out a sheet of the thick, chalky stationery. Cora traced the letters, earnestly squeezing the pen. Dear Daddy, Come home for dinner. Love, Cora.

Behind, a car stalked her. Cora's shadow, long at first, shrank as the headlights came nearer. The car crawled around her and parked at the curb, the exhaust smell staining the air. The window slid down.

Del Somer propped his arm on the door. "I've got enough bodies to keep me busy. A frozen fool, I don't need."

9

Abby

January 1917

During the long ride to Tully, Abby's body shook with cold while her seared feet burned. Pain drove her thoughts like stinging pellets of snow. Would the doctor cut off her feet? Could she stifle her cries for one more minute?

The horses' sides steamed as they struggled through the drifts up a series of hairpin turns. The exposed ridge above them was shrouded in cloud, but they could hear the wind shrieking. Abby whimpered. She counted to a thousand.

When they crossed the crown of the hill, wind battered the cutter. The horses scrambled to gain footing on the ice. "Haw, Luke—goddammit, come on." Seamus half-stood, working the reins. The sleigh lurched, teetering on the edge of the steep drop. Abby slid along the seat. Her feet struck the wooden side. She screamed, pain stretching her torso until she thought it would split. The horses' hooves found traction; the sleigh righted itself and sank with a thump into the road's icy grooves.

She continued to howl, angry at a lifetime of admonitions to be brave. "Abby, shut up. Stop it." Seamus, breathing hard, dug his fingers into her shoulder and shook her until her head wobbled. His voice gentled. "Come on, Tiger Stripes. Try to think of something to keep your mind busy. I remember when Doc Cuthbert set my leg, I recited the Rosary. Ten decades."

She swallowed. "I don't know the Rosary, but I'm pretty sure it's Popish. How much longer?"

"I don't know. Depends. A couple hours, maybe."

The year before, each of Miss Miller's students from third through eighth had had to memorize one of Robert Service's poems about Yukon prospectors and recite it in front of the class. Abby had practiced "The Shooting of Dan McGrew" as she walked home from school, swept the store, and washed windows. She'd declaimed the poem again to great applause at the Macpherson family picnic that summer at the Old Farm.

She launched into the first stanza that came to her, snatched through the haze of cold and pain. "When out of the night, which was fifty below, and into the din and the glare/There stumbled a miner fresh from the creeks, dog-dirty and loaded for bear.'"

Seamus laughed. He tucked the buffalo skin more firmly around her and picked up the familiar lines: "'And watching his luck was his light-o'-love, the lady that's known as Lou.'"

Sun stole briefly through the clouds before it disappeared again.

———

Only one lonely set of footprints marred the snow on Laurel Street when Abby and Seamus dragged into Tully hours later. Seamus halted the exhausted team in front of a two-story clapboard house with a sign in front: Edwin Cuthbert, M.D., General Practice.

"I'll make sure Doc is home." Seamus left Abby in the sleigh. Snow plopped from evergreen branches when he opened the gate. He rapped several times before the doctor, dressed in a robe over his pants and white shirt, opened the door. He held the screen as Seamus carried Abby in, feet first.

Cuthbert walked across the foyer and unlocked his office. "In here. On the table." He removed his bathrobe and hung it over the back of his swivel desk chair. "I was about to go to bed," he said, rolling up his starched cuffs. "Put some coal in the stove." Seamus nodded. Black lumps thumped into the stove's belly.

With a foot lever, Cuthbert cranked up the head of the leather-cushioned exam table so Abby was half-sitting. Her feet were propped in front of her like gorged slugs. An ague of fear shook her. The office looked like a necromancer's chamber: glass-fronted cabinets were crammed with bottles of sickly green and brown medicines, racks of evil scissors, jars of syringes and needles. On the counter, the doctor arranged various sizes of forceps poised, Abby imagined, to pull fingernails or tongues.

Cuthbert spread a towel over the end of the exam table. "So, young lady, you cooked your feet like steamed puddings?" His hand shackled her ankle to stop its trembling. With a pair of long tweezers, he unwound the wrapping from her right foot. Her torso jerked as air touched the skin. She raised her head. Her feet were swollen, running with fluid, blanketed with yellow blisters. She dropped back, squeezing her eyelids shut.

"Hmmm. Second degree scalding—perhaps some third degree." He tweezed away torn bits of stocking clinging to the burned skin and placed them on a square of gauze. "Get me that brown bottle," he said to Seamus. "Third shelf on the right. Come. You can hold her down."

With Seamus gripping her ankle, Cuthbert punctured and drained the blisters, swabbing each with alcohol. Abby concentrated every scrap of will on Seamus. She memorized his chin, its curved fleshiness, a white scar to the right of his mouth, one front tooth lapping over the other, individual lines of stubble on his cheeks. She gathered the colors of him like bits of glass in a kaleidoscope—ruddy skin, copper hair, green eyes. She willed herself to become lost in the tilt of his head, his shoulders retreating from his thick neck.

————

The next morning, two hands appeared around the door, fingers intertwined, wriggling. She giggled. "Seamus, that is so infantile." The morning was improving. Abby had been dosed with several tablespoons of Lydia Pinkham's Vegetable Tonic, and she could no longer feel her feet.

At dawn, Abby had upset the bedpan while she peed. Dr. Cuthbert's wife, who had come to check on her, gave one sniff and called her daily house girl to clean up. Abby cringed with embarrassment, but the girl was kind, relieving the bedding's pressure on Abby's feet with a dusty hoop skirt from the attic slipped under the quilt.

Abby was propped now on a stack of pillows in the third floor maid's room, her feet protected like hothouse flowers. Seamus moved inside the bedroom, a pocket of cold accompanying him like an old friend. He wore the wrinkled clothes he'd worn the day before, but his face was smooth-shaven, and he smelled of bay rum.

"A devil of a night." He plucked her dress and knickers off the straight-backed chair, hung them on the doorknob, and moved the chair beside her bed.

"I feel strange," Abby said. "Like I'm sledding down Knox's Hill and the trees are swooshing by."

He peered at her eyes. "You've been nipping at a bottle?"

"Don't be shilly—silly, Seamus. I took some herbal tonic."

"Same effect. With thanks to Mrs. Pinkham."

Out the window, snow slid off the porch roof and hit the ground with a muffled thump. "I got through to your ma and pa," he said. "They should be here today. Maybe tomorrow." He reached inside his sheepskin-lined coat and pulled out a package wrapped in brown paper and tied with string. He looked at the plaster ceiling as if he were embarrassed. "A little something to make you feel better."

Abby unwrapped it slowly, savoring the texture of the string, the crackle of the paper under her fingers, the turns as she unrolled it. Seamus had never given her a gift before.

It was a doll with a china head, real hair, and a kidskin body, dressed in a silk dress and tiny leather shoes. The doll's eyes opened and closed. Abby's head buzzed and the room seemed to tilt. "I hate you, Seamus."

His mouth dropped open. "What the devil's the matter?"

"I don't want this stupid thing."

"Are you drunk on that infernal tonic?"

Abby tossed it on the quilt. "This is a present for a little girl. I'm not a little girl. I'm grown up."

"That's blarney. Even in the old country, twelve is still a child."

"I'm nearly fourteen, and don't you ever call me a child again." Abby's voice sounded high and childish.

"Right now, you sound drunk and seven." His face reddened and his brogue thickened.

"You can go to the devil and take this with you!" Abby snatched the doll and threw it at him. Seamus caught it before the china head shattered on the door frame.

"And you can stew in your own juice until your parents arrive, you spoiled brat." Seamus slammed the door as he left.

Abby stuffed her fingers in her mouth to keep from crying. Her childhood skin felt as though it was splitting like a pomegranate, with bloody seeds waiting to spill out.

A few minutes later she heard the front door close below her window. Seamus and Doc Cuthbert, hidden by the porch roof, talked in low voices. "Up the coast, all the way to Boston," Cuthbert said. "Another month, perhaps two, and we'll have enough."

"We've got to move quick. Shipping is going to be a problem," Seamus said.

"Not so much as you might think. The Kaiser would be very appreciative of any group that distracts the British from the Western Front. I have guarantees our boat will slip through the blockade."

"Will it now?" Seamus sounded unconvinced. "Gun manufacturers are tooling up, and factories have a backlog of government orders. I'm in contact with a dealer, but he needs a month's time, once we have the money in hand."

"We're certainly not paying him in full until the weapons are delivered," Cuthbert said.

"No, no. But he is a sharpster. He may demand earnest money in advance."

"Our group is fully capable of providing it."

Abby exhaled carefully, afraid they might hear. Seamus had found another contact.

10

Cora

April 2000

Once she was buckled in the seat with the heater blowing on her feet, Cora began to shiver, tremors that penetrated to her back teeth and the folds between her legs. Del brushed her arm as he twisted around to fish a sweatshirt from the rear seat. He leaned around the barrel of his upright shotgun to drape it over her shoulders.

"You drunk?"

"Not too bad." Her voice was high and shaky. She struggled to thread her fingers into the sweatshirt's right sleeve, but kept missing the opening. The loss of her mother seemed fresh, more vivid than it had ever been, each detail sharp. She thought of the bright blood on the sidewalk on Sutter Street.

"Thinking about offing yourself?"

"No." She wrapped the edges of the sweatshirt around her bare neck and let her legs splay open like a tired whore, abandoning her efforts to press her knees together to keep them still. It didn't seem worth it to keep her legs and arms aligned, her thoughts organized, her life on the proper freeway.

He guided the Crown Vic away from the curb, the stubs of his fingers sliding across the top of the wheel. She wondered if he had phantom pain similar to what she'd felt as a girl, a sudden ice pick thrust for her missing mother. When some part of you is gone, there is no predicting when or where you'll feel its loss. She wanted to tell him that, but it was too much. The radio unit crackled with traffic from the dispatchers. She knew their number-coded language, but tonight it seemed muffled, as if she were hearing it from another room with the door closed. She breathed a cloud onto the car window and the ghost of her face reflected back.

Somer plucked an insulated aluminum mug out of the cup holder and handed it to her. She smelled coffee, tasted his mouth on the rim. Panic ballooned in her throat. Too near. He was too close, Alice was too close, they were stones on her chest, present and past, cutting off her air. The hot coffee went down her windpipe. She coughed, spraying coffee on the dash, and thumped her chest with her fist. She took a deep breath that scraped her throat. Her mother's ghostly scent and touch faded.

"I ought to have you committed on a seventy-two hour hold," he said.

"You'd have three days of peace, and then I'd be back."

His chest rumbled, but she couldn't tell if he were growling or laughing. "You're a pisser, aren't you?"

"Only in my better moments."

Somer's turn signal clicked. He made a right on Clinton, then headed north on Highway 81, the route Cora had taken that afternoon. The speedometer needle pulsed at fifteen miles over the speed limit. Typical cop. She tucked her hands in her armpits. Too tired to brace herself, she allowed the car's sway on the curves to shift her from side to side.

The Preble off-ramp flicked by. They weren't driving to the O'Brien farm or past the farm to the site of the old store shown in her mother's photo.

"Why didn't you tell me you were once married to Judith O'Brien?" she said.

"I don't exactly keep a scrapbook."

"You had a major conflict of interest. You should've called in another agency to investigate."

"What for? Everybody in the area over eighteen knows Judith dumped me, and nobody's upset about my handling the case. Except you."

"But I could be kicking up some very smelly shit, and Troop C doesn't need another scandal."

"That was a long time ago. Before I came here."

"The Internet has given people long memories."

"Nobody will believe you. You're a head case too dumb or too crazy to come in from the cold." He turned left onto a dark side road. The hum of the engine deepened as the car climbed.

"Conflict of interest may be the least of your problems," Cora said.

In the dash light, she saw his eyebrows lift. "You're going to try to implicate me? Good luck."

"It's a legitimate line of inquiry."

"I had no reason to be angry at Sean. My only regret about our divorce was its impact on Tyler. A good kid, but very shy. He and I did a lot together when Judith and I were still married: fishing, hunting, and playing baseball. Since then, he's had a hard time. Never took to Sean."

"Judith sounded like she was in bad financial trouble, and she'd have a hard time supporting him."

"Judith always has a financial problem. It's part of her act—the gifted artist forced to work for the Philistines, looking for a benefactor."

"She has a point. It's tough to be creative and support a family."

"She's been creative. At spending Sean's money."

"Do you still love her?" Cora asked.

Cora thought she felt the car swerve a little, but maybe it was dizziness. Somer tightened his hand on the wheel. "Lady, I don't know you. My personal life is private. Keep your nose out of it."

"Not so private. You're investigating the death of the man who stole the woman you loved." Cora tried to imagine Stephen driving through a storm to rescue her, as Somer had done for Judith the night Sean died. It wouldn't have happened. Why was it that some women were so memorable that men were willing to be chained to them forever? Whatever it was, she didn't have it.

Once Stephen had moved into a condo with Tami, he neglected Nathan and never really looked at Cora again. When she tried to meet his eyes, he turned his face slightly away, as if he were discouraging an over-friendly supermarket clerk. He didn't seem to hate or even dislike her; he was just indifferent. But not Del. He was still involved with Judith somehow.

"I saw her in the parking lot at the supermarket tonight," Somer said. "She wants me to get rid of you."

"You mean, bump me off? I thought we were getting on so well."

His voice lightened. "Nothing that drastic, although it does have a lot of appeal." He was quiet for a minute, apparently savoring the thought of some violent felony. "She was thinking more in terms of my diverting your attention by reopening the investigation with Santerra as the suspect."

"And he can't prove himself innocent, since he's dead. I assume your reward for this favor is the return to your embrace of the fair Miss Judith."

"Something like that."

"So you were on your way home to change the sheets and open a bottle of wine when Debbie called."

"Actually, I turned her down."

"Honor raises its ugly head."

"Not really. I was just tired of it." They left the highway. There were no lights to illuminate the narrow, curved road as it wound uphill. Trees pressed close to the asphalt and blotted out all but a narrow strip of stars.

Cora swallowed some of the coffee, which was cold and acid now. "Where are we going?"

"Song Mountain. It's at the top of the next hill. There's a ski area here, but the snow's about gone. I've always liked the view."

"In the dark?" She realized she was in a car with an armed possible homicide suspect on a deserted county road. It sounded like a slasher movie, but she was too drained to care, and somehow, she didn't think he was a killer. He steered the car into a turnout and snapped off the lights. The idling engine vibrated the soles of her feet. Stars were scattered to the western horizon, and below, darkness ironed out the hills to a flat plain. Wind hit the car, a rush in her ears and a half-felt impact against the door.

He released the seat catch and stretched his legs. "There's Otisco Lake, the dark oval area with no lights that looks like a finger in a glove. It's where the glacier withdrew to the north."

"I feel like I'm sixteen and I'm parked with my boyfriend on Twin Peaks. He's about to put his hand down my pants."

He gave her a slow look, half mocking and half serious. "If that's an invitation, I'll take a rain check. Conflict of interest and all."

The dispatcher's voice blended with the hum of the engine and the whine of the wind. "I come up to this place every ten days or so," he said. "It helps me put things in order. I know every road, every pond, every house and barn. When I get them all arranged in my mind, I'm ready to tackle whatever's bothering me."

"And tonight, you're bothered by Sean O'Brien's death."

The lines in his face were deeper and his jowls sagged more than they had that morning. "I answered Debbie's call to prevent something happening to you on my watch. I don't need a confidant."

"So why don't you confide in Judith? Because she might have killed her husband?"

He looked in her direction, but didn't seem to see her. "Problem is, the facts aren't right."

"Oh?"

"Statistically, males who commit suicide rarely poison themselves. They use a gun or commit suicide-by-cop. If they do use poison, it's not strychnine. Too gruesome and painful."

"Do you think Sean was involved in the scam? Buy registered Holsteins, inject them with some lethal but undetectable substance, and inflate their value for the insurance money?"

"Probably. I've talked to Len Crutcher, the insurance investigator, and he thinks it could have been Sucostrin, which suffocates the animal by paralyzing the respiratory system. Sucostrin is virtually impossible to detect if it's injected into the tail vein."

A rising sensation of violence rose from the darkness below, where thousands of years before, ice had ripped a black wound in the earth's flesh. The melting ice, the movement of huge frozen sheets embedded with dirt, dead trees, animal carcasses, and perhaps even human flesh, had ripped and scarred this land. She shivered with the sensation that the slow, violent movement continued even now. Huge animals writhing in terror, Sean O'Brien convulsing on his study floor, Franklin Santerra blasting his head with a shotgun. Any trace of humor she originally had seen in the story of two men and three cows vanished. She rubbed her hands on her thighs. Her fingers tingled. This was a good story.

"Santerra and Sean, they had some other relationship, something besides an insurance scam, didn't they?" she said.

"What makes you think so?"

"Either they both committed suicide over a messy but minor crime—which seems unlikely—or Franklin was so devastated by Sean's death he killed himself, or someone murdered them both, for unknown reasons. None of those scenarios makes sense unless they were linked in some way," Cora said.

"I never heard rumors about them being queer, but if they were, so what? Rural New York isn't San Francisco, but even here, gay relationships aren't uncommon. Even if they were outed or fighting, that's not dire enough for a double suicide." He moved restlessly beside her. "My legs are cramped. I'm getting out."

"I'll come with you." Possibilities swirled inside the car, and she wanted to keep them moving.

He turned off the engine. "That sweatshirt isn't going to be enough." He popped the trunk lid, climbed out, and removed a blanket. "Here."

A plow had scraped the turnout, mounding the snow, now diminished by the spring thaw. They walked to the edge, Somer's bulk shielding her from the wind. She hugged the blanket and rubbed her cheek against its rough fibers. She suddenly remembered a time, as if she were watching two actors in a movie, when Stephen had abraded her nipples with his unshaven beard.

"If you look straight down my arm at those three pinpoints of light, that's Sean's place," Somer said.

"I'm told there's an old store, fallen to ruins, not too far away," Cora said.

"I know it. Just over the line, in Onondaga County. From up here, it's about a finger width north of Maple Leaf Farm, in that black area." He tugged his hand out of his pocket and waggled his little finger alongside a trio of tiny lights.

"My mother, Alice Macpherson Brooks, lived right there when she was young." The wind shifted, snatching at her hair and whipping it around her face. "She ran away from me one night and I never saw her again."

Somer turned to stare at her.

"She took a brown leather suitcase, an avocado-green knit dress that I didn't like, and a purse with a short handle and a gold clasp. She took a picture of a giraffe I'd made in school that was taped to the refrigerator." Cora took a breath. "When I put on my nightgown, I lied to her that I'd brushed my teeth. When I woke up the next morning, she was gone." Cora's memories were new to her, hot, and dangerous.

Somer cleared his throat, as if loosening a response. His boots creaked with the shift of his weight. "She didn't abandon you because you lied to her."

"I know." Cora intended to say it firmly, but her voice turned quavery.

"You can search out every liar, write a thousand stories, expose them all, but it won't bring her back."

"I didn't become a journalist because of some repressed guilt over telling my mother a fib when I was six."

"Okay."

What did Somer think of her? Did he see her as a minor irritant or a candidate for serious psychotropic medication? The cumulative impact of bad sherry, no dinner, and the empty void below them threw her off balance. It reminded her of standing on the fulcrum of the seesaw when she was a kid, shifting her weight and feeling the solidity of her footing disappear from under her.

He scooped up some dirty leftover snow. The ball hit a tree trunk with a thump. "Anyway," he said, "you have your own family now."

"My son." She cocked her head to one side, surprised by his change in subject.

"That makes up for it."

"I guess."

"Of course it does." He sounded angry. "The family part passed me by. I was an only child, and I knew I wanted three or four kids. I met Judith in college, but she left me just before graduation. By the time I came back here and found her again, she had Tyler and didn't want another. I was positive she'd change her mind, but she didn't. She divorced me, married Sean, and took Tyler with her."

"My son's also gone. To school in Boston." The wind seemed to dig at her eyes, and they blurred with defensive tears. "I'm driving to New York Saturday to meet him."

11

―――――

Cora
April 2000

On the return trip from Song Mountain, Del's cell phone interrupted the dispatcher's crackling voice. He flipped it open with his thumb.

"Neville. Yeah, what? Christ, when?" The engine surged, thrusting Cora back against the upholstery. "Who found him? He's at General? I'll be there in ten." He snapped the phone's cover shut and clenched it in his palm. A strong hand. Not to be trifled with.

"What's wrong?"

"Tyler. Judith's son. He's at the ER. Looks like an OD." Del lowered his window and slapped a flashing red light on the roof. The car barreled south, then west over Cortland's empty streets. He braked to a stop in the No Parking zone outside the emergency room lobby.

He ducked his head and scrambled from the car, slamming the door. Cora trotted at his heels like a hunting dog. Inside, they met Neville, pacing between the hard plastic chairs, his normally ruddy face blue under the florescent lights. In the background, the cries of a sick child mingled with a Broadway show tune from the PA system.

She felt the prick of Neville's stare; he probably was wondering why she was here. The two men hurried through the double swinging doors, and Cora darted after them like a child afraid to be left behind. A nurse in rubber-soled shoes pointed them toward an alcove screened with a gray sliding curtain.

"Wait outside, ma'am." Neville's fingers clamped firmly on her elbow as he guided her toward the lobby.

"No." Heat rushed to her face, and her heart beat against her ribs.

Behind the curtain Judith gave a brief, hard cry. Del turned to Cora briefly. "Go outside. I'll come as soon as I know something."

"You promise?"

He nodded. In the curtain's gap, Cora saw the muddy soles of a pair of Air Jordans lapping over the edge of a gurney, the feet splayed outward as if the patient were napping. Three people clustered at the other end, bent over Tyler's head. An intravenous line pierced his arm and it looked as though the medical personnel were trying to install an airway. Judith huddled against the wall, her hair falling like a torn headdress around her face, her features skeletal, twisted in anger. The curtain closed again with a slide of metal rings.

In the waiting room, Cora wished she smoked. The ritual of the package, its crackle, then the lighter's click, the inhalation, the smoke, the ashes. Nearby, the mother hunched over the baby as if she were convulsed with a stomach ache.

Through the window, she saw a pickup truck drive up with a squeal of brakes and stop behind Del's car. A teenaged boy jumped out and ran around to open the passenger door. The teen, first hitching up his baggy jeans, slung a man's arm over his shoulder and hefted him out. "Dale, goddammit, not so fast. Whaddare you doin'?" Blood spattered the man's pajama bottoms and drenched a makeshift bandage on his foot. A watermelon stomach sagged under the hem of his plaid wool shirt.

"Come on, Pop. It's just a little way."

The older man sank back on the seat. "Get a wheelchair, you fucking idiot."

The injured man's skin was clammy, and he was breathing heavily by the time the boy pushed him to the admissions window. "Cut his foot with an axe." The clerk nodded and handed the injured man a clipboard with forms to fill out. The spittle of his profanity filled the air. The clerk admired one French-manicured nail while she notified someone by telephone.

Cora went to the vending machine in the hall. A cup of coffee would taste good now. She'd thrust her hand into her pocket before she realized she still wore Del's sweatshirt. She had left Seneca House hours ago with no wallet. She fiddled with the cord on the hood. What part did Tyler, troubled sixteen-year-old, play in the deaths of Sean O'Brien and Franklin Santerra? Maybe the kid's OD wasn't directly related. Youngsters were susceptible, easily consumed by unforeseen tragedy. She'd covered a story last year involving the suicides of three teens following the death of another in a crash. Two were friends of the victim, but one had never known him.

What had been Tyler's real relationship with Sean? Hours earlier she'd stood in the room where Sean died. The moment seemed fuzzy, with indistinct edges. Judith had said Tyler wasn't home that night. Del had said Tyler was failing in school. Cora frowned. What did the boy look like? She had seen no pictures of Tyler hanging on the walls at the farm. Dozens of Sean and over a hundred of prize show cows. Judith was a professional photographer. No photos of him in his baseball uniform or with a girlfriend at the lake? How did Tyler fit into Judith's life? It seemed unlikely he traveled with them on Sean's trips to livestock shows; Tyler would have missed too much school.

She flinched to think what would have happened to Nathan if she'd traveled on assignment during the months after Stephen left. It had been a terrible time, but Nathan had never tried to kill himself. Had he taken drugs? Probably. She'd searched for signs, but hadn't unearthed any baggies, needles, or unfamiliar tablets.

The automatic door wheezed. Cora glanced over her shoulder to see Rico, the ranch hand from Maple Leaf Farm, and his hatchet-nosed sidekick, Pedro. They hovered close to the exit, hands stuffed in their jeans pockets, talking in Spanish.

"Hola. Are you here to inquire about Tyler?" She stirred her memory like cold soup to bring up her Spanish vocabulary. "Doctors are with him, but there is no news yet."

"Gracias." Rico combed the coarse hairs of his mustache with his nails.

"I'm Cora, a friend of Señora O'Brien," she said. "I met you today at the farm."

"I remember, Señora," Rico said. He slid Pedro a swift glance.

"Do you know what happened to Tyler?"

"We don't know nothing. We only see him and tell Señora."

"You discovered him?"

"Si. We went to the *mercado*, I bought a money order for my wife. And some Dos Equis. On our way home, we see his car by the lake."

"Was he conscious?"

Pedro spoke for the first time, his gold front tooth winking. "We think car was empty. We think maybe he drown himself. Then we opened the door …" He demonstrated, slumping down, twisting his head to the side and dropping his jaw. Like a hanged man.

"You didn't call 911?"

Pedro's eyes crept toward the door as though contemplating leg bail. Of course he hadn't called. Even though they had work visas, they were suspicious of law enforcement on general principles

"We called *La Jefa*," Rico said. "She come pretty quick. Drive very fast."

"While you waited—did you try to revive him?"

"Oh, si," Rico said. "We did the …" He imitated shaking a limp body and slapping the cheeks. "He very white, like a ghost."

"Judith arrived, and then what happened?"

"We carry him to *La Jefa*'s car. She drive away." He gestured a racing car with his hand.

"Why did you think he'd drowned himself? Do you know him well?" Cora said. From the corner of her eye, she saw Neville walk out of the emergency suite, a weapon on his hip under his suit jacket.

Rico and Pedro hit the door running, Rico's New York Yankees cap flying off his head.

"Hey—shit," Neville said. "I wanted to have a chat with those two." He pulled a notebook from his shirt pocket and wrote a reminder to himself.

"How is he?"

"They won't know anything for awhile yet. They're putting a tube down his throat to suck all the fluid from his stomach. It looks as though he drank a snootful of alcohol along with codeine-laced Tylenol."

Cora's legs trembled, and she collapsed with a thump in one of the hard chairs. She was so tired.

"Ma'am. Do you need to lie down?"

"Only in my bed. Don't even think about wheeling me in there."

"Right. The boss—Major Somer—asked me to take you home."

"I'm waiting here."

"Ma'am, we'll give you a thorough briefing as soon as we know something." Neville brushed his bristle haircut to attention.

"Great. I'll be right here." She wiggled her body in the chair to demonstrate how ready she was to wait.

"I'll be in deep shit, like permanent graveyard shift, if I don't deliver you to the B and B," Neville said.

"I tell you what, Neville. If you buy me a cup of coffee, I'll tell the major you tried oh-so-valiantly, but I was intractable." Neville scurried out to the vending machine in the hall, his hand jingling the change in his pocket.

When he put the paper cup in her hand, Cora blew on the coffee's oily surface. "Is he conscious?"

Neville looked blank for a second. "Oh. Tyler. Not yet. Two or three hours, maybe." He excused himself and walked outside to take a call.

Cora looked around. The mother and baby had disappeared; into a treatment bay, she hoped. An ER orderly pushed the axe victim through the swinging doors in a wheelchair. The lobby smelled of blood from his wound and a stronger odor that she associated with anger and fear.

The teenager, sitting on his tailbone, thumbed the keypad on his phone. He wore a pair of very expensive sports shoes with molded uppers that reminded Cora of space helmets. He ignored her with such chin-thrusting attitude that Cora took a chance. "Do you know him?"

"Who?" As if he hadn't been eavesdropping on her conversation with Neville.

"The boy we were talking about. Tyler O'Brien. He's in there, almost dead from an overdose."

Dale continued to move the keys on his phone. "I might have seen him at school." A scattering of chin hairs wiggled when he talked.

"Is he a stoner?" She hoped her teen vernacular wasn't too out of date; Nathan had been gone nine months.

"I dunno."

She must have been even more tired than she felt. "What I meant was, have you heard anything, any talk around school about Tyler using drugs?"

He scratched his stomach under his T-shirt. "There's been some kids saying stuff. But not exactly about using."

Cora waited without moving, as if trying to catch a glimpse of a feral cat. The background music played "Red Roses for a Blue Lady."

"He be, you know, doing business," Dale said.

"Selling, that is." Disappointment clogged her throat. She knew Tyler, she thought she did, actually she didn't, but she'd been cheering for him, living with the silent barns and the wind and the grunting pig and the new father.

"How did you find out?" Cora asked.

A nurse from the ER poked her head around the door and waved to Dale. "He wants you." Dale slid his skinny ass off the chair and hitched up his pants. The nurse turned back inside to speak to someone.

"Dale," Cora said. "It could have been you with a tube down your throat getting your stomach pumped. Facing brain damage. You and Tyler can't be that different."

"I'm not one of them."

"Absolutely not."

"Once, you know, I might have taken a little hit, and O'Brien all of a sudden, was the go-to guy."

He shouldered open the door and disappeared inside.

12

Cora

Cora
April 2000

There was a hole in her mother's torso. Cora knew she was asleep at the same time as she watched the dream unfurl. Through the opening, she saw the tree and the lake again, like looking through a peephole. Her mother stared at her and Cora looked down at her own stomach to see a matching round gap.

All at once, she was awake. Somewhere in the house, a washing machine hummed. She raised her head a couple of inches to look at her wrist. Eleven-thirty in the morning. Her cheek felt sore where it had pressed against her watch. On the West Coast, Stu Manion would be in his office. He'd left two messages last night, but she hadn't called him back. She fell asleep again and awoke at two. Tyler O'Brien probably felt like this, his forehead glued to the bed. If she sat up, she'd have to lift the full weight of the mattress.

Tyler had been wheeled to an inpatient room sometime after two-thirty in the morning. Judith had stayed to watch over him, but Del barred Cora from interviewing the boy. Del drove Cora home to ensure she didn't make a nuisance of herself.

Cora's cell phone whirred like a rattlesnake against the bedside table, stopped, and began again. "It's me." Del sounded annoyed. "I've been calling all day."

"I've been busy."

"You're in bed, aren't you?"

"I'm up." She propped a pillow against the headboard and bent her knees to hold herself in a half-sitting position. She squeezed her eyes shut to ease her headache.

"This is your lucky day. I've got chili cooking," he said. "Come by at seven."

"Chili sounds so terrible right now, I'd leave town to avoid it."

"You haven't tasted mine yet. The heat will incinerate your hangover. My mother will be here, too. She's lonely and likes to meet new people."

She opened one eye. "Is this a date?"

"Absolutely not." Del sounded annoyed, as if she'd caught him eating a third cookie.

"Good. If it were a date, I'd have to say no. Conflict of interest." Was she flirting? God, she couldn't remember what it was like. It had been, what, twenty-five years? Since she first met Stephen. A generation.

"I'll send an e-mail with directions. See you at seven," he said.

"Wait, don't hang up. How's Tyler?"

"He feels lousy, and he's climbing the walls at the hospital. He'll be released tomorrow, hopefully to drug treatment if I can find a space."

Cora showered, dressed in jeans and a navy pullover sweater, took two Advil, washed them down with a glass of metallic tap water, and brushed her teeth. She shouldered her rucksack, and as she descended the stairs, called the hospital on her cell. Tyler had been admitted to room 243. No visitors or calls except family. And law enforcement, she assumed. If Tyler was being shipped to rehab, probably tomorrow, she needed to see him this afternoon.

Outside, the sunlight was filled with tiny meteors of excruciating brightness. Paul Landesdowne and his handyman pounded on a dry-rotted side porch with a regiment of hammers. Her eyelids and temples were tender to the slightest touch.

She slipped on her sunglasses and drove to a florist shop to buy a cluster of latex balloons embossed with "Get Well" messages. They bounced against the ceiling in the car's back seat and obscured her view out the back window, so she drove at exactly thirty to avoid the notice of the Cortland cops. In the hospital lobby, she waved at the volunteer who manned the information desk, caught the elevator, and got off at two. The bobbing balloons screened her from the attendant at the nurse's station, and Cora slipped into 243. No one was monitoring the door. Judith must have taken a break. A rumpled pillow lay on the floor beside a chrome-footed visitor's chair.

Tyler lay in a bed with metal sides, his head and the knees raised, his hospital gown drooping off one pimply shoulder.

She released the balloons and they floated jauntily, anchored only by the weights tied to the ends of the strings.

"Hello. I'm Cora."

His thumb worked the television remote, flipping from channel to channel. "There's no cable in this shitty place." He threw it on the coverlet without giving her a look.

"Enjoy it now, because tomorrow you'll be at rehab, with no TV for sixty days," Cora said.

Despite Judith's assertion he was sixteen going on twenty, Tyler was young looking, with his mother's thin, light bones. He'd bleached his dark brown hair at the tips. Nathan had been small like Tyler for awhile—five three or five four—before he got his last growth spurt. During that period, a neighbor had asked Nathan if he'd graduated from the sixth grade yet. The neighbor's house was egged at Halloween.

Tyler's face shone with sweat, his eyelids were puffed, and his skin held a greenish undertone. An intravenous tube taped to the back of his hand dripped clear liquid into a vein. A monitor traced his life flow in a thin, nervous line on the screen. Tyler's jaw muscle was a knotted clump of misery under his skin. He jabbed the remote again to increase the volume.

Cora slid the straight-backed chair alongside the bed and sat down. She removed a notebook, a pen, and a palm-sized tape recorder from her backpack.

Oprah was interviewing a doctor, a psychologist, and a menopausal woman about hot flashes. Tyler watched without blinking, his chin tucked against his chest. She guessed he was angry and scared. This was a good development, She waited, her hands crossed in her lap. Ten minutes.

"So you have forms and stuff," Tyler said.

Cora held her breath. He thought she was from the agency that ran the county's drug diversion program. She considered whether to go along with the pretense, pose as a social worker. A juicy interview she'd never get otherwise.

On screen Oprah put on her caring face, batted her ten-pound eyelashes, nodded her head sympathetically. Her varnished hair shone like a black hard hat under the lights. Subtly, she worked the audience, encouraging the woman to over-dramatize her life.

Cora sighed, clicked on her tape recorder, and flipped open her note pad. "I'm a news reporter writing a story about your stepfather's death. I want to ask you about it."

Tyler pressed the mute, shrank further into the pillow. The voices of two nurses echoed in the hall. A bathroom faucet dripped. The metal bed rail rattled as Tyler jiggled it with his foot.

"Mom told me you'd been around. She doesn't like you."

"It's your choice, whether you talk to me or not," Cora said. "I don't get the feeling you and Sean were pals."

"Go away."

"You didn't kill him," Cora hoped it was true. "I'm going to find out who did."

"Del is doing that."

"He and I are working together," Cora said.

Tyler's mouth twisted. He grabbed a kidney-shaped pan and retched miserably into it. "I wish I'd done it. Wish I'd killed him."

"Wish you'd committed a crime that could land you in prison? How come? He adopted you, gave you and your mother a chance to travel. Owned a farm that you'd inherit someday."

"That fucker didn't want me. And I didn't travel with them. They left me at that stinking farm, smelling the cow shit, because I had to go to school."

"So who stayed with you while they were gone?"

"You mean who babysat me?"

"You're pretty old for that."

His head rolled back and forth on the pillow. "Sometimes I'd stay with Del at his place, but mostly I'd sleep down at the trailer."

"With Rico and Pedro?"

"Yeah."

"They don't speak much English."

Tyler gave her a sideways glance as if to say, what did we need to talk about?

A big, empty white house, mother gone with her new husband, a bed in a crowded, drafty double-wide with lonely adult men who drank away their time in a foreign country. "I remember the smell," Cora said suddenly. "Stale liquor, it clings to the upholstery, and the rug, and the kitchen linoleum."

Tyler shot her a look of disgust. "On a farm, who'd notice?"

Cora's mouth felt dry, her tongue coated with fuzz from last night's drinking. Father. Daughter. She'd think about it later. She clicked the Pause button on the recorder, went to the bathroom, and filled a paper cup with water. As she drank, she heard Tyler talking in a low voice on his cell phone.

" ... find it. I'm going to be in for two months."

The phone was resting on the bedside table when she returned. She switched the recorder on. "Your mother said the night Sean died you weren't home."

"I stayed over with Dale Tilly from school. There was a big storm, and I decided not to drive home."

"You have your own car?"

"Truck. An F-150 with a 5.4-liter engine."

Poor little rich boy. Nathan had driven a used Geo Metro when he was in high school, small enough to squeeze into one of San Francisco's hard-to-find parking spaces. Not a truck on steroids that got twelve miles to a gallon.

"Fancy, for a kid whose stepfather was going broke."

"I saved my lunch money." Tyler scratched the back of his hand near the IV needle.

"You got the money for the truck selling drugs at school. Isn't that right?"

"Nope."

"I talked to someone who said you were the guy with the goods. Where were you getting your supply? From your stepfather?"

"That fucking Dale. I heard he was here last night in emergency with his meth-head dad. Actually, you've got it ass backwards."

"Dale was selling drugs?"

He belched.

"Were you a buyer?"

Tyler rolled onto his side. The loosened ties of his hospital gown revealed pale skin and bony, vulnerable spinal knobs. She felt sorry for him. It was unlike her, she realized ruefully, to jump on the sympathy train for a foul-mouthed, obnoxious, and possibly drug-dealing felon.

"Del talked about you last night," she said.

Tyler's stiff bones relaxed when she mentioned Del. "He probably said what a fuckup I am."

"Actually, he talked about the good times the two of you used to have, fishing and playing ball."

"Yeah. Del, he liked baseball." Tyler turned onto his back and drew his mouth into a straight line. Cora had seen Nathan do that to prevent his lips from trembling. Outside, an ambulance siren brayed.

A plastic bag containing Tyler's clothes sat on a shelf under the television set. The dirty jeans and huge, muddy sports shoes looked like trash dumped from a garbage can. Tyler must have felt like soiled clothes after Judith left Del. She'd married Sean, aggressively severed Tyler's ties to Del, and left the boy alone while she traveled with her rich new husband. What capped it for Tyler must have been the adoption. He'd signed his despised new name on every school form and class paper.

Even now, with Sean dead, Tyler didn't get consolation from Del, because the kid was in the center of what could be a murder.

Tyler's leg muscle twitched under the sheet.

"You were there, weren't you?" Her voice seemed muffled at the same time her thoughts were clear.

"I told you, I was with my buddy."

"No, you'd driven home. Your truck was parked behind the trailer, maybe. Del spotted it, and that's why he stayed, while Neville investigated the so-called suicide. He wanted to protect you."

Tyler shot her a scared look, as if a glimpse might damage his eyes. "Okay, I was watching TV at the trailer, but I didn't see nothing. I swear."

"Why did you leave your friend's place?"

"His old man was freaking."

"Pedro and Rico were at the trailer?"

"Pedro and I switched between MTV and soccer on Telemundo. Rico was asleep in back."

"Why didn't you go to the house? Your mother was there the whole time."

Tyler pressed a fist against his mouth. The monitor beeped as his blood pressure spiked. A nurse in scrubs—lavender pants and a flowered top—hurried in. Her thumb stabbed at the monitor reset button, and the signal fell silent. Her cold gaze settled on Cora.

"Ms. Brooks? Major Somer called. The patient is to have no visitors except family. If you don't leave immediately, a trooper will escort you off the premises."

The nurse lowered the head of Tyler's bed.

"I just wanted to ask …"

The nurse clamped her hand over Cora's arm. "Out." She outweighed Cora by fifty pounds. Why was it that so many nurses were fat? Well, hefty, like their clunky shoes. Cora looked over her shoulder at Tyler to get in a last lick. "What is it you're hunting for? That you won't be able to locate until you get out?"

He watched the TV screen and didn't turn his head. The nurse's SUV-sized hip shoved Cora out the door.

———

Cora perched beside a split-leaf philodendron in the hospital lobby while she waited on hold for Manion. A couple tottered past her in perfect step, the man's shoulders age-hunched under his wool jacket, his wife clasping his sleeve as she led him along. Cora imagined them sharing the bathroom sink in the morning, or stepping around each other in an evening waltz as they cooked dinner.

Stu interrupted her thoughts. "Manion here."

"It's Cora."

"Do you work here? I think I recall the name."

"Sorry I haven't checked in more often, but I don't have much progress to report."

"So, put together what you've got."

"I don't have enough. The more I work on the story, the more complicated it gets."

"D'Arcy is giving me heartburn. He asks for a status report every damn day."

"Stu, we're in a situation where we can't run one of those, 'It's a mystery, sure enough,' stories like they do on television. The *Standard* has got to solve the thing, and I don't have the answer yet."

"How long?"

"That's what I'm telling you, I don't know."

"Ramp up. You're bankrupting our travel budget. I wouldn't have sent you, except D'Arcy wanted it."

A nurse assistant pushed a mother and a swaddled baby through the lobby in a wheelchair. A pink cap covered the infant's tiny head. Alongside shuffled the father, loaded with bags and a blooming yellow chrysanthemum.

"By the way," Manion said, "you'll be happy to know Traci is keeping up with your beat. She broke a terrific story Tuesday on a terrorist cell in the Mission. Excellent enterprise."

"I've been following that story for months, waiting for an arrest. I had a tip from the detective inspector."

"Yes, well, she's doing a great job. Real aggressive, but gets along with people. Doesn't give me heartburn."

"A Tums with big tits."

"One more comment, and I'll write you up. I want you back in San Francisco a week from today."

13

Abby
April 1917

It had been two months, and the skin on Abby's feet was pink and healthy but still tender when she pressed it with her thumb. She spun on the piano stool. At each turn, it squeaked.

"Abby, stop that." Her mother's mouth twisted oddly, talking while she held several straight pins between her lips. She was on her knees, measuring the hem of Rose Conklin's wedding dress.

"Go downstairs. Work at the counter," her mother said. She sat back on her heels and surveyed the flow of the batiste skirt.

Rose twitched the cuff. "I think it needs another row of lace." She was set to marry Ed Tinsley Saturday. Ed had enlisted in the army to fight the Germans, a week after President Wilson stood before Congress to ask for a declaration of war. Monday, Ed would join the others from the National Guard at the Cortland train depot.

Abby felt achy and bursting, as if something under her skin was trying to escape. "I waited counter all day yesterday. I want to go to Emily's."

Ruth took the last of the pins out of her mouth and stabbed them in her wrist pincushion. Before her mother changed her mind, Abby stuffed her arms into her coat sleeves and ran down the back stairs. After so many days inside, the cold made her face feel alive, and the air sang in her throat.

Patches of snow still lay on the hills like spots on a hunting dog. A breath of green fuzz lay in the folds of the land; leaves grew secretly on the larches and elms. Two blood-red cardinals called from the woods near where the faint trail of compacted dirt led between the trees in the direction of her father's still.

Abby glanced around. She wasn't going to Emily's or the still. Instead, she crossed the muddy ruts in the road and started down the hill toward Maple Leaf Farm. She'd taken a few steps when she heard the plop of hooves. George Wright and his team slogged toward her. She swallowed, humming the Doxology to herself. If he stopped, he'd try to put his hands on her. All the girls knew.

He pulled the wagon up short. The horse on Abby's side reared a little as the bit pulled at his mouth. "Where you headed, Missy?" The filthy man called her the same nickname as her father.

Abby forced her lips into a little smile. "Looking for flowers. Mama needs a bouquet."

"Need some help?" Wright rubbed his thumb and forefinger together.

Abby looked away, making her eyes focus up the road toward her father's hay barn, where the loft door stood half-open. "I have to be quick. Mama is watching from the window," Abby said.

"Oh, well." He picked up the whip and lashed the horses' backs. They leaped forward, sending the wagon onto the driver's side wheels before righting itself. She didn't move until it rolled around the curve.

She walked quickly to the farm, passing the O'Brien's stone-fronted icehouse, much larger than her father's, dug deep into the hill to cool the milk before it went to the co-op. She avoided the O'Brien's house, its paint bone white after a winter of punishing storms. Old Mrs. O'Brien always asked her questions, then stared and pursed her lips as if she sucked some meaning from the words. Abby felt the same kind of pull in her stomach now, just thinking about her, a green-apple feeling.

As she neared the barns, cows bawled in different pitches, like human voices. Abby darted between the silos, their height throwing cold shadows. Ahead, she saw Seamus open the gate, as if he were inviting guests, and let in about twenty cows with swollen pink sacs. At the milking shed, Seamus' brother, Leland, hosed off their hoofs and udders, protected by a rubber apron and tall rubber boots.

Abby crouched in the shadows. Seamus herded the last of the cows into the enclosure, closed the gate. His red hair glowed, vivid against the muddy cattle pens and gray fences. Leland's hair was paler, a sandy brown, as though God had run out of color by the time he was made. Abby wanted to stare and stare and never glance away.

Seamus slapped his palm on the fence post and headed in the direction of his farm office. When she tiptoed inside without knocking, she saw him leaning over an open ledger on his desk. She sniffed, her nostrils spreading, and caught the scent of his tobacco. His pen scratched. His eyes flicked up to see who was there.

"If it isn't my Tiger Stripes." He smiled, his beard stubble glinting in the crinkles around his mouth.

"I'm better,' Abby said. "I walked here, and I'm going back to school next week." Her voice was lower, heated somewhere in her chest.

His swivel chair squeaked as he leaned it back, his chapped hands resting on the arms. "You're different. Taller."

"I'm fourteen now. Two months until I graduate." She moved a chair close to the desk and sat down. "It's okay about the doll, Seamus."

He clicked his fingernails on the desk. "I may have made a small error, not noticing you were almost a young lady."

"Did you get the guns?" she whispered.

Seamus paused, like the second before a match touches a firecracker. "I was never serious about buying guns. I would be a traitor if I did that, wouldn't I?"

"I heard, Seamus, that day at Dr. Cuthbert's."

"Christ's blood! Don't you ever mind your own business?"

Anger burned her cheeks. "You were talking loud. If you have a secret, talk quiet."

"It's unsafe, your delving into the affairs of others."

"Did you get them? Are they on the ships yet?"

He moved his jaws, as if he were chewing gristle. "Have you told anyone?"

"You asked me not to. Before."

"Good lass." He slid the ledger aside and rolled his chair to the window, squinting toward the main road and the hill beyond.

"Are they going to arrest and hang you Seamus?"

His face whitened until she saw some freckles on his cheeks. "I'm in no danger unless someone yammers." He rolled the chair close to her and murmured, "My safety depends on you, Tiger Stripes."

The office door scraped open, swollen from the winter. Seamus rolled his chair away.

"The seed delivery is here. Fellow wants to be paid," said Leland. The bill of his cap settled over his eyebrows, putting his eyes in shadow. He had graduated eighth grade from Miss Miller four years ago, but hadn't continued to high school.

"I'll be back in a wink, Abby," Seamus said. He strode out the door and stumped down the steps. Leland waited with his hand on the knob as if he listened for something; then closed the door behind him.

Abby hooked her heels over the chair rung. Seamus's pen lay crosswise on the blotter. The ledger entries from this angle looked like Chinese writing, his pen strokes flattened, like a warped reflection in a carnival mirror. Some of the ink flowed into the crevices of the paper, blurring the numbers.

A flow started inside her, like peeing but a little different. She pressed her legs together and felt a dampness on her drawers. Her stomach cramped again and she hunched over. Seamus had told her to wait, but she needed to go to the outhouse. She stood up. She reached beneath her skirt and touched between her legs. Blood stained her fingers.

———

Abby's breath hung around her head in the chill air of Seamus' ice house. Her stomachache blended with the pain in her legs and buttocks from sitting on the ice. The blocks rose as high as her shoulder, and the grainy sawdust that slowed melting covered her hands.

Blood was bad. When someone talked about it, her mother spoke very fast and pinched the edge of her collar between her fingers. Once, Abby had seen a pail filled with rags and bloody water sitting by the back door. She'd wrinkled her face and put her finger in, but Mama jerked the pail away and gave her a spanking.

She hunched over, curving her back over her stomach. How long did it take for all your blood to run out? Abby pressed her elbows against her sides. The sod walls smelled of damp and dirt, like a grave might smell if you were alive in your coffin.

Slow steps approached from outside. The door swung open and a shadow climbed the wall.

"Who is it? Who's there?" It was Maggie O'Brien's cracked voice.

"Go away!" Abby squeezed her eyes shut. "Leave me alone."

"You be daft, girl? Why are you lurking here?" Maggie raised the oil lamp and narrowed her eyes.

Smell rose from Abby's clothes: blood, and bloody wool, and underwear.

"Your mother will take a rod to you, certainly." Maggie circled her one way, then the other, leaving tracks in the sawdust.

Water trickled from the ice block, a pink track. "I'm dying." Abby wanted to keep her secret from Maggie, but she wasn't strong enough. "All my blood is leaking out my bottom."

Maggie snorted. "You've never had a talk with your mother about this?"

"It started all of a sudden." Abby rocked, her forehead touching her knees, her hair falling like blinders around her face.

"You're not sick, dearie. It's the curse."

"I'm not going to die?"

"No, but sometimes you'll wish you had, when the babies come. Baby's blood, that's what you've got. Blood that will make you sons, if you're lucky."

"I don't want any babies."

Maggie grunted. "You don't have any choice about it. It's up to men and God. You may not want to, but you're ready."

Abby began to cry, or laugh, some funny squeeze in her throat that let all the tightness out, forcing more blood from between her legs.

Maggie took off her lumpy sweater, stretched at the elbows, and wrapped it around Abby's shoulders. When she lifted Abby off the ice block, the girl's ankles buckled. Maggie drew Abby's arm around her waist. "We'll go in the house, and I'll get you some rags."

14

Del
April 2000

Del checked his wristwatch. Six-forty. By the time he got home, Cora would be there, having her arm twisted. His mother could teach The Mob a few things.

He slapped the palm of his bad hand on the conference table, and a couple of captains jerked awake. "Roger, this is so damn boring, it must be important. Let's continue tomorrow. One o'clock." His administrative captain halted his budget presentation mid-sentence. Chairs scraped and executive staffers gathered their notebooks and binders.

Del took his Stetson off the hat stand and held it by the point of the crown while he waited for the office to empty so he could snap off the light.

"Got a date?" someone said.

"With the Mets." He drove eighty on the way home. Every trooper in the area knew enough to back off when they saw his car with 01 painted on the trunk lid. He spewed gravel as he raced up the driveway, where a Neon and his mother's tank of a Mercury were parked in the turnaround. He left the Crown Vic by the old cider house. He needed to do something about the building, either tear it down or rehab it.

Light streamed from the kitchen windows. In the half-dark, he looked through the glass. Cora's hair gleamed like toast and honey. His heart beat against his throat; he was irritated over her visit to Tyler, excited over a lingering dream from last night about fucking her. Why he was attracted, he wasn't quite sure. She was jangled, skinny, fraught. He was going crazy.

As he opened the door, he heard his mother. "You obviously don't moisturize, young lady."

Cora's butt was propped against the kitchen cabinet, but even so she towered over Frieda, and Del was aware for an instant how much his mother had shrunk over the years. He wished she'd also gotten more tractable. Cora had her arms crossed over her chest, clearly not in a buying mood. "Look at my face," Frieda said. "This is what happens if you don't moisturize." She pinched a fingerful of skin from her fleshy little chin.

Cora threw Del a defiant look. They would exchange words later about the scene at the hospital. She turned back to Frieda. "Your skin looks very nice to me, ma'am," she said. "I'm afraid my face has never been one of my priorities."

Del shut the kitchen door, rattling the glass. "Mom, you promised." He put his Stetson on top of the refrigerator and smoothed the hat line out of his hair.

"I know, honey, but she asked." Frieda turned to Cora, the top of her curly white head just reaching Cora's shoulder. "You asked what I did to keep busy, didn't you?"

"Yes, Ma'am." Cora kept a straight face, but he caught a flash of amusement, either at his mother or his own discomfort.

"No more arm-twisting about Mary Kay. Everybody runs when they see you coming." Del tried to sound stern.

"Not true." Frieda squinted at him. "You should use some Man Lotion. Your face looks chapped."

"That'll be a cold day in hell." Del stashed his coat and his weapon in the hall closet, jacked up the thermostat and opened the front door for Drago, who thumped his tail against Del's leg. Del hadn't thought he'd ever want a dog after losing his fingers, but this one, a lab who'd showed up on his porch a year ago, was a gentle guy. Drago trotted into the kitchen and went directly to Cora, sticking his nose into her crotch. Damn, she was having her period.

Cora circled his muzzle with her fingers, pushed it away, and gave it a little shake. "Sorry, old man. We haven't been properly introduced."

"Things are going great." Del fished two beers from the refrigerator. He hesitated before shutting the door. "Cora, can I offer you something to drink?"

"Some wine, in about forty years." She didn't look too bad after last night's drunk, except for the dark rings around her eyes, and that was probably a lack of iron.

He popped the tab on a Coke, and the caps on two beers. He handed a beer and a glass to his mother. "I thought you were going to reheat the chili."

"I got here just as Miss Brooks drove up." Frieda sipped her beer and licked a bit of foam from the corner of her mouth. "Do you remember the radio show, 'Our Miss Brooks?' About the school teacher? Were you ever a school teacher, Miss Brooks?"

"I was never a teacher, thank goodness, and call me Cora."

Del lifted the cast iron chili pot from the refrigerator and set it on the stove burner. The chili looked a little greasy. The sirloin must have had too much fat on it.

"Neither was I, but I wanted to." Frieda said. "The university here used to be called Cortland Normal School." She unloaded lettuce, cucumber, green onions, and mushrooms from a brown paper bag and stood on tiptoe to pull a salad bowl from the cupboard. "I married Eddie when I was sixteen and never went to college. I left the teaching to Del."

"Del was a teacher?"

"He taught nights for awhile at community college." Frieda nibbled a piece of cucumber as she chopped vegetables.

Drago, after scavenging the kitchen floor for stray morsels, did his circle dance at Cora's feet and flopped down with his head on her shoe.

By the time Del had sliced French bread, chopped onion, grated cheese, heated the chili until it bubbled, and ladled it into bowls, his mother had filled Cora in on his entire career. Behind Cora's back Del signaled Frieda with a slicing motion across his neck—stop with the resume and cut to the important stuff. Cora's husband, ex-husband, soon-to-be ex-husband. Once she got started, his mother was a hell of an interrogator.

They sat at the scarred plank table like poker players in the circle of brightness from the hanging light. His shirt was sweaty under the arms from the stove's heat. Spoons clicked against bowls. Every time he took a bite, his eyes darted across the table to gauge Cora's reaction to the chili.

"Are you married, Cora?" Frieda sprinkled cheese on her chili.

He waited, like a drooling idiot, his spoon halfway to his mouth.

Cora sucked a mouthful of chili. A red-pepper stain crept up her neck, and she blinked furiously.

"You've got tears of joy in your eyes. I told you I make great chili," he said.

Cora croaked a word or two before she gulped a long draught from her Coke. She dabbed her eyelids with her napkin. "Hot doesn't necessarily indicate quality." She turned to his mother. "Actually, I was married for twenty years, but now I'm divorced."

Del swallowed some beer. It tasted so good, cold and crisp, plenty of hops. Tomorrow, he'd send his mother an azalea bush from the nursery.

"Do you have a lover?" his mother asked.

"I don't think that's any of your business, pardon my frankness."

Frieda leaned over to Drago, who lay beside her with his chin lifted in supplication. She tossed him a chunk of bread. "Generally, being old is sewage. My hip aches, my fillings fall out and I can't sleep at night. But one great thing, I can say whatever I want. So, about the lover," Frieda continued.

"I work ten- to twelve-hour days as a reporter," Cora said, "but after work I prowl the San Francisco bars to find a straight man I can drag home for meaningless sex."

"I knew it. You don't have a lover," Frieda said.

Cora shot Del an accusatory look.

"What can I do?" he said. "Get a restraining order? Send her to journalism school?"

His cell phone vibrated against his hip. He moved into the back entryway. Zone Captain Craig Mollineux was on the line to brief him about a traffic stop on the 81 near Binghamton. The fenders and dashboard of a Honda Civic were stuffed like a Thanksgiving turkey with plastic-wrapped bags of cocaine. At the same time Del listened to Mollineux describe how troopers had torn the fenders and dashboard apart to get into the secret compartments, Del tried to keep up with his mother's questioning.

"You didn't have a mother? Last time I heard, that was impossible," Frieda was saying.

Cora began telling Frieda some of what Del had heard the night before. There was less pain, but more encompassing sadness with the way she told it this time, as if her sorrow had been compressed all these years and was expanding as it escaped from some hidden cache.

"She didn't telephone or send a gift or write a birthday card. She just left," Cora said. "Later on, my dad heard she died in Maryland having another man's baby."

Del switched attention back to the phone. "Do you need any help out there?" Mollineux said no, the trooper was trying to identify the suspects, who had given false names and offered fake vehicle registration. Del glanced out the back window. Moonlight slipped over the weathered wood of the cider house, painting it silver.

Cora propped her elbows on the table. His mother scooped more salad onto Cora's plate. Del suspected Frieda was already at work to add some weight to Cora's bones. Frieda and Judith never had gotten along, right from the first when his ex-wife told her there would be no Somer grandchildren other than Tyler. Judith ignored Frieda's telephone messages and forgot her birthday; his mother retaliated by displaying pictures of her grandnieces and grandnephews, and, to underscore Judith's lack of attention, bought Del shirts and socks.

Tonight, he couldn't decide whether his mother and Cora were getting on. They weren't talking in those sweet, sing-song voices women used when they hated each other. On the other hand, they weren't exactly trading recipes.

"Why didn't you have any more children?" his mother said. "I had seven brothers and a sister. It's not good, being an only child." Del, taking a beer from the refrigerator, shot his mother a look over his shoulder. Frieda met his gaze and bit her lip. He remembered her doctor visits, special diets, prayers to the saints, but none of it had done any good. Del had remained an only child.

"I had a couple of miscarriages. After that, I stopped." Cora brushed her fingers over the back of Frieda's hand. "Enough with the questions. You don't have to be worried. I'm only here for a week or two, and I'm not interested in your son."

Frieda's white poodle haircut quivered. "Why not? You'll hardly find a man his age who has all his hair."

It was past time to create a diversion. "Mom, did I see a chess pie sitting on the shelf?"

Frieda explained to Cora that a chess pie contained a mixture of eggs, butter, nuts, and raisins. "It's a poor man's pie, no fancy ingredients. My mother taught me how to make it during the Depression."

"I've never baked a pie," Cora said.

Frieda poked Cora's thigh. "I don't think you've ever had a bite of one. Come to my house some afternoon, and I'll teach you."

Del ground beans and brewed two pots of coffee, regular for Cora and him and decaf for his mother. He watched the two women across the table as Frieda sliced the pie and slid it onto plates. They resembled each other in some way. Not physically—Cora was an exotic bird with her extravagant hair and prominent nose, and Frieda, a wrinkled, tart little apple.

Drago's cold nose touched his hand. Del retrieved the dog's bowl from the back porch and scooped kibble into it. He called Mollineux, who said the suspects were in jail and the cocaine secured in the evidence room. "Have a draft press release on my desk in the morning," Del said.

Back in the kitchen, Cora rinsed the dishes as his mother stacked them in the dishwasher. He listened to them mine each other for information. Cora's job and his mother's Mary Kay business gave them each a perfect opportunity to ask embarrassing questions. They were investigators, he realized. They wanted to know how did this happen, what did you think, what did you do then. He wasn't sure which of them was more dangerous.

"I'm going home. My night vision's not too good," Frieda said.

Del held her coat and settled it on her shoulders. "Do you want me to follow you home?"

"No, no. I won't get lost." She hoisted her purse strap on her arm and cradled the clean pie plate against her chest.

Cora walked with them to the back entry. "I think you've forgotten something."

Frieda *tsked* at herself. "My address. For the pie-baking lesson."

"That. And a Mary Kay catalog in case I want to place an order."

———

When his mother had roared away in a puff of cold exhaust, Cora picked up her coat from the top of the washing machine and handed him the sweatshirt he'd loaned her the night before. "I didn't wash it, but at least there's no vomit."

"Thanks. It's vintage state police."

It was folded neatly down the center, the arms caught inside the pocket of cloth. He reached across her and hung it on a coat peg. The house creaked, curling up for the night. Drago finished crunching his food, flopped, and yawned a goodnight song. On the uninsulated utility porch, the air moved uneasily with currents of heat from the kitchen and chill from the windows.

They were close in the narrow space, but he caught no scent of perfume or one of those creams that women use. She hadn't dressed up for dinner; her straight-leg jeans drooped a little in the hips as if she'd worn them for a day or two without washing them, and her turquoise turtleneck shirt was faded.

With one finger, Del lifted her hair as if he were a shut-in moving aside a curtain. The strands were so light he barely felt them brush his skin. He slid his hand up her cheek to her ear. There he found what he'd glimpsed earlier, a small gold stud in her pierced right lobe. It was only a tiny indicator, the barest hint of femininity, but his cock hardened nevertheless. With both hands, he traced the curve of her ears, feeling the tiny contours with the sensitive stumps of his fingers. Her lobes stretched as he tugged the gold, warmed by her skin. He watched her face as he pulled, her eyes dark and unblinking. Her nostrils flared and her shoulders rose and fell with her breathing.

He drew his thumb across her chapped lower lip, then slid it inside her mouth. She wet it, circling the tip with her tongue. He shivered with lust and foreboding. He'd wanted to touch her since he first met her, and now he cupped her head between his palms and kissed her, giving her plenty of tongue, exploring her lips' soft lining, sliding over the sleek surface of her teeth.

"I thought we weren't on a date." She breathed like she'd been running.

"We're not." He worried her lip with his teeth. "We're too old." He led her into the kitchen, flipped off the lights, and started for the stairs.

"I can't," she said.

"Oh, for Christ's sake."

"I have my period."

"I know. Drago's got a very sensitive nose."

"There'll be blood. On your hands, your sheets."

"It doesn't put me off."

"No, no. I haven't been with anyone for years. And the first time, all that red …" She began to shake so violently he imagined pieces of her flying away like leaves in a high wind.

He cupped her shoulders and ducked his head to catch her eyes. She averted her gaze. He heard the involuntary clatter of her teeth.

"Cora, it's okay, it's okay. I can see this is a terrible idea. Don't go crazy on me again." He clasped her hand and guided her stumbling steps through the dark hall to his study. A brass lamp was lit on the walnut kneehole desk. He moved a stack of books off the leather sofa and Cora curled up on it, her face buried in the cushions.

Del sat on the front edge of the desk, legs dangling. He ran his tongue across his lip, tasting her. "May I ask you something?"

She raised her head, not looking at him, but at a picture of him in uniform when he was sworn in as a state trooper.

"Did he kill her?" he said.

"Who?" She shrank against the cushions, her body stilling to stone-carved.

"You know."

"He said she went away, but now I'm seeing. Hearing." Eerie, how now she spoke in a high, thin child's voice. "I saw spots on the floor. Small. One in the hall. It turned brown, stayed there for years."

15

Cora
April 2000

"He hurt her," Cora said, and a black space grew in her. It pushed at her brain and heart, at her stomach and legs. She didn't think about her words, which erupted from her like vomit. "I don't know how often, but he hit her. More than once. I mean, more than one night. Funny, not funny but strange, odd, I don't remember voices, I remember the sound. A crack from an open hand. And other sounds, a smack, a blow that hit a target with more liquid in it, soft tissue, not muscle. With a closed fist."

"Jesus, Cora." Del slid from the edge of the desk and reached out to touch her, but her breath caught and she shrank further into the upholstery. No shoes on the furniture—her mother had said that. She wanted to make herself smaller, tighter, roll herself up in a hard shell like a sowbug.

"I was so scared I opened my eyes to let the air touch my eyeballs. It hurt, opening my lids wide so I wouldn't be overwhelmed by those sounds. I'd climb out of bed, drag my blankets into the closet where the clothes muffled the sounds. I closed the door and stuffed socks in the crack. Crouched on the floor. It was in there, black and muffled and smelling of sweaty shoes, where I was safe."

Del collapsed in a leather chair, rubbing his eyes as if they pained him. "Did she ever call the police? Make a report?"

"I never saw a policeman. Remember, it was around 1960. No one whispered, much less spoke out loud about wife beating. If they had, they'd just have been told it was a private matter."

"How about running away? Leaving him?"

"I don't think she had a place to go. She never played bridge or invited a friend over for coffee. My father might have sabotaged her friendships. I know he forbade her to work. Any family she had was in New York. I remember her waiting every afternoon for letters to slide through the mail slot."

Cora opened her eyes wide, like she'd done as a child, to invite more light to come in, more memory. "She tried to cover it up, I think. Once, she said an allergy made her lip swell up. Another time, I saw a mark as big as a plum on her upper arm.

"I was an active kid; I knew bruises. But I didn't ask how she got that ugly mark. I might have been too frightened."

Why was all this floating up forty years later? The sight of this lake, these fields and wooded hills, and the rotting boards of the old store stimulated a fold deep in her brain. Cora rubbed her forehead. She could almost touch it—a cluster of memory cells handed down from another generation.

"That night, what do you remember?"

She jumped at the sound of Del's voice and began to tremble. He sat forward in his chair, forearms on his thighs.

"How was it different from the other times?" she said, half to herself. "The blood. Streaks on the soap in the bathroom. A stain on a towel stuffed in the trash can out back. Two dots on the rag rug by the back door.

"Then there was the spot of blood in the hall just where it merged into the living room. Where the baseboards joined. After she disappeared, Dad never cleaned the house. I swept sometimes, but that speck was never washed off. I didn't think about her when I saw it close to my shoe every time I walked by. But then, I never wet my finger to rub it away, either. That drop stayed there until Dad died, and I sold the house."

He sighed. "No DNA typing back then, no way to tell if it was hers. The house, his car, his clothing—all of it could have yielded evidence."

"That night, when I told her the fib about brushing my teeth, she seemed just as usual. Her letter-writing box was on her desk in the bedroom. She wrote letters all the time, but I don't have any idea who she mailed them to."

With a hard knuckle, Cora rubbed a stinging tear from the corner of her eye. "What I think about now, is how little I knew. What was wrong with him?"

"Who cares about the condition of his fucking psyche? He was guilty of assault; possibly murder."

"Did she stay because she loved him in some sick way?"

Del sighed. "Those aren't things a child knows. Your parents probably didn't have a clue themselves. It's very likely your mother endured the beatings because of you."

"Oh God, I've hated her all these years. Him, all along, I thought he was a good father, other than the drinking. That's what I told myself."

"You were protecting yourself."

"Sort of the Stockholm Syndrome, family style." Her chest hurt, and she rubbed the spot with her fist, but the pressure intensified.

"Something like that," Del said. "What's the matter? Are you sick?"

"I've got terrible heartburn the chili."

" It wasn't that hot. Are you having a panic attack?"

"I'm not melting down; I just need an Alka-Selzer."

"This has been heavy stuff. Maybe you should go to emergency. Get an EKG."

He was probably right, but Cora couldn't move. The corner of his couch was safe; the vee formed by the back and the arm protected her back. She sank further into the pillows.

She asked again for an Alka-Seltzer, and he returned after a few moments with a tablet bubbling in a glass of water. Drago trotted at his heels. The dog sniffed at Cora's shoe, climbed onto the leather couch and curled at her hip. She drank the glass down, stroked the dog's ears, and her pain eased.

Del gave Drago a look, half rebuking, half envious.

"So, yes, it could be." She felt thin and gray. "That he killed her. I went online today to the Bureau of Vital Statistics in Maryland. They have no record of an Alice Macpherson Brooks dying there."

16

Abby
June 1917

Abby's graduation day hadn't turned out as she envisioned. No sunshine, no joy. Instead, she was filled with brown lumps of feeling, as ugly as potatoes. Grandma Miller had died of influenza a month ago. She had been buried in the Miller family plot at Dutch Hill. So many people had died, that the undertaker sold out of coffins. Her father had hammered one himself for Grandma, a yellow pine box small enough for a child. Abby blinked away tears. She'd never thought of Grandma Miller as a small woman, though she'd drawn Abby's eye to her like a hummingbird, sweeping, scrubbing, talking nonstop. Her German accent had filled her throat.

Grandma Miller wasn't the only one who'd died. Rose Tinsley's husband, Ed, was gone, too, along with two hundred other recruits at Camp Dix who'd been training for the war in France. Rose and Ed had been married only six weeks. Miss Miller had considered canceling the graduation ceremony to prevent infection, but the state and federal governments had announced just days ago that the disease had abated. Still, the ceremony felt like a burden.

In the front seat of the buggy, Abby's mother plucked off her wide straw bonnet, and used it to shield the honey cloud cake sitting in her lap. Her father clucked to the horses and shook the reins.

Abby glanced back. They were putting distance between their buggy and Seamus's. She wiggled her fingers at him, close to her shoulder, hidden from her parents. Seamus lifted his chin. A spot of heat, like a red ember in a pile of ashes, warmed her stomach.

She'd sneaked off to Seamus's farm twice since the day she'd gotten the curse. Seamus and Leland were running the farm without hired help, because so many valley men had joined the army. He had looked very tired, and Abby had wanted to run her fingers through his hair.

The buggy jerked as her father reined the horses to avoid a knot of horses, buggies, and wagons. They clogged the road and churned up mud as they pulled off into the trees near the white frame schoolhouse. Her father tied the horses and stood close to Ruth to hand her down the step, holding the cake. Her mother was pregnant. Abby knew this because Maggie O'Brien had told her. Now, Abby could see Mama's little bowl of bread dough rising under her skirt. Abby decided she would knit the baby a little sweater. Grandma Miller had been able to knit so fast the needle tips blurred. But Abby couldn't start the sweater until Mama admitted she was pregnant. Ruth had gotten very quiet in the last few weeks, and Abby imagined she was listening for the baby's voice.

Why had Ruth never said anything to Abby about monthlies? Why did she never mention the babies she'd miscarried? When Abby looked at her mother, she sometimes wanted to snatch the spectacles off her face and force her to tell her secrets, stored like jars of dark fruit in the cellar.

The school yard bubbled with activity. Small children bounced on the running board of the superintendent's new Franklin sedan. Mothers in starched shirtwaists scurried around like plump-breasted hens, arranging the food on long tables and covering the dishes to keep the raindrops off. Miss Miller directed the one-through-seven students as they lifted wooden chairs off a wagon, unfolded them, and set them in rows on the playground.

Miss Miller paused to survey the clouds, then spotted Abby. "The others are all here." She pointed in the direction of the school's cloakroom. Inside, Edna and Emily, who usually finished each other's sentences, were fighting.

"You're doing it wrong. You should have left it the way Mother tied it," Emily said. She peered over her shoulder at Edna, who was retying Emily's green satin sash.

"It looked stupid," said Edna. Tears of frustration gleamed in her eyes.

Abby tried to remember the first sentence of her graduation speech so it would be on the tip of her tongue when she stepped up to the podium. Ralph Waldo Emerson said ... What was it Emerson said?

To distract herself from panic, she looked out the cloakroom window. A few drops still fell intermittently, but the crowd was sitting down. Abby spotted her mother and father moving their chairs so Grandma Clemmie Macpherson and Uncle Will could sit beside them. Abby felt sad that only one of her grandmothers would watch her graduate, but happy Grandma Clemmie was able to come. She had been delivering a baby for a down-valley family. Mother had told Grandma Clemmie to leave as soon as the baby was born and make sure she didn't have any blood on her shoes. This because of how Grandma Clemmie had arrived after delivering a baby on Ruth and Jack's wedding day.

Emerson said ... Abby's heart beat fast. John Goins marched around the schoolroom blowing into the mouthpiece of his trumpet, making odd, squealing sounds and scattering spit. The twins practiced their song, but Edna was a little flat. What would it be like, boarding with them next year at Miss Truk's in Tully? Abby wondered if she snored or slept with her mouth open. She would remind herself every night to bury her face in her pillow.

Outside, Seamus sat down in the front row with the other trustees. She stole a look at him. His stiff shirt collar poked against his chin and his buttoned shoes gleamed with polish. He looked very fine.

Abby closed her eyes for a second. Emerson said, "Nothing great is ever achieved without enthusiasm."

———

Graduation was nearly over, but the Reverend Topham's closing prayer dragged on. From the front row, her aunt's hands flexed, as if she wanted to wring the reverend's neck. The audience had applauded Abby's speech; Edna and Emily remembered all the verses of the "Battle Hymn of the Republic"; Melvin said the Gettysburg Address almost as fast as Lincoln: and John Goins missed the two top notes in his trumpet solo. The superintendent handed them their certificates decorated with a gold seal and a piece of blue satin ribbon. Abby fingered the thick ivory paper. Her muscles jumped.

The Reverend Topham didn't let them go. "Oh Lord, bless those who have been taken from us, and welcome them into eternal life."

Abby was supposed to keep her head bowed, but instead she watched the clouds sail north, sparing them any further rain.

"And accompany those who have been left behind in this vale of tears."

In the field to the south of the school, the alfalfa grew as high as the fence, the stalks fat with moisture. Abby's eyes widened. A goat ambled through a hole in the fence, a strand of alfalfa hanging from its mouth. The animal's nostrils distended. A hoof clicked against a stone. It trotted toward the trestle tables heaped with food.

"Bless those who labor in the fields, and those who battle the evil Huns on the continent of Europe," Reverend Topham said.

Abby searched the audience. She was stuck on the podium and couldn't interrupt the prayer. Everyone's head was bowed except her aunt's.

The goat stopped, stretched its neck, tendons rigid, and sniffed the air like a connoisseur.

Abby held her hand close to her chest and signaled to her aunt, who fixed the reverend with her most quelling teacherly glare.

At the table, the goat pushed its nose under the napkin covering a plate of Mrs. Spellman's baking-powder biscuits. It emerged, its black lips peeled back from its teeth, laughing at her while it ate.

"And now, oh Lord ..." The reverend apparently had received an infusion of inspiration.

The goat circled the table, eyed a glass dish of what looked to Abby like Grandma Clemmie's marinated green beans.

Abby's armpits were damp. Her new dress would be stained with perspiration. She took a deep breath.

"Ow, oww, owww!" She made the scream as loud as possible, and high-pitched. "My foot, a bee stung my foot!" She held her hands over her stocking-clad foot, rocking and moaning.

Miss Miller jumped from her chair, as quickly as if someone had goosed her, and ran to the podium. The goat backed away from the table a few steps and cocked its head.

"In the name of the Father, the Son, and the Holy Ghost," the reverend said snappishly.

"Let me see, Abby," said Miss Miller, prying Abby's fingers off her instep. Abby whispered to her the impending disaster at the luncheon table. Her aunt shot a quick glance at the goat, then dispatched John to run it off. She wet a pad of gauze with water from the pump and tied it around Abby's foot.

Abby got a hug from Mama, who flashed her a sharp look that promised questions later. Her father lifted her bangs and kissed her on the forehead. He looked down at her, his shaggy brows half-screening his eyes. "I'm proud of you, Missy," he said. Abby slipped her hand into his suit coat pocket. When she was a little girl, her father often had hid a treat in his jacket pocket when she'd done something good. It was empty, and Abby gave him a mock pout.

Her father smiled. "Check again later."

After a few minutes, Abby abandoned any pretense of pain from her foot. Voices from the picnickers, sitting in circles of chairs and on blankets spread on the ground, seemed far away. Insects buzzed in the air. Daisies and wild roses blooming at the edges of the schoolyard scattered their fragrance. Light glittered on the lake's surface. Her dress brushed her skin. Her silk stockings clung deliciously.

A hand touched her back. "Very nice job." Seamus said. Abby whirled. He blocked the sun for a second, a tall, black silhouette. Then they moved, as if they were dancing, and she saw him clearly, the collar of his suit loosened and the hair in front of his ears darkened with perspiration.

Words crowded her mouth.

"The speech, I mean." He tapped his shoe against her gauze-wrapped foot.

"I almost forgot it," she blurted, ignoring his insinuation.

"No harm done. That's a very fetching dress, by the way." He touched the sleeve, and his knuckles brushed her arm.

"I've missed you." Her face ached, the bones damming up a flood of feeling.

Three weeks and two days ago. It had been the day after Grandma Miller died; her mother and aunt had begun laying her out for the funeral. Abby, feeling sad and useless, walked to Maple Leaf Farm. Seamus was hunched over his office desk, the sleeves of his brown shirt rolled to his elbows. The window was open and a breeze riffled the pages of his ledger. She talked to him while he added the columns of figures. The soft scratching of his pen seemed immensely important, like his hand resting on the page, the nails still dirty from work, like the bright hair grazing his collar. He winced and kneaded his shoulder. A cow had kicked him while he milked.

She stood behind him and kneaded the spot until his skin warmed through his shirt. Her finger traced the creases in his sunburned neck. She had moved around in front of him, propped her hands on the chair arms, and kissed him.

The clink of plates and forks seemed far behind her. "I've missed you," she said again.

"It's been awhile. I haven't had time to visit the school as much as I did last year. I've left it to the other trustees." His gaze traveled over the crowd, as if calculating who was close enough to hear.

"Did you miss me?" Abby hated herself for asking, but the whispered words forced themselves out.

"I enjoy keeping track of the students' progress," he said.

Abby scanned his face for a sign, even a quiver. He'd been surprised at first, his shifting weight creaking the chair, his eyes widening. Their mouths parted for a second and their breaths converged, warm and damp. Seamus tipped his head so their noses wouldn't bump, and the second kiss was different. She'd imagined kissing him would be like honey, slow-running and sweet. She didn't expect the surge of painful joy. It seized her muscles, weakened her legs. She stumbled and nearly fell.

He lifted her into his lap and kissed her again.

Abby had told no one. She wasn't ashamed, but she was afraid if she told someone, the magical feeling would disappear, like the evaporation of the moon's mystery once the sun rose.

She remembered the taste of Seamus's tobacco, the scent of sun and soap on his clothes, the throb of her lip, the shock of his wet tongue. Those sensations seemed as real to her now as Uncle Will, sitting on a plaid blanket with a plate of food on his lap.

"So we'll lose you in the fall," Seamus said, glancing down at her.

"Monday through Friday. I'll be home Friday night," Abby said quickly.

"You'll meet new people. Make new friends," he said. Abby strained to hear what he felt, but his words were flat.

"I'll be waiting all week to come back."

"You'll get a boyfriend." He seemed to be pushing her away from that magic circle of feeling that had surrounded them.

"Boys are loathsome. They have pimples and their socks smell. They play tricks and say stupid things and punch you in the arm and make jokes about titties. I hate all of them." Her throat was raw, as if she were screaming.

"You'll change your mind, I expect. The boys will gather around, and you'll have your pick." Seamus refused to meet her eyes.

"I don't change my mind, Seamus. I have never changed it." Anger filled her throat.

Her father startled them. "O'Brien. Take yourself off." He thrust himself between them, forcing Abby to stumble backward.

Seamus reddened. "I don't take orders from you or anyone else."

Her father stuck out his chin. "I'll not have Abby influenced by you. Corrupted by your shady connections."

"You filthy Scottish bastard. I've a mind to teach you a thing or two with the tops of my knuckles." Seamus loosened his tie and shoved it in his pocket.

"Abby. Hie yourself away." Her father was tall, six feet two, but he looked thin and bony beside Seamus's broad shoulders.

Seamus shook his head in disbelief as her father edged closer, his fists raised. "Macpherson, what's the matter with you? I was the one. I took her to the doctor in the midst of the winter's worst storm. I'd do the same for any hurt child."

Child. At his words, Abby wheeled and stumbled along the path across the school yard, past the tire swing and up the hill.

17

Cora

April 2000

Drago climbed off the leather sofa and settled on the carpet. Cora squinted at her watch. Seven. This is your life, she thought, sleeping with the dog instead of his owner. She remembered an argument last night with Del. He'd been trying to get her to sleep in the guest room, but she couldn't move. Some delicate interior structure had threatened to collapse if she stood up, so she slept the remainder of the night in his office. She rubbed her cheek on the blanket. The whoosh of the furnace filled her head, and the brass lamp cast a circle of light on the desk.

Her stomach growled in concert with Drago's doggy snores. No one was stirring. Del's chair was rolled back slightly from his desk. He'd sat there until late.

She shut her eyes. Memory rolled back to swamp her. She felt scraped and raw. All of it sickened her: her mother, her father, darkness, sounds, fists, blood, the smells of her childhood sweat and terror. She longed, to the soles of her feet, to have her ignorance back. It was simple when she believed Alice was dead. Having abandoned them for some man, having died bearing his child. Her ashes in an urn somewhere, black and enclosed in brass.

This morning Cora felt as though each of her billion synapses was screaming with frightening possibilities. Her father a wife beater. Her father—

She struggled to stand and knocked her shin against the coffee table, startling Drago. Her jeans and shirt were twisted on her body, and her hair felt like jungle undergrowth. She reached for her boots, which were aligned neatly beside the sofa where Del must have put them last night. She laced them and left the rumpled blanket for Del to put away. On the desk, she saw an insulated mug with a note taped to it. "Left early. Here's coffee. Talk to you."

As Cora sipped, she paced his study. She opened the drawers, poked among his books, rearranged a dozen pictures of Little League baseball teams he'd sponsored, studied a black and white of Frieda and a man in a World War II army uniform, glanced at autographed publicity shots of Stan Musial and Bob Gibson.

In a niche in one of the tall bookcases she caught a reflection off a glass surface. A small, framed Michelangelo print of a human hand was tucked between two heavy volumes. The fingers, drawn in red chalk, curled upward. Cora swallowed coffee. The lamp shone on a pile of pink message slips beside his telephone, probably calls taken at the office he hadn't had time to return. She needed to go back to Seneca House. Take a shower. Brush her teeth. Read Sean O'Brien's preliminary autopsy report.

Instead, she scooped up the messages. Two from Judith. One from somebody at county rehab services about Tyler. Dr. Byrne, regarding a dental appointment. Len Crutcher. Absently, she combed her fingers through a snarl in her hair. Crutcher. The name was familiar; Del had mentioned him. Ah, yes, the farm insurance investigator working on the trio of cow deaths. He'd left a number at the Comfort Home Inn in Tully. Cora slipped the message in her pocket and drained the mug. Del made a great cup of coffee.

———

On first glance, Cora would have called Len Crutcher sloppy.

"Your telephone call barely caught me," Crutcher said. He cracked the door to room 116 open just enough to frame his face. "I'm packing my suitcase."

"I know you're terribly busy. I brought doughnuts and coffee to save you time." She waved the paper sack in front of his nose, spreading the smell of grease and sugar like a censer at morning mass.

"Well, a minute or two, maybe." He opened the door slightly, and she slid past him.

She was glad she hadn't wasted any more time at Del's. Despite feeling shaky, she'd hurried to Seneca House, showered, grabbed a change of clothes, and headed for Crutcher's motel.

When she glanced around the investigator's room, however, she saw no evidence he was about to leave. The credenza was covered with four bags of chips, a package of Mother's shortbread cookies, two bags of microwave popcorn, and a quart of Diet Dr. Pepper. She unloaded the doughnuts and the two paper cups of coffee onto the desk, where the chair seat held two piles: one of John Grisham novels, and one of microcassette tapes.

"I hear you've dug up the real story on the death of Holland's Queen Beatrice and the two other cows," she said.

"Where'd you hear that?" Crutcher popped the lid on the coffee and plunged his hand into the doughnut bag. He was a short man with a terrible comb-over. His sport jacket resembled a poorly plowed field, lumps of brown tweed rising here and there.

"From the state police," she said.

"I haven't told them anything yet," he said, chewing noisily.

Cora took a chance. "You let Major Somer know about the possibility of Sucostrin."

"I can't talk about it until I've submitted my final report," Crutcher said. "The folks I work for hate it when they get back-doored on the results of an investigation."

He made no move to clear the chair, so Cora sat on the bed. She unslung her rucksack from her shoulder, snapped on her tape recorder, and opened her laptop.

"Aren't the three insurance companies kissing your feet? You've saved them a bucketful of money."

He gulped hot coffee and fished another doughnut from the bag. "There may have been a dollar or two involved."

"Come on."

"I'll have to admit, this was one of the Fat Man's better cases." He rocked back on his run-down heels. "That's why the guys at Great American have my number tattooed on their arms."

"What are your conclusions?"

Crutcher glanced at her. "I haven't given Great American my report yet. It'll be another two weeks before the final, final lab reports are in."

Cora wanted to snatch his comb-over out of his scalp. She didn't have fourteen days. Her job could be gone by then. "I'm going to write this story next week. I won't use your name, word of honor, but I have to address your investigation."

He shook his head. "Can't take the chance. I don't know you, never seen you before in my life."

"I'm an investigator like you. Here's my card."

He slipped it in his pocket.

"We're both looking for the right story, the correct facts, Mr. Crutcher. I need to get it straight, like you."

He pursed his lips and nodded.

She hoped she wasn't going to regret depending on Crutcher's report. He looked like a disorganized slob who probably didn't get his assignments in on time. "How did you get involved in the cases?" she said.

"Great American calls me to review all their big claims," he said, strutting between the bed and the credenza. "I give them the benefit of the Fat Man's eagle eye. Only the third death, Queen Beatrice, was insured by GA, but it didn't smell right, so I decided to drive up and do some field investigation."

He fished a nail clipper out of his pocket. "That's when I learned about the two other claims, so I began at the beginning. The first one, Cayuga's Princess Honor, was shipped to O'Brien from Santerra Farms on September 10 of last year. The Hartford wrote that one, for eighty-five thousand dollars. She died a week later."

He clipped each nail as he talked, snip, snip. One of the rinds landed on Cora's sleeve, and she flicked it off.

"Santerra sold him the second cow for fifty thousand. Arrived on November 1. Died on November 13. An Aetna Farm policy."

Cora's fingers tapped the keyboard. "How did you find out about the policies if they weren't from your client's company?"

Crutcher winked. "Professional courtesy. The Hartford was about to cut a check when I opened my investigation. We pooled our information, so to speak." He returned to his nails.

Cora said a quick prayer he didn't start on his toes.

"Now we come to the third one, Holland's Queen Beatrice. That was our policy. Two hundred and fifty thousand, her value declining 12 percent a year. She was trucked to Maple Leaf on December 5."

"Slow down," Cora said.

Crutcher folded the clipper with his thumb. "She was a prime exhibitor in October at the Dairy Expo in Madison, Wisconsin. Her dam was a top producer, and Queen Beatrice, milking twice a day, produced sixty-seven thousand pounds of milk last year."

Not as sloppy as Cora had thought. "What documentation was there that Queen Beatrice—the one that arrived at O'Brien's farm—really was this fabulous cow?"

"Franklin Santerra attested to it." Crutcher studied the bags of potato chips. "I tracked down a relief milker that was working at Maple Leaf Farm the day Queen Beatrice arrived."

"Rico and Pedro weren't there?" she said.

"Supposedly, they were home in Guatemala for a month."

"What did the relief guy say? Queen Beatrice stepped out of the cattle trailer onto a red carpet?"

"Even more interesting. He tells the Fat Man that this $250,000 cow was wearing an udder halter."

Cora frowned and stopped typing.

"Like a bra," he said. "A sling to give the udder more support. But a winner like Queen Beatrice wouldn't need any support."

"She wasn't a glamorous, firm-bodied young star. Instead, she was a middle-aged, menopausal gal whose boobs were sagging."

"Right. She was worthless as a dairy cow. Overdue for the slaughterhouse."

A hot flash burned Cora's cheeks. She took a deep breath and pressed her arms against her sides. This story had to be good, or she was headed for the unemployment line. "Doesn't the seller have to certify that the animal he sells is genuine?"

"It's like buying a car. You go to a dealer you trust, you look the car over, kick the tires."

"Sean O'Brien, who was a highly respected cattle judge, would have known the cow that arrived at his farm wasn't a show winner or a big producer," she said.

"Either that, or he was going blind."

"So your conclusion is that O'Brien and Santerra were in it together."

"You might assume that." Crutcher leaned over to restack the paperbacks and the cassettes on the chair, tapping them so their edges aligned.

Crutcher's room, which had appeared to be a cluttered rat's nest when she first arrived, now seemed to have an odd orderliness to it. Her mind clicked off each detail she'd observed earlier. "Okay, Len. Where is it?"

"What?"

"The recorder. Microcassettes but no recorder."

Crutcher looked unabashed as he pulled the palm-sized recorder from his jacket pocket. "Never can tell when I might need some backup."

"That was damn sneaky. I told you I wouldn't print your name in connection with the investigation."

"In my business, I find that most people are welshers," he said.

"I'm surprised you aren't wearing a wire, it being your business," Cora said.

"Who says I'm not?" For the first time, Crutcher smiled. "Not today, but I've done it in the past. Have a recorder in your pocket, meant to be found, and a wire, that won't be."

Cora got up and stretched, leaning away from the laptop. "What happened to Queen Beatrice?"

"On December 22, Pedro went into the barn at 4:30 a.m. and found her dead in her stanchion. No marks on her."

"Do they do autopsies on cows?"

"You bet. A large animal veterinarian named Angela Troppi did the autopsy. Queen Beatrice apparently suffocated, but there was no sign of the cause."

Cora remembered Del's speculation about how Queen Beatrice had died. "Then it was Sucostrin? The cow suffocates because it's paralyzed and can't breathe." The room seemed airless and she had difficulty getting her own breath.

"That's my educated guess," Crutcher said. "It's a skeletal muscle relaxant. Anesthesiologists use it when they put an airway down a human patient's throat. In a cow, a big injection works quickly and leaves no trace."

Crutcher fished another doughnut from the bag, inspecting it before he took a bite. "There are other ways. One case I investigated, the owner shoved ice cubes up the cow's nose and down her throat. She suffocated, but the ice melted before the vet arrived."

Cora struggled for air. Her father's violence, the increasing possibility of her mother's murder, the terrible suffering of the men and cows, all these events seemed to suck up the oxygen.

"You're not looking so good, girlie." Doughnut crumbs fell on his brown jacket.

Only the disgusting thought that Crutcher might give her mouth-to-mouth kept Cora from fainting. "Give me a minute. Asthma," she said, and leaned over, breathing shallowly.

The doughnut bag rustled. "Funny thing. O'Brien reacted the same way when I told him he wasn't going to get any money."

18

Cora
April 2000

Cora listened to her voice mail after she left the motel. Del had left a message: he'd received the autopsy report on Franklin Santerra and he'd discuss it with her. He used his behind-the-desk voice. She felt an irrational disappointment.

Stu Manion had left two messages. His second, "Brooks, call me immediately," sounded like he was chewing glass. And Frieda had called to invite her to a pie-baking lesson the following afternoon.

The two-lane road between Tully and Santerra Farms wound over ridges that trembled with a green tint that had grown more brilliant since she'd arrived in New York. The rise of the hills and their fall to gouged-out, glaciated valleys seemed endless. She wished she'd consulted the map and driven north to catch the Thruway. Small farms flipped by, white houses, silos, red barns weathered to silver on their exposed sides and falling off their granite foundations. Villages, a handful of houses, a church and a fire station.

Her stomach growled. She hadn't eaten breakfast. She should've stolen one of Len's doughnuts. No. She wasn't that hungry.

She squirmed in the seat. Fiddled with the radio, but couldn't get a station. Her interview with Crutcher left little doubt: O'Brien and Santerra had needed big sums of money. Judith had told Cora that Sean had invested in some failed foreign companies, but that didn't explain why Santerra had agreed to collaborate with him on the fraud scheme.

Judith presumably knew what Sean had needed the money for, and why he'd been so frightened he was almost sick. Tyler almost certainly knew. Convenient, that Tyler now was headed for a rehab facility where he would be tucked away incommunicado for sixty days. A commitment greased by Del.

The landscape of working farms was broken more often now by expansive, contemporary houses with paved driveways and painted fences. Must be city people looking for acreage—farmers here weren't prosperous enough for five bedrooms, three baths.

She puzzled over where Del fit in. The key must be Tyler or Judith. Last night, she could've sworn he was over his ex-wife. Over enough that he wanted to get into her pants. Men didn't usually sit for hours and listen to a woman's traumatic stories when they had commitments elsewhere.She considered the pictures she'd seen that morning on his study wall. Tyler stood in the midst of the team members in each of the Little League photos. She chewed a fingernail. There was something ...

Her cell phone rang. "Cora, it's Chris Myerling." The newsroom assistant at the *Standard*. Cora idled at a four-way stop while she disengaged her mind from her train of thought.

"Hold for Stu," Myerling said. "He's finishing up another call."

"Hey, Chris. How's the weather in the City?" Cora said.

"Foggy." She heard the juicy snap of his gum. "Listen, Cora, things are really a mess. Everybody's jumping like they've been goosed."

In the rearview mirror, she saw a pickup behind her. She crossed the intersection and started down a steep grade.

"Management is ..." Chris whispered, then raised his voice. "Yes, Stu, I've got her on the line."

"I've been trying to reach you since yesterday," Manion said.

"Sorry. Cell phone coverage here is spotty."

"Do you have a fax where you're staying?"

"Probably, but I'm on the road."

"E-mail the number to me as soon as you get back."

"What's going on?"

"The fax will be a management memo issued to The Newspaper Guild yesterday. The Standard Newspaper Group experienced a third year of circulation losses. Fifteen editorial positions are being eliminated."

The road's twisting decline made her feel as though her guts were outdistancing the car.

"I wanted to reach you before you heard from someone else," Manion said.

"I'm number one, aren't I?" she said suddenly.

Manion cleared his throat. "Yes, but the list is alphabetical, not in preferential order. I regret this, Cora, but management offered a buyout last year, and you didn't take the option."

"Using that rationale, I loved my job, didn't want to quit, therefore, I'm being eliminated."

"Logic never seems to be a reporter's strong point," Manion said. "We offered a very attractive package that benefited long-term employees by escalating payout substantially for extended periods of service."

"Cut it, Stu. The strategy is to axe the experienced workers. They cost too much."

He didn't answer.

The car's speed increased, and tires squealed around a turn. Heat burned her face and sweat popped out on her skin under her yellow turtleneck.

"Layoffs become effective two weeks from today, and each former employee will be given two weeks' severance, plus accumulated vacation time. Sign the memorandum when it arrives by fax and send it back to indicate you've received it."

The Neon cut over the center line on the turn. A liquid propane truck lumbered up the hill, and Cora hesitated for a split second before she jerked the wheel to the right and straightened the car's path. She barely saw the road until she came to a turnout. Her fingers squeezed the wheel at eight and four. The cell phone had skittered to the floor under her foot, and when she picked it up, the line was dead.

19

Cora
April 2000

At Santerra Farms, Cora switched off the ignition but didn't open the car door. After a minute, a barking collie appeared and jumped off the porch of the double-wide trailer, berating her for the intrusion.

"Look," she told the dog from behind the closed car window, "I don't want me to be here, either." The reality of her layoff hadn't quite hit her yet, like bad food that had to work its way to your guts before it made you sick.

The dog's noise didn't raise anyone. The farm perched above Cayuga Lake on green hills broken by the plow into beaten, striated fields. Clouds fought overhead, throwing shadows down the slope and across the water, where the surface darkened from gray to oily black.

The farm's center was a large graveled turnaround. On the right was a one-story white house with the shades drawn and grass sprouting a foot tall in the yard. Across the farmyard from it sat a double-wide mobile home, a mop standing upside down by the front door and muddy shoes, soles up, on the porch rail.

The dairy occupied the rest of her view. In contrast to Maple Leaf Farm, this one was in full operation. A herd of Holsteins clustered in a holding pen between four rows of polyvinyl cow sheds and a long milking parlor. A ponytailed man in a white T-shirt opened the gate to send more of the cows into an automated cow washer. The car's closed window didn't block the hot, solid smell of manure.

A stocky woman, her rubber boots climbing to the knees of her jeans, threw an exasperated glare at the Neon as she crossed the farmyard from the milking parlor. Rather than changing course to greet the visitor, she continued to the calf pens with a five-gallon pail in each hand, the milk slopping over the rims as she walked.

Cora hugged the wheel, watching the woman pour milk into the calves' troughs. From his online obituary, she knew Santerra's survivors included four grown children and one grandchild upstate, plus three sisters who still lived nearby. Whether Franklin Santerra's gruesome death was murder or suicide, they must be suffering.

The woman—one of Franklin's sisters?—finished feeding the calves and strode toward the car. Her green John Deere cap shaded her face. With a sharp word, she called off the dog. Cora fumbled with the window button and rolled it down.

"You're the reporter, I suppose." The woman set one of the empty pails on the ground and rubbed her chest with the heel of her hand.

"Maybe I'm selling magazines."

"Del Somer said you were nosing around." Her thick, ebony hair exploded from a ponytail threaded through the opening in the back of her cap.

"One of the rewards of my job is the way people welcome us," Cora said. "They usually offer a cup of coffee and a piece of cake."

The woman snorted. "Turn around and get out of here."

Cora's fingers rattled the car keys, but then paused as if she'd just realized something. "You're his sister, right?"

"What if I am?"

"I'm sorry for your loss."

"No, you're not. You're glad, because now you have something to write about."

"There are a hundred deaths I could write about. I'm writing about Franklin and Sean because there are questions—mysteries that haven't been answered. You know that better than anyone."

"Maybe I don't want to know," the woman said.

"We always want to know. There's nothing worse than not knowing." Cora spoke more loudly than she'd intended. "I'm Cora Brooks, by the way."

The woman chewed the inside of her cheek, then offered her hand in a sandpaper grip. "Yolanda Santerra."

Yolanda was opening her mouth to say something else when a cow began a great bellowing in a pen across the farmyard. The enclosure was a sea of heaving black and white animals, one with its front hooves on another's back.

"Oh, for God's sake. Bobby, Bobby!" Yolanda steamed across the yard. She grabbed a long prod and clambered up the fence rail, continuing to call for Bobby, presumably the employee Cora had seen earlier.

Cora climbed out of the car, sucked along in Yolanda's boiling wake, curious to see what would happen next.

Bobby ambled from the milking parlor, a hose in his hands, and squirted a blast of water in the aggressive cow's face.

"You've got to keep 'em moving," Yolanda yelled. "You're slow today." She disappeared into the milking parlor.

Cora crossed the yard and peered inside. Yolanda was removing the milking lines from a cow's udders. She opened the gate around its neck, and on its own the animal walked, rump swaying, down the sloping floor and outside.

Four more cows entered, two on each side of the parlor, hooves clacking on the concrete. Yolanda secured two, swabbed each of their udders with a cup that smelled of iodine, and attached the milking lines. She scooped a measure of grain into the trough in front of each cow. On the other side, Bobby hooked up one cow, gazed out the high window at the clouds, scrubbed his face on his T-shirt, and started on the second.

Cora listened to the hum of the machines. Milk poured into the plastic milking tubes.

Yolanda picked up a bit of trash from the floor and hurled it in the refuse barrel. "Bobby, what's the matter with you? You're not worth a damn, haven't been all week. We could have had a broken leg out there."

"I haven't been feeling all that good." His voice was slow and contemplative.

"You've been late three mornings. Screwed up on the feed mix." Her voice rose, and the sound echoed off the concrete walls. She massaged her chest again.

"Couldn't help it. My alarm didn't go off." The cows flicked their ears, and one stopped chewing.

The smells of iodine and manure quivered in the volatile air.

"That's all right, Bobby. You sleep in tomorrow," Yolanda said.

"What?" His body tensed.

"Turn off the alarm clock. Make yourself a big breakfast."

Cora slipped her hand in her jacket pocket and turned on her tape recorder.

"Now, Yolanda."

"You're just as bad as Franklin. Never here, dumping the work on me: the herd, the feed, the bank, the roof, the Harvest Store. Oh, yes, the wonderful Harvest Store, Cadillac of silos." Spittle flew from her mouth.

Bobby raised his hands, palms out, to deflect her tirade.

"If I had a stick of dynamite, I'd blow this place into hamburger meat." Yolanda laughed.

Someone appeared in the doorway at the far end of the parlor. Another sister, with the same black hair and olive skin. "Yolie. Shut up. And Bobby, you're not fired."

She turned to Cora, her silver belt winking. "Who are you?"

Cora introduced herself and the newcomer responded that she was Cruz Santerra.

"She's a reporter, here about Franklin, that's what." Yolanda's face reddened and she breathed quickly. "As if that lazy, rutting bastard hadn't caused enough trouble. He's in the ground, and that self-centered bastard is still doing it. My God, I can't stand it!"

Cruz ran down the steps, drew back her arm, and slapped Yolanda in the face. "Don't talk about him like that. He was my brother."

A red mark blossomed on Yolanda's cheek. "So you're going to get your fancy pants dirty running this place? Get manure on your cute boots? Freeze your ass at three a.m.?"

Bobby, in his first show of energy, quickly disconnected two cows from the milking machine and tugged the levers on the neck gates. The pair trotted out. He let two more in, keeping his eyes on the animals, the milking machine, and the measure of oats in each trough.

Cruz, meanwhile, turned her back on Yolanda and regarded Cora with narrowed eyes. "What's your interest in my brother?"

Cora gave her the usual pitch. God, she was tired of saying it.

Cruz rubbed the toe of her roping boot in a puddle of water on the floor. "That reporter from the *Times* swore he'd find out what happened, but his story left it hanging. Franklin didn't commit suicide. I've never believed it."

———

Cruz led the way, out of the milking parlor to a huge elm tree across the farmyard. She dusted off a metal storage box and perched on it while Yolanda paced. Cora found a seat on a wooden bench littered with fallen tree buds.

Cruz combed her artificial fingernails through her long, dark hair. "Franklin was a terrific older brother. He was a great guy—funny, liked to have a good time. When boys came around to take me out, he always made sure they treated me right. When I was about ten, he took me to Guatemala with him to visit Tio Ernesto and Tia Cruz, our uncle and aunt. Not many guys in their twenties would do that."

Yolanda kicked up a spray of gravel with a muddy boot. "Hardly the loving brother. He took you because Mama and Papa said they'd buy his ticket if he did. He told me he dumped you with Tia Cruz for a month while he shacked up in the village with a woman who had a dope stash. Babysitting wasn't his idea of a great vacation."

Cruz's eyes narrowed. "You're jealous. You wanted to go."

While she listened to the sisters quarrel, Cora shook her pant leg to dislodge a cat that had sunk its claws into the denim. The farm swarmed with cats, skittering around the grain silos, slipping under the green tractor, stalking unseen rats in patterns of sun.

"Of the three of us, I knew him best," Cruz said. "He took me with him in his pickup. He bought me little things a girl would like, a pair of flip-flops. Some pop beads."

Cora thought she saw Cruz as a girl, much younger than her brother and sisters, hungry for attention from her busy parents.

"Were you all born in Guatemala?" Cora pulled her collar up. She'd been warm in the sun a minute ago, but now clouds darkened the sky, and a cold blast of wind blew down her neck.

"Franklin was born there," Yolanda said. "Marie and I were born here, in a dumpy little building on the property we use now for storage. At that time, Papa was the milker."

"Then Papa bought out the Van der Horns," Cruz said. "I was the only one born in the white house. After Papa died, it was Franklin who really turned the dairy into a showplace." A cat jumped into Cruz's lap. She stroked it and watched the wind carry away tufts of loose hair.

"Were you surprised when Franklin sold Queen Beatrice to Sean O'Brien? Winning prime exhibitor must've added to the dairy's prestige." Cora caught an exchange of glances between the two sisters. It was their first hint of unity.

"Sean didn't buy Queen Beatrice. She was sold to a dairy in California and shipped directly from the show," Yolanda said.

"You're sure?"

"I helped load her into the trailer myself."

"What about Cayuga's Princess Honor and Baca's Lady Lenore?"

Yolanda rubbed her rubber boots against the edge of an overturned wheelbarrow to scrape off the mud. "They're still in the herd. Numbers 106 and 257."

Cora pulled her already running recorder from her jacket pocket. "I'm going to record this, okay?" She wanted perfect sound.

Cruz's chin quivered. "Yes. Go ahead. Maybe you'll find out what really happened."

"Oh, for God's sake," Yolanda said.

"Back on the subject of the cows," Cora said, "is each one marked?"

"With a number in its ear," Yolanda said. "I was the one, not Franklin, who installed the spreadsheet software to track each cow in every string. Her feed, age, date of insemination, production."

"Were there two other cows missing from the herd? Wouldn't you have noticed?" Cora felt the knotted story begin to loosen, like a snarl in a piece of twine.

"Two were gone," Yolanda said. "But not part of the herd. Two old sisters, big prize winners in their day, that we showed years ago. They should have been sent to slaughter, but Marie's girls loved them. We kept them around, and they ate up tons of feed."

"Who's Marie?"

"The third one of us sisters. Marie came over with the girls when they were home last Thanksgiving. They went to the barn to say hi, and the old cows were gone."

Cruz lifted the cat from her lap and set it on the ground. Her nails flashed as she brushed her fingertips together to remove any cat hair. "We don't know if Franklin sent them to Sean's. Maybe they died, and Franklin had them hauled away."

"I would have noticed the tallow truck," Yolanda said.

Cora couldn't believe her luck. The fight between the sisters was as good as the old TV show, *Point Counter Point*. "What about the phony Queen Beatrice? Did she come from your herd?"

Cruz stood and brushed the seat of her tight jeans. "No. Other than the two old gals, the farm's cows are all accounted for. That's what your records say, don't they, Yolie?"

"He could have bought one at the slaughterhouse. Anywhere, just to have a bogus winner for O'Brien," Yolanda said.

Cruz gave Yolanda a poisonous look.

When had the relationship between Cruz and Yolanda soured? Probably when Cruz was a pretty little toddler and Yolanda was a pudgy teenager. Cora had never had a sister. It must be odd, knowing there was someone in the world with the same genetic strands in each drop of blood. Although the sisters pummeled each other with words, they were still hitting familiar flesh, like slapping yourself to keep awake. Yolanda and Cruz might feel safe, in an odd way, knowing there was another like them in the world, solid, real.

Not an ephemera like her, Cora thought. She didn't even see her real self in the mirror, because her face was reversed. She had no relatives in whom she might catch sight of a shrug or twitch that she recognized as her own. There was Nathan, but he looked like Stephen.

Cora squeezed her eyes shut and took a deep breath. The loneliness that always accompanied her swelled until an obstruction rose in her throat. She swallowed painfully and opened her eyes to see the sisters watching her strangely. She cleared her throat.

"If Franklin and Sean really cooked up this scheme together, why did they do it? The dairy was successful. He had a winner at the big national show. Why would he jeopardize his reputation?"

Pain twisted Yolanda's face. "After the funeral, I found out he'd taken out first and second mortgages on this property, which Papa had paid off in his lifetime. The Harvest Store company, among others, has a lien. Franklin's dead and we're facing bankruptcy."

She assessed the old white house, the shade tree, the fields sloping down to the lake. "I was trying to get Franklin to give up dairying and convert the property to grapes. Start a winery. He said yes, maybe next year."

"He never would've done it," Cruz said.

Yolanda's story reminded Cora of her visit with Judith. Sean's widow also was angry, left with debts and struggling to meet huge loan payments. Sean and Franklin must have gleaned five hundred thousand dollars from their mortgaged properties, but whatever they'd gathered wasn't enough.

"Why did he need money?" Cora said.

"You think he told me? He signed the loan papers without one word," Yolanda said.

"He didn't give you any hint?"

Cruz rubbed a fleck of manure off her boot. "Franklin wouldn't have squandered everything. It must have been Sean who invented the whole thing, whatever it was, the money, the insurance scheme."

"Don't make me laugh," Yolanda said. "Sean was no mastermind. He was a puffed-up little Chihuahua. Franklin was always looking to make it big. He didn't care about this place. I was the one that kept it going, not Mr. Pussy Hound."

Cora wondered what tack to pursue next. If the Santerra sisters knew something, they didn't realize it or weren't saying. "

"Cruz, you think it was Sean who got Franklin into some scheme?" Cora asked. "Judith O'Brien is pretty sure it was the other way around." Not exactly true, but maybe the white lie would loosen things up. "She thinks Franklin got Sean mixed up in gambling, maybe, or a shady land deal."

They were distracted by the sound of an engine, a truck tractor hauling a shiny metal tank trailer marked Hinkle Dairy. It swung into the driveway and stopped next to the milking shed with a hiss of brakes. Yolanda waved to the driver, who clambered from the cab. He carried a test kit and drew a sample from a spigot that led to the bulk storage tank.

"Franklin was proud of this place. Santerra Farms is one of the top ten shippers—best mix of solids, fats and proteins," Cruz said.

"Who gets the farm?" Cora said.

Noise from the unfed calves increased, and Yolanda swayed, first toward Cora and Cruz, then the pens. "I have work to do." She sidestepped for a yard or two, then headed for the milking parlor.

"We do." Cruz shivered and rubbed her arms.

"You and Yolanda?" Cora tried to imagine the two sisters running the dairy. Not without bloodshed.

"And Marie. Franklin's will didn't include his kids. They aren't interested."

"Who found him?" The *Times* story said he had been discovered dead in a rural cottage a gunshot wound to the head.

"Marie did."

"How did she happen to go to the cottage?"

"Marie lives in Ithaca with her husband and kids. She was going to have lunch with him in town, but he didn't show up. She tried his cell all that day. When she couldn't reach him by the next morning, she went out to the cottage."

Cora reminded herself to get the medical examiner's reports. "What made her decide to check on him there?

Cruz pulled on a strand of hair. "Franklin, well, he had relationships."

"He was with a woman?"

"I don't know. Marie thought maybe, but when she arrived the next morning, he was the only one there."

Cora could see Franklin, flung onto his back by the force of the blast, the phone ringing, ringing, drops, pools, patterns of red fanned out around him, small spatters of brown, larger patterns shading to bright red in the center. Bedding underneath him wet. Soaked.

Cruz touched her eyes to blot her tears, her polished fingernails red wounds against her skin. The hills cast blue-gray shadows on the farm, and far out on the lake, a white sail glowed in a last ray of sun. The watchful wind dropped, waiting for night. The pump on the dairy truck stopped and in the silence, a calf bleated.

20

Cora

April 2000

To avoid the roller coaster over the hills, Cora took the Thruway east from the Santerras' farm, then turned south on Highway 81. Rush hour in Cortland had passed, and traffic thinned on Main Street. Vacant Victorian store fronts greeted her on either side, relieved by a book shop with half-empty shelves, an auto parts store, and a tattoo parlor. The city should dynamite the downtown and start over, she thought. No redevelopment plan was going to succeed in turning it into an urban shopping mall.

While she waited for a long traffic signal, her eyelids drooped. When an SUV behind her blew its horn, she struggled to raise her head. The weight of her thoughts seemed about to topple her. She guided the Neon into a diagonal parking space and switched off the engine. With the seat back reclined, she rested awhile. What was Marie Santerra like—did she resemble her hot-tempered, volatile sisters? What did she do to escape the memory of discovering her brother with his head shot off? She might pick a fight with her husband, letting the heat of anger burn away the images of Franklin's wounds. Or she might crowd them out with work.

Cora thought of all the news stories she'd written, the ring of the telephone, the police report, the weapon, the suspect's prior record, the family's grief, the victim's age, the year and make of the car, how the details helped blot out her own memories of blood.

And now she had no job. Free to sit home and think about her father's long fingers, which might have wielded a pen or a brush, but instead had been crushed by machines and permanently blackened by printing ink. Plenty of time to remember the flesh on his meaty palms, which had pounded her mother's fine bones.

After a few minutes, she sat up. Lights from the Downtowner restaurant painted squares on the sidewalk. She hadn't eaten since dinner at Del's the night before. She gathered herself as though assembling a sack of bones, and went inside.

The hostess showed her to a dark wood booth in the back. Cora slid across the plastic seat and propped herself upright in the corner. A waitress with a missing eyetooth and bleeding red lipstick recited the specials, and Cora said yes to something.

She tried to lift her mood by concentrating on the coming weekend, when she'd see Nathan in New York. They'd do the museums. See a show. Play tourist. She called him, but he didn't answer.

Dishes rattled as the waitress delivered the meal. A small plate of iceberg lettuce with Thousand Island dressing. A dish of canned beans. A plate with a breaded pork chop and a mound of mashed potatoes and gravy. The greasy, fried smell of the chop was perfect.

She dipped a morsel in gravy. Thoughts of the three sisters, Franklin Santerra, her parents, all faded in the face of salt and pepper, a forkful of potato and animal fat. The chop was eaten, and she'd picked up her knife to cut the lettuce wedge, when Del appeared beside her table. She could see from his face that he was angry.

She asked, "Are you following me? I got a back booth so I could interview my confidential sources—if any happened to show up. You're cramping my style."

Del's eyes narrowed under the Stetson's brim. "I was worried that some semifamous San Francisco nut case might have died in my area."

"Semifamous?"

"All right. Famous. Notorious." He slid into the booth across from her. With a napkin, he polished a patch of tabletop and put his hat on it.

The waitress hurried over with a coffee carafe and poured him a cup. "Thanks, Hannah. And bring me one of those." He tilted his head toward Cora's plate. "I was damn worried. I put out a BOL on you, and one of my troopers on break spotted your parked car."

"Sorry. I spent the afternoon at the Santerra farm." She didn't mention her visit to Len Crutcher.

The deep lines around his mouth smoothed out.

She leaned over the table and tapped his hand. "Thanks for the morning coffee, Major," she whispered.

He studied her bitten nails resting on the stubs of his fingers. "I'll ignore your not-so-subtle attempt to divert me. How are you feeling?"

"Like I've been kicked by a prize-winning cow."

He chewed the inside of his cheek for a second. "I did something today you might not like. I called the SFPD."

Her stomach clenched on her half-digested food.

"They ran a DOJ check on Roy Edward Brooks. He had one drunk driving conviction, but no arrests or convictions for assault or domestic violence." He turned his cup in the saucer. "No missing person report was ever filed on Alice Macpherson Brooks."

If there were no white pages in manila folders stored in a police warehouse, no blood samples or X-rays of broken ribs, did that mean her memories of that terrible night were part of a demented fantasy? Or if they were true, why had no one, not a neighbor, friend, minister, been suspicious of Roy Brooks? Did he tell people quietly, with his face averted, the story about the lover?

The dinner, which had seemed so appetizing a few minutes ago, smelled like garbage. She had believed her father. She had accepted the story, yet she knew more than anyone alive.

"San Francisco and the nine Bay Area counties have no unidentified remains from that period of years that fit your mother's profile."

"You spent a lot of time on this," she said.

"Only a day. You've been on it, one way or another, for nearly forty years."

She ducked her head so he couldn't see her tears. She was falling apart again. Without meaning to, he seemed to have a marksman's aim for her vital organs.

Cora pushed her plate aside. "He could have buried her somewhere."

"It's possible. But usually, bodies have been discovered after this much time. In a crime of passion, the murderer doesn't hide the body well enough or dig a grave deep enough. The elements expose it, or the city excavates to construct a new road, or somebody finds it spading up the garden."

The waitress arrived with the plates containing Del's dinner balanced on her arm. She put his dishes down and carried Cora's away. He gave Cora a sheepish look. "This is what the state police calls dinner conversation. Sorry."

"We crime reporters only converse about classical music and German philosophers at meals," she said.

Del laughed, a deep, easy sound that made her want to touch his face. As she leaned forward, Cora glanced at the restaurant's front door, where she saw Mimi Shafter and a male companion waiting for a table. Cora shrank back against her seat. "Oh, no. The big-mouthed woman from the historical society just walked in."

Without peering around the corner of the booth, Del said, "Mimi and Dick? They eat here several nights a week. "

In about twenty seconds, Mimi's infrared gossip detector had homed in, and she stood at the table, with Dick on tiptoe to see over her shoulder.

"Del and Cora. Aren't we cozy?"

Dick and Mimi Shafter were at opposite ends of the bell curve. Mimi was broken glass you didn't walk near if you were barefoot. Dick was soft and pear shaped. His head was sunk between his shoulders, and his lack of a neck seemed an attempt somehow to protect his vulnerable spots.

"I'm re-interviewing Major Somer for my story," Cora said.

"Have you solved Sean's murder yet?" Mimi's voice ricocheted off the high ceiling. Several diners glanced up from their food.

"Our preliminary conclusion was suicide, Mimi. If we get some evidence to the contrary, I'll let people know directly," Del said.

"It's strange coincidence, don't you think," Mimi said, "how the O'Briens have had two mysterious tragedies in their family?"

"What? Has something else happened?" Cora said.

Del sat up straighter, and Cora saw the bulge under his arm. He carried his weapon in a shoulder holster even at dinner. "Not in recent memory," he said. "Mimi is talking about the old missing person case. I told you about it the first time we talked."

Dick Shafter craned his head around Mimi. "Sean's uncle, Seamus O'Brien. There was talk of buried treasure."

"That's, what, eighty years ago? You folks have long memories," Cora said.

"Have you been out to the site of the old store?" Mimi asked.

"Not yet. I've been busy."

Mimi smirked and rolled her eyes toward Del. "Why don't I take you? Give you some local history."

Cora tasted a bitter resistance in her mouth. She was afraid of what feelings might arise if she went to the spot where Alice had lived as a girl.

"Nine o'clock tomorrow. I'll pick you up," Mimi said.

The pressure of Mimi's will pressed on Cora. "Okay, but I'm not at my best in the morning," Cora said.

"I can deal with it. Come, Dick, let's eat." He raised his shoulders as if to deflect her order, but at the same time moved after her.

On the way out of the restaurant, Del turned to her. "The forensic toxicologist's report on Sean O'Brien is back, and I've got a copy at the office. I can drive, if you like, and we can talk about it." He settled his hat on his forehead.

The streets were quiet. She noticed the absence of cars with thumping sound systems. In San Francisco they sent her blood pressure soaring. A luminous moon shone behind the budding branches. Through the half-open car window, the cold air smelled of wet earth and some fragrance, snowdrops, maybe, or crocuses. The beauty of the evening made her sad.

"The paper is laying me off. I've been given two weeks' notice." She felt ashamed, as though she should cover her mouth as she spoke. She hadn't been unemployed since she graduated from Berkeley.

"So the story's dead?" He sounded so hopeful, Cora hated to disillusion him.

"You're not off the hook. I'll finish the story, and the paper will run it before I leave." She hoped.

"You sound confident you'll have something to write."

"This will be my last story for the *Standard*. When I leave, I want this story to show them how wrong they were."

Del parked near the side entrance to his office. He held up his key card to the reader at the side door. Better than sitting in the drafty lobby with no magazines, as she had on her first visit. On the third floor, the lights in the reception area were off and the only illumination was the glow from the digital clocks and screen savers. He used a key to open his office door and snapped on the desk light.

Cora noticed again the bareness of Del's office. He deliberately left no clues to his personal taste, as if his private life were too fragile for even the most superficial scrutiny. The only hint was the aerial photo of the Finger Lakes reflecting the sun like gold ingots.

He perched his hat on the hat stand and thumbed through an accordion file on the credenza behind his desk for the toxicology report.

The photo took on more meaning now that Cora knew Judith had been the only passionate attachment in Del's life. Did the picture remind him of his loss or his foolishness?

Was he still mourning her? If he were disgusted with himself for making a mistake, the picture might be a sticky note not to commit the same error again. It felt strange to be speculating about him. In the two years since Stephen left, she hadn't spent more than sixty seconds thinking personally about any one man. Romance, even casual sex, seemed to be located in someone else's neighborhood.

Cora imagined what Del might be telling himself about her: Here's a skinny woman who doesn't cook, lives three thousand miles away, and comes from a dysfunctional family. She's working on a story that will make you look bad and might cost you a promotion. Hot prospect.

She laughed.

"What's so funny?" The lines between his eyebrows deepened.

"I was thinking about what a poor candidate I am for a relationship." Relationship? When the word dropped from her mouth, she was appalled.

"With me?" His desk clock clicked off the seconds.

"No, of course not." Her face burned. This was being thirteen and taller than all the boys, this was going to the senior prom without a date, this was trying to attract Stephen's attention, but not knowing how to flirt.

"Yes, you are."

"I just want you." Last night her head had teemed with mothers, Alice and Frieda, and with blood, Cora's and Alice's. Tonight she just felt the emptiness.

"You hardly know me," he said.

"I don't care."

They met at the corner of his desk. He buried his fingers in her hair, cupping her head between his palms. His blue eyes darkened as he looked at her, and Cora's breath was trapped in her chest. Then his arms went around her, and she pressed against him, breasts, stomach, legs, saturating herself with him. Taller than Stephen, but not as lean. His muscle and bulk made her feel safe, and blocked out everything that disturbed her: age, parents, job.

She kissed him, searching his lips and mouth with her tongue. The moment extended, wet and heated, until their two tastes blended. With her eyes closed and her mouth still touching his, she felt for his belt buckle.

His quick breathing tickled her face. "Not here. There are people in the building all night."

"Now." Her head whirled, and she rocked on her feet.

He steadied her with a hand between her shoulder blades. "I'm too old to screw on my desk. Come on, let's go home."

She squeezed her eyelids tighter, not wanting to see the spare office chairs, the metal blinds, her reflection in the window glass.

He laced his fingers between hers. "You'll like it. I promise."

21

Abby
June 1917

Abby crouched on the glider swing under the grape arbor. It was after nine and nearly dark, the reluctant dark of midsummer. A swollen moon hung on the horizon. Sweat collected in Abby's bent elbows and in the folds behind her knees. Mosquitoes buzzed around her face; one bit her cheek. The store was locked, but upstairs lamps were lit and windows open to catch a ripple of air.

"We'll wrap it up. Bury it as soon as it's light." Grandma Clemmie's voice drifted down from above like chimney ashes.

"Is she awake?" her father asked.

"She's crying. I gave her some laudanum."

Abby shifted to set the glider in motion. Her mother had lost another baby. A boy or girl. Brother or sister. What would Grandma Clemmie wrap the baby in? A dish towel or a luncheon cloth, maybe. Abby dug her thumbs into her eyes. Would her father make a box for it, like he had when Grandma Miller died of influenza? Mama's stomach under her long skirt had been small, the size of a two-pound bag of flour. The baby was probably tiny enough to fit in a metal cracker box like the ones in the store.

Abby pumped the glider faster. It squeaked, grinding on its corroded track.

Her father leaned out, his words thick with whiskey and misery. "Abby, stop that."

Another mosquito bit her face. How could the world be so full—insects buzzing around her, honeysuckle scent everywhere—and yet be so lonely?

She left the arbor and walked down the center of the empty road in the direction of Seamus's farm until she spotted the almost invisible ruts that marked the track to the still. The moon was bright enough that her misshapen shadow slid along beside her. She turned and followed the path uphill, through the grove of ash trees, over the grassy knob at the top, and then down. When she heard the trickle of the spring, she slowed. The cove was tucked in an odd fold of the hills, screened by a stand of huge elms. Moonlight didn't penetrate here, but the cove swirled with the smell of cold wood fires and the sharp tang of whiskey.

Abby felt another presence somewhere in the ash-stained black ground. Her father recognized it, too; he said the prickly presence was the faeries. She groped her way across the clearing until the rough wooden door to the distillery rasped against her fingertips. She pushed it open and fumbled for the matches in the metal dispenser hung beside the door. The lantern's wick caught with a whoosh.

In the flickering light, the coils of copper tubing writhed like iridescent snakeskin. Last year's ashes lay piled in the drying kiln. Her father wouldn't come here again until late summer, when the barley was nearly ripe.

Abby carried the lantern outside and sat down under the grandfather elm that hid the cove. She'd first followed her father here when she was seven. He'd been turning the sprouting barley on the distillery floor when he glanced up.

"What the Sam Hill are you doing here?"

"It was an accident, Papa."

He hunkered down eye to eye, one knee in the wet barley. "Swear to me, on the holy head of Saint Andrew, that you won't tell a soul about this place."

"Not even Mama?"

"She knows as much about it as she wants. But she's the only one, you hear?"

Abby swore, and her father had put his palm to her forehead to seal the oath.

Abby tried to remember how many of her mother's babies had died. Four, she thought. When she was younger, she didn't realize what was happening, because Ruth never talked about female troubles. Abby imagined the lost babies like four dark places in her mother's heart that she never had time to visit. Would Ruth stay in bed for a long time? Probably not. Abby didn't remember a morning when she hadn't heard the pump handle creak as her mother drew water for breakfast.

Abby cradled her cheek against her knees. The water trickled over the rocks and flowed through the channel her father had dug under the still house. The tip of the lantern flame smoked, coating the glass with a black, greasy residue. Humid air pressed her eyelids. She hadn't seen Seamus since graduation day. She savored the memory of his kiss in the farm office, how she'd felt the slow, delicious revolution of the earth under her feet, how her body had become an exquisite landscape under the pressure of his hands, and her mouth throbbed with an unexpected pulse.

A harness jingled, and metal hit stone. Someone was bringing a wagon up the track to the still.

She closed the lantern slide. Holding her breath, she moved swiftly inside the distillery. She'd never seen anyone in the cove except her father and Uncle Will. Government agents and thieves both wanted to discover its location, her father said. She was angry, suddenly, at her father for all this trouble. He'd made her swear; he broke the law. Even worse, he'd told her to be quiet while she listened to Ruth cry over her baby.

The clop of horses' hooves stopped, and a wagon brake squealed. Abby peered through a crack in the door. A tiny flame ignited a lantern. A bare arm gleamed as the man raised the light. It wasn't a government agent. It was Seamus.

He set his lantern on a rock, propped a rifle against a tree, and began to dig.

Abby eased open the distillery door. He was here about the guns, either making a hole to bury them or digging them up. The wagon sat high on its springs, so it wasn't loaded. He must be here to retrieve them. Why were the guns here in the cove rather than in Ireland?

As Abby descended the steps, one of the horses rolled an eye at her and jerked its head. Seamus lunged for his rifle.

"It's me!" Fright turned her voice to vapor, so she took a deep breath. "Seamus, it's Abby."

He froze with the rifle midway to his shoulder. "Christ, I almost put a bullet through you." He didn't lower the gun, but gazed slowly around the clearing. "Who else is here?"

"Nobody. I'm alone."

"Meeting someone?"

"Don't be stupid, Seamus."

"Then what the hell are you doing, running about in the middle of the night? Go home before Jack finds out and takes a belt to you." He kept the rifle in the crook of his arm. His legs were bent, ready to leap or run.

"I'm not going home—I'm staying here. And no one will punish me, because you're not going to tell."

Abby crossed to the spot where he'd been digging and peered into the hole. Dirt loosened by her shoe dribbled onto the top of a wooden crate. "How many guns are there?"

"There aren't any guns."

"No guns? Then what are you digging? A grave?"

He sighed. "I can't tell you."

"Why didn't you buy the guns for Ireland?"

He lifted a water jug from the wagon bed and drank deeply. "I'll tell you, but this is our secret. Understood?"

Abby felt the weight of yet another secret adding to the heap of stones on her chest.

"You're the only one who knows." His voice was deeper, inviting. "We're friends, aren't we?"

Abby resisted that beguiling sound. "I told you we were. Before."

"I remember; it was in my office." He rubbed the pulse point on her wrist with his thumb. "There was something more about that day."

Just thinking about the scrape of his beard, the pressure of his mouth, created an ache in her body's soft places. He pulled her closer, bent his head, and slid his lips up the curve of her neck.

"I don't know if I want to," she cried, dizzy with the smell of his soap and skin. She was unsure what to say and feel, whether she wanted to keep the tender spot behind her ear to herself or tilt her head to offer it to him. Coolness touched her back as he unbuttoned her bloomer suit and slid it over her shoulders.

"I do. This will be our secret, you and me."

His chest vibrated against her when he spoke, and the folds between her legs picked up the small tremor. He slipped his thumbs under the straps of her chemise. Her nipples felt strange as they were exposed to the air. His cheek burned against her breast.

She tried to gather her resolve. "I want you to come calling on me, Seamus. I want a gold ring."

A distance opened between them. "Marriage? Let's wait until after I finish this shipment. Then we'll talk about it."

Abby knew she needed a better promise, but while she tried to form the words, he undressed her. She waited with her arms wrapped around her nakedness until he had spread a canvas from the wagon on the ground. The horses shuffled their hooves, and a mockingbird sang its stolen songs from a nearby tree.

Her mother never talked about sex, always averted her eyes when someone made a joke, but Abby had watched the mating of dogs and cats, horses and cows. The act looked ludicrous, undignified, far from becoming one flesh like it said in the Bible. She'd imagined the mating of men and women was different, as if some veil was cast over them to shield the awkwardness of it. Seamus took off his clothes, pulled her down beside him, and laid her on her back.

Over his shoulder, the lantern winked, dark, light, as he moved in and out of her, his weight robbing her of breath. She felt odd. A change was about to happen, and then he cried out and she went spinning into another place for a few long seconds. He rolled to one side, and she saw a moth fluttering round the lantern.

The tender place between her legs was swollen and hot, not really painful, but extraordinarily sensitive, the way her lips felt after she ate spicy food. She stroked his back with her knuckle from his hips to his neck. With her nose to his shoulder, she inhaled his musky scent. He threw his arm around her and hummed into the curve of her neck, a rhythm that might have been a tune. Remember this forever, she told herself.

———

Abby's fingers stumbled over each other, anxious to fasten the openings in her clothes. She sat on the canvas as far away as possible from the bloody spot that marked where they had lain.

Seamus jumped down into the hole and used the blade end of the pickaxe to loosen the packed dirt, then snatched the shovel. He grunted as he hefted a wooden crate out of the hole. The box was unexpectedly small, two feet square at most. Sweat streamed off him as he lifted more boxes until twenty sat in a line along the lips of the pit. His chest heaved as he hoisted himself out and sat on the ground, his elbows propped on his thighs.

"I couldn't hide anything at the farm. Leland has learned of our project somehow, and he's been doing some searching on the quiet. I can see him playing light-fingered Harry."

"If my father sees someone here, he might mistake you for a government agent and shoot you," Abby said.

"Stop fretting. He only comes here two months a year for distilling. The barley's nowhere near ripe."

"Why didn't you move the guns earlier? The navy has set up a blockade now. It could sink your ship."

"Half the shipment is gone. Shipped and received." Triumph hardened the lines around his mouth. He unplugged the stopper from the water jug and held it out to her. Dirt clung to the hairs on his arms. She tilted her head and swallowed, letting some run down her neck. The clean, wet spot made the rest of her feel soiled.

He took a long drink. "Abby, let down the backboard on the wagon."

She unfastened the metal hasps on either side and lowered the wagon's heavy wooden end. The horses shifted uneasily, clicking their hooves and rattling their harnesses.

"Getting them down there was a sight easier than pulling them out. They must weigh a hundred pounds apiece."

"It's not guns, is it?"

He flipped his hand in an invitation. She squatted beside one of the dirt-stained crates and loosened a groaning slat. She pushed aside the cotton wrapping.

Three ingots lay there, gleaming like huge gold teeth.

"We couldn't get the guns. Every shipment of iron ore and every factory assemblyline is reserved for the army's weapons orders. The armories are being guarded. We're sending gold, instead," Seamus said.

22

Cora
April 2000

Cora hated the trip to his place, isolated from him by the police radio, hands-free phone, and laptop between the seats. She wrapped her coat around her and brooded about Traci Knapp, the reporter who slept with the captain from Bayview Station. Cora had complained about Traci's unprofessional conduct, but she was committing the same offense. What did it matter? In two weeks, she'd be unemployed, without a job to be professional about. She sighed.

Del made two or three telephone calls while he drove, rescheduling a seven a.m. breakfast, talking to Frieda.

"She wants to know if you're coming for your pie-baking lesson tomorrow afternoon," Del said.

"Yes. Tell her four o'clock, and I'm sorry I didn't get back to her."

The porch light was on at Del's. He parked in back beside the ciderhouse. Cold air in the kitchen made her shiver. She wrapped her arms around herself and watched as he turned up the heat and set his briefcase on the table. Although she'd been hot for him forty-five minutes ago in his office, now she'd cooled. She wanted to return to Seneca House.

Drago scratched at the back door, and Cora let him in. He barked at her while at the other end his wagging tail whacked the table legs.

She scratched him behind the ears. "Hello to you, too."

When Del returned from the front of the house, he had taken off his sports jacket. His white shirt retained the imprint of his holster strap.

"Is that the report?" Cora tapped his briefcase.

"Yeah. I've found that a really effective way of getting women into bed is to go over toxicology results."

She remembered, suddenly, the bare floor in the O'Briens' study, lined with tacks that once had anchored the carpet.

Del touched her cheek, and Cora jumped. "Hey, it was a joke."

Before his face stilled, she saw a twitch of hurt around his mouth. He quickly put his hand in his pocket.

She struggled to shift her focus to Del. "I told you we should have done it there. I'm having second thoughts."

He looked at her closely as if assembling bits of evidence. "We don't need to make love. I have a guest room, or you can sleep on the couch again."

"I don't know." She blew on her hands and shoved them into her jacket pockets.

"Come on." He held out his hand.

She clasped it, and he led her up the back stairs from the kitchen to the master bedroom. The scent of aftershave lingered on the gray and blue spread that covered the king-sized bed. A terrycloth robe was thrown over the arm of a chair, and a dent in the bedclothes showed where he probably sat to put on his socks in the morning. On the dresser a collection of baseball caps was lined up like new recruits.

Del kicked off his shoes. As he walked into the bathroom, his feet left prints in the thick carpet. She hesitated a second, then followed. The bath had been remodeled with twin marble sinks and a whirlpool tub. The shower could hold a basketball team and was fitted with multiple nozzles.

The luxury seemed out of character for Del. "You lived in this house when you were married?" she said.

"I've owned it about twenty years and thought it was fine, but Judith wouldn't move in until I remodeled."

Did Del's bedroom and bath retain memories, like hers in San Francisco? She'd hauled to the dump the mattress she'd slept on with Stephen, where he'd lain with his hard, bony back to her and told her he was leaving. When the new bed was delivered, she'd felt a surge of angry satisfaction, but the change didn't erase the memories. A floorboard on his side of the bed still squeaked, as it had when he'd gotten up to use the bathroom. A lock that he'd installed on the bedroom door after Nathan walked in when they were making love was still in place.

Del crossed her line of vision, unbuttoning his shirt and turning on the shower. The multiple jets threw a fine, steamy spray. He came close, spread the edges of her jacket, slid it off her arms, and tossed it on the floor. His hands were warm on her ribs as he slid her turtleneck over her head. He knelt down to untie her boot laces.

"I can do that," she said.

He looked up and shook his head. Feeling very vulnerable, she put her hands on his shoulders to steady herself while he slipped her shoes and socks off. His face was close to the zipper on her jeans, and she tilted her hips toward him.

Steam drifted over the top of the shower door.

He rubbed his face between her legs. Cora fumbled with the hook on her bra and snatched it off. In a moment, she had tossed aside her jeans and white cotton panties. She pulled him to his feet and kissed him, sucking at his lips, biting his tongue as she unzipped his slacks and slid her hands into his shorts. When she touched his penis, she drew back from his mouth. For two heartbeats, they didn't breathe. She caressed it, circled it with her fingertips.

"Let go for just a second." He slid his clothes off, opened the shower door and drew her inside. The hot water sluiced over her, drops stimulating her skin until every cell seemed to vibrate. He plucked the soap out of the dish and rubbed it over her nipples.

The hair on his chest tickled her palms, and she twined her arms around his neck. Standing on tiptoe, she wrapped her legs around his waist.

"Wait. Let's slow down," he said. "We've got all night."

"Now. Quick!" If she didn't fuck, she'd be in tears.

He slid his hands under her ass and entered her in one juicy motion. She came, crying out at last, her muscles going slack. She bumped his chin with her head.

She wrapped her arms around his neck and worked his cock in and out of her. She rode his hips, surfed on his movement, felt the impact of his climax.

He leaned against the shower wall, his eyes closed, gasping for breath. The folds between her legs throbbed in rhythm with her heart. He set her down, and she fell abruptly on her ass.

"Jesus, are you okay?" He turned off the water and lifted her to her feet.

"I feel strange. As if I'm not here all of a sudden."

He dried her with a towel, rubbing her back and thighs, running his fingers through her hair to untangle it.

———

In bed afterward, she lay on her stomach and buried her face in the pillow instead of curling against him. It was hard to breathe, and she caught the toasty scent of his hair on the pillowcase. Del lay beside her, not touching. His body made a separate dent in the mattress.

Loneliness crept up on her again. Her isolation felt worse now than earlier, before they'd had sex; the brief moment of wholeness faded until all that was left was the puffiness of her lips and stickiness between her legs. She pulled her arms close to her sides, turned her feet in, toes touching like a child, and listened to the whisper of her skin against the sheet.

"Cora?" He pressed his thumb against her tailbone, and the firm touch made her want to cry.

"I think," she swallowed to keep her tears in check, "I think you should see a shrink."

"Me?" He jerked up onto his elbow, as if he'd been peppered with buckshot.

She took her face out of the pillow. "You're suffering from an unhealthy compulsion to get involved with needy women."

"What the hell are you talking about?"

"First Judith, now me. There's a pattern," she said.

He spun her onto her back and lay half across her, pinning her to the bed.

"Hey, it was a joke," she said.

His eyes narrowed, and his mouth thinned into a hard line. He was furious. "Stop it, Cora."

"Get off me." She squirmed, then punched at his arms and shoulders, but he didn't budge. He must weigh one-ninety, she thought.

"You kid around, like if you make enough jokes, then you're not really messed up."

She averted her face, straining the tendons in her neck, so she wouldn't have to look at the angry lines around his mouth. "I want to get out of here."

"Not yet." He clamped his hand onto her chin and turned her face back toward him. "What was that all about, in the shower? It sure as hell wasn't about love, and, at five minutes, it was hardly even about sex."

"You're complaining? I don't believe it."

"If I wanted a quickie in the shower, I could have more fun by myself, and I wouldn't have to strain my back doing it."

She tried to get her knee up to his crotch, but couldn't free her legs. His weight pressed on her chest and her pulse pounded in her throat. A hot flash started in her face, burning its way down her body. "I can't stand it," she screamed. "Get off me."

Heat spread over her chest, and he flopped onto his back, his arms rigid at his sides and fists clenched.

In the bathroom, she splashed cold water on her face. She returned and sat on the edge of the bed, not looking at him, but at a LeRoy Neiman baseball print on the wall.

"I wanted to forget about all of it for awhile. Take a break," she said.

"Don't you think you need help?"

She raised a hand, warning him away.

"A therapist, maybe."

"For God's sake! Stop it."

"You go ballistic when I even mention it. Has someone else told you the same thing recently?"

"Maybe I'll do it," she said to put him off. She snatched her clothes from the bathroom floor and began to dress.

He watched as she fastened her bra and stepped into her pants. "That's a real commitment."

"I might have some time after I wrap things up at work."

"In other words, no."

She was short of breath. She wouldn't think about therapists. They were for whiny society women and fucked-up teenagers. "What is it with you? You make it your mission to save distressed women? Are there so few in New York State that you have to rescue visiting journalists?"

"No, only you, for some strange reason."

"And Judith."

"That's over. Stop harping."

She shoved her feet into her boots and tied the laces. "If you're not trying to rescue her, then what is it about this case? I don't believe for a minute you believed her version of Sean's death. Why didn't you investigate whether it was really a suicide?"

He swung out of bed. "Go home, Cora. Forget this story. Get some help." He stepped into a pair of jeans and pulled on a Mets T-shirt.

The shirt reminded her of the Little League photos on the bookshelves in his office. "Oh, God, it's Tyler. He did it."

He scooped up his wrinkled dress shirt. "Don't go there, Cora."

"You're protecting Tyler. That's why you've left loose ends all over the place. Completely uncharacteristic for someone with law enforcement training."

"Goddammit, Cora, butt out."

"You saw something. You know something."

"Finish dressing. I'm taking you to your car."

They faced each other toe to toe, she in her pants and bra, he with his shirt hanging open and his belt unbuckled. Cora's panic about therapy faded and she was diverted by the story again, unearthing small bits, arranging the pieces until they fit. She'd done it dozens of times. In the story, she knew her route; she was focused and capable.

"I'm not leaving until you tell me," she said. It was ridiculous. If he wanted, he could snatch her off her feet, throw her in the car.

His lips thinned, and he radiated frustration.

"Let's go downstairs," he said. "I'll make coffee."

23

Del

April 2000

He sat across from her at his kitchen table. The coffee maker burped. His watch read 1:53, a time of night when regret flourishes.

She was on the right track, and it wouldn't be long before she knew everything. Drago bumped their legs under the table, excited to see someone at such a late hour. Del pointed to the floor, and the dog sank at his feet.

Cora was vibrating like a piano wire, he could feel it, anxious to be on the trail, arrange her facts, erase all ambiguities while she ignored her own conflicts. The light over the kitchen table seemed extraordinarily bright, and he hunched like a suspect from a B movie.

He spread his hands, the whole one and the ruined one. It was a gamble to tell her, but he had to delay or derail the story. Tyler's life could depend on it. Luckily, Cora had a soft spot for Tyler, who was so close in age to her own son. He sniffed the residual spicy burn of last night's chili, and began slowly.

"The night Sean died, it had been snowing since about nine o'clock, not much wind, but very cold. The roads were slippery, even with snow tires."

"What time did you arrive at the farm?" The tip of her ballpoint tapped on the paper as she wrote.

"At 3:42. Same as I told you the other day."

"Tell me again what time she called you."

"It was 3:09." He remembered it clearly; he'd risen on his elbow and reached for his watch and cell phone, which lay close to the lamp on the bedside table. Exactly the same place every night.

"Dispatch shows you called 911 at 3:12," she said.

"Yes. I pulled on some clothes and called before I left the house. When I got to the farm, there was a light in the house. A set of tire tracks led from the road around to the rear of the property where the milkers' trailer is."

Cora's pen hovered over the page. "No way to tell if the tracks were coming or going? Did you see the vehicle?"

"Not then. I didn't have time." He had tucked the sight of the tracks in his memory as his car chewed through the unplowed drifts to the house.

He remembered the dread. Its weight had bent his back and made his head feel too heavy to hold up. "Judith was waiting for me by the study doors."

He remembered the snow swirling around her; she had run outside without a coat. When she hurled herself against his chest, he awkwardly patted her back, feeling trapped. He hadn't wanted to see her, didn't want to feel again the regret of his failed marriage.

Del's chair scraped the floor as he got up and went to the cupboard. He poured coffee into two mugs and set one in front of Cora. Her eyes moved to the cup and then back to her notebook.

"As soon as I saw Sean, I knew he was dead. His face was in rictus and rigor had begun." He'd dreamed about it since, Sean's retracted lips and gleaming teeth in a final white smile.

"I covered Sean with a blanket, then took Judith into the living room so she wouldn't have to see him while I waited for Neville."

"What about the ambulance?" Cora took a sip of coffee, grimaced, then touched her burned tongue to her lip.

"It arrived at 3:55, but there was nothing they could do except to confirm he was deceased. At 3:57, Neville arrived. At that point, I turned things over to him."

He heard his voice slowing by degrees. The closer he came to the heart of the matter, the larger the words seemed, hunks of emotion stuck in his throat.

Cora tapped her fingers on the table.

"I told Neville to call the medical examiner and walked through the snow to the double-wide. The tire tracks were pretty much gone by then."

Cora crossed her forearms atop her notebook. "Tyler was there, wasn't he?"

Del remembered bypassing the mobile home, his footprints leaving holes in the snow. "I found his truck in a shed behind the milking parlor. The hood was cold."

"He'd been back at the farm for awhile, not at Dale Tilly's," Cora said.

"I banged on the door of the trailer, but when I couldn't rouse anybody, I went inside. Beer cans were everywhere and the place stank of vomit. Pedro and Rico had passed out in the living room."

The corner of Del's mouth was trembling. To stop it, he pressed a knuckle against his lip. "Tyler was in the back bedroom, asleep in his clothes. I woke him up. Told him Sean was dead. He made this strange sound, like something was caught in his windpipe. When I bent over him, I saw he was pissing himself."

How could he explain it, what Tyler had been like when he and Judith were first married? A kid with two missing front teeth who stole Del's change off the dresser and screamed at his mother. A kid who followed Del around pointing out all the things he did wrong.

He wanted to tell Cora how, night after night, he'd gotten up to find Tyler asleep in the hall outside their bedroom door. Del had picked him up, the boy's face cold against his neck, knowing this was all he would have in the way of children, and lain Tyler in his bed.

Del was surprised to see the glint of tears on Cora's eyelashes.

"He was very, very scared," she whispered.

Del studied her a minute. Her emotions were involved, and that was good. "He told me he did it."

"Oh, God."

From under the table came the wet sound of Drago licking a sore.

"According to Tyler, Sean had lost huge sums of money a year or two ago in a Mexican investment scheme. Judith ragged on him constantly." When they were married, Del remembered, Judith had been relentless if she wanted something, until Del would have done anything to shut her up. He gulped a mouthful of scalding coffee.

"Tyler wanted to come back here. He wanted Judith and me together again. I knew he'd fantasized about it when we first split, but I thought he'd gotten over it. You'd think at sixteen—anyway."

He wrapped his hands around the cup, embracing the pain of its heat. "Sean traveled a lot, all over the world, judging at livestock shows. He always brought something home for Tyler as reparation for being gone so much. Last summer, immediately after Sean and Judith got back from a trip that included a detour to Central America, Sean was hospitalized for a few days. He'd picked up dysentery somewhere."

"Come on, Del, get to the point." Cora scribbled notes again, as though to make up for her moment of weakness over Tyler.

"Tyler had asked Sean to bring him back some electronics, so Tyler went through Sean's luggage. Under a false bottom in the suitcase, he found thirty pounds of cocaine."

"Sean was smuggling drugs to recoup his losses," she said.

"Apparently."

"So Tyler stole the coke and sold it," she said. "Dale Tilly told me that all of a sudden Tyler was the source for drugs at high school."

"No!" Del slapped the tabletop, and the cups rattled. Drago slunk to the service porch and scratched at the back door. "Tilly is a low-life little punk who'll be in prison by the time he's twenty-one. He'd lie about anything."

"Okay, okay."

"Tyler didn't steal the coke for money."

"Then why?"

Del let the dog out. The cider house canted in the moonlight. "Tyler was afraid that if Sean became a regular mule—running coke all the time—the money would be good."

"And things would be hunky-dory in the O'Brien household."

Del nodded. "Tyler figured if the shipment disappeared, Sean would have to sell everything to pay back the Central American cartel."

"A sophisticated scheme for a sixteen-year-old."

"It was goddamn naive," he said. "Hatched by a kid that's been watching too many movies."

"But still, events developed the way he wanted," Cora said. "Sean sold off most of the herd and mortgaged the property. Judith began hankering for the good old days with you."

"Sean's problem was, there's no way he and Franklin could have scraped together enough to buy their way out. Not even with the phony insurance deal."

Cora pounced on his words. "You knew it all along! The two of them were conspirators in the smuggling plan."

He shrugged. "I've known both of them for thirty years. Actually, Sean for longer than that. I didn't have to be Einstein."

"And Tyler set the whole thing in motion," she said.

"He didn't realize. When Tyler saw Sean unable to sleep, drinking a lot, he thought about giving back the cocaine. But he didn't have the chance." Del rubbed his dry eyes with his thumb and forefinger, wishing he knew more. "When I told him Sean had died, Tyler assumed the cartel had pulled the plug, and it was his fault."

"Those bad boys don't poison people with strychnine. They do infinitely nastier things," Cora said.

Del turned his back on her to hide his fear. He'd read reports, seen pictures, listened at drug enforcement conferences to the horrors committed by the cartels.

"Why is Tyler continuing to hide the drugs?" she asked.

"Don't know. I've tried every coercive trick I use on hardened suspects, but he won't say."

"You should have called in another agency to investigate the suicides," she said. "Tyler's not a misunderstood little boy any more. He's a thief, concealing a huge drug stash."

"And the secret could get him killed. That's why I kept the case, why I got him into rehab. At least he'll be safe for sixty days."

She tugged her hair in frustration. "Lots of information, but it still doesn't tell me who killed Sean O'Brien."

"It may not be a murder or even a suicide." On the table, he unsnapped the fasteners on his briefcase and took out the toxicology report. She reached, but he turned it upside down and spread his hand over it.

She shook her head. "I can't leave Tyler out of the story."

There was nothing for it, he had to beg. "Please, Cora, give me a chance to find out. Tyler's not a bad kid, and there's a lot we don't know." He gazed at her steadily, not blinking. If she wrote the story tomorrow, the spotlight would be on his evasions and conflicts of interest. If he was able to find the answers, the focus would shift to the suspect. He had to believe it was someone beside Tyler.

Cora drew a circle on her notepad. "Tyler's thin. He hasn't been eating well."

"That's true."

"Probably very frightened."

He held his breath.

"You have to tell me everything you find out. All of it."

The paper crackled as he flipped it over. "Sean had both strychnine and cocaine in his system when he died."

24

Abby
August 1917

Her father used rope to lash two gouged cardboard suitcases to the bed of the Model T truck, parked in front of the store. He lifted the hood, adjusted the choke, and cranked the starter. With a tubercular cough, the engine shuddered to life.

Abby was imprisoned between him and Ruth in the truck's small cab; her father's elbow jabbed her side as he worked the accelerator lever, her mother's hard shoulder allowed her no room to lean away. The smell of truck exhaust and her father's perspiration incited a knot of bile in her throat. Cold drops sprang from her skin and dampened her forehead.

"Let me out!"

Ruth slapped the balky door open and scrambled down, her long skirt swirling. Abby raced to the bushes at the end of the porch, pulled aside her motoring veil, and lost her breakfast. Inside the truck again, her parent's anger sucked up the air. Please God, maybe if she pressed her shoe heel deeply enough into her other foot, if it hurt very badly in penance, she and her mother wouldn't have to go to California.

At Rice Hill, her father put the truck in reverse and backed up the long incline so that gasoline would flow from the rear fuel tank to the engine. The tendons in his neck stretched long and ropy; he leaned out the window into the billowing dust, and Abby watched the land drop away in front of her, the lake, her school, Seamus's farm. This long haul up Rice Hill was the same route she and Seamus had taken last winter, wrapped in a thick buffalo robe against the snow and wind.

Today, Seamus seemed as far away as that long-ago blizzard. A small, greasy bug flew in the open side of the truck, and snared itself in her veil. Steam hissed from under the truck's hood, and her father cranked the wheel and pulled into a turnout. He cursed when he touched the hot radiator cap.

Two weeks ago, she and her mother had hiked up the hill to gather strawberries, carried two basketsful back to the kitchen, and picked them over for jam. Abby lowered the empty Mason jars into a bath of boiling water to sterilize them, accompanied by the soft thumping of her mother's mallet as she crushed the berries. All at once, the noise stopped, and Abby looked over to see Ruth's hand poised over the bowl of glistening red pulp and juice.

"I haven't washed any rags," her mother said.

Abby tried to keep her hands still, but the jars clinked against each other.

"How long as it been?" Ruth's eyes pinned Abby like a frog on a spike.

"I scrubbed them myself."

"There were no rags on the clothesline."

Abby swallowed. She was probably pregnant. Two months without the curse, and after breakfast she sometimes threw up her food.

She hated secrets: her mother's, her father's, Seamus's. Now she harbored in her belly the biggest one of all. She wanted to be with Seamus, feel the solid flesh of his chest, hear his deep voice in her ear. Since the night at the still, she had seen him only once, at the annual fish fry at Munger's Resort. Abby had tried all evening to speak to him, but he had warned her away with a shake of his head.

Her mother had sunk her fingers into the soft part of Abby's upper arm. "Who is it? Tell me."

Abby snatched her arm away. Her chest burned with misery.

"Is it the Goins boy? Don't look at me that way. Your father will beat it out of you."

Abby concentrated on the fine golden hairs on her arms. She mustered every particle of her strength and said nothing about the gold, the still, or Seamus.

Papa had locked her in her room, where she cried until her tear ducts were empty. A fever of anger infected her, and she lay in her bed burning with fury at her mother, who brought meals and emptied the chamber pot, at her father, who carried the key in his pocket, and at Seamus, who had not come to call on her nor asked her to marry him.

At Tully, her father turned north toward Syracuse. A three-thousand-mile journey faced Abby and Ruth before they reached Oakland, California. Four days by train with a change in Chicago. Aunt Mary would meet them at the station and escort them by ferry across the bay to San Francisco.

In the Pullman car, a Negro porter lifted their suitcases into the overhead rack. Abby slid into the window seat. An older couple in dark clothes settled into the two facing seats. Ruth stashed the basket of sandwiches and fruit and a vacuum flask of lemonade under the seat. Abby turned to the window. The glass bore the oily imprint of someone's hair. A whistle blast reverberated across the dozen rows of steel tracks, which reminded her of prison bars.

A belch of steam and black coal dust erupted from the engine. The train crept along, gained speed, and emerged from the station into the gritty machinery of Syracuse—smelters, drayage companies, slaughterhouses, and breweries.

Ruth unpinned her hat and stood up, legs apart under her long skirt to absorb the motion of the train. She placed the hat carefully on top of her suitcase in the overhead rack. Returning to her seat, she plucked a handkerchief from her sleeve and cleaned the dust from her glasses.

Abby saw that Ruth's eyes were drawn by the magnet of Abby's belly. *It's flat*, Abby screamed inside her head. The horrid baby is no bigger than a seed. Maybe there is no baby. It's all a mistake.

Her mother reached to touch Abby's skirt, but jerked her hand away.

Abby turned her back. The click-clack of the train wheels echoed from her ears to the muscles in her buttocks. The sound and motion numbed the ache that had overcome her in the station when she had caught a glimpse of a man at the ticket counter with red hair. It wasn't Seamus, but she had wanted to touch it, nonetheless. She twisted restlessly, infected with longing for Seamus one instant, loathing the next. She had no desire to have his penis inside her again, but she yearned to feel him panting and trembling over her, bound to her.

Her eyes stung, with a sandy residue under her lids. She burrowed her nose into the stale-smelling seat fabric, missing her feather pillow from home, and fell into an uneasy sleep. When she awoke, it was evening. The clouds ahead were discolored by a storm that sent flumes of rain slanting into Lake Ontario.

Ruth handed her a sandwich, cheese slices with mustard on thick, homemade rye. Abby chewed a few bites before wrapping the remainder in a cloth napkin.

"You're not eating enough." Her mother's hard eyes probed her again. Ruth tucked the sandwich remnants back in the basket and unscrewed the metal cup from the vacuum flask of lemonade. "We're stopping in Buffalo soon. Do you want to get out and stretch?"

Abby shook her head.

Ruth put on her hat and waited, spine not touching the seat. When the train stopped at the terminal, she moved down the aisle and exited onto the platform. A group of soldiers gathered at the far end, military coats unbuttoned in the heat, cigarettes glowing in the dusk.

Clustering at the Pullman doors, incoming passengers tugged at their suitcases. A newsboy hawked papers, a vendor sold meat pies from a wheeled cart, and a striped kiosk offered roasted peanuts steaming in paper bags. The couple across from Abby rummaged through their belongings. Outside, Ruth took a turn down the platform.

Abby slipped from her seat, squeezed past the boarding passengers, and scrambled outside. Workers hefted mail sacks, trunks, and even animal cages into the wide-open doors of the baggage car. Her mother stood half-turned toward her at the far end of the platform, talking to a soldier.

Abby ducked her head as she raced across the platform. The terminal's marble floor and walls were cool, with just a few people slumped on the oak benches. Gas lamps were turned low to save fuel for the war effort.

When Abby saw that the ticket windows were all closed, her determination faltered. She twisted right, left, uncertain. Then a scraping sound caught her attention, and, collecting her nerve, she approached the window where an agent behind an iron grating had opened the wooden shutter.

"Can I help you?"

Abby peered through the bars. She wanted to scream at him, *I don't want to go to California, I can't have a baby, in seven months Seamus will have forgotten me.*

Instead, she said, "I want a ticket to Syracuse."

"Three dollars." He wasn't that old, maybe twenty. One eye squinted in her direction, the other slid sideways, as if he was at war with himself.

Abby's eyes widened. She'd had no idea the ticket was so expensive. She fished her leather wallet from her skirt pocket and poked at the coins inside.

"I only have $2.26."

Both the agent's eyes flicked over her before the errant one drifted toward the ceiling. "Three dollars."

"My grandmother is dying, and I'm an orphan. I have to get there before she passes." Abby tried to make her face look piteous.

The agent folded his hands on the counter.

Behind her, someone touched Abby's shoulder. "Miss, the train is about to leave. Aren't you coming? I saw your mother get on board."

Abby swung around to see the older man in the black suit who'd been sitting across from her. He had a newspaper tucked under his arm. She stood for a long second, hearing someone's voice echoing off the terminal's high ceiling.

"I'm coming," she said.

25

Cora
April 2000

Del drove fast, as usual, but he watched the road with obsessive care, as if everything depended on his avoidance of any given pothole or rabbit.

Cora sat beside him with the toxicologist's manila envelope on her lap. At Del's kitchen table, she'd picked up the report and asked him to drive her to her car, still parked downtown. She wanted to read it without Del looking over her shoulder. It was nearly four a.m., and Mimi Shafter was scheduled to pick Cora up at Seneca House at nine.

The interior of the car smelled like sex. His legs spread wide as he drove, his knee nearly brushing hers on the turns. She tried to ignore the hypersensitivity of her labia, which made her aware of him whenever she moved.

She felt dangerously open to sensation, the rasp of her jacket against her wrist, the acid taste of Del's coffee, the hiss of the air on the window glass, flashes of moonlight through the trees.

Those touches, scents, sounds, were fissures in the great dam of numbness she'd built over the years. Since the murder and suicide on Sutter Street, Cora had endured a painful heightening of her senses, and tonight she was terrified. How would she endure all of it, all her losses, her mother, her husband, and soon, her job?

She touched a tender spot where Del had nipped her in the cleft of her neck. Every hair crackled with electricity, and each toe felt separate as it pressed against her shoe.

Trees flowed past, caught in the headlights, their dark, arterial trunks branching into a million capillary twigs. She squeezed her eyes shut until flashes of color erupted under her lids. Careful, don't lose it now. Focus on the story, the last story for the *Standard*.

Del cruised through a stop sign on the dark, empty road. "O'Brien died of asphyxia. He had elevated levels of carbon dioxide in his blood." He hadn't spoken since he switched on the ignition. In the low light from the dash, he looked exhausted, his skin gray and his eyes receding into their sockets.

She listened to the dispatch traffic on his radio. "You said at the house it was strychnine and cocaine."

"Asphyxia is the outcome of strychnine poisoning. The muscles convulse nonstop until the victim is too exhausted to breathe. Essentially, he dies of suffocation."

"The cause was the poison, right?"

Del nodded. "They found strychnine in his blood, urine, and gastric fluid. The poison was the same elemental compound used in a common rat poison. There was a container of it in a storeroom at the farm."

"No fingerprints on the container?"

"The instructions are explicit. Use a mask and gloves to prevent inhaling it or having it enter through a break in the skin," he said.

She heard a hum in her ears, and shook her head to clear it. "Was the strychnine in the pizza that Tyler brought home?"

"No. Evidence technicians collected samples from the leftovers in the refrigerator. There was none there, and none in O'Brien's stomach contents."

Cora had watched an autopsy a few years ago, and now she regretted it. Images crept in, the gruesome Y cut from neck to groin, the examiner inspecting the organs, collecting tissue samples, the flash of the knife.

"In addition to the strychnine, he had coke in his system?" she said.

Del nodded. "The blood vessels in his nose were distended and some of the capillaries were broken. Consistent with cocaine use. The blood sample also tested positive."

"So the strychnine could have been in the cocaine."

The car accelerated. Barns, houses, low hills whipped by. Del's fingers kneaded the wheel.

She shook somewhere, but she couldn't locate the tremor. "Slow down, Del."

"I'm driving the way I always drive. If you don't like it, go home to San Francisco."

"Let me out here." She leaned over to pick up her backpack, but bumped her forehead on the dash.

The tires skidded as Del slowed, but he didn't stop.

The speedometer read fifty now. She massaged her head with her knuckle. "Tyler's fingerprints were on the container, weren't they?"

"Judith says she told Tyler to put rat poison around the feed bins about three months ago. He says he forgot to use gloves when he handled the container." Del's voice held a world of weariness.

"Someone else—a dealer—might have cut the coke with strychnine."

"It does happen, but rarely. Tends to reduce the client base," he said.

Cora bent over and pressed her cheek against her knees. Tyler was linked to both ingredients in the lethal mixture that killed Sean, strychnine and stolen cocaine. She felt words forming on her lips, a halting prayer that startled her as she said it under her breath. *Please, God, don't let it be Tyler.*

The lights of Cortland appeared in front of them, and Del slowed to thirty-five.

"You knew all of this practically from the beginning, didn't you?" she said.

"Pretty much."

"You've got to turn the case over to another agency."

"Not yet. Not until I get him out of this."

"It's already too late. Your reputation will be on life support if the facts get out."

He laughed, not a pleasant sound. "You think my only concern is my reputation?"

"Your judgment is impaired, Del. Refer the case out."

"I need ten days."

"What if you've got nothing in ten days? Or a hundred? Maybe this is a case that will never be solved."

"It's got to be."

"Maybe he's guilty, Del." The words dropped like stones as they left her mouth.

"He says he didn't give him any adulterated coke, and I believe him."

26

Cora

April 2000

Sun struck the bleached damask in the Seneca House dining room, and Cora felt the glare at the back of her eyeballs. A white tablecloth at breakfast was very wrong, against all principles of decency and humanity. She imagined Debbie arising at five to flip the cloth over the table and set it with antique silver. Cora hoped there was a circle in hell reserved for morning people who inflict themselves on night people.

"Sit right here, Cora." Debbie slid out a chair across from the other guests and poured coffee into a flowered china cup. "You can start on the champagne fruit compote. I was lucky to get pears and oranges from Florida; nothing local at this time of year except mushrooms."

Other guests made annoying noises that passed for conversation. A Canadian couple yammered about their road trip back from winter in Florida. A German woman chewed each bite thirty times and talked throughout. Cora speared a chunk of orange from the fruit compote. It tasted bitter.

"The Seneca House Surprise, everyone," Paul said. A spot of powdered sugar rested on his nose. "Our secret recipe makes it puff like that." A plate slid in front Cora stacked with pieces of French toast, each the thickness of a dictionary.

In a minute, he returned with two more plates of food. "The maple syrup is made locally. My brother-in-law has a wood lot near Homer."

The German tourist flooded the plate with syrup and gobbled the toast. Cora sipped some coffee, and it perched for a moment on the back of her tongue.

The bell rang in the front hallway, and the door banged. Mimi Shafter blew into the dining room on a swirl of cold air. "Finish up your breakfast, or we'll miss the best part of the day." She tossed the words at Cora over her shoulder while she poured coffee at the sideboard. She scooted a chair up to the table, her jagged coral earrings swinging.

"I'm not up for the trip," Cora said.

Mimi's voice dripped honey, "Did you have a late night?" as she exploited her sighting of Cora at dinner with Del. Cora pushed to the back of her mind images of herself, hot and slippery, in Del's shower with her legs wrapped around his waist. She didn't want to send out any guilty signals.

"I was up early, working," she said, keeping her voice as colorless as possible. She hadn't slept after Del dropped her off. She'd combed the toxicology report until dawn for any additional information that might implicate someone besides Tyler, but there was no opening that suggested another culprit. Her fingers and legs had jumped with ragged nerves, and she'd never fallen asleep.

"If you want to get your story right, you've got to understand the Finger Lakes: the nooks and crannies, the history," Mimi said.

"Which story? Personal or professional?"

"Both." Mimi's eyes glittered over the top of her cup.

"Thanks for the offer, but no thanks."

"You need a tour guide that speaks the local language," Mimi said. There was something watchful about her, an intentness hiding behind her dark brows and spiked cheekbones.

Cora turned the cup in her hands. Mimi might have some key fact about the case stored in her encyclopedic memory bank. Besides, what harm could it do? Assuming Mimi wasn't plotting to stab her with those pointed earrings. "Wait about twenty minutes. I have to shower and make a couple of calls."

In her room, Cora punched the number for Maple Leaf Farm. A man answered. Cora stuttered in surprise, then asked for Judith.

"Who calling?" the man said.

"Cora Brooks. I visited Mrs. O'Brien at the farm a few days ago."

"*La reportera.*"

"Right. Is she there?"

"What you want?"

"I'll discuss it with her."

He hung up. She'd try later in the day. For a nanosecond, Cora considered returning the signed fax acknowledging that she'd received the layoff notice. She thought better of it, and rang Frieda instead.

"Are you ready for a potential kitchen disaster with a difficult student?" Cora said when Frieda answered.

"I've got my rolling pins and pie pans all set out. You want to do chess or lemon meringue?" Frieda sounded so excited that Cora was sorry she'd be gone in a few days, and would never see the old woman again.

"Do I have to choose?" Cora said. Maybe if Frieda were kept busy instructing her about pies, she'd be diverted from high pressure sales tactics for skin cream. Cora showered, then stared in the mirror for a few minutes at the dark circles around her eyes. With the night's adrenaline finally wearing off, she was achingly tired. It took all her willpower to change clothes, toss a notebook and tape recorder into her rucksack, and layer a sweater over her turtleneck shirt.

"I'm going to take a short detour," Mimi said in the car. "A couple of miles to Homer." Her old, diesel-powered Mercedes clattered along the road. The weather had done an about-face from yesterday, and sunshine glinted on the windshield.

"What's the deal with names around here?" Cora said peevishly. "Greek and Roman for a hundred miles. Homer, Syracuse, Marathon, Seneca, Tully, Cato, Ovid, Ithaca."

"It happened after the Revolutionary War," Mimi said. "At a big meeting in 1790, Governor George Clinton's cronies divided up all of central New York into townships. About that same time in England, John Dryden published his translation of Plutarch's *Lives of the Noble Grecians and Romans*. All the educated people— meaning men—were reading it. Apparently, the naming committee opened up Plutarch and went down the list."

"Most of them are little villages. Spots on the road. It's as if they had high aspirations that never materialized." Cora felt sorry for the little places with the grandiose names.

Mimi gave her an odd look. The car turned into the town of Homer and cruised down a wide street lined with two-story homes as trim as Victorian women in new hats. Mimi eased to the curb in front of the block's eyesore, a clapboard house with a sagging front porch and a weather-stained plywood addition hammered onto the rear. A sign stood in the front yard, but the words were too small to see.

"This is the birthplace of Amelia Jenks Bloomer, to whom I give thanks daily," Mimi said.

Cora raised her eyebrows. "The original Bloomer Girl?"

"The very one," Mimi said. "Ms. Bloomer revolutionized the way women dress by writing an article in her women's newsletter about the new Turkish pants. They were worn under a knee-length skirt. Until then, women wore at least four layers of flannel petticoats, three cotton ones in summer."

Amelia Bloomer's contribution to feminism apparently hadn't inspired the cottage's owner to do any maintenance. Cora rubbed the fabric of her jeans and imagined Amelia Bloomer sashaying past these trim houses in her bloomers on the way to the market. It must have been strange, unburdened of all that weight. The women had probably felt exuberant, loved being free to run or kick their legs.

"Women began swimming in them, that's certain." Mimi adjusted her seat back. "My mother was the first woman to swim the width of Otisco Lake. I have a picture of her in her Bloomer bathing suit. I haven't worn a skirt since I was seven, and I'll probably be buried with pants on."

She shifted from park to drive, and the Mercedes bumped over the winter cracks and potholes, its suspension definitely not doing the job. Cora reminded herself to get new shocks on her Toyota Tercel when she got back to the City. Out the window, Cora spotted a rusted double-wide trailer with three weathered pickups squatting beside it. "You're a real estate agent. How do you make a living around here? With the economic slump?"

"When sales are slow, I give blow jobs," Mimi said.

Cora laughed. "I'm shocked."

"Actually," Mimi said, "real estate has been picking up. Bill and Hillary vacationed at Skaneateles Lake a couple of years ago, and the wine industry is increasing land prices."

"Plus you blackmail people into listing with you because you've got the dirt on them."

"There's that," Mimi said.

They left Homer and headed north, climbing through the same countryside Cora had driven to Maple Leaf Farm. When Cora had first arrived, the New York hills seemed like lap dogs compared to the ferocious granite of the Sierra, but the more she saw them, the more comfortable they felt, rising and falling like deep, regular breaths.

Since she'd arrived, a green mist of leaves and tiny white blossoms had appeared on the trees. Bottomland was a patchwork of emerald grass and chocolate-brown fields where geese pecked for last year's grain. As soon as the ground dried, farmers would begin planting corn, alfalfa, and rye.

"Eighty years ago, there were more than a hundred barns in this eight-mile-long valley," Mimi said. "There was a cheese-processing plant, two schools, and a store. Do you know what its downfall was? The tractor." She sounded regretful.

"Didn't tractors make the farms more profitable? I'd think owners could work more land, bring in more money," Cora said.

Mimi's mouth pulled down at the corners. "In this case, the horse-drawn plows and harvesters were actually better. Look at the hills. Now they're covered in woods, but in those days, they were cultivated. The horses were surefooted and the equipment had a low center of gravity. Farmers were able to grow enough oats and alfalfa to feed their animals. But the hills were too steep for tractors. A couple of farmers were killed when their tractors overturned and crushed them, and eventually people stopped working the hills altogether. They had to buy cattle feed, and it was too expensive to make a profit."

"You sound as though it's very personal, like it happened to you," Cora said.

Mimi's lips twisted. "Isn't all history personal? My grandmother's family bought land here in the 1850s, about a mile north of the store in your picture. But my parents couldn't make a living on the farm, and my dad ended up as a janitor for the county."

The road to Maple Leaf Farm slid by the driver's side window. Above the curve of a hill, Cora saw the tops of its silos.

"How did Sean earn a living? There aren't enough cows at the farm."

"I didn't know Sean that well. He and Franklin were ten years older than I am. I suppose he owned some milkers, did some breeding, and in the summer, boarded other owners' cows."

"Did he own many acres?" Cora said.

"Maybe three hundred or so. It's one of the bigger places left in the valley."

Mimi steered into where the shoulder widened into a graveled turnout. Two red barns stood side by side on the downslope of the gentle hill, separated by a muddy blue trailer. A sign was nailed to the heavy sliding door of the nearest barn: *Antiques Tues. Wed. Sat. Sun. 10–4.*

"Speaking of personal history, there's the old store," Mimi said, pointing across the road.

Cora stepped out of the car, unaware she was leaving the door open. A creek splashed somewhere close, and the metal in Mimi's car pinged as it cooled.

The store's tangled rubble rose on the road's uphill side. Thick wooden beams that had once been joists and rafters jutted from the pile. Boards bristled with rusted nails, window casements gaped with broken glass, and a smashed porcelain sink lay half hidden in the mud. Sun had burned the paint off, and snow had clawed chunks from the wood. A flour of rot puffed around her feet.

Blades of new grass sliced through gaps in what had once been the porch. Cora shivered. The flesh of her mother's legs had touched these boards. Her palms had been planted on their rough surface. Alice had smiled as she sat here, the eager curve of her hair swinging forward.

Cora kicked aside a plank and retrieved the Daniel Webster Flour sign from the rubble. The tin was cool, and rust powdered her fingers. Red and yellow paint still clung to the raised lettering. She scratched a loose flake with her fingernail. In the picture of Alice, the sign had hung in the store's front window, above and to the right.

Cora put the sign to her ear. She wanted to hear whispers of long-ago secrets, quivers of meaning, the sound of her mother's voice.

Muscles in her face ached with pent-up frustration. She wanted a blinding flash that solved the mystery of her mother. Why had Alice left her, a vulnerable child, in the care of a brutal alcoholic?

Cora moved the sign to her other ear.

"You are one weird broad," Mimi said.

Cora jumped. Her nerves vibrated from a lack of sleep. "Why the hell do you care?"

"You were the one who said you came here to research your family history."

"I'll do it on my own. Butt out."

"I just wanted to help." Mimi's face was smooth and unruffled. "This was Alice Macpherson's home. She grew up in this building."

"Not true. She wasn't born here. She didn't die here. I've checked the records. What could you possibly know about her?"

"My family's lived here for five generations. I still own their farm, which is just up the road. I thought I was doing you a favor."

"I'm not in the market for favors," Cora said.

Mimi raised her hands. "I only wanted to tell you …"

Some internal twanging string snapped. Rage scorched Cora's face. "You're nothing but a small-town gossip. If my mother really lived here, she left and went to San Francisco twenty years before you were born. You don't know a damn thing!" Her hands flexed with the urge to smash something.

"I do, too. Alice Macpherson lived right here, in a flat above the store, from 1919 to 1936, when she graduated from Tully High and went away to school. My mother remembers her—smart, and anxious to get out of this backwater place," Mimi said.

Cora threw the rusted sign onto the mountain of rotted lumber, shoved her hands in her jacket pockets and took off at a half-jog in the direction of Cortland. Her feet slapped the pavement to the beat of her racing pulse. A woodpecker drilled furiously into a dead tree.

She was staggered by the unfairness of it. A stranger she'd met only three days ago knew more than Cora about her own mother. She, Cora, was the one who knew nothing. Her grandparents were as unsubstantial as ghosts; any aunts, uncles, and cousins, hypothetical. She didn't have a fund of family stories to draw on, didn't even know her mother's birth date. One torn picture, that's what she was left with. Mimi, the self-satisfied bitch, had no right to know anything. Cora was the one who had touched Alice's skirt and buried her nose in the crook of her mother's arm. Cora was the one who'd had to force herself to look without flinching when someone hugged or kissed their mother, after her own was lost. Mimi hadn't earned the right to know anything about Alice Macpherson Brooks, not one tiny fact.

Cora slowed to a walk. The barns and silos of Sean's farm were partly hidden beyond a grove of larches, but the house's white siding was visible through the trees. Had Sean's ashes been scattered on these plowed fields, or had he been buried in the small graveyard along the valley road?

After a quarter of a mile, Cora heard the engine knock of the Mercedes behind her.

Mimi drove alongside and called through the open passenger

window. "Get in. It's fifteen miles to Cortland."

Cora didn't turn her head.

"Come on. I've got your backpack."

Damn. Her new digital recorder was in it.

"If you don't get in, I'm calling Del," Mimi said.

27

Abby
August 1917

As the weeks went by, Abby's life in San Francisco took the shape of an ill-fitting shoe.

She and Ruth rose at five a.m. from their cots on the enclosed porch at the back of Aunt Mary and Uncle Emmett's house. Wind slithered between the cracks, and gulls called over the roof.

During breakfast, Mary, Ruth, and Abby dodged each other around the kitchen, cooking ham and eggs, brewing coffee, making pancakes, and slicing apple pie for Uncle Emmett's breakfast. He presided at the table like a king, while the three women waited on him. His cup was refilled and his lunch made while he solemnly chewed his food.

Abby longed for breakfast at home, the enameled coffeepot with the chip on the spout, Ruth's hot porridge, and her father's wink as he surreptitiously fed toast scraps to the dog.

At 5:45 Emmett rose from the table. The front steps groaned under his weight, and he was off to catch the trolley to the Bethlehem shipbuilding yard, where he worked as a carpenter on one of the dozens of war vessels under construction.

"Weeell, that's done for another day." Mary dumped two spoonfuls of sugar in her coffee. Her Scottish accent was stronger than Papa's, more like Grandma Clemmie's. Abby suddenly wanted to hear one of Grandma's Scottish tales, though always before she'd ignored them.

Mary divided the leftovers from Emmett's huge breakfast between their three plates and loosened the sash on her wrapper. Abby and Ruth sat elbow to elbow against the onslaught of the day as Ruth sipped her coffee. Abby drank tea and ate soda crackers from a blue crockery dish.

Ruth poked at a bit of ham with her fork. "They say, if you have morning sickness into the fourth month, it will be a boy."

Abby inhaled a lungful of air. In the last two weeks, her nausea had eased, and she hadn't vomited for ten days. For the time being, she and Ruth seemed to be together about the baby. Abby had stopped hating it, and her mother seemed to have stopped wishing it was hers and hating that it was Abby's. A smile tickled the corner of Ruth's mouth. "There's another school of thought that if the baby starts out high, it's a boy."

The baby did seem high to Abby, a tiny mound pushing up toward her ribs, toward her heart, rather than down between her hipbones like she'd expected.

Mary scraped her plate into the garbage pail. "Maybe it's twins."

Sweat burst out on Abby's face. She chewed several crackers and sipped her tea. She knew nothing about babies. Whenever she had picked up Emily and Edna's baby brother, Eric, he screamed. What if it were twins, and they cried and cried and wouldn't stop? What if they wouldn't eat? The thought of babies sucking at her breasts seemed obscene. Would one of them die like the weaker of twin calves? She felt dizzy, as if she were twins herself, one growing a baby and one who wanted to crawl under a blanket and cry childish tears.

"Mary, shame on you, you're scaring her," Ruth said. She tucked Abby's hair behind her ear.

"A wee joke," Mary said. She slid the dishes into the sudsy water. "We must hurry now."

They washed and dried the dishes and swept the kitchen floor. In the tiny bathroom, they squeezed past each other as they washed in the small sink dotted with clots of shaving cream and Emmett's whiskers. By seven-thirty, they were ready.

Mary had removed the cover from her sewing machine, folded the lace doily on the dining room table, and set out her dressmaker's dummy, racks of thread, patterns, scissors, and needles.

The knocker sounded on the front door. Mary scheduled fittings for her dressmaking customers on Mondays, Wednesdays, and Fridays. On Tuesdays and Thursdays, clients dropped off fabric and picked up finished gowns. Mary and Ruth pumped the treadle in shifts. They cut out silks, satins, and gabardines on the dining room table. Abby pressed seams, basted darts, and sewed hems.

"No, lookit here," Mary said, her twisted, arthritic finger pointing to Abby's crooked hem. "This is not good enough for my ladies."

Abby bent over the vile, slippery silk and ripped out the stitches. At home, the leaves would be turning wine red on the hills around the lake, and night bringing a nip of frost. Emily and Edna had begun school in Tully. Abby imagined her cousins and the other girls at Miss Truk's, laughing as they cooked dinner together and whispered secrets to each other under the quilts at night.

And Seamus—Abby pricked her finger but quickly sucked the blood before it stained the silk—he was probably bringing in the last crop of hay and slaughtering all but the best of his herd. Her life shifted, memories of Seamus becoming farther away yet sharper, as if she glimpsed them through the wrong end of a telescope.

After lunch Abby studied algebra, English, ancient history, and geography for two hours. While she worked, Ruth read Jack's daily letters and wrote him back.

Abby galloped through the lessons. Once she'd given her work to Ruth to correct, she was free until dinner. She wrapped a shawl around her shoulders, conscious of her swelling stomach, though it wasn't yet large enough to attract any attention, and escaped outdoors. The four Nesbitt boys, who lived next door, argued in loud, aggressive voices over a stickball game on the uneven brick street. She walked west, up the steep hills, past the narrow houses on cramped lots, and down the sedge-covered dunes to the ocean.

Although winter was arriving in New York, here in California nature ran askew. San Francisco emerged from the fog and cold of summer into long, glittering hours of sun. Blue sky merged with the ocean on the horizon, and warm wind blew in her face.

Her first glimpse of the ocean had been from the ferry as they crossed from Oakland. Then, the water hadn't seemed much different from Lake Ontario. But here, where the blue-green water and choppy waves stretched to China, Abby felt the overwhelming emptiness of it. A huge freighter sat like a dot on the horizon, of no more interest to the vast sea than a floating wood chip.

The baby floated in its own watery world. Here it caught the ocean's rhythm, and she imagined it kicking slowly, a lonely swimmer in its own sea, unheralded and unwelcome. Anger and determination formed a knot in her chest. Her child would be assured its place in the world. It would receive the love and attention it deserved. It would be acknowledged.

On the way home, Abby passed a post office, where the United States flag snapped briskly on its pole. That night, she tiptoed from bed to avoid awakening her mother, who slept on the adjoining cot. The house creaked with the nighttime secrets of its joists and timbers. Abby moved from the enclosed porch to the dining room. In the dim glow from the streetlight, she drew her tablet from the window seat.

My Dearest Cousin Emily,

I'm sorry I left without saying goodbye. I have taken a long journey to California, where Mama and I are living with my aunt and uncle.

I have to tell you something that you must keep in the most solemn secrecy. I am—how can I say this except to take a deep breath and write it swiftly—I am with child.

I imagine what you must think, that I am a fornicator and sinner. It is true. I am those things, but, God strike me down, I do not feel guilty.

She told Emily everything: the secret still, the elm tree, the gold, the night with Seamus. Each pen stroke as it scratched a fine black line on the white paper made it real again. She signed her name, then added a line at the bottom.

P.S. Enclosed is an envelope. I beg you to deliver it to Him. DO NOT TELL ANYONE.

Abby littered the table with beginnings of his letter. A shadow appeared in the hall, and Abby sat like a statue until Emmett had shuffled to the bathroom and returned to bed.

When she heard him snore again, she hurriedly scratched out the bare words.

Dear Seamus,

Mama and I are living in San Francisco. I will have a baby in March 1919. I would not be unhappy if it had red hair. Please write to me and give the letter to Emily Spellman to include in her envelope.

Sincerely,

Abby

The next afternoon, she bought a stamp and dropped her envelope in the slot at the post office.

28

Cora

April 2000

Cora held up her arms like a surgeon about to do a heart transplant while Frieda wrapped the strings of the chef's apron around her waist.

Frieda eyed Cora critically. "I'm not sure how much that will help. You're already covered in flour."

"And these are my best clothes," Cora said, gesturing to her jeans.

The oven in Frieda's kitchen was set for four hundred and the small room was warm. Cora had taken off her sweater when she first arrived, and now she used her thumb and forefinger to push up the flour-laden sleeves of her shirt.

"You're going to do two single crusts," Frieda said, climbing back onto her tall stool. She leaned an elbow on the blue and white tile counter.

"With your help and advice, right?" Cora stifled a smile. Del's mother's cheeks were rosy, and her white hair curled around her small face. Anyone meeting her for the first time would mistake her for a sweet old thing.

"Don't worry. I'll be right here, but you're the one getting your hands messy. Pie crust is all in the touch."

Cora had returned to Seneca House in the thick silence of Mimi's car. She'd dropped into bed for a couple of hours of sleep and awakened a few minutes before she was due at Frieda's. When Cora drove up, Del's mother hadn't waited for the doorbell, but hurried down the front walk to meet her.

Cora peered into the mixing bowl, where she'd dumped three cups of flour and a teaspoon of salt. "What's next, Madame Chef?"

"Measure six tablespoons of shortening. Not neat little spoonfuls, but generous. Too little fat, and your crust will be dry." Frieda had the flour, salt, shortening, spoons, measuring cup, and rolling pin laid out on the counter beside a pastry board.

"Now," Frieda said. "With your fingers, work the shortening into the flour. Not squeezing, just gently."

Immediately, Cora had flour and shortening wedged under her nails. A lock of hair fell across her cheek and she brushed it aside with the back of her wrist. As she worked, she was reminded of making mud pies when she was four.

"Del threatened me with dire consequences if I tried to sell you any Mary Kay products," Frieda said after a short silence.

"Any transactions will be kept in strictest confidence." The flour mixture was turning the texture of corn meal under Cora's hands.

"You've changed your mind?" Frieda lowered her voice. "I have some miracle lotions for the older woman."

"I might be interested in doing some business later," Cora said.

"Speaking of secrets, how is your story coming?"

"Is there anyone in town who doesn't know my every move?" Cora shook her hands over the bowl, dusting it with crumbs of pastry.

"College kids, maybe." Frieda looked at the dough and patted Cora's arm. "That looks great. Now add another six tablespoons of shortening."

"Why didn't I put in twelve to start?"

"The texture wouldn't be right. Flour has to be worked in slowly."

Cora dug six more greasy tablespoons from the round container. "What do you know about Mimi Shafter?"

"Her Highness?" Frieda wrinkled her nose. "I first met her when she was working at the recorder's office, before she got into real estate. She grew up along the lake, but her family didn't have much money."

"What you think of her?" Cora looked doubtfully at the dough, which was studded with walnut-sized lumps of shortening.

"She's a hard one to figure. Smart as a whip. Went to SUNY Binghamton on scholarship, but always had to have her foot on someone's neck, even her husband's."

"Any children?"

"It's okay, keep going, even though it looks disgusting," Frieda said. "That's interesting about Mimi. She has twins. The third generation of the Spellman family to have twin girls."

"How do you all know this about Mimi?"

"Every year, Eddie and I used to drive up to her grandparents' place at Otisco Lake to buy maple syrup and damsen plum jam."

Frieda told Cora to pour ice water into the dough and stir it with a fork to moisten the ingredients. "That was before I knew Mimi. When I first went there, her grandmother, Emily, was a widow who lived with her twin sister on the farm. They were an odd pair, those two."

"Two old ladies?" Cora stopped working the dough.

Frieda shrugged. "They were very poor. Secretive."

Under Frieda's direction, Cora floured the board and pounded half the dough into a mound with the heel of her hand. Rolling did not go well. The dough stuck to the rolling pin, ripped, and in response to Cora's efforts, spread into a lopsided triangle.

"That's the world's ugliest piece of dough," Cora said.

"It's so ugly, it's cute," Frieda said. "Looks about like my first one, when I was nine. Cheer up. After you've done forty or fifty, your pies will be pretty enough to take out to potlucks and Thanksgiving dinners."

Cora recalled the previous Thanksgiving, when Nathan had been away at school, and she'd eaten turkey at Chris Myerling's. He and his wife had fought, and his aunt got drunk. Cora had brought two beaten-up pies that she'd snatched the night before from the nearly empty shelf at Safeway.

"Knead the other half," Frieda said. "This time, flour the board. Coax it along a little at a time. Keeps it from getting tough."

Cora tipped the sticky mass onto the board, and in a few minutes had worked it into a smooth rounded ball.

"When you're ready to roll it out, I'll help you," Frieda said. "Start from the center with each pass." She sat high enough on her stool that their shoulders and elbows brushed as they worked. Cora moved away a foot or so. Frieda wanted someone to mother, a surrogate daughter, or even better, a daughter-in-law. Cora wasn't the one.

If Alice had stayed, perhaps she would've taught Cora how to cook. Did Alice ever bake? Cora couldn't remember. She imagined herself as a child bending over the kitchen counter while her mother guided her hand. Their faces might have glistened with the stove's heat.

She was getting maudlin. Even if Alice had tried, her efforts would have failed. Cora's only interests at that age were creating intense dramas between GI Joe and Barbie and pedaling around the playground blacktop with Andrea Chan.

Frieda's arms crossed Cora's in a duet, sprinkling flour on the pastry as Cora pressed the dough with the roller. The older woman's enlarged knuckle trapped her gold wedding ring permanently on her finger.

Years ago, Cora had considered becoming more domestic. Baking. Making pickles. Sewing. There was an ad saleswoman at the *Standard* who sewed quilted potholders and sold them from her office cubicle at Christmastime. Cora had imagined herself at the sewing machine, using one of those fancy stitch thingamajigs that embroidered names and flowers on the pockets of ruffled aprons. A laugh welled up inside. When the *x*s and *y*s had been handed out, her nesting gene had gone missing.

"Del came by this morning," Frieda said. "He brought me two doughnuts and offered to fix the back porch."

Cora concentrated on the crust, which was thin and even, almost circular. "Sounds like he was feeling guilty about something."

"Really?" Frieda gave her a speculative look

"I mean," Cora said quickly, "he was sorry he hadn't been over to repair it earlier. Probably."

"That's good. Now transfer the dough gently to the dish. " She watched Cora pick up the smooth, elastic round and drape it over the pie plate. "Would you say he was guilty enough to take down the storm windows?"

"Not that much."

Frieda turned away, but not before Cora caught a look of disappointment on her face.

She liked Frieda, but it had probably been a mistake to come. Her visit only encouraged Frieda's hopes that Cora and Del might start something long-term. "I'm about to make a mess crimping the edge," Cora said. "Give me some help here."

———

The pies cooled on the shelf, one lemon, one pecan and raisin. Both were topped with meringue. Cora and Frieda sat at the yellow Formica table with their coffee cups. Scents of lemon, cinnamon, and browned pastry rose in the warm air.

Light faded, and the low sun gilded the trees and garden in Frieda's yard. Cora let her back and shoulders curve momentarily, released from the tension that had stiffened them all day. She brushed her hair away from her face and, without any conscious intention, told Frieda about the morning's trip to the ruined store.

"I remember the place," Frieda said. "It was still standing when Eddie and I were first married. We stopped once for a Nehi on our way to a fish fry at Munger's Resort. How interesting, you're connected to it."

"To me, it's strange."

"Now that I'm old, I notice connections everywhere," Frieda said.

"Did you see anyone? A young woman about your age?" Cora sat very still and focused on Frieda's tiny chin.

"To tell you the truth, we didn't pay much attention. No customers, I think. Only the old couple that owned the place."

"Do you remember anything about them?"

"I'm afraid not. Mimi's family was connected to them somehow, through the Macphersons, I think. They used to be a big clan around here."

"Mimi and I are shirttail relations? That's a scary thought." Cora closed her eyes and pressed her eyelids. She wanted to see the couple who owned the store, the glint of blue in their eyes, prominent cheekbones, brown spots on the backs of their hands, yellow-white hair worn thin with the friction of age. She wanted to see them and be certain.

She was unaware how hard she was pushing until she felt a flash of pain in her eyes and lifted her hands away. The clock ticked on the kitchen wall, and frogs croaked outside.

They were startled when Del hallooed from the front door. He'd changed from his work clothes to jeans and a long-sleeved T-shirt. A late-afternoon beard darkened his cheeks.

"This place smells incredibly good." With his eyes on Cora, he stooped over to kiss Frieda.

Frieda gave the two of them a speculative look. "You can have a slice of each pie as soon as you finish the porch."

"I've got some other things to do tonight. Is there any way I can postpone it until Saturday?"

"I might fall through before Saturday and break my hip," Frieda said.

"The porch has been bad for months. Can't you get Hank to do it?" Del inspected the two pies.

"He could, but why pay him when you can do it for free?"

Del broke off a piece of crust and popped it in his mouth.

"I saw that," Frieda said.

"I tell you what. I'll pay Hank. Does that get me off the hook?"

"You don't want to spend time with your mother?" Frieda took three plates from the cupboard and three forks from the drawer.

Frieda and Del, Cora thought, were two opponents who had battled their way to a loving truce. Del had forgiven her for the relentless nagging—get married, give me grandchildren—he'd endured when he was younger. Cora guessed that Frieda had pardoned him for waiting until he was in his forties to marry Judith, a woman who didn't want more children. Frieda, she sensed, had overflowed with vitality and sexuality when she was young. Life had denied her the rollicking family she'd dreamed of, and she clung, in her own way, to this only son.

Frieda carried the pies to the table. She insisted the cook must serve, so Cora chopped the pies into wedges. Cora's fork rested beside her plate while she watched Del and Frieda dig in.

"It's the best thick crust I've ever had." He waved his fork.

"Del, stop that. It's very good."

Cora ate a bite, her first food all day. The pie was a communion wine of tart and sweet flavors in her mouth. Dizzy with fatigue and emotion, she touched Frieda's hand. "I owe it all to my coach."

29

Abby
October 1917

Four weeks had passed without a letter from Seamus or Emily. A rhythmic crick, crick, came down the sidewalk outside Aunt Mary's house and ascended the stairway to the front porch. Abby ran to scoop the letters from the entry floor beneath the mail slot. She riffled quickly through them, but there was no letter from Seamus, not even a return note from Emily. She touched the stack of stiff, white envelopes to her mouth to stop herself from crying.

The war had slowed the mails, she knew, because her father's letters took nearly a week to arrive. Emily was away at high school and only home Saturday and Sunday, so she might not have had time to answer. Perhaps Abby's letter had been lost. She repeated those excuses as she set the mail on the dining table for Aunt Mary.

The baby moved, but Abby kept her hands away from her abdomen. She wanted Seamus to be the first to touch her belly, his fingers cupping it as if he were holding the world in his hand. She kept this fantasy secret, even from herself, except late at night when the household was asleep. Then it crept in like a burglar.

It went like this: Seamus comes to San Francisco and knocks on Mary and Emmett's front door. Abby opens it and there he is, his red hair parted on the side and combed smooth. He wears a suit with a starched white shirt and a necktie. He reaches for her hand and kisses her fingertips. Marry me, Tiger Stripes, he says, and she says, Yes, yes I will. The judge reads the vows and Seamus slides a beautiful gold ring on her finger. Their first night together he cups the curve of her stomach and tells her how happy he is.

A streetcar rolled by outside, clanging its bell. Once Abby's swelling stomach became obvious, she would have to hide in the house. Mary had told the neighbors that Ruth was pregnant and her husband had been sent to France. The baby moved again. Seamus wasn't here. He hadn't answered her letters and she was alone. Her eyes filled with tears. She picked up the hateful letters, none from him, and threw them in the fireplace. Coals from the morning's fire ignited them, and they slowly burned to ashes.

———

After dinner, Abby washed the dishes in a white enameled dishpan while Ruth dried and put them away. Through the window over the sink, Abby saw Emmett sitting on a bench beside the vegetable garden smoking a cigar. His head tilted as he watched the smoke drift upward.

Mary turned up the gas lamps in the parlor, and the women gathered there with their work bags. Needles glinted as Ruth and Mary knitted brown wool socks for the soldiers in France. Abby labored on a khaki wool scarf, not meeting their eyes.

"Did you ever hear the tale of Big Archibald and his encounter with the lowlander?" Mary's burr was stronger in the evening when she was tired. She and Jack were the two oldest of Grandma Clemmie's eight children. Their childhood seemed woven with her Scottish legends.

"I may have heard it a time or two," Ruth said. Knitting needles protruded from four angles like instruments of torture as she turned the heel of the sock.

Emmett came inside and sat in the big armchair. Mary never sat in it; instead, she maneuvered Abby and Ruth to other chairs to leave it empty for him. Mary flapped her hand in front of her nose at the cigar smell. He clicked fasteners on his leather-covered flute case.

"I'm giving Abby and Ruth a tale," Mary said in an aggrieved tone.

Emmett blew a few experimental notes. "They already can recite all the Macpherson stories from memory, isn't that right, Abby?" His work at the shipyard had weathered his face like a piece of driftwood, but below his throat where his shirt was unbuttoned, his chest was white.

"I can't wait to hear what happens," Abby said, her voice as innocent as a bleating lamb's.

Ruth pursed her lips with a schoolmarmish gesture Abby had seen on Miss Miller.

Emmett began to play a bony, Scottish melody.

"Anyway," Mary said, "Big Archibald was passing by Achnacone one fine day when he met a lowlander. Being a good highlander, he greeted him politely, '*Beannachd Dhia dhuit, a dhuine*!' That means, God's blessing on you, sir. The lowlander, a rather stupid fellow, had no Gaelic, but had the bare wit to know some response was needed."

Emmett's tune wove itself among them, between their fingers and the strands of brown wool.

"The lowlander replied that it was a very fine day. 'Foolish man,' Archibald said, 'do you despise the word of God?' Before the lowlander had a wee moment to gather his brains, Big Archibald drew his sword and ran him through."

Mary's face thinned as she told the story, her nose grew longer and sharper. "Big Archibald took the dead man's shoes, his musket, and a guinea from his coat pocket, and went to the village of Ballachulish. There he told the laird that in his view the morning had been a profitable one."

Abby's father told the story slightly differently. In his version, instead of running the lowlander through, Big Archibald whacked off the offender's head. Jack always swung his arm at that part, adding a little twist of his wrist at the end.

The sock grew under Mary's nearly imperceptible movement of needles and yarn. "The laird sent his men to bury the lowlander, and they, being less simple than Big Archibald and more wise in the ways of southern tailoring, searched the secret pockets in his breeches, where they found sixty more guineas. Big Archibald, while never in trouble with the laird for the murder, nearly lost his head for the near-loss of the guineas."

Abby half-expected Emmett to stop playing the flute with the end of the song, but instead he began another. This one, "The Thistle and the Plaid," her father played at home on his violin. Ruth must have been thinking of him too, because she dropped her knitting in her lap. "I think it happened differently," she said, picking it up.

Mary arched an eyebrow.

"After Archibald turns over the single guinea," Ruth said, "the laird sends the women, not the men, down to bury the lowlander. They are the ones who find the sixty guineas. I know this, because it is women, not men, who are familiar with tailoring. They sewed money into their own clothing to hide it from thieves and foreigners."

"The women never would have gone. They would have had to carry their babes." Mary folded the sock and shoved it in her work bag. "Are you coming, Emmett?"

After Emmett laid his flute back in the case and the couple disappeared into their bedroom, Ruth heated water and brought two cups of tea into the parlor. Glancing uneasily at her mother, Abby held her cup near her mouth and blew on the surface. To conserve gas, Ruth usually turned out the lights and went to bed at the same time as Mary and Emmett.

"Have you given any thought, Abby, about what you will do after the baby is born?"

"Do?" Tea sloshed over the cup's edge and burned Abby's fingers.

"You can't stay at home. People in the valley would shun you. Everyone would stop coming to the store, and it would ruin our business."

Abby held her cup and saucer poised in midair, fearful any small motion would scald or shatter something. She felt the baby cowering, imagined its eyes wide open.

"You can't keep the baby. Where would you go? You have no skills, no way to make a living." Ruth's voice was as calm as the surface of Otisco Lake on a summer's day.

Seamus, Seamus, help me.

"You see, don't you, that you must give the baby up." Ruth sipped her tea.

Abby heard voices passing on the sidewalk outside, the flow of water in the bathroom sink, the snick of her mother's cup against the saucer. She tried to remember the lilt that sometimes crept into Seamus's voice at the end of his words.

"Abby, listen to me."

She heard something swimming beneath her mother's tone. "Give my baby away?" she said carefully.

"That would be one way." Ruth set her cup down and twisted a blouse button between her fingers.

"Couldn't I keep it at home?"

"Your father and I have a suggestion."

Abby, unable to move, stared at her own reflection in her mother's glasses.

"Give the baby to me. Everyone knows I've been trying for years to have another. I'll pass it off as my own."

———

Abby pulled the blanket up under her chin and watched Ruth extinguish the oil lamp. Ruth was the one who did that, never Abby. It was Ruth who decided when Abby had done enough algebra for the afternoon. Ruth who said, let's wash before supper. These small thoughts hurried through Abby's mind while the large, painful one sat unmoving in her chest.

"I'm not giving it away. It's mine." Abby was surprised that she'd spoken aloud.

"That's what you said earlier, but I urge you to think about it. There's plenty of time."

Abby rolled over, facing away from Ruth. She hunched her shoulders. Ruth was always the mother, and now she wanted to take Abby's baby and be its mother, too.

"You wouldn't be giving it up. You'd see it every day," Ruth said.

Abby looked over her shoulder. "You'd let me quit high school and stay home?"

"Of course not. You need an education."

"I'd hardly ever see the baby." Abby felt her cheeks growing hot.

"It needs a father and a mature mother. Jack and I can give it what it deserves."

"You want to steal it so you can have it all to yourselves." Words pushed rudely past her lips.

"Listen, you selfish girl, if you don't do it, people will be ruined—your father, me, Flo, even Emily and Edna. The scandal will touch everyone." Ruth threw back the bedclothes and shoved her arms into her wrapper, put on her glasses and moved quietly into the dark house.

Abby drew her legs up and curved her shoulders. It saddened her that she had to wrap herself around the baby, protecting it. If only she had been able to see Seamus before they left for California. The baby wasn't tickling her softly tonight as it usually did when she lay down. It was waiting in the darkness too, its eyes open wide, for a letter from Emily, a letter from Seamus, an answer to the question.

Ruth spoke from the doorway. "This is about the baby's father, isn't it? That's why you're so stubborn."

"Stop talking, Mama."

"Is it John Goins? Come now, don't be afraid. Tell me."

Wind pressed against the house, and the weather vane flapped on the roof. Abby pressed her thumb to her lips.

"I assure you, Abby, whether it was John or someone else, he won't come to help you. Males who take advantage of young girls don't do that."

She wanted to escape, go to sleep. She whispered into the quilt, "He's not like that." She struggled to remember the world she'd left behind in New York, her bed at home, its height, the nick in the finial where she had tried to carve it with a knife when she was six. Seamus' hands, the fine red hairs that curled on the backs. It all seemed pale now, like a faded dress.

"You could see the baby as much as you want when you're home on weekends, feed it, hold it, change its messy diapers."

"I want to stay here in San Francisco."

"You'll have no money, no way to support yourself." Ruth sounded less sure of herself.

Abby turned on her back and spoke to the ceiling as if she were delivering the commencement address at PS 12. "Mary needs someone to help her. I'll be her assistant and care for the baby right there beside me."

"You can't do that. We've told neighbors I'm the one that's pregnant."

"I could move away from the neighborhood."

Ruth inhaled sharply as if to stop her panic. "California isn't home for you. This windy, foggy place isn't home. No one knows you, how old you were when you first walked, your favorite blue wool dress, your favorite chess pie. No one is here to love you."

"Mary and Emmett are here."

"They came here to be by themselves, away from family. They took us in because Papa is paying for our board."

Abby didn't reply. She'd write another letter tomorrow.

30

Cora
April 2000

Del started down Frieda's front steps, then looked up at Cora on the porch. "Thanks for humoring my mother. She can be a pain in the ass."

"Don't you dare talk about her that way," Cora said. "Your mother's a terrific woman who's gotten old with enthusiasm."

Del pressed his lips together. Her defense of his mother seemed to move him. The years of warfare between Frieda and Judith must have made him defensive about Frieda; perhaps he expected Cora to dislike the old lady.

"I called Judith this morning," she said. "I got the feeling that something's not right."

The light went off in the house, and they were in shadow. He sighed and moved his shoulders to bring himself back to the mess involving his ex-wife and stepson.

"What did you get out of her?"

"We didn't talk. Rico answered, the milker who wears the Yankees cap. When I told him who I was, he hung up."

Del rubbed his cheek with the stub of a finger. "Odd. Those guys hardly speak English. Why would she let them answer the phone?"

"It was like he was in charge. Screening her calls."

"Neville has been trying to interview Rico and Pedro for a week. They keep ducking him," Del said.

"I saw them Monday at the farm and Tuesday night at the hospital," she said.

He rattled his keys in his pocket. "They're like fleas on a dog, too quick to catch."

"They were there at the farm when the first two cows died," Cora said. "They were there when Sean died, and close when Tyler ODed."

Del headed for his car. "I'll check on her."

The burn of a hot flash hit her. "I was the one who told you about the call. I'm coming, too." She raced down the steps after him.

"This isn't one of those buddy deals like you see on TV." He unlocked his car. "You're not in law enforcement, and you're not coming."

She ran around the car, jerked open the passenger door, and hopped in.

"Come on. Out."

"If you don't take me, I'll call the farm and tell them you're on the way."

"For God's sake, Cora, it might be dangerous." Del ducked his head and shot her an angry look through the open driver's door.

She clicked her seat belt.

He sighed and climbed in.

"Look, I can be useful," she said. "I could go up to the door. They won't be as threatened by a woman. It might be safer than the state police thundering in."

Del ignored her. As he drove, he thumbed the keypad on his cell phone and left a message. "Neville, call me. It's now 19:57. I want you to meet me at the turnout on Plato Crossroad, just above the farm."

For once, Del's high-speed driving didn't bother her. It hadn't occurred to her when she called Judith this morning that she might be in danger. Dark trees, barns and occasional houses flipped past with satisfying swiftness.

"When we arrive, you're staying in the car," he said.

Cora nodded, the same way she did in high school when her father told her, no weed, you hear?

At the turnout, Del backed in, which Cora knew was standard training for law enforcement officers, to give them a fast break. He switched off the lights and stopped the engine. It was dead quiet. Through the trees, high-intensity lights bleached the farm buildings bone white.

They looked straight out the windshield toward the empty road. "We've spent how many hours in the car together?" she said.

"We could make out until Neville arrives." Del sounded distracted.

"How about climbing in the back?" She knew he wouldn't do it.

He slid down a little in the seat and leaned back against the headrest. The glow from the dash highlighted the deep lines in his forehead and touched the silver in his hair. His eyes were in shadow.

He turned toward her. "We'd have to be really quick."

"I'm as fast as the next girl."

"I don't think so." His deep voice held a note of approval.

"People who are right all the time can be very annoying," she said.

"Then you haven't slept with anyone else since your husband left you?" He watched his hands as they tapped a rhythm on the wheel.

"Don't ask me that, it makes me sound so … so stricken."

"You weren't?"

"Yes, I was. He found someone else, and I wasn't expecting it. Like you and Judith."

He squirmed and adjusted the seat to allow him to stretch his legs.

"What is it about a car and a dark night that makes me say things I don't want to say?" She leaned against the door to widen the distance between them.

"If I were an egotist, I'd say it wasn't the setting, but the company." He kept his voice neutral.

"Maybe. It's the mark of a good investigator, to lure people into telling you things."

He swung around to look at her. "This isn't about work."

She heard the anxious sound of her own breathing. The car ceiling was too low and the interior was getting very warm. She changed the subject.

"What was your appointment this evening? You told Frieda you couldn't do her repairs."

"I was going over to see Yolanda Santerra."

"What's up with her?" Cora felt steadier, shifting the subject to the newspaper story.

"She sent me a photo. Said she'd pulled it out of Franklin's wastebasket when she inventoried his house." He reached into the back seat and extracted an envelope from a pile of papers.

The photo was in black and white. The lack of color made it worse, because she knew red was everywhere, smeared on the chest and sleeves of a shirt that might have once been white. She focused on the victim's hands, palms up, stared at the splayed fingers with every bit of her energy, to prevent her from looking higher. The victim's head was missing.

"It's not Franklin," she said.

"No."

"Who is it?"

"Don't know. The postmark on the envelope is LA, but the murder could have taken place anywhere," he said.

"The photo's a warning," Cora said.

"You bet. It's the hallmark of Latin American drug cartels. Illustrates the punishment. Rip us off, we'll rip your head off."

She turned the glossy surface face-down on her knee and spread her fingers over it, as if to divine its meaning. "Sean and Franklin were in the smuggling business together. Franklin had the family contacts in Central and South America, and Sean made frequent business trips overseas."

The two conspirators had probably felt buoyant after the first few successful deals, amazed at how easy it was. All they had to do was pass the drugs on to the next level of distribution, and count their money. Then the previous summer, immediately after Sean arrived back in the states, he'd gone to the hospital with a gastric infection. Cora imagined him arriving home, saw him pawing through his dirty travel underwear to reach the suitcase's false bottom. What had he thought when he found the coke missing?

Out the passenger window, the house lights struggled through the screen of pines. Each small opening in the branches created another point of brightness, until it seemed a thousand eyes peered out.

Cora imagined Sean ripping out the lining, tearing the bag to pieces, unable to believe it. Probably he'd hurried outside, whispered to Franklin on his cell phone. Met him on an abandoned road where they'd screamed at each other, where Franklin had punched him, where Sean had waved a gun, blaming his long-time friend.

Months passed, but the pair failed to gather enough money to repay the cartels. Threats from overseas escalated. Photos had been sent, perhaps one to each of them. She pressed her hands between her knees to stop their shaking.

Del's phone rang. "Good, it's Neville." Del unfastened it from his belt and flipped it open.

"Judith?" His voice lowered to a whisper. "Talk slowly. I can't understand you." He bent over to concentrate his hearing. "Okay. I'm close by. Exactly where are you?"

Still holding the phone, he popped open the glove box and lifted out his weapon. "Don't move, and stay calm. I'm going to keep you on the line." He set the phone on the dash while he checked the clip and tucked the gun in his waistband at the small of his back.

"What's happening?" Cora said.

He turned off the interior light, scooped up his phone and a small flashlight, and stepped out of the car. "I can't wait for Neville. Our friends are talking knives and cleavers with Judith. When he gets here, tell him I'm going into the house through the cellar door on the northwest side."

Cora zipped up her coat. "I'm going to help."

"You stay out of the way. I don't want to shoot you by mistake. I'm very serious, Cora. Don't leave the car." Her stomach clenched over the pie she'd eaten.

"Have they locked her up? Is she hurt? Where is she calling from?"

"She's wedged herself inside the laundry chute, and they're searching the house for her." He closed the car door quietly. His face flashed white as he slipped along the boundary fence, and then he was gone.

Mist rose from the fields as the soil cooled from the day's heat. An owl hooted, and Cora caught a glimpse of its dark outline on a bare tree branch. She ignored her stomach pain and tilted her head to listen. Something. She tried to remember her first visit to the farm. Where was the dog that had made so much racket? What if the dog alerted the kidnappers to Del's approach? She shivered. Cora climbed out of the car and leaned against the door. Her eyes strained to catch the beams of Neville's headlights turning off the main road, but there was no illumination moving through the trees. She blew into her numb hands. Off to her right, more lights snapped on in the house. Muffled shouts floated on the air like carrion birds. She visualized Rico charging Del with a machete or Pedro with a pruning knife, slashing Del's face. Her legs trembled, and her heartbeat thumped in her ears.

Pushing herself away from the car, she ran across the road and squeezed under the fence. She staggered awkwardly across the fields, tripped by heavy clumps of mud on her boots. Ahead towered the barns, silos, and grain bins. She stopped beside the nearest barn, her warm, moist breath writhing in the cold air.

She scanned the buildings, trying to get her bearings. On her right was the cluster of silos and further back, the farm office and the trailer. Alongside the driveway sat Tyler's F-150. The milkers' Ram 4x4 stood near the murky outline of the pig shed.

To get a clearer view, Cora scurried across an open area and dived into the shadow of the shed. She crouched against the weathered boards and heard grunts and uneasy thumps from inside.

From this vantage point, light from the study where Sean had died illuminated the house's back garden. A silhouetted figure in a baseball cap slid past an upstairs window. Glass broke and wood splintered.

Suddenly, the house went dark. Del was inside; he must have switched off the breakers in the cellar.

There was a horrible pause, then voices sharpened. If the two kidnappers found Del or Judith now, the prisoners would be hacked to death. Cora rocked on the balls of her feet to calm the twisting in her belly. Neville wasn't coming. Maybe she should go back to the car and call dispatch on Del's radio. It would look bad in the press, a state police major launching himself into a hostage situation without backup. But a bad rep was better than dying. And there was Judith, mother of a troubled son.

She started back to the car, stumbling over the wedge of mud on her boots. She'd barely left the shadow of the pig shed when she heard a woman's scream coming from the house. She gulped a mouthful of cold air. Del and Judith might be dead before anyone came.

The 4x4 was parked fifty feet away. When she reached it, she crawled inside, using the door that was shielded from view of the house. Her fingers fumbled with the dash buttons until she located the headlamps and switched them on. The beams snaked across the farmyard, partially illuminating the interior of the pig shed.

She raced across to the shed and ducked inside, ignoring the stench. The shed had been dark last time, but in the headlights she saw the animal more clearly—a massive boar covered with coarse black hair. Razor tusks jutted from a pointed face. The creature squealed and jumped up with amazing agility, its hooves sinking into the muck of its filthy pen. The boards creaked as it butted against the sides, its misshapen shadow dancing against the walls in the light from the truck.

Cora surveyed the shed's interior—grain sacks, piles of rotten boards, rusted scrap metal—before she found what she was looking for. She extracted a pitchfork from a shroud of cobwebs and perched on the fenced enclosure of the boar's pen. Leaning over the side, she unlatched the gate. The boar, flanks caked with muck, swayed on its feet. It gave a phlegmy, drawn-out grunt.

Cora lifted the pitchfork, but caught her sleeve on a fence nail. She ripped the cloth free. The pitchfork was unwieldy, and she was breathing hard as she maneuvered the long hickory handle in the cramped space. She balanced it on the top rail of the pen.

With every bit of strength in her arms and belly, she drove the glittering steel tines into the boar's fleshy backside. The animal screamed, a high, earsplitting squeal of pain. Its lunge sent the pitchfork flying. The animal's shoulder hit the gate, and it thundered into the barnyard screaming and shrieking, pounding the gravel with its hooves.

Cora jumped down from the rail, looking for a place to hide. If her diversion worked, Pedro and Rico would come bursting from the house soon.

Outside, the boar thrust its tusks straight into the front of the 4x4, smashing a headlight. Cora heard three gunshots over the sound of shattering glass.

31

Del

April 2000

Del held the slender flashlight in his mouth while he pried open the rusty lock on the cellar door with his pocket knife. At the bottom of the steps, he paused to quiet the sound of his breath. Dread filled the damp black space, thick enough to touch. This fucked-up deal was infinitely worse than the operation in Saranac Lake. There, he'd had a plan. Backup. Still, he'd messed up his hand.

He tensed as the kitchen floor above his head creaked with the pressure of a heavy boot.

"Donde se escondio esa puta?" Probably Rico. The voice faded as the hired hand moved to another room.

Why weren't they looking for Judith down here? It was a great place to hide, with possibility of escape. A thin slice of light showed at the top of the stairs where the door was slightly open. Apparently, they'd already searched the cellar.

From his whispered conversation with Judith, Del knew the breaker box sat on the wall to the right of the cellar door. He scanned the floor for a few seconds with his flashlight to avoid tripping over the buckets of nails and clusters of rusted tire chains. Past shelves set with rows of dust-covered Mason jars. Curves of the discolored fruits in the jars, probably there for fifty years, seemed as malign as body parts in formaldehyde.

He eased open the breaker box and flipped the rows of switches to the Off position. In the cellar, the blackness deepened. Upstairs voices got louder, raised in pitch, woman-like. They were afraid, the most dangerous kind of bad guys.

Del dodged the junk in his path and slipped outside, fastening the cellar door silently behind him. They would be thundering down here in seconds. In the farmyard, the moon was a frigging snitch, bright enough that he saw his shadow. The moon had been full that other night, too.

He stooped low as he ran under the kitchen windows and around to the northeast wall close to the front porch. He spotted the open window where Judith had said it would be, small and stuck slightly ajar. He worked the sash, held his breath when it squeaked up and hefted himself—he needed to get back to the gym—through the opening into a cloak room.

He pressed his ear against the door panel.

The kidnappers cursed as they stumbled down the back stairs from the second story.

Del cracked the door open and peered into the front hall. He sniffed. Something burning. Were they torching the place? He heard Rico shrieking and Pedro's muffled reply. They were in the cellar, maybe lighting newspaper flares.

He touched the weapon at the small of his back and ran lightly up the front stairs two at a time. The carpet runner deadened the sound of his feet. On the second floor, he guided himself by touching the wall with his fingertips. His feet crunched on broken glass and his toe struck something large and wooden.

He passed the doorway to Judith's office and tiptoed into the master suite. Moonlight rushed in the windows, illuminating smashed mirrors, dresser drawers dumped on the rug, and an overturned armoire stomped to kindling. He looked around to get his bearings. Judith had said the laundry chute was in the wall behind the bathroom door. In a moment, he was holding his flashlight high, peering at her dirty, terrified face. Her back was pressed against one side of the narrow chute and feet braced against the other, knees bent.

No matter how much he disliked, even hated Judith, he felt a surge of pity. She was filthy, her hair matted, and face covered with dirt. A bloody scratch tore across one cheek. Her eyes rolled before they focused.

"It's Del. Come on."

She lurched, her trembling legs gave way, and she began slipping down the chute. Her scream drilled into his ear. He clung to her arm and shoulder, his right hand almost useless. Grunting, he wrapped his arm around her torso and hauled her through the opening.

She swayed on her feet. "This is all your fault," she spat.

"Judith," he whispered, "for God's sake, shut up."

"Sean would be alive. Tyler on the hockey team. I'd be exhibiting in New York."

He clamped his hand over her mouth and felt the depth of her terror. His face came close to hers. "Judith, be quiet or I'm going to gag you, understand?"

She nodded.

He picked her up and put her over his shoulder in a fireman's carry.

"You should have given up on Tyler. Not tried to be his buddy." She was crying.

He reached into the back of his belt for the Glock. Pedro and Rico would be stationed at each stairway by now, and they were sure to have semiautomatic weapons.

It was strange to be trapped with the one woman above all others he didn't want to be with. Virtually no chance they would escape. Why was it that only the little things mattered when you were looking at death? Not his hand, not the long detour in his career. Instead, he remembered two things: a hot summer afternoon when he'd played catch with Tyler, and the way Cora's long nose had looked last night, with its cute little bump in the middle.

The front stair tread squeaked. Someone was coming up.

Swaying under Judith's weight, he side-stepped toward the stairway, alert for more sounds. Judith breathed heavily, and he hoped she wasn't about to vomit. He stopped just short of the landing.

The stair banister squeaked. He glanced over his shoulder and backed up a few paces, his side pressed against the wall. They'd be clay pigeons if he stood at the top.

Suddenly an unholy shrieking arose from the farmyard, as if hell's gates had opened. Glass broke and metal screamed.

A low exclamation from the landing below him.

Del squeezed Judith's thigh, warning her to keep quiet. Taking two steps to the center of the hall, he raised his weapon and fired three shots at a faint, dark shadow.

The explosion in the narrow hallway deafened him. For ten seconds he was a moth in a jar beating silently against the glass. His head throbbed with images of what was going on outside, Cora, not safe in the car but lying in the farmyard with her face in the cold gravel. Injured or dead.

Del's nasal membranes stung from the smoke, and he rubbed his dripping nose with the back of his hand, gun still clutched in his fingers.

From the landing, he heard ragged breathing and a low sob.

"*Pedro! Que Chingada. Ven, ayudame. Estoy herido.*" Rico stumbled, half-falling down the stairs.

After a long moment counting his heartbeats, Del heard Pedro's muffled voice berating Rico from the study in the back of the house. The outside door slammed.

Del cautiously descended the steps. As he reached the landing, the farmyard was rocked by a staccato burst of semi-automatic fire. Del lurched as if a bullet had entered his chest. Rico and Pedro were fighting it out with whomever had created the diversion in the farmyard. Suddenly, Judith's weight was more than he could bear.

"Can you walk?"

She arched her back. "I'd crawl if it gets me down from here."

He knelt, his legs trembling, and slid her to the floor. "Hold onto the back of my belt," he said. With Judith in tow, he inched out the front door and crept alongside the porch to an opening in the lilac bushes.

From the distant mobile home, he heard the sound of an engine roaring to life. Pedro and Rico were getting away. He freed himself from Judith and raced into the driveway turnaround in time to see taillights bobbing across the bare fields.

As the two red eyes disappeared, a car barreled through the front gate, emergency lights whirling on the roof. Neville's tires skidded on the dirt as he braked to a stop. In the hallucinogenic flashes of red, blue and amber, Del saw the bullet-pocked 4x4 with a dented fender, door panel, and shattered headlight. Beside it lay the steaming corpse of a huge black boar.

Neville crouched behind his car door, shotgun in hand. Del raised his hand, signaling him to stop.

"Cora! Where are you?" Del's voice ricocheted among the listening buildings.

There was a cough and a splintering of rotted wood. Cora staggered out of the dilapidated shed, covered in pig dung.

32

Cora
April 2000

It was a threesome in Debbie Landesdowne's second-best bedroom. Steam from a recent hot shower still misted the air. Judith was propped up in bed, a stack of lace-trimmed pillows at her back. Cora, fresh from a shower in her own room, sat in an overstuffed chair wishing she was in bed but not with Judith, and Del occupied the rocker. He had an odd, flushed look on his face, as if he'd had a quick sexual fantasy about being in bed with both of them.

"And when that despicable insurance man started investigating, Sean told me everything. Nearly everything." Judith picked disdainfully at the cuff of Debbie's spare nightgown.

Del had turned over his weapon to Neville and given him a statement. Judith would be available in the morning, he told Neville, but she was too traumatized to say anything tonight. The state police issued an APB on Rico and Pedro.

At that point, Cora had sensed that Del was uncertain what to do with Judith, because his former wife refused to return to the house where Pedro and Rico had held her prisoner for two days. Judith was a pain in the ass, but in a weak moment Cora suggested that Judith ride to town with them and sleep in one of Debbie's rooms at Seneca House.

Judith touched the long scratch on her cheek, which looked worse since she'd showered. "When the coke turned up missing, Sean was insane with fear. He and Franklin had been smuggling. Their third shipment was the one that disappeared, the one Sean brought in from our stopover in Mexico City."

Del stopped rocking and leaned forward, his eyes red-rimmed but alert.

"In Mexico Sean had eaten something from a street vendor— can you imagine, a man who travels all over the world stooping to eat from a street vendor? By the time we arrived at the farm he was ill with amoebic dysentery. He was in the hospital three days, and when he got out, he opened the secret compartment in his luggage. The coke had disappeared."

"It seems strange Sean didn't suspect Tyler right away." Del said.

"I knew Tyler was involved somehow. Sean kept prodding, so finally I told him Tyler had stayed with you while we were gone. I told him Tyler couldn't have been the one." Judith looked at Del over the rim of her cup of hot chocolate.

"Thanks for involving me in your mess," Del said.

Cora ran her fingers through her hair. Despite the shower and shampoo, she still smelled of manure. The pig shed had seemed the least likely place Pedro and Rico would search. She'd only lain on her belly in the pen for a few minutes, but now she realized it might be a week before she got rid of the stink.

She watched Judith do, what? Flirt with Del? No, no, Cora thought, she wasn't jealous of Del's ex-wife. He'd said he didn't care a thing about her.

"Sean and Franklin tried everything to raise money," Judith said. "They took out second mortgages on their properties, but only raised half a million, a fraction of what they needed."

Cora gathered her wits and focused on what Judith was saying.

"Then they approached a realtor about listing the farms, but there wasn't enough money between the two farms to buy a doobie, much less what they owed," Judith said.

"Even with Franklin's acreage?" Cora said. "Wineries are opening up all over that area along Cayuga Lake."

"The Santerra place had a problem with soil contamination on the southern side. At least, that's what Franklin said."

There was a tap on the door. "Here's a fresh pot of chocolate, you poor thing." Debbie's eyes swallowed every detail of the bedroom tableau, titillated by the sight of Del, his ex-wife, and his new girlfriend. She set a tray on the bedside table and rearranged Judith's pillows.

Del pursed his lips and gave her a dark look. Debbie scurried out.

"Was it then they concocted the insurance scheme?" Cora asked.

"Sean was really excited about it, but it was a bad idea from the very beginning. After New Year's, when Great American started its investigation, he finally told me everything." Judith looked into the cup with distaste, as if she were angry not so much about her husband's smuggling and stealing but that he had handled it so amateurishly.

Del's rocking chair squeaked, and Cora felt the sound in her joints. Her body wanted sleep, but her brain kept churning. "Why did the cartel give Sean and Franklin so much time? Drug lords aren't into monthly payments. If news leaks out they've been ripped off, it's bad for discipline."

"One of the cartel's leaders is a relative of Franklin's from South America. That's how he got into it to begin with. I guess when the cocaine disappeared, Franklin's relative kept his partners from killing them outright," Judith said. "Instead, they sent Rico and Pedro to the farm."

Del paced the small room from the rocker to the bed. "Pedro and Rico were there to protect the boss's interests and commit mayhem, if that's what it took."

"But now Sean's dead," Cora said, "and it's certain the cartel didn't do it. Not messy enough. Why were Pedro and Rico sticking around the farm?"

"Just before he died, Sean had concocted another plan.'

"Guaranteed to fail," Del said.

"No, this one might really be it," Judith said.

"Does this have something to do with Tyler? Actually finding the coke?" Cora sat up straighter.

"No, no. This is about the gold. Sean's uncle's Irish gold."

33

Abby
November 1917

My *Dear Friend Abby,*

Forgive me for not answering your letter sooner. It has been a terrible time. The Spanish influenza struck the valley again. Indeed, it seems that the devil, not content with the deaths he caused in June, returned to finish his work.

Our little Eric died three weeks ago today, and Mother and Edna have both been very ill, near death. John Goins expired last Tuesday. To Father and me have fallen all the duties of care and nursing.

To avoid the contagion, Edna and I have not been to high school in Tully since the term opened. I am sick with grief for my little brother and my only comfort is that he is an angel now.

We were unable to care for our winter herd during this trial, and it is only due to the assistance of Uncle Jack, who came every day at dawn to feed and milk, that our cows survived.

I should have been shocked to hear your news, but with all that has happened, I can only rejoice that you are alive and safe. I have been very tired and hardly able to cook a meal without going to my bed for sleep.

As to your request that I give your letter to Him who resides here, I have been unable to do so, as you may well imagine.
Love,
Your Cousin Emily

At first, the Spanish influenza seemed to have bypassed San Francisco. As a precaution, the schools had been shut. The Bethlehem yard, considered one of the potential contagion sites, had been closed. Few people had become ill.

"Damn waste. Nervous Nellie health department putting thousands out of work. Might better quarantine Italians and Chinamen." Emmett stirred his oatmeal and the spoon clicked angrily against the dish. Mary hadn't fried ham or steak for breakfast since he stopped bringing home a paycheck. The women sat alongside him at the breakfast table rather than waiting on him, reflecting his lowered status, since he was unemployed.

After the meal, he remained in his chair, the *Standard* spread on the oilcloth in front of him. "Abby, you should pour boiling water over those dishes. And use a towel on them. Don't leave them to dry in the air. Keep the flu away."

Mary paused in the kitchen door and anchored her hair with a tortoiseshell comb. "Emmett, I want you out of this house in twenty minutes. One of my ladies is coming."

"It's raining. I haven't shaved, and my flannel shirt hasn't been ironed."

Abby rinsed another plate, watching her aunt and uncle from the corner of her eye.

"The chess players at the Taravel Club will care if you're shaved? Go. When you're here during fittings my ladies get nervous, and I don't need to lose any more customers. Too many are staying indoors because of this terrible plague."

"A man should have a place in his own home."

"Fifteen minutes. Abby, go iron his shirt."

———

As the disease spread, she saw fewer people from the front window. The only vehicle that drove by for days was a health department truck. From the window she watched it disgorge a team of workers, who canvassed the block distributing white gauze masks to every house. A man with a badge on his chest knocked on the door and instructed Mary that no one was to go outside without covering his mouth and nose.

Mary's clients became ill, and her business dwindled to nothing. Instead, she went to the Baptist church each day to cook meals for policemen and public health workers. The *Standard* ran stories that the Yerba Buena naval training station had been quarantined, and hundreds of new cases were reported each day. Mortuaries were staggered by the numbers of the dead, but the paper assured readers that the epidemic was still less severe in San Francisco than in other cities. After seven of Emmett's coworkers at Bethlehem fell ill, and two died, he spent the daylight hours with a crew of volunteers who moved from house to house. They hauled corpses, wrapped in stained white sheets, by freight wagon to makeshift morgues and even icehouses.

In the evening, Mary's house was filled with the stench of disinfectant. Emmett used it to scrub his skin, and Mary poured it into the wash water to purify his clothes. He ate less and less, and his ruddy face became grayer, as if he were absorbing the human decay.

It was during this time that Iris, the young woman who lived in the next house to the west of them, fell ill. Her husband was in France, and Abby had imagined Iris writing letters and biting her fingers until they bled as she waited months for a reply. One morning, Abby heard mournful yowling and looked outside to see Iris's ginger cat alone at the woman's back door. "Iris hasn't fed her cat for two days," Abby said at breakfast.

"I'll stop to see her on my way out," Mary said. She was back in a few minutes, breathing hard. "She's sick. Very bad. Ruth, could you come?"

Ruth's skin turned moist and white.

"This is the city," Abby said. "There are doctors. Can't you call?"

Mary's lip twisted. "There isn't a decent doctor in San Francisco. All the good ones are in the army. The drunks, adulterers, and drug fiends are the only ones left, and they're working twenty hours a day at the hospitals. Which are overflowing."

Ruth nodded. She took off her apron and tied the white mask around her face.

During the next three days, Iris defied Mary's predictions by hanging onto life. Ruth, Mary, and Emmett left before dawn, as if they plunged into the black heart of the disease, and returned after dark. Abby became the mistress of a small, lonely kingdom. After everyone had gone, she washed the sticky oatmeal bowls, made up the beds, and rolled the carpet sweeper over the rugs. By midmorning, she had run out of chores. It was shameful that she was filled with resentment when people were dying, but she couldn't help it.

"Hear that? It's the fog dripping off the eaves," she told the baby one morning. A voice, even her own, kept her from going mad. Did the baby hear her?

Did *she* hear, because Abby suddenly knew it was a girl, a tiny little version of herself, except she had red hair. The baby seemed to respond to her voice, rousing a little when Abby spoke in that empty, fearful house.

One evening Emmett came home early. Wrinkles were collecting under his chin from lost weight, and his face seemed grayer than usual after his day with the dead.

"The radical Bolsheviks have taken over in Russia," he said as soon as he sat down to supper. "There's talk the Ruskies will sign a treaty with Germany."

Abby set a bowl of the vegetable stew and a plate of biscuits in front of him. "What difference does a treaty make?"

"The Allies will lose what little help we were getting from Russia." Emmett peered at the vegetable stew in his bowl. "The army will get more of my meat."

"Doctors are what we need now," Mary said.

It rained the next day. Long, slanting sheets of water encased the house and the dampness penetrated Abby's bones. Ruth said at breakfast that Iris probably would die today.

Toward afternoon, the background noise of the rain was broken by an argument among the four Nesbitt boys next door, who were stomping in puddles to splash each other. Abby felt as though she were floating alone in an endless ocean. She started a few pieces of coal in the fireplace and huddled in her rocker close to the grate. She lifted her skirt, untied the drawstring on her underpants, and surveyed her stomach. "I want to see him." Tears slipped down her face and rolled into her mouth. She rocked with her hand on her bare skin, hardly aware of her surroundings.

Outside, there was a small roll of thunder, and she heard herself say, "Wake up!" Her pulse surged to the tips of her fingers. The baby quivered, and the skin fluttered on the left side of her abdomen.

Abby fumbled to tie her clothing and went to the sleeping porch. She reached under her mother's bed to draw out a shoe box. The cardboard container was filled with her father's letters to Ruth, arranged neatly on their edges. The envelopes bore red one-cent stamps and the stains of travel. Ruth had used a knife to slit them open along the fold in the flap.

Her mother rarely discussed what was in Jack's letters, other than to say, "Papa is fine. He says hello."

Abby fished out the first envelope, postmarked in mid-August. A slight scent of her father's bay rum clung to the paper. He began it, *My Sweet Ruth*. Abby squirmed. Her parents were too ancient to spout lovey-dovey words to each other. Her mother—pregnant only five months ago—Abby refused to think about it.

Papa related a dispute with a supplier who had reduced the store's ration of coal. The second hay crop was cut and baled. He and Will had been at the wood lot splitting and hauling for the winter. Abby folded the pages exactly along the creases and slipped them back in the envelope.

Late in August, he'd attended the fish fry at Munger's, where he'd played the violin for dancing and made discreet inquiries. "I gleaned no information but returned home covered with insect bites," he wrote.

"I am not convinced by your argument," he concluded. "I think Wright, while he is in fact a sordid lecher, might be the type that would appeal to an impressionable girl."

Abby laughed. George Wright, with his wolf-like teeth and dirty fingernails. Ridiculous.

Word in the valley, he wrote on August 30, was Leland and Seamus O'Brien had netted a tidy amount from selling their summer herd to the government to feed the troops. A week later Papa had dashed off a hasty letter. The Spellmans were very ill. Grandma Clemmie worked around the clock caring for the sick. Leland O'Brien was abed and Maggie O'Brien had died.

Abby buried her face in the paper on her lap. Last spring in the ice house, Maggie's hands had been rough yet consoling as she'd tucked her own sweater around Abby's shoulders. It was Maggie, not her mother, who'd told her about monthlies. Yet Abby felt a rush of relief that if death had to come, it was Maggie and not Seamus.

Abby's eyes raced over the letters while her ears were tuned to any hint of a voice from the front door.

In early September her father's writing changed; the even rhythm of his pen strokes became focused and driving. "I have had little success in finding the vile man responsible for Abby's plight. Miss Miller said she saw no partiality on Abby's part for John Goins or Melvin Watkins, the only boys her age at school. "

A few days later he wrote, "Last night I drank several glasses of my best with George Wright, sipping until he was quite overcome. I am satisfied he is not the one. Where else do I turn? I had thought early on it might be one of the O'Briens, but we have had nothing to do with them, not even in the store, since before the war."

Didn't he remember about her foot? The trip to Tully in the snow? Abby's fingers ran through the envelopes now. Two weeks ago he'd written, "I have tried for some time to speak to the

Spellman girls, but I hardly need tell you that the epidemic has made the timing unpropitious. I am hopeful, now that the family is on the mend, the girls may shed some light on the matter. I assure you that I will persevere. I would sooner slit my own throat than fail to protect my little girl."

Her hands trembled and it made it hard to stuff the letter back in the envelope. She had pulled out the last one when she was startled to hear movement in the kitchen. Ruth had returned through the back door. Abby called out a greeting while she jammed the letter back into the stack and slid the box under her mother's bed.

Ruth leaned against the counter. Her umbrella, held at her side, shed teardrops of rain on the floor. She seemed so small, her hair rolled bravely above her ears. She didn't look up when Abby entered, and her lowered lashes smudged her blue-white skin.

"Is she ..."

"Who?" Ruth licked her dry lips. "Oh, Iris. Yes, it's done."

Abby took the umbrella from Ruth's flaccid hand and eased the coat off her shoulders. "How long have you been sick?"

During the evening, Ruth's chest filled; Abby heard the liquid sound of her respiration, as if she were drowning in her own fluids. Abby and Mary concocted a hot poultice of oatmeal and mustard, and Abby carried the stinking mess to Ruth's bedside.

"Mama, I'm going to bind up your chest."

Ruth's eyes were half open. She raised one hand and let it fall, then murmured some strange, dark words. Abby hesitated, gathering courage to violate her mother's intense and rigid privacy by lowering her nightgown. Ruth coughed, and Abby unbuttoned the gown to her mother's waist. She slathered the poultice from her mother's collarbones, over the long thin bones of her ribs, between the rise of her breasts. The mustard powder's heat made Abby's nose run and the thick, glutinous oatmeal congealed on her hands and under her nails.

"Now wrap her with the strips," Mary called from the doorway.

Abby wound the bands of cotton around Ruth's chest, threading them under her body. She breathed hard with the exertion of leaning, lifting her mother's torso and tugging the strips tight, all the while with her ear close to Ruth's chest. Only a thin stream of air was being drawn into Ruth's lungs.

Abby took a deep, unsteady breath, as if hoping in some childish way, her easy breaths would be transferred to her mother.

With her chair at the foot of the bed, Abby sat for two days, changing the poultice, listening to the rain pummel the roof. In the middle of the first night, Mary handed a bowl of soup to Abby through the opening in the curtain. Abby held it on her lap and sipped a spoonful. The thick soup tasted good, but her throat felt constricted. She narrowed her dry, stinging eyes. The face on the pillow with the bluish skin and sunken flesh was a stranger. Only the gold ring tilting loosely on her thin finger was familiar. The ring reminded Abby how her mother, in late afternoon before she started dinner, sometimes used to look from the window above the store and turn the ring around and around. The night wore on. Every few minutes, Abby took a hot iron from the stovetop, wrapped it in a towel, and slipped it under the blankets at the foot of the bed to warm Ruth's chilled feet. The white curtains around the bed shivered at the onslaught of the wind against the house. Abby kept watch from the straight-backed chair, the wicker seat biting into her thighs.

Toward dawn, Abby braced her hands on the sides of the chair and pushed to her feet. She touched her mother's face, which was clammy, but no longer cold. Her breathing was easier, and the fluid in her lungs seemed to have declined. The iron under the bedclothes was cold. Mary was in the kitchen. She began to sing the strange, sad notes of "Macpherson's Lament."

Fare thee weel, you dungeons dark and strong,

Fareweel, fareweel to thee ...

Abby had last heard the song at her Grandfather Macpherson's funeral. "Stop it! Mama is strong. She has strong blood." Abby ran a basin of warm water from the tap and gathered a towel.

"We'll see." Mary's mouth turned down.

Abby returned to the bedside and unfastened the bindings that held the poultice, which stank of sour oats, mustard, and Ruth's clammy sweat. She wet the towel and washed the crusted mixture from her mother's skin. Abby swallowed several times to keep from vomiting.

"You've eaten nothing," Mary said at the noon meal. She cleared Abby's nearly untouched plate of hash from the table.

"It hurts to chew," Abby said. At her aunt's sharp look, she added, "No, I'm not getting sick."

"Think of your baby, then. It needs nourishment."

Abby had been almost unaware of the baby for awhile. It was hiding from the disease as best it could. She ventured outside on the porch. The wind blew against her cheeks, and she gulped lungfuls of air, feeling a rush of freedom. How long had it been since she had been outside or gone for a walk? A siren blew. Two skinny boys who lived next door hurried past on their way to the trolley, their feet pounding on the bricks, masks bouncing against their chests.

The older boy shouted at Abby. "Hurry, there's a war bond rally at Civic Center. Speeches. Bands."

Mary leaned over the stair rail to watch them. "It's criminal. They'll go down there, catch the disease, and carry it home to the few of us who are still healthy." She worried her lip with her teeth. "Where's Emmett? He should have been home for lunch by now." She went inside and returned with her coat and hat on, and the mask covering her face. "I'm going to find him before he wanders to Civic Center."

Abby remained on the porch, her arms folded across the rise of her stomach. A Velie roadster hummed by with a banner hung out the window. After a few minutes, she went back inside. As the day wore on, Mary did not return. Ruth was feverish and only half-conscious, but she clenched her fists, moved her feet, rocked her head on the pillow.

Ruth seemed to sink further as night came, her habitual ordered way of thinking now a jumble of disjointed phrases. Abby leaned close to her mother's face, trying to follow the meaning, but captured only a bit here and there.

"Five gone." Ruth's voice cracked.

"Mama, shhh, it's all right." Abby knelt by the bed.

Ruth lowered her voice to a whisper. "No, Jack, not now. We can't. Five fingers, one hand, five of them gone, all fallen out."

Abby's stomach brushed the bed frame, more sensitive than it had been for many days, the skin stretched tighter across her belly. The baby moved, high up, as if seeking the shelter of Abby's breastbone.

"I said no, Jack, don't, but then I said yes." Ruth cried, dry sounds with no tears. "Maybe this time, don't tell anyone, not yet."

Abby wanted to run from the story.

A drop of blood glistened at Ruth's nostril. "Squeeze your knees, hold it in, lie still, no it mustn't come, oh God, help me."

Abby wiped the red spot away with her sleeve, staining the cuff of her blouse. She laid her face against her mother's hot, arid cheek, smelling the odors.

The baby's movements darted and plunged in disquiet. Abby was captured by the bond between the three of them, like three strands of a braid. As she watched, her mother's features seemed to melt for a moment, and Abby was unsure if the face, so pale and helpless against the pillow, was her mother's, the baby's, or her own. Abby's breath merged into the rhythm of Ruth's, as the baby's flutters and darts mirrored Abby's longing to be a child again and wriggle into that special spot against her mother's side. The enclosure around the bed seemed to swell to contain it all, until the cracked lips, the breath, the memories, the small, quick movements in her belly were all melded into one.

"You can have her, Mama." Abby felt the unity of the three of them, their flesh bound together, the way each hair, every tiny vein was linked. "You and Papa can have the baby."

34

Cora

April 2000

Cora stood under the hot water in Del's shower, washing herself for the second time that night. The smell of pig dung had lingered in her nostrils and under her fingernails. Del was downstairs talking to Neville on the telephone, although it was after two in the morning. The shooting investigation team would be interviewing him sometime later that day.

She unfastened her hair and let the water run over her head. It seemed ridiculous that she was back here where last night they'd had quickie sex and a nasty fight. After they'd finished interviewing Judith, however, Cora wanted to get as far away as possible from the memory of the boar's pen and gunfire at the farm.

Cora rubbed the bar of Del's Irish Spring soap on the back of her neck. Judith's account did add some interesting details to the whole tangled story. Sean and Franklin must have been two of the most naive drug smugglers in history, leaving the cocaine unprotected in a suitcase for three days, running around for months concocting inept schemes to reimburse the cartel.

And now Judith's new information about their hunt for a cache of lost gold. A San Francisco homicide inspector had told her once that all murders were local. If he were right, Sean and Franklin's deaths weren't the result of the drug cartel's retribution. The solution was right here, in the soil and rocks and the people who lived in this strange part of the country. The Burned-Over District, the nineteenth-century historians had called it. A niche in the landscape where the fires of unconventional thinking—Mormons, Shakers, free thinkers, feminists—blazed, as had some other passion that left these two men dead.

Slowly, she soaped her nipples and the thick, curly hair between her legs. Steam rose around her, and she felt excited. Sexy, yes, with the slickness of her skin and the luxurious weight of her wet hair around her shoulders, but also stimulated by the possibilities for the story.

As she stepped out of the shower, she noticed that a fresh towel had been laid on the laundry hamper. Del must have put it there for her while she was washing. She wondered if he'd watched the soap part.

She rubbed herself slowly, taking in the homey sight of Del's terry robe hanging on a hook and a pair of stretched-out slippers beneath. Beside the sink, he'd lined up two razors and a can of antiperspirant. She folded the towel with the edges touching and hung it on the bar. She ran her fingers through her hair. Toast, that was the color Stephen used to call it. Toast—tasteless, prone to crumbling, needing jelly to be palatable. A hot babe she was not.

When she opened the bathroom door, the lamp was on and Del was lying in bed. The covers were thrown back. She came close and saw that he was aroused.

"Even after last night's fight?"

He nodded at his penis. "Doesn't have an ounce of sense."

"And speaking personally, I'm pleased about that," she said.

He reached out and touched the curve of her hip, drawing her into bed. She straddled him, the hairs on his chest and legs tickling her thighs. He was solid, graceful, even, despite some extra weight around his waist.

He played with her damp hair. He licked her eyelids and the curve of her ear. Why wasn't he going faster? She moved lower to take him inside her.

"Not yet." His tongue touched the hollow in her throat.

She moved her fingers from between his legs. "Don't you want to?"

"You can tell I do."

She felt the heavy length of his erection against her thigh. "Yes, but …"

"You expected slam, bam, thank you ma'am? Again?" His voice was low and amused.

"A little quicker, I guess." She looked at him warily. How strange this was, talking while he stroked the soft skin of her inner thighs with his thumb.

"Nope. Not in this bed." He drew her face close and kissed her, and she recognized his taste from the night before, like a favorite dish she'd been looking forward to. Using his uninjured hand, he explored her in a leisurely way.

She wanted to cover herself, hide from his slow, demanding touch. He looked at her too closely, saw her small breasts where the nipples seemed grossly large, touched the wrinkled skin on her stomach, stroked her legs that were too thin. He seemed to see all of it and more. His breathing quickened. Cora didn't meet his eyes. She didn't want him to see all of it, the lovemaking with Stephen when he'd asked her to get breast implants and ran his fingers over the stretch marks on her hips. Where she urged him, forced him to come quickly and then, later, pleasured herself alone. Guilty for doing it, but angry and defiant too. Her refusal to surrender to his lovemaking had been retaliation.

Del, who was stroking the arch of her foot and the back of her leg, pinched the tender skin behind her knee.

"Stay with me," he said.

She drew a sharp breath. "I was."

"Liar." He didn't look angry so much as focused on her. Intent.

The pinch tingled, and the sensation spread upward. She felt the slipperiness grow between her legs, her nipples swell, her skin flush.

Before he played the waiting game any further, Cora drew him inside her with a quick twist of her hips. Del dug his hands into her waist to keep her from moving too fast.

It had been so long since she had been on this slow, voluptuous journey, it was like learning to walk again. Every small motion, each tightening and loosening of their flesh seemed perilous and full of danger. She marked the milestones in the wet click of her sex, in the rasp of his breathing. When she came, the power of it flung her forward onto his chest, and she cried out in rhythm with her climax.

———

The sky was bright when Cora awoke. Del's maimed hand lay open on the coverlet. He usually kept the stumps of his fingers in his pocket or half-closed in his palm. When they made love during the night, he had used his good hand to touch and caress her. She studied the stumps of his three injured fingers closely. They were of uneven lengths, as if the doctors had saved as much as they could on each one. The ends were blunt and red.

It surprised her he was still hiding his hand twenty years after his injury. How did he feel when he hid his hand and used the other to trace a path down her breastbone?

He rubbed his cheek on the pillow and nuzzled her hair. "Mmmm. Smells like sex."

She stroked the length of his leg with her foot. "At least I don't smell like pig." She shuddered at the thought of the huge body, dead in the farmyard. "I wonder what will happen to him."

"Go for tallow. Too old for meat."

"As opposed to you and me, who are not at all old." Cora slid her fingers down to his penis.

Del glanced down. "Just now, that guy could probably go for tallow."

He clasped her hand and gently manipulated the delicate bones at its back. Pleasure rumbled at the back of her throat.

"Did you ever wear a wedding ring?" he asked.

"I had one when we got married, but never liked it. I only wore it for a few years before I put it in my jewelry box and left it there. After the divorce, I had the diamonds taken out and sold the gold."

She drew her hand away. "Why?"

"The whole thing about women and rings. Frieda has never taken off Dad's ring since the day they were married."

Cora propped her elbows on his chest. "And you? What about men and rings?"

He tilted his head on the pillow to regard her sternly. "Real men don't wear rings. And yes, I wore a gold ring, for whatever it's worth."

Cora sat up. The talk of gold made her nerve endings come alive, her nipples, tips of her fingers, end of her nose. "What do you think about Judith's story?"

"It's possible. There's always been a legend circulating about buried gold somewhere around Otisco Lake. Every decade or so, somebody with a wild hair goes up there and digs around for a few weeks."

"Could Sean O'Brien have figured out the location?"

"So what? He didn't find it, and he's dead."

The secret had been hoarded for sixty years, Judith said. Sean got the story from his father, Leland O'Brien. Cora imagined Leland in the aftermath of his brother's disappearance, turning the story over in his mind, thinking about gold bars when he arose at four a.m. on a subzero morning to milk cows. He might have thought about the gleam of gold while he hosed the manure off them, dipped their udders in iodine, shoveled oats.

Leland may have guessed his older brother Seamus had gathered gold and hidden it not too far away. Somewhere in the valley. Over the years, Leland may never have gone anywhere without a shovel and pickaxe rattling in the back of his wagon and, as the years passed, in the bed of his truck. He may have broken the earth in a hundred places, trying to follow Seamus's path and locate the cache.

Since Sean was a boy, he'd known the story of Seamus, how his uncle threw himself into the fight for Ireland's independence from British rule. Sean never figured out how his father learned about the gold, whether by eavesdropping or reading Seamus's private correspondence. Sean knew what Leland knew: the British heavily blockaded shipping to Ireland during World War I to prevent weapons falling into the hands of anti-British elements. Free Irish sympathizers in the U.S., like Seamus, tried to equip the rebels, but the blockade prevented a suitable ship from getting through. Then, in early 1918, Seamus disappeared. Rumors swirled, but no sign of him was seen again.

"He might have taken the gold to Ireland himself and joined the freedom fighters," Cora said.

Del wedged the bed pillow behind his neck. "Or an accomplice might have killed Seamus and grabbed the gold for himself."

"Judith didn't mention anything about an accomplice." Cora scrolled through the notes of the interview with Judith, her laptop balanced on her bare thighs.

Leland continued to run the dairy farm even as it shrank in size. The hills that ringed the valley were too steep for cultivation, once tractors had replaced the horse and plow. Alfalfa and corn fields on the hillsides disappeared, and Leland couldn't raise enough of his own feed to maintain a big herd. Trees grew to wipe out landmarks that had been clearly visible in Seamus's time.

"If there was an accomplice, that person has turned to dust," Cora said. "The thing is, Leland seemed to think the gold hoard was still intact."

She squinted at the screen in the low light. "Judith said rumors back then put the value at a million dollars. There were no forklifts in those days, and I don't think one person could have moved it." She typed an Internet search request. While she maneuvered through several sites, she felt Del's eyes on her and glanced up. She pulled the laptop over her pubis. "You've never gone online naked?"

He rubbed his lip with his thumb. "Once or twice, maybe."

She looked at him from under her lashes. "You were conducting an investigation?"

"I was looking for chili recipes." He said it without a hint of a smile.

Cora laughed, then focused her attention back on the screen. "Here it is. The price of gold in 1920 was twenty dollars an ounce." She frowned. "The government must have controlled the price for decades, because it was exactly that price in 1910 and 1930."

He leaned over and kissed her shoulder as she switched to another site.

"If Seamus had a million dollars in gold at twenty dollars a troy ounce, that would have been fifty thousand ounces," she said.

Del shifted closer so he could see the screen. "What's the price of gold now, 265 bucks?"

"Close: 272." She let her breath out slowly. "That's 13.6 million dollars."

The light seemed to dim, and gold glittered in the air.

"Enough to pay off their debt to the cartel and have millions left to buy a prize cow or two," he said.

"Or get off the farm entirely."

Del hopped out of bed. Cora heard his footsteps retreating down the stairs. In a little while he returned with the investigative report on Sean's death. He flipped through the pages.

"Here it is. Judith said he was excited that night. Upbeat. Not at all in a suicidal mood. He and Franklin had been away for two or three days. So they'd discovered the gold."

Cora shook her head. "If they'd found it, why didn't Sean tell Judith? She knew about the disappearance of the cocaine and had been crazy with worry for months."

Life at the O'Briens must have been intolerable, Cora thought. Sean besieged by debt. He and Judith twitching with nerves. The insurance investigator snooping in their affairs. Threats of torture and death coming from the drug cartel. Judith trembling for her husband and hiding her suspicion that Tyler had stolen the drugs.

"Maybe," Cora said, "Sean and Franklin had finally pinpointed the location of the gold, but they hadn't begun digging yet. It was winter, and the ground was frozen."

"They might also have been dealing with the problem of moving it." He took the laptop and set it on the blanket in front of him. "So, 50,000 troy ounces ..." he worked the keyboard, " ... equals 4,166 pounds. Men like Seamus O'Brien were probably more fit than we are today for lifting and carrying by hand, but even then I'd think 100 pounds is about as much as he could lift comfortably. That's 41 lots of 100 pounds apiece."

"A good-sized hiding place." Cora grabbed his arm. "In an old barn. Under the floor of an old barn. Mimi told me at one time there were a hundred barns in the valley."

"It's a good theory. There are three barns on the Maple Leaf Farm property. One is probably from that era."

"But I suppose Leland or Sean would already have searched there."

"Probably." He slid out of bed. "I've got to talk to the shooting investigation team at eleven and give a statement to the Bureau of Criminal Investigation at one." He showered, and Cora watched him as he dressed. She decided she liked the small fold of skin under his chin.

After he left, she got out of bed, wrapped herself in Del's terry robe, and went downstairs. She made herself a cup of tea in the microwave, and carried it into Del's office. On the sofa, she studied the now-familiar objects: his brass desk lamp, the wedding photo of Frieda and his father, the Michelangelo print of the perfect hand, and in the most prominent spot, the picture of Tyler in his baseball uniform. Perhaps Del felt it too, a surge of life that infused the house when a child came home. The rugs seemed softer, the furniture more solid, the food fragrant and delicious.

Cora sipped the warm tea and suddenly felt tears on her cheeks. She didn't have space for these lumps of emotion that were growing like a child in her belly. Feelings for Del, for Frieda, for Tyler. She felt painfully stretched, as if her skin would split.

She was going back to San Francisco soon, and she wouldn't see them again. Her story would run in the paper, maybe getting some favorable notice, and she'd use the clip to get a new job. If she was laid off before the paper ran it, she'd turn it into a magazine piece or a book.

She wouldn't get any more caresses from Del's battered hands or cook pies using Frieda's recipes. Tears wet the collar of her robe. She wiped her cheeks with the couch pillow.

At least Nathan was coming home for the summer.

35

Cora
April 2000

He was late. Cora craned her neck to see if she could spot him amid the herd of tourists that entered through the tall granite columns of the Metropolitan Museum of Art. There he was—no, shorter than Nathan and without his springy walk.

Cora wrapped herself more tightly in her black gabardine coat. She had this one dressy coat labeled by some demented California retailer as a waterproof garment, but it didn't keep out the rain that gushed from the clouds in New York. She wiggled her toes in her dress shoes. Boots and a waterproof parka would have kept her dry. Why did she have to impress Nathan? He was well acquainted with her many flaws.

The lobby was packed with visitors, who eddied around their tour guides and queued up for tickets. Echoes bounced off the trio of domed skylights in the three-story-high ceiling. Cora had already purchased two tickets to the Met's featured exhibition, a display of Walker Evans photographs. Evans's powerful images had drawn her to study closely his haunting, unposed 1930s portraits of farmers, subway riders, and pedestrians. The exhibit was coming to San Francisco in June, but she wanted to enjoy it with Nathan—at the moment, however, all she could think about was why he might be late.

She twisted on the carved wooden bench to take another look at the entrance. Nathan had agreed to meet here at ten, and it was nearly eleven. He wasn't answering his cell phone. She imagined him in bed, too sick to call. Maybe the train from Boston had been wrecked.

Yesterday morning, Del had bent to kiss her, before he left for his interview with the shooting investigation team, but her face must have held some warning. He paused, as if checking traffic for oncoming cars, and touched her shoulder instead.

"A storm is coming in," he said. "Are you rested enough to drive?"

"I'm fine; don't try to talk me out of this trip."

Cora had left most of her luggage in her room at Seneca House, after tapping out an e-mail to Stu Manion that she would be away until Monday. She didn't mention the layoff memo. Rain began to fall as she drove through Binghamton, the cold fogging the car windows. It was nearly seven before she arrived at the Benfield Hotel in Midtown, after laboring through rush-hour traffic and streets clogged with construction scaffolding. She registered and booked a room for Nathan down the hall. The rain, traffic, and unrelenting city noise set Cora's nerves abuzz. She woke every few minutes to the scream of sirens on the street below. The curtains were thrown open and she let the glare of the millions of city lights burn flowerets on her retinas.

She used to love New York. Its tempo moved faster than San Francisco, and her body matched it; her arms pumped faster when she walked, words leaped from her brain to her mouth. The first time she visited, she'd been on her high school's junior class trip. The anti-Vietnam war movement was roaring, and New York boiled with rock-throwing protesters confronting baton-wielding police. Cora, Samantha Dane, and Andrea Chan eluded their chaperones and linked arms to march under a red-lettered banner urging the impeachment of Mayor John Lindsay.

For that week, she'd escaped her father and his quiet rage. Cora had decided sometime during those seven days that she could leave him; it was possible he'd survive without her, and she without him. Someday, she might eat dinner or go to bed without rolling his clean socks and laying out his razor on the bathroom sink so he'd remember to shave before work despite his hangover. Someday, she wouldn't need her father to have someone solid and safe nearby.

On the school group's last night in New York, Cora had bought a hand-tooled leather belt with an intricate silver buckle for twenty dollars from a vendor who spread his wares on the sidewalk like a string of bright fish. His eyes took a trip over her, and his long yellow hair brushed her arm as he threaded the belt through the loops in her bell-bottomed jeans. She cocked her elbows and smelled the patchouli on his skin. She felt weightless, the scent, the sun on her shirt, the opening of green desire.

The street vendor, she almost remembered his name—Todd or Ted—had taken her hand and walked her to his crowded apartment in Hell's Kitchen. Samantha and Andrea lied to the chaperones about where she was. He lit a dozen candles in the soot-darkened single room while Cora stared at the mattress on the floor piled with wrinkled bedding. He put a vinyl record of sitar music on his stereo. She lay on her back on his wrinkled paisley bedspread and had sex for the first time. Her body was tight, and he was thin and pale, but she liked his weight, liked winding her legs around him, liked the momentary fantasy that someone was taking care of her.

———

"Mom."

Cora's hair flew as she swung around. Nathan was here. His long nose was cold and wet against her cheek as she hugged him. While she held him at arm's length, rain dripped off his eyebrows. She hugged him again. His slippery jacket muffled the feel of him against her palms.

"You look—different," she said. He had the aura of a Sicilian fisherman or a longshoreman, a navy blue watch cap pulled down over his hair and ears. His beard, darker than she remembered, stubbled his cheeks.

"Same old guy." He smiled, an uncertain grin, his lips dipping a little and then gaining confidence. His hazel eyes were more green than gray today. She'd loved their changeability since he was a child.

Happiness fizzed through her. She was inflated, as if the cap and the grin were sparkling soda that filled her to bursting.

"I was so worried about the derailment between Boston and New York," she said.

"There wasn't …" Then his eyes widened and he stifled a grin. "Terrible. Bodies scattered all over. I spent a good hour digging out of the wreckage, because I knew I had to meet you."

"And without a scratch," she said. She put her cell phone back in her purse. "I've bought tickets for the Evans exhibit. You'll love his work. And afterwards, I thought we'd get tickets for a show. There's a new one starring Patrick Stewart from Star Trek."

He dug his hands into his jacket pockets. "Mom."

"The reviewers say the exhibit is great."

He turned away from her and reached out to someone, a round-cheeked girl with gray eyes. He clasped the girl's fingers and tugged her to his side. "Mom, I want you to meet Shanley Cort." A note rumbled in his voice, deeper, more complex than she remembered. She felt dizzy.

The girl—what do you call a female old enough to enter college and have sex, but with blonde, strawberry, and royal-blue extensions woven into her black hair? Is she a woman if she wears pink high-top tennis shoes, bell-bottomed jeans, frayed and muddy around the hems, and a shirt that bares her midriff to the cold? The girl gave her the unblinking look of a cat on a lap.

"Hi, Mrs. Brooks," Shanley said. A mascara-darkened mole wiggled at the corner of her mouth. "I've heard a lot about you."

"I haven't heard a thing about you," Cora said.

Nathan hunched his shoulders. "I've been meaning to e-mail you, Mom, but we've been busy with classes, and then we went to Stowe on break." He and the girl gazed at each other and exchanged a slow, private smile. Nathan broke off the eye suck. "Shanley's in my Western Civ class. We found out she lives just down the hall from me in the dorm."

"How nice." she said. Behind them, the echo of voices ratcheted up a decibel.

"Each suite has its own bathroom," Nathan said hastily.

"Well, I bought two tickets for the exhibit. Let me stand in line and get a third."

Shanley stood on tiptoe and whispered into the approximate spot on Nathan's watch cap where his ear was. He swung their clasped hands and nodded.

"Shanley doesn't care much for traditional art. She's more into surreal and avant garde stuff," Nathan said.

"In the thirties and forties, Evans's work was considered extremely unconventional," Cora said.

Shanley's mole squirmed. "But he's so last century."

"What we're thinking about, Mom, is touring the city on one of those double-decker buses and then taking off for Chelsea or DUMBO."

"I'd have two useless tickets on my hands. And what's DUMBO?"

"Down Under the Manhattan Bridge Overpass. It's where the really cutting-edge artists have space," Shanley said.

Words pressed against Cora's forehead, Shanley's unwelcome words mixed with the babel of French, Japanese, Spanish, Chinese and German that churned around her.

"It'll be okay about the tickets, Mom," Nathan said, misunderstanding her grimace. He reached for them, and before Cora had gathered her wits, he crossed the lobby and sold them to someone walking in the door.

He returned and stuffed the money into her coat pocket.

Cora shook the rain off her umbrella, scattering drops on the terrazzo floor. "All right, then." She pursed her lips at Shanley's bare navel. "You're not dressed warmly enough for an open bus. It's only supposed to be forty-five degrees today." She sounded motherly. Nagging. Old.

"I'll be fine, Mrs. Brooks." Shanley rubbed her and Nathan's clasped hands against her cheek.

Cora bought tickets for the hop-on, hop-off tour from the driver of the red double-decker. A plastic cover like an oxygen tent shrouded the open upper tier for the winter season, and they trudged up the stairs. Nathan and Shanley snuggled into one bench, and Cora sat across from them on the aisle seat with an empty space beside her. The bus tossed her from side to side as it lunged along. The tent belled and flapped, pumping rain and air through the vehicle like a bellows. Cora's gabardine coat leaked body heat and her high-heeled shoes felt like ice trays.

"Isn't this great?" Nathan propped his foot on the empty seat. He rubbed the condensation off the plastic window. The bus looped down Fifth Avenue, through Midtown and up Eighth and Central Park West. It was Saturday, and there were few cars on the streets.

The tour guide, a woman in a red parka and a pair of imposing mountain boots, studded her commentary with celebrity nuggets as they passed the place where Jacqueline Kennedy had lived; the beaux arts Ansonia building, where Babe Ruth once had an apartment; the restaurant run by the Soup Nazi from the Seinfeld television series; and the Dakota, where John Lennon had died from an assassin's bullet.

It was raining too hard to walk in Central Park. The night before, Cora had imagined Nathan and herself on a stroll among the budding trees to see Strawberry Fields, the sidewalk mosaic commemorating John Lennon.

"Let's get some lunch," Cora said when they stepped off the bus in Midtown. "We passed an Italian place a few blocks back."

Shanley whispered again into Nathan's wool cap.

"Shanley doesn't eat meat," Nathan said.

"Then she can eat pasta with mushroom sauce," Cora said. A trickle of rain slithered down the back of her neck.

"The thing is, the utensils have all been used to cook and serve meat dishes," Nathan said. "Shanley's read about the harmful effects of flesh residue."

"There's a vegetarian place, maybe on Seventh Ave," Shanley said.

They hiked the Trail of Tears looking for the place, discovering it wasn't on Seventh Avenue, anywhere between Forty-Second and Sixty-Seventh streets. On the crowded sidewalks, Cora's umbrella clashed with the one Nathan was holding over Shanley's head.

"How about a deli?" she pleaded.

"I think it's near here. This bookstore looks familiar." Shanley looked obscenely perky, despite her wet hair and her drooping little blouse. Raindrops glittered on the tips of her lashes and a faint pink flush colored her cheeks, as if she were a china shepherdess.

After a few more of New York's interminable blocks, Cora was astonished when they did, indeed, find the place, a tiny restaurant warm inside and fragrant with curry and cardamom. Bright enameled leaves and red and pink hibiscus were painted on the walls with a flowing brush. She ordered lentil soup and green tea, wistful for a cup of something with a major dose of caffeine, but unable to find coffee on the menu.

Nathan slid his wet jacket onto the back of his chair, but didn't remove his cap, which dripped spots of water onto his shirt. He chose soba noodles in broth and fried tofu.

Shanley pinned the waiter with a rapier stare. "Are the vegetables in the Greens-and-Beans Salad certified organic?"

"Absolutely." The waiter tapped his pad with his pencil and studied a bougainvillea blossom above his head.

"I don't think I'll have that. Can I get the fruit smoothie with soy yogurt? Good. And do you have bok choy to substitute for spinach in the stir fry?"

After the waiter gathered the menus, a silence fell among them. Cora wrinkled her nose at the odor of her wet shoes and damp hair. A rustling from Nathan and Shanley's side hinted they were doing something with their hands under the table.

Nathan cleared his throat. "Shanley's majoring in journalism, Mom."

Cora sipped her tea. "The newspaper industry isn't very robust right now. Jobs are disappearing."

"I'm not interested in newspapers," Shanley said. "The stories are really long and boring. I want to write for a 'zine or a blog. Something that talks about what's happening."

"Last time I checked, that's what newspapers were doing," Cora said. The waiter slid a bowl of soup and slice of French bread in front of her.

Nathan ate a forkful of tofu. "The media has been taken over by corporations. They're just one more conglomerate trying to meet earnings projections."

"I want to write about electronic music and dumpster-sourced art, things people are really interested in," Shanley said.

The soup tasted bad.

They took several incorrect subway lines, and it was getting dark by the time they arrived at DUMBO. Traffic roared overhead on the Brooklyn Bridge. Brick warehouses lined the dimly-lit streets. In every doorway lay a homeless person talking on a cell phone, ears illuminated by blue light. Cora stepped into the gutter to avoid someone sleeping on the sidewalk, and trod on a pile of dog shit.

Up ahead, people mingled in the street, dark outlines against dim light trickling from a warehouse. The buzzes and squawks of electronic music hovered like a cloud of insects.

"Omigod, isn't this great? My sister told me about this show. She knows one of the artists." Shanley splashed ahead of them through the puddles. The warehouse had been gutted, painted white, and divided into exhibition space for several artists. A student group crouched over a computer and synthesizer, creating a dense atmosphere of sound. Colored lights flashed in coordination with the noise. Shanley greeted a woman whose brown dreadlocks were woven with drinking straws. "Alix, this is unbelievable. It makes such a statement about our throwaway culture."

While Nathan and Shanley chatted with Alix, Cora wandered through the crowd, stopping to look at an exhibit of a restroom roller towels embroidered with verses from the Quran. In another room, Cora sank onto a low bench. Her feet hurt and her legs felt too heavy to lift. Her eyelids had almost closed when the crowd parted for a moment and a sculpture loomed above her.

It was eight feet high, a monster beast from a dream. Its evil head was the white skull of a cow stripped bare of flesh, and hard, blunt teeth grinned in its jaws. The artist had fashioned a wooden cone and attached it to the end of the nose to lengthen the snout. A pair of pointed horns extended from its forehead. Molded white plaster formed the body and legs, which were held together with hardened green foam dripping from the seams. Legs ended in real cow hooves. The center of the beast was hollow and inside the shelter of the rib cage huddled rows of tiny plastic dolls.

The crowd closed around her again, blocking her view. The room was dense with humidity, wet clothing, clashing perfume smells, and the weight of human flesh.

She lurched to her feet and climbed onto the bench, searching the huge space. When she spotted Shanley's multicolored hair and Nathan's wool cap, she jumped down, tossed an apology for stepping on a man's foot, and elbowed through the crowd.

"How could anyone have conceived something like this? It's fabulous." Shanley gazed up at the beast.

"It's a psychological break from reality," Cora said. "Also known as psychotic."

Shanley lifted her chin, daring Cora to hit it. "I think it's very good. Justin, the artist, thinks it's going to be selected for a big joint show."

The bare white surfaces of the bovine's teeth in the lipless mouth and the sickly green bond between the seams took on new depth, radiating malignity.

"Somebody like Walker Evans is an artist. This person is a refuse collector," Cora said.

"The beast is a real creation. Justin collected stuff, it's true, but he combined the elements to create something entirely new."

A pulse beat in Cora's eye. The beast had been created from hooves sawn off a cow's leg bones. From the skull of a dead cow frozen in a storm or stripped of flesh by animals. The skull could even be one of Sean O'Brien's cows, Queen Beatrice, maybe, rendered at the slaughterhouse. The Queen, who'd won top honors six months ago at the Dairy Expo.

"The beast makes a statement, just like photographic art," Shanley said. "It says, this is what happens to dead things. They rot. They stink. They turn to dust, and then they become something different." For the first time, Shanley faced Cora full on.

"What do you know about dead things? You're twenty." An itch crept up Cora's forearm, urging her to slap the girl. A glance at Nathan stayed her hand. His face twisted with the indecision over whom to support, his new, exotic woman or his familiar, neurotic mother.

Cora wanted to sink onto the gallery floor among the dense forest of legs. She imagined herself for a moment lying there, watching the shoes move past, enduring the glancing blows of feet.

"I'm going back to the hotel." Cora said.

Nathan told Shanley he'd find his mother a cab and be right back.

The two of them walked to the end of the block, and waited on the curb for a taxi. He plucked her umbrella from under her arm and raised it over her head. Rain fell in slanted sheets.

His tall form was visible over the parked cars, and soon a cab driver spotted him and splashed up to the curb. Nathan opened the door. She handed him the key card for his hotel room.

"It's paid for," she said, and settled herself inside. Her body shook with a deep, gray cold.

He propped his forearm against the top of the door frame and leaned inside. "I know this didn't go very well, but Shanley's really great, Mom. Give her a chance."

Cora shook some droplets off the umbrella onto the cab floor. She looked up at him, the long nose and crooked eyebrow where he'd had stitches when he was six, his face so lovely she wanted to grasp it between her hands.

"We'll talk more when you come home during summer break," she said.

Rain dripped from his cap to his cheekbone. "About that ..."

The periphery of her vision darkened until she saw only the red reflection of a neon light in his eye.

"Shanley and I are staying in Boston. I'm not coming home."

36

Abby
February 1918

Ruth stopped cutting a length of China silk. "What's wrong.?"

A strange sound rumbled in Abby's throat. "I think something has happened to the baby. All her blood has run out." Her lips were swollen and rubbery.

"Let's see." Ruth knelt on the floor and touched the fluid on Abby's stocking with her fingertip. "It's not blood. Your bag of waters has broken."

Abby stripped off her wet shoes and stockings, and Ruth brought her a nightgown.

"She's too early," Abby said. Her abdomen tightened, a pang that could have been a labor pain or anger. She was supposed to have nine months with the baby—all hers—when its flutters and tremors were a secret between the two of them. Before the day was over her belly would be empty, and the baby would belong to Mama and Papa.

"Eight months is not bad," Ruth said. "Not at all. It should be small, but healthy."

She handed Abby her own flannel wrapper to put over her nightgown. "Come. We need to get you walking."

Walking? She's a lunatic, Abby thought.

"Grandma Clementine has delivered a hundred babies, and she does this every time. Walks the mother to bring the baby down quicker. I walked when you were born."

Abby paced from the sleeping porch through the length of the house to the parlor. Ruth rolled the China silk carefully, then changed into an old housedress and rolled up her sleeves. While she and Mary ate soup and toasted cheese sandwiches, Abby walked the path of her labor from the front to the back of the house: the frayed edge of the oriental carpet, the soft runner in the dining room, the cool, oily linoleum in the kitchen, and the loose board on the service porch. She used each spot as a milestone, stepping on them every time, counting the circuits as her pain mounted.

Ruth and Mary chewed slowly and turned their heads as Abby passed, like spectators waiting for the play to begin. The parlor clock chimed the quarter hours. The baby moved downward on a journey of its own. Abby hated the baby, loathed its uncaring march. She dug her nails into her abdomen as if to tear it out.

The rags between her legs were wet with fluid again, but now Abby couldn't bear to stand still. She walked, bent over to scream in anger and pain, paced on.

Finally, her mother took her arm. "Come, it's time."

Abby lay in Mary and Emmett's bed. It was dark, and Mary lit the single gas lamp. Ruth, sweat shining on her forehead, curved her palm around Abby's belly. She monitored the contraction from a watch pinned to her blouse.

Mary sat on a low stool beside her, and Abby squeezed her aunt's hand as if to transfer the pain to their clenched fists. She cared nothing for her nakedness or her widespread legs.

"Push now," Ruth said.

Abby rose out of herself, to the night on the slippery canvas, Seamus's face dark above her, lantern light shining in his red hair, his skin hot. The desire of every leaf overhead, each speck of dirt beneath focused on the space between her legs. This small patch of flesh was what longing was all about, her triangle of pale hair pointing down, to where she was swollen with desire and pain. They all wanted something from this wonderful, terrible spot. Seamus wanted to keep his secret safe, Mama and Papa, to get a baby. Abby had wanted something, too—a little girl, completely her own, if only for a few months.

"I can see the head. You're doing fine. One more." Ruth's voice was faint but clear at the end of the bed.

Abby tensed every breath, muscle, and drop of blood in one final push, yelling for her baby to take its final step into the world. With a rush of fluid, the child slid into Ruth's hands.

"Oh, my God, a girl." Ruth was laughing and crying.

"More's the pity," Mary said.

Abby released Mary's hand. She saw the top of her mother's head between her legs. Ruth held up the baby, barely larger than her two hands. Her blossom toes were curled, not yet ready to open.

Mary took the tiny child, pinched her heel and started the baby's breathing. Ruth rubbed her tears away with her forearm to keep from touching her face with her bloody hands. Swiftly, she tied and cut the cord. Mary held a basin of water while Ruth wiped the baby's face and head with a cloth.

"I want to see her." Abby struggled up onto a shaky elbow. Ruth hesitated a few seconds, and Abby saw the truth. It was her mother's baby now, not her own.

37

Cora
April 2000

Cora gripped the wheel. If she let go to turn on the heater or adjust the mirror, she was sure the wheel would fall apart. The wipers pummeled the windshield, and she felt each thump. After she'd returned to the Benfield Hotel, she stuffed her clothes and toiletries into her suitcase and left without checking out. The storm continued as she drove back to Cortland.

He wasn't coming home. The words drilled into her chest. She couldn't stop turning over every detail of the summer plans she'd made for them: a week at Bodega Bay, backpacking in the Sierra, ocean fishing. More than that, laughing with their mouths open at dinner, ridiculing the anchors on the television news, reweaving their lives after nine months apart. Nine months. It was a reversal of pregnancy, the slow loss of a child where once he'd grown in her cell by cell.

After some miles on the road, she began a series of admonishments. Stop wallowing. Nathan is your son, not the great love of your life. He's not going to spend his life at home, caring for his neurotic mother. Then her bravado collapsed. Trees lining the road bent under the whip of the wind.

She stopped at a self-service station and filled up with gas. Hers was the only car, and the overhead lights cast blurry reflections on the hood. Inside, the clerk stood behind the counter, his arms folded over his chest. He looked like Nathan, his long, lank hair falling to the neck of his T-shirt. Nathan's hair curled like that when it got long. The clerk raised his hand in a wave. Nathan had waved for a second before Cora's taxi had pulled away from the art gallery.

With a shiver, she slid inside her car and locked the door. When he was in high school, Cora had nagged Nathan constantly to get a haircut, keep his hair cropped close to his scalp. She'd told him that long hair gave him acne, but the truth was, he looked like Stephen, and she'd wanted to excise Stephen from every part of her life.

Finally, she had dragged a set of clippers from the back of a closet shelf and sat Nathan down in a kitchen chair with a towel around his shoulders. Nathan groaned with each pass of the clippers, but she was inexorable. His hair dropped to the floor in a soft carpet, and she stepped on it as she circled him, left to right, the clippers vibrating under her fingers. Afterward, her arm was numb.

Nathan jerked off the towel. His eyelids were pink, as if he were about to cry, yet his face was hard and unforgiving. "Give me those." He snatched the clippers from her hand. Later, she found broken bits of the plastic case in the alley near the garbage can. That night and the next, he hadn't come home.

Cora steered the car back onto the highway. Her speed climbed to eighty, and oncoming cars shot their lights into her pupils.

When she arrived in Cortland, she parked at the curb in front of Seneca House with the engine running. The porch light was on, but the house was dark. Debbie wasn't expecting her back until tomorrow night. Cora pressed her cheek against the cool window. She didn't want to go to Del's. She felt too unprotected, as though a single word from him could shatter her into tiny bits.

She drove away. The rain had stopped, but under the canopy of trees, water dripped steadily on the pavement. A light glimmered in the kitchen of Frieda's house. As Cora walked up the driveway, the fragrance of lilacs washed over her. In a moment, Frieda appeared in the lighted window, tucking the collar of her bathrobe under her chin.

The old woman pushed up the window sash. "I'm disappointed. I thought you might be a handsome burglar."

"Burglars aren't handsome, Frieda. They're drug addicts with AIDS and missing teeth."

"You're ruining my fantasy." She slid the window closed. After the rattling of deadbolts and chain locks, the kitchen door opened.

"I saw the light, or I wouldn't have stopped," Cora said.

"Insomnia is the curse of people my age. These eyes pop open, and I know it's two a.m." Frieda waved her inside. The old woman's gray-white hair was flattened on one side where she'd lain on it.

Cora leaned against the counter watching the movement of the blue veins in Frieda's hands as she sliced the last of the pie and poured hot water for tea.

"You look terrible," Frieda said.

"And you'll sell me a face cream that'll take care of it."

"No cream is going to take that away." Frieda studied her over the rim of her cup.

"I suppose not." Cora fingered the pouches of fatigue under her eyes. "I just got back from New York City. To see my son."

"It didn't go well?"

Cora looked away. If she met Frieda's sympathetic gaze, she'd start to blubber. She concentrated on Frieda's breathing—slow, but with a little catch in her chest.

Frieda said, "It's hard to have a child that age. Like picking blackberries. You get scratched all over for a few sweet morsels."

"There wasn't any sweetness on this trip." Cora found herself telling Frieda about Nathan and Shanley and the shattered summer plans.

Frieda nodded. "Children ignore us, slander us, trample us, bump us off. All to be free to grow up." She sounded different now, not like an old cutie-pie, but tough.

"Children should love us. Be our best friends." Cora rubbed her cheek with her knuckle and found it was wet.

"Let me tell you a secret." Frieda's thick, yellow fingernail tapped the table. "Your son will never be your best friend."

"But you and Del are friends."

"No. We're mother and son. I boss him around and he ignores me."

A mockingbird sang in the darkness outside the window. Inside, odors floated up like memories: cinnamon, old linoleum, bacon grease. Had her mother's kitchen smelled like this? she couldn't remember.

"My Eddie was a house painter," Frieda said, "made good money in the summer, but not much in the cold months. When Del started high school, Eddie worked Saturdays, and Sundays during the season. Saved every penny to send Del to Cornell. My husband wasn't a talker, but all those words stored up in his brain were like a bank account. Gave him determination—Del would be the first one in both our families to graduate college.

"Funny thing. Not so funny, I guess. He had a heart attack six months before Del got his university diploma."

Cora struggled for the right words but could find nothing to say. Del's father had died many years ago, and Frieda had been a widow longer than Nathan had been alive.

"I wanted Del to move back to Cortland after graduation from Cornell, marry a local girl." Frieda tossed her remaining tea into the sink and cocked her head as if listening to the liquid trickling down the drain.

"Do you like bananas?" Frieda said.

"Not much."

"They're Del's favorite fruit. All those years he lived in Ithaca, I bought a bunch every Friday. Put them in a bowl on the kitchen counter in case he came to visit. They turned from green to yellow and then got brown spots. By Thursday he hadn't come, and they were rotten. I threw them out."

Cora covered her face with her hands. Behind her closed eyes she saw the yellow bunches perched hopefully in the bowl. The smell of their ripening was on her palms. Tears dripped between her fingers.

Frieda squeezed her shoulder. "None of my plans worked out, of course. Del enlisted in the military and then joined the state police. I hardly saw him for the next six years, except for a few days at Christmas."

———

It was Sunday, and Frieda had arisen early. Through the adjoining wall, Cora heard the sounds of the toilet flushing and shower running. She opened her eyes. The room Frieda had given her to spend the night was scuffed like a pair of boy's shoes—the headboard and dresser dented and the door paint chipped where Del had kicked it long ago. She decided to stay here all day under the cotton sheet, thin from many washings.

Her house in San Francisco would probably become like Frieda's, a tombstone to the years when she and Nathan had been a family. She buried her face in the pillow. It was too soon, too soon to give him up.

She fell asleep again and dreamed about Franklin Santerra. He listened to the small movements of the cottage's joists and studs, fearful of assassins. He checked the shotgun to make sure the shells were in place. He clicked the breech closed. He peeled off his shoe and sock. He placed his toe inside the trigger guard, where the metal usually pressed his finger like a wedding ring. He inserted the barrel delicately into his mouth.

Cora staggered out of bed, fully awake. As she pulled her clothes on, the pant legs and shirtsleeves caught on her skin.

In the kitchen, Frieda was about to leave, her purse strap over her wrist. She straightened her yellow suit jacket. "I'm going to Sunday service. Want to come?" She looked sweet and buttery. The flinty woman who had given Cora advice in the dark, hard night seemed never to have existed.

Cora shook her head.

"Del will probably be there."

"Thanks, but I'm going to Santerra Farms."

Frieda swallowed and pressed her lips together, making an unspoken request. She wanted Cora to stay, and knew she wouldn't.

Frieda seemed gallant just then, dressed in the yellow suit, her low-heeled shoes too large for her thin feet. An unfamiliar tenderness rose in Cora. She leaned over and kissed Frieda lightly on the cheek.

38

Abby
February 1918

Abby held her daughter for two hours before she gave her to
Ruth. "Her name will be Alice," Abby said, "From the song 'Alice
Blue Gown.'" Alice stared at the gas lamp, her gray-blue eyes
blinking when Abby talked.

Ruth and Mary cleaned up the afterbirth, the towels, the basin
of water, the sharp sewing scissors. Alice was wrapped tightly in a
receiving blanket, but as soon as the two women left the bedroom
and closed the door, Abby unwrapped her, lifted the flannel gown
over her head, and took off her cotton diaper. Alice's arms and legs
jerked in protest against the cool air.

Abby laid her cheek against the baby's chest and listened to
her heartbeat. She whispered against the bottoms of the baby's tiny
feet, the palms of her hands, and the coil of her bloody cord. Later,
Abby didn't remember the words, but she breathed to her daughter
quietly, quietly, everything about Seamus.

She dressed Alice again, awkwardly folded the blanket around
her, and fell asleep with the baby in the crook of her arm. When she
awoke, her arms were empty.

Abby and Ruth had agreed, before the baby was born, that it
was better for her to become accustomed to Ruth, but Alice was a

picky baby. When Ruth offered her milk, Alice sucked the nipple on the glass nursing bottle only a minute or two before jerking her head away and crying fretfully.

"It's the California milk. There's something the matter with it. Not like the milk at home." Ruth spooned the skin from the top of the scalded milk and put it in the icebox to cool.

Emmett snorted. "An udder's an udder. A cow's a cow."

Mary bought goat's milk from a neighbor, but little Alice was not appeased.

Hardly bigger than a five-pound bag of flour, she filled the house with her cries. Ruth rocked the low wooden cradle with her foot, jiggled Alice on her shoulder, fed her warm water, turned her this way and that, but the baby could not rest.

Abby didn't offer to help, and Ruth didn't ask. Abby moved from the wide bed in Emmett and Mary's room back to the sleeping porch with Ruth and Alice. Abby lay ignored on her cot. Her belly shrank, but her breasts were painfully swollen. Directly after the birth, Ruth had shown Abby how to pin a towel tightly around her chest to keep her milk from coming in.

She listened night and day to this angry infant who wailed at the disturbance in her tiny intestines. She wasn't the child Abby had imagined. The two of them had been so attuned to each other during pregnancy, they might have been dancing. A walk, meal, even a heartbeat had evoked a response from the baby in her womb.

This baby, her Alice, was colossally angry. Sweat and soured milk clung to her hair and dirtied the flannel gowns Abby had sewn for her. The stink of diapers saturated the air on the sleeping porch. Alice's cries drilled into Abby's ears.

Alice wanted to suck milk from Abby, but Abby wouldn't—couldn't—reach out to take her. Alice was promised to Ruth and Jack. Abby couldn't take her back now. Ruth focused entirely on this small, outraged collection of nerves, as if she allowed herself no leeway for failure as a mother, after her years of longing and disappointment.

The constant pressure of the towel squeezed out Abby's milk, and within a few days the desire to let the baby suck disappeared. Her breasts sagged like scooped-out potato skins, but she continued to wear the voluminous blouses and large-waisted skirts she had worn during her pregnancy. She felt a great sadness as she pinned them together, as if they were her mourning clothes.

Aunt Mary had received five orders for wedding dresses and hired Abby as her assistant. "Ten cents an hour," she told Abby, "provided your work is satisfactory."

Abby cut, hemmed, and stitched. Her fingers worked more quickly than they had before Alice was born, and she discovered she was particularly good at basting the huge puffed sleeves into the armholes. She and Mary often returned to the dining room work space after a quick dinner to spend the evening with the needle and sewing machine.

With Mary's long hours and Ruth's struggles to feed Alice, it took Abby several days to steal time alone to write a letter to Emily. Again, she enclosed a note to Seamus. The dry scratching of her pen on the paper reduced Alice's birth to something small and compressed, not the triumph Abby had felt when her last great push sent the baby into the world.

She slipped down the front steps late that afternoon to hand the envelope directly to the mailman. It had been weeks since she'd been outside, and she was immediately embraced by the odd phenomenon of spring in late February. Pink blossoms opened on the flowering plum trees and a bed of jonquils erupted from the earth in Mary and Emmett's tiny front garden. The air was saturated with the scent of tender bark and translucent petals.

Wind caught strands of her bobbed hair, and she leaned back to let the air touch her throat. She wanted to go home. More than anything, she yearned to race down the road to Seamus's farm office and feel the warmth of his breath on her face.

"Going out?" The postman pointed at the letter and shifted the shoulder strap of his leather bag.

"Yes, yes." She handed him the envelope, took the incoming letters from him, and used them to fan her hot skin.

After dinner, Mary lit the gas lamp and spread the fabric, a length of Belgian lace for a wedding dress mailed home by an infantryman to his fiancée. As Abby worked the sewing machine treadle, she recalled Ruth pinning the hem of Rose Conklin's wedding dress, nearly a year before, the same day her first monthly had come. Her memory flowed in a powerful stream to the moments before Seamus had pushed himself inside her under the elm. She had asked him about a wedding, but Seamus had put her off. He'd said they would talk about it later, after he finished shipping the gold.

A stabbing pain jerked Abby back to her work. The sewing machine needle pierced her finger.

"Dear God." Mary rushed to her side. "Don't let any blood fall on the fabric."

Abby closed her eyes to keep from fainting. Mary reversed the fly wheel and eased the needle out. With her handkerchief, she cradled Abby's finger. Tiny red drops oozed from the twin holes, one in her nail and the other in the pad of her index finger.

"No harm done," Mary said.

39

Cora
April 2000

Cora slid into the rear pew at St. Cecelia's Catholic Church. Ahead a few rows, she spotted Yolanda Santerra, her hair as glossy as the rump of a black Angus.

Before she'd left Cortland, Cora phoned Santerra Farms. Yolanda's niece answered. Yolanda wasn't in. After some manipulation of the girl, for which Cora was only mildly sorry, she learned Yolanda was at church.

During the drive, mist rose off the hills as the sun evaporated yesterday's rain. The iridescent green hurt her eyes, and the roller-coaster hills made her carsick. She wanted this story over, so she could go somewhere dark and sleep for years.

St. Cecelia's priest faced the congregation over the altar. "And after supper he took the cup of wine, and blessed it and gave it to them, saying, 'This is my blood, which is shed for you'." Cora leaned around a woman in a large hat to see Yolanda bury her face in her palms.

Cora huddled in the pew until the end of the service before approaching Yolanda. Maybe church was a good location. Yolanda might be filled with peace and tranquility afterwards, and curb her impulse to whack Cora across the face. Cora wondered if Cruz

Santerra had sported a black eye after the fight with her sister in the milking shed.

Worshippers blocked Cora's path, and by the time she reached the center aisle, Yolanda had disappeared. Cora scanned the parking lot, then ducked back inside. The sexton had snapped off the lights. Smoke from the snuffed-out candles took on the rose-colored tinge of the stained-glass windows. When her eyes adjusted, Cora spotted Yolanda on her knees in the flickering candlelight of a side altar. Yolanda lit a votive candle and shook out the match.

"It's not going to help." Cora sat on the carpeted step beside Yolanda and propped her forearms on her knees.

"Get lost."

Cora scooted closer. "You can't pray yourself out of it." Yolanda had changed in the last few days. The flesh around her eyes had shrunk back against her eye sockets, and her formerly aggressive chin sagged. She pressed her palm against her breastbone.

"I hope God strikes you dead for violating the sanctity of His house to go after your filthy story," Yolanda hissed.

"God wants justice. And you ..." Cora let the silence ripen. "You lied."

Yolanda tried to say something, but one side of her face seemed to be numb. She crawled to a corner of the altar and vomited on the hem of the embroidered drape.

Cora reached for her cell phone on her belt. "Hold on! I'll call 9-1-1."

"No!" Yolanda scrabbled at her pants pocket with a trembling hand. She grasped Cora's wrist. "Nitro."

The clamminess of the suffering woman's body dampened Cora's hand as she searched Yolanda's pockets. For a second, she wanted to wipe her fingers on her jacket. She overcame her distaste and fished out a vial with a screw cap.

Cora shook out a tiny white pill and slipped it between Yolanda's lips. "Please let me call," Cora pleaded. Yolanda shook her head.

The two of them sat on the altar step without saying anything, smelling vomit and candle wax, and in a few minutes Yolanda's breathing returned to normal. "Look at what you've done." She tapped her breastbone with her fist.

"Don't blame me," Cora said. "Franklin got himself in trouble and committed suicide. You lied. You cooked up the deception that he was murdered. That's what's ripping you apart, not my poking around."

"If the word had gotten out, Franklin would have been buried in unconsecrated ground."

"So you deceived the priest about Franklin's suicide, and you haven't gone to confession since. How many times have you taken communion in a state of sin?"

"I didn't like Franklin—he was a self-centered ass—but how could I deny him the chance to lie beside Mama and Papa?"

"Did Franklin leave a note?" Cora knelt to help Yolanda to her feet. The woman's clothing smelled.

"My God, can't you leave it alone?" Yolanda exhaled with a rush of breath.

"How come the Police missed the note?"

"Because he didn't leave it there. He pushed it under the door of my place before he drove off with the shotgun. I didn't find the envelope until he was gone."

A subtle movement of air made the candles flicker on the small altar. Yolanda slipped on her shoe, which had dropped off her foot. "His whole life, Franklin pushed responsibility off on me—the farm, the dairy business, the breeding program. I've cleaned up after him since he was eight or nine."

Cora leaned close to Yolanda's ear. "You kept it. You didn't show it to anyone, not the police, not even your own sisters. They're living in fear the cartel will come after them for Franklin's debts."

Yolanda tottered unsteadily toward the church door. "I took care of him. I did what I've always done, even after he died."

Cora wanted to shout. She longed to thrust her face inches from Yolanda's and say, you knew how he died. You had a body. You had a funeral. People said nice things about him and remembered him. You were lucky, even though you whine about it now, because you can see his gravestone any time you want, whether or not it's in some holy dirt. You don't have to wonder for years whether he's dead, whether he's alive and has forgotten you, or worst of all, whether he's alive, remembers you, and just doesn't care.

Cora pinched out one of the candle flames with her fingertips. It hurt. "Did you save it?" she called after Yolanda.

Yolanda stepped outside and the church door wheezed shut.

Cora ran out after her. "I think you've got it. Let me see it, so we can put this horrible thing to rest."

Yolanda crossed the parking lot and hoisted herself shakily into a dirty red pickup.

Cora rested her hand on the pickup's window frame. "The note might shed some light on Sean O'Brien's death. If that's settled, the threat ..."

"It doesn't, and I don't give a damn about Sean."

"What about the living? Your nieces? What's it like for your sisters, knowing their families are in jeopardy? They're at risk of being tortured or killed."

The pickup's window began to close.

Cora put her hand on the window edge, ignoring the risk of broken fingers. "Those girls are young and innocent. Aren't you afraid for them?"

Yolanda's jaw moved off kilter, like a ruminating cow. "Okay, I'll show it to you because of them, but afterward I never want to see your skinny ass again."

She gunned the engine and roared away. Cora followed her to the farm. The same rigorous line of tall, muddy boots perched on the double-wide's porch rail. Yolanda entered through the unlocked door and hung her keys on a pegged board alongside a dozen other sets marked with colored tags. The place was scrupulously neat, plates lined up in the dish drainer, copies of *Holstein World* aligned precisely on the desk. In the corner near the television set was a small altar to the Virgin Mary decorated with a bouquet of plastic flowers.

Yolanda disappeared into the bedroom. Cora inspected the family photos arranged in a straight line on top of the bookcase.

One showed a tall man with dark hair, gleaming white teeth, and 1970s-era sideburns. His head tilted to one side as if to dodge the next responsibility traveling his way. He had his arms around the shoulders of an older couple. The woman wore a lace-collared dress and the older man was unsmiling beneath a black mustache.

When Yolanda emerged, she'd changed her church slacks for jeans and was pulling a sweatshirt over her head. "That's Franklin and my folks. The year he finally stopped fooling around and graduated from Cornell." Her nostrils were red and raw, as if this tender part of her face were her only vulnerable spot. From the bottom desk drawer, she lifted out a flat metal box. She set it on the table in the dining nook.

The envelope seemed light. It should have been weightier, more significant. Inside, a note was written on a page ripped from a spiral notebook. Small scraps of paper clung to the edge.

Yolie,

Sorry.

Sean's new contact had the last few pieces of the puzzle. With the stuff we had from Sean's dad, we were home free. But without him, I'm screwed. Another threat this morning. Serious.

You can't get me out of it this time, mi hermana.

F.

Yolanda lowered herself onto the edge of a reclining chair as if it were a bed of nails.

"Do you know what he was talking about in the note?" Cora asked.

"The ridiculous gold scheme."

"You don't think there was any gold?"

"In eighty years, don't you think someone would have found it?"

"Not if it was well hidden. Or buried," Cora said.

"Except for a few fools, the people who believe in fairy-tale gold all ran off to California a long time ago." She pulled on a pair of heavy work socks. "It was Sean, always him. Got Franklin into that import furniture business. As if American furniture wasn't good enough. Then the Mexican investment scheme. The evil, sinful drug thing, and, finally, the gold."

She was fooling herself, but Cora didn't say anything. "Do you know who the third person was?

Yolanda shook her head. "Another of his *friends*, I suppose." Her voice was saturated with loathing.

"I'd like to make a copy of the note."

"Why are you digging up all this putrid stuff? No one in California gives a rip about how Franklin died."

"That's what I said, but the publisher was a friend of Sean's."

"Then don't use anything about Franklin. He's a poor messed-up suicide. Depressed over financial troubles."

Yolanda was right. Despite D'Arcy's enthusiasm for the story, Manion would oversee the editing, and he'd cut it to nothing. She was a has-been, not one of his young, award-hungry reporters. They would be at the paper for years to come, scraping by on lower wages, after the experienced staff with higher salaries had been laid off. But Cora didn't want to open her fist and let the story go. She wanted to shake and pummel it until every bit of truth tumbled out: the unknown conspirator, the dates, the cows, Sean's pizza, the poison, the photo of the headless man, the missing cocaine.

More. Even more than that. She felt a flash of heat and dislocation. Sweat ran down her back, and she smelled its odor on her clothes.

Yolanda stepped into a pair of thick-soled clogs waiting beside the front door. "You and I are alike, I think."

"Not that I can see." Cora slipped the note into her pocket with a trembling hand.

"We are. We both want things our way. Neat. Organized." Yolanda opened a metal tin of dog kibble and dished out two scoops. The collie sat until Yolanda snapped her fingers; then he began crunching the food, his long white teeth showing.

"I don't want it neat," Cora said. "I want to know why. Why a handsome, restless womanizer like your brother risked everything in a naive drug scheme. Why his friend, with a wife and son, wanted to join him. Why they got in trouble, why they kept going from one outlandish solution to the next. Why did it happen?"

"See what I mean?" Yolanda fingered another nitro pill from the bottle. "You want everything in the right stall."

40

Abby
March 1918

Emmett was turning fifty. Mary had dithered about throwing him a party, concerned about a resurgence of influenza cases and a shortage of butter, eggs, and cream for a cake. Ruth finally weighed in. "Emmett might be dead next year. He might have run away with another woman or developed stomach ulcers. You'd better do it now."

Party preparations had increased Abby's deep restlessness. She'd received no reply from Emily. Meanwhile, letters from Papa arrived almost daily. Ruth read snippets aloud; snowstorms were sweeping across the northeast, and he'd teamed up with Uncle Will to cut ice from the lake. Abby wanted to be quit of San Francisco, go home to the blanket of silent snow on the fields and the snap of cold air in her lungs. She longed to be herself again, not this stranger, this girl-woman.

Mary, Emmett, and especially Ruth ignored her, as if to reinforce the lie they told everyone that the baby was Ruth's. Her father had spread word at home: Ruth had given birth to a girl prematurely in San Francisco and would return to the Otisco Valley when she was well enough to travel.

On the Sunday of the party, Abby tried on a favorite skirt she'd brought from home; it fit around the waist. She stared at her belly.

A month after Alice's birth, all that was left of her pregnancy was a soft little hump.

The shades on the sleeping porch were closed to coax Alice into napping before the guests arrived. A brief cry and the sound of sucking plucked a response from connective fiber in Abby's skin. She was still extraordinarily sensitive to the baby's moods, as if the two of them were a wireless telegraph, sending and receiving signals.

The first guests were from Emmett and Mary's church. Drops beaded the ends of Emmett's hair where he had tamed it with a wet brush, and when his friends from the shipyard arrived, the atmosphere began to simmer with the rough male energy. The shipyard workers were loud and boisterous, awkwardly holding dainty punch cups in fingers scarred from saws and chisels gone awry. As the men drifted in and out of the kitchen, they doctored their punch with spirits and laughed at jokes about Emmett's age and sexual vitality.

Abby passed trays of cucumber sandwiches, cookies, and nuts, and on one of these circuits she noticed a man apart from the others, in the alcove formed by the Queen Anne window. He was about Seamus's age, with skin so pale his natural color seemed to have been leached away by some caustic substance. He leaned heavily on a cane and lowered himself into Emmett's favorite chair.

"Good to see you out and about." Emmett pumped the usurper's hand. "Abby, bring Alan something to drink."

Abby dipped a cup of punch, which Emmett splashed with a dram of spirits from a hip flask. Emmett introduced the soldier, recently returned from France, as Alan Murtha. He'd been gassed and hit in the thigh by a piece of shrapnel.

Alan's mother fluttered around him with small plates of sweetmeats and cookies, which he refused with a shake of his head. He followed the crowd's noisy laughter and movement with detachment, as if observing an exotic species.

"There will be birthday cake soon," Abby said.

His shirt collar drooped away from his thin neck and his pants wrinkled around his injured leg. Her own clothes were beginning to look the same around her belly and hips.

"It will be tasty, I'm sure, Miss, especially if you made it, but I'm somewhat off my feed," he said.

"Can I get you something special? Some custard or rice pudding?"

He kneaded the muscles in his thigh. After a moment he said, "Another cup of your uncle's punch."

Abby smiled. Alan's mother undoubtedly was unaware he was imbibing. She refilled the cup and added a generous splash of whiskey from a bottle in the kitchen. She wove through the guests and set the cup on the small table beside Alan's chair.

"Thank you, Miss."

"My name is Abby."

He sipped the punch; his eyes watered as he swallowed.

Over the sound of a fiddle, Abby heard a cry from the sleeping porch. In a few minutes Ruth returned with Alice tucked in the crook of her arm, decked out in a pink crocheted dress and matching cap tied under her chin. Women clustered around Ruth and Alice, nipping the baby's cheek with their fingers and twiddling her small toes inside her booties. Ruth's skin was burnished with joy. Alice didn't cry for once, and she ignored the invasion of her person as though distracted by an internal conversation.

Abby couldn't stand to look at Alice for more than a second or two at a time. When she saw Alice's delicate eyelids and pinkish-brown lips, she wanted to snatch her baby and run.

"Your sister is a very pretty child," Alan said.

Abby scrutinized him closely. There was something about him, a note that hovered beneath his words that made Abby want to hear him speak again.

"Her name is Alice, after the song 'Alice Blue Gown.'"

Alan nodded. "My mother has the sheet music." He took another sip of punch. His forehead bloomed red and shiny against his white skin.

At that moment, Mary carried the birthday cake triumphantly from the kitchen and set it on the table. She lit a single candle with a sulfur match. To applause from the women and catcalls from the men, Emmett clutched his chest, coughed theatrically, and blew the candle out with a great expulsion of breath.

Abby passed out cake squares on Mary's Haviland china plates. When she was finished, she pulled a footstool in front of Alan's chair.

"Here. For your leg."

He shook his head. "I'm already too much cosseted by my mother. I only want to be left alone." He flipped his hand toward his mother, who hovered over Alice, blocking the baby from Abby's sight. Alice began to cry.

"Ah, the wee baby wants a little solitude, as well," Alan said.

Abby knew, all at once, what it was about him. "You're from Ireland." She seated herself on the stool at his knee.

He rolled his head against the back of the chair to regard her closely. "You're very quick. My grandmother is Irish."

"I have a friend, at home, who's Irish." Restlessness swept over her, and she nearly screamed with longing to leave this city, the houses with barely three feet between them, the smell of sewers strong on warm days, the mean, grasping calls of the gulls. She wanted to tell Alan about Seamus, about how the baby had floated in her belly on a calm sea of birth waters, how Abby had walked the steps that brought the baby out, how Alice now was lost, fretful, and searching.

"I lost my friend in France," Alan said. "We were boyhood mates and enlisted together. He died in the Argonne Forest." The flush in his cheeks deepened.

Abby leaned nearer, until her face was close to his shoulder. The sterile scent of despair clung to his body.

"The baby is really mine," she whispered. It was a relief to tell someone, as if she'd lanced a boil and pus had spurted out.

His eyes widened a fraction, and he nodded, as if his head were immeasurably heavy. "And you've lost her."

41

Cora
April 2000

Cora called Del from her car, still parked in front of Yolanda's trailer. While the phone rang, she watched Yolanda back up a tractor and hitch it to a feed wagon.

"You're back." Del said. "I saw Mom at church."

"I'm at Santerra Farms, and I have something you'll be interested in."

"I'm free now."

In the enclosed car, her clothes, stiff from yesterday's rain and mud, smelled even worse. "Later. I need sleep."

"I've got a bed at my place."

Cora started the engine. "I don't think so. Maybe breakfast later?"

"It's one o'clock."

"Food of some sort. The Downtowner at four?" Cora tooted at Yolanda, who had towed the wagon under the grain chute. She acknowledged Cora with a half-wave of her hand.When Cora arrived, Seneca House sagged in Sunday afternoon torpor. A bald man snored in one of the living room's overstuffed chairs. Debbie's soft voice droned from the open door of her office, where she took a telephone reservation. Cora had hated Sunday afternoons when she was a girl. Life seemed suspended. The house smelled, her father was hung over, and her friends were doing family things— bicycling, playing soccer, eating Sunday dinner with relatives. After sitting through church on her search for Yolanda, the world seemed fraught with contradiction and sin.

Cora carried her overnight bag up to her room, where she'd left her computer, tape recorder, and most of her belongings during her trip to New York. She took Franklin's letter from her pocket, unfolded it, and smoothed it on the desktop. The pen strokes contained a slight tremor that gave the message a lacy appearance. She brushed the letter with her fingertip, tracing the indentations that Franklin's pen had made in the paper.

She sealed the letter in a plastic baggie. Del would want to see it.

She stripped off her reeking clothes and dropped everything in the wastebasket, including her muddy, misshapen shoes. She was rubbing her skin dry after a scalding shower when her cell phone rang.

"It's me," Del said. "I just went over last night's dispatch log. The remains of the country store burned last night."

Cora snatched a pair of underpants from the drawer. "Let's go out there."

"I'll swing by in fifteen minutes."

Cora was waiting on the porch with a baggie containing Franklin's note when Del's Crown Vic pulled up at the curb. Her hair was still damp, curling wildly around her head. Del leaned over to open the passenger door. When she climbed in the car, he brightened, like embers that ignite under a breath.

"I like the hair." He touched a strand, and, completely against her wishes, it wound around his finger.

"It's a mess." She scraped it back from her face.

"Give it some slack." Del touched her cheek.

"Not now."

He sighed. "I was thinking, Sunday afternoon sex in the car in front of the B and B."

"I think there's an ordinance."

Northbound on Highway 81, Del flipped off the dispatch radio. He rubbed her knee gently with his palm. "I'm sorry about your visit with your son."

"How?" Cora demanded. "Oh, Frieda."

They turned left at the intersection and headed up the valley. Cora read Franklin's note to Del.

"Jesus."

"I thought about him all the way home, this third person, and I can't figure out how he fits in. I feel like I'm in a tunnel, getting deeper, the sides closing in on me until I can't go backward or forward."

Del's foot was heavy on the accelerator now, his speed keeping pace with his thoughts. "This is good. There's someone out there—alive—who has a piece of the puzzle. I've got to talk to Judith and Tyler again."

'We. We've got to talk."

"Right."

A thin column of smoke curled up from the dimple in the hill where the store had stood. Across the road from the charred ruin, the blue trailer and the antiques in front of the barns were covered with a layer of ash. Cora rolled down the window. The penetrating smell of the fire in the cool air ate at the membranes in her nose. Somewhere close by, the scream of a power saw rose and fell as it ripped a stubborn tree. Del got out and walked up the rise above the fire site, where a state police investigator in a navy T-shirt poked a boot into the soft earth.

To keep from crying, Cora pressed her upper lip hard with her thumb. She had a brief memory of doing this often to stop tears when she was a girl, but couldn't remember why she'd been so often upset.

She walked across the road on shaky legs. The store, which on Thursday had been an eight-foot-high mound of siding, thick wooden beams, rotting planks, and window casings, had collapsed. The tangle reached only to her knees: charred wood and ash, discolored pipe, daggers of glass, remnants of the porcelain sink.

She stepped on new spring grass coated with a black, oily residue. Her mother had sat on this ruined porch. Alice might have buckled her shoes, studied fractions, and dreamed about falling in love in this building. Then sixty years ago, she'd said goodbye and traveled west. Met Roy Brooks. Cora supposed it was possible that wood hoarded physical remnants from the past. A delicate flake of skin, a hair, teardrops. But the fire had incinerated any residue. Cora felt a physical impact from the fire—sweat again. Heat crept up her chest, over her face, and into her hair. A week ago, she'd barely known the store existed, but now she mourned its loss as though a finger or toe were missing.

Del interrupted her thoughts. "Our investigator thinks it was arson. There's evidence of an accelerant, gasoline or kerosene."

"Why would anyone want to burn a wreck?"

"Could've been kids with an itch for excitement or destruction." Del rubbed his sooty palms on his thighs.

"The store stands empty for thirty years. It's been falling down for ten. And seven days after I arrive, somebody burns up the remains. What does the fire have to do with Sean and Franklin?"

"Hell, I wish I knew. The arson investigator should have more details once he finishes."

Cora folded her arms over her chest. "I don't know what to feel. About its being gone."

Del kicked a charred beam which collapsed into powder. "What's there to feel? Ashes, broken glass, and hot nails."

"Easy for you to say. You talk to your mother twice a day." Torching the wreckage of the store seemed personal, not about the deaths of Sean and Franklin, but something closer. Cora imagined someone lighting a match close to her face.

He pursed his lips as if about to answer, then changed his mind. He crossed the pavement to the other side of the road. The heavy barn door rattled as he checked the lock on the antique shop. "One lucky thing, sparks didn't jump the road. The dry wood in these old men would have sent flames a hundred feet in the air."

She walked past him to stand at the edge of the road looking down on the rust-stained roof of the blue trailer. The sinuous green hills fell away toward the flat bottom of the former lakebed. Somewhere close by, she heard a tractor chew its way through a winter-ravaged field.

Gravel crunched under Del's boots, but she didn't turn.

"A bunch of rotten lumber isn't a connection, Cora. A connection is an application for Social Security and Medicare, or a death certificate."

She swallowed to dislodge an obstruction that closed her throat. "What would that information give me? Born, married, died. Facts—facts but not her." Cora had been close to some revelation on her first visit; it hovered slightly above her range of hearing.

"Never know. If you really dug in, you might turn up school records, pictures of her, even letters. Learn what she was like, why she left here. Whether she deserted you, or whether your father killed her."

His logic angered her. He was diverting her from a feeling, not a fact, that would explain everything.

Since that night at Del's when she'd relived the trauma of her last day with her mother, Cora had tried to lock the memory away. She imagined a steel safe with a combination lock. Later, she told herself, she'd explore the sound of the blows and cries, the sight of red drops, when she was stronger. More stable.

But the fire showed her she couldn't wait. No documents, no records would give her answers. Only something here on this spot. Above her, two hawks screamed. They swooped past, their six-foot brown wings nearly touching, before they veered apart and drifted downwind toward Maple Leaf Farm.

The sun dipped from its zenith, illuminating tiny bits of incandescent spider web swimming in a sea of bright air. Her mother, her grandparents, Sean, his father, his uncle. They were the core of it, not the gold. The answer nearly brushed her face, as fragile as one of those glowing filaments. She turned to stare directly into the sun and felt the pain in her eyes. She began to cry, unaware of her tears, a shower in a clear, heartless sky, moisture dripping from her face onto her T-shirt.

Del grabbed her and held her head tightly against his shoulder. His skin smelled warm and spicy like his chili. His hand moved in slow circles over her back. She felt the warmth of his lips against her temple. "I want you to stay, Cora. Leave San Francisco."

With her ear pressed to his chest, she heard his voice boom in her ear, loud and phlegmy, as if he had a cold. "We'd be good together," he said. "I don't want to lose you."

She reared back. "I can't do that. We've only just met."

"It's a beginning. We need to build on it. Be together."

"I'm not ready." Tears distorted her surroundings into streaks of red and blue, flashes of almost unbearable sunlight.

"We're as young now as we'll ever be. Let's not waste time."

"Not right now." She scrubbed her cheeks with her shirt sleeve.

"What's holding you back?"

"That's not the question. The question is, what would lure me here?" The meanness of what she'd said made her turn away in shame.

"Your old life is done. Exactly like the store is over. What I'm talking about is the future," he said.

"It's not over. I have a house, a beautiful city, a son ..." Cora blinked away more tears. A car approached from the north. As it neared, she recognized the engine knock of Mimi's Mercedes.

Mimi braked in the middle of the road and rolled down the passenger window. "I heard about it this morning," she shouted across the front seat. "Too bad. Somebody might've paid money for the old timbers."

"I can't imagine they're worth much." Cora walked slowly toward Mimi's car window.

Mimi tilted her head. "I see you've got the law on your side."

"What?"

"Nobody would suspect it was you, given that you and Del are an item," Mimi said.

"You think it was me?" Cora backed a couple of steps away.

"Who else has been interested?"

"And I torched it because ..."

"Who knows?" Mimi said. "Who knows why you would come three thousand miles to write about two suicides?"

Cora felt Del come up alongside her. "Why are you so interested?" he ducked his head to look in the window.

"I inherited my grandparents' farm, which is a mile north of here. Dick and I come up on weekends." She fingered one of her long earrings. "What does the fire investigator say? About how the fire started?"

"Mimi, give it a rest. It won't hurt you to learn the news the same time as everybody else, when the report comes out," Del said.

"Inside news is money in the real estate business, Major."

Cora stirred restlessly. "Who owns the property now?"

"I do, actually," Mimi said. "I bought it for back taxes at a county auction."

"Then why didn't you clean up the place?" Del sounded angry. "The investigator said the fire could have spread, lit up those old barns, even burned out the neighbors."

"I was getting around to it."

"What did you want with the property? It isn't big enough for a farm," Cora said.

Mimi started the engine. "That's an interesting story, Cora. I'm on my way to Seneca Falls. Come along, and I'll tell you about it."

"I wouldn't have any way of getting back to Cortland." Traveling anywhere with Mimi right now seemed like a suitcase too heavy to lift.

"I'll drop you off," Mimi said.

Cora shot a quick glance at Del, whose face twisted with a subtle pain that tugged at his usual calm features. As much as she wanted to avoid Mimi, she was even more anxious to abandon her discussion with Del.

"See you later," she said not looking him. As soon as she slammed the door, Mimi did a U-turn and headed north along the lake.

42

Abby
March 1918

The next morning, Abby picked up the dirty punch cups, cake plates, and ashtrays. She opened the windows to blow out the fug of cigar smoke. The oriental carpet was littered with broken nuts and bits of cookie, which she cleaned up with the carpet sweeper.

While Abby worked, Mary stitched the seams of an organdy blouse. She finished a seam and broke the thread with her teeth.

"Sophie Murtha has been a friend of mine for thirty years," she said. "Alan is such a nice young man."

"Alan is an old man," Abby said.

Even so, he had music in his voice, she thought, golden Irish notes. She drew a sink full of scalding water and slid the crusted plates into it.

"Not so old. Twenty-four." Mary's voice, usually rough with a Scottish burr, was smoother. "I first met Emmett when he was twenty-five and I was sixteen."

A china plate slipped through Abby's fingers. It hit the side of the porcelain sink, and sharp, flowered bits scattered on the floor. "I don't like Mrs. Murtha. She has a mustache." She swept up the pieces and carried them outside to the garbage bin. The remainder of the morning, she spent bent over a *peau de soie* skirt, hemming it for one of Mary's clients. During the afternoon, she thought about Alan Murtha, his wounded leg, his lost friend. At 3:45, she heard the gate click. Putting aside her work, she ran down to meet the postman.

A letter from Emily. Dated three weeks before, correctly addressed but misdirected to San Diego. She moved into the shadow under the steps. The space smelled of rotten wood and cat urine. She held her breath and tore at the envelope flap.

My Dearest Cousin,

I received your letter about little Alice. I am relieved you and the baby are well. As your True Friend, even twenty mules could not drag your secret from me.

Please forgive me for not writing sooner. It took me awhile to devise a plan whereby I could deliver your letters to The One.

Saturday, I went to the store. It was crowded, since the snow had let up for a time. While Uncle Jack was busy drawing a gallon of kerosene for a customer, I slipped behind the postal counter and placed your letters in His box. On the way out, Uncle Jack gave me a long, long look. I stammered a little, but told him I had purchased stamps and put money in the drawer. I think his suspicions were put to rest.

Abby, I SO look forward to seeing you again. I told Miss Truk the two of us would be sharing a room when you got back.

With much love,

Emily

Abby folded the letter, creasing and creasing it until it was no larger than her thumb. She slipped it into the heel of her shoe, where a sharp folded corner dug into her foot. Three weeks since her letter had been placed in Seamus's box, and still no word from him.

After dinner, Abby opened a novel, carefully turning the pages. Her mother's head drooped like a heavy melon as she struggled to stay awake for Alice's ten o'clock feeding. Emmett ground the lighted tip of his cigar in the ashtray. Mary coughed twice, her signal she was going to bed.

Abby was still reading when she heard Alice's first hungry whimpers. She bent her head over the novel and pressed her heel against the letter, reminding herself not to get up. Alice's cries mounted until the clamor filled Abby with a wild tension. Ruth finally shook herself awake, picked up Alice, and held the screaming baby over her shoulder while she tested a drop of milk from the bottle on the skin of her inner wrist.

Alice sucked, her wide eyes blue and unreadable. She raised her hand as she drank, fist open and pink fingers searching like slow antennae to catch the emotion swimming in the air.

The yellow strip of light under Emmett and Mary's bedroom door blinked out. Ruth lifted Alice to burp her and murmured impatiently as the baby spit up on her shoulder. Ruth wiped the baby's face with the burp cloth and clicked off the kitchen gas lamp.

"Coming?"

"Soon." Abby held up the book, her finger marking the place.

She breathed the minutes away. After an hour, she crept to Ruth's bedside. Alice was awake in her bassinet. Tap, tap, her hands thumped softly against the sides.

Abby squeezed her eyes shut. Don't cry now, Alice, please don't. She knelt, her cheek close to the cold floor. She swept her hand through the dust under her mother's bed until she touched the shoe box containing Ruth's letters from Jack. Abby inched it out. Alice made a small breathless sound. Ruth turned over and rubbed her cheek against the pillow. Abby allowed the silence to descend again.

In the small entry near the front door, she lit a candle. No one could see the light here, so far from the bedrooms. She settled on the floor beside the console table with her back against the wall. Dirt from the box smeared her skirt. The candle flame nodded at a breath of wind that crept around the cracks. Next door, tomcats wailed around Iris's abandoned kittens, now in their first heat.

The letters were closely packed, tighter than the last time she'd spied on her parents' correspondence. She tugged at the first envelope, postmarked five days ago. Papa and Uncle Will had been to the lake with their drills and saws to cut ice. The ice house behind the store was now stacked to the ceiling with blocks ready for warm weather.

She drew out her father's next letter, dated eight days before. It was a short note. "My Dearest Ruth, I see that California has jumped aboard the prohibition train. The amendment is foolishness, although it may be advantageous to my enterprise. I miss you, Jack."

Nine days ago. The ink was darker, the words deeply impressed in the paper.

Ruth,

I made you a promise last fall that I would search out the man who defiled our Abby. How can you suggest, now, that we drop the matter without retribution? It is a blessing that you have another child to raise, but do not forget a great wrong has been done. Would you allow such a thing to happen again, to our little Alice?

At any rate, I will tell you this: I have learned the truth, and I have wielded the sword of justice. The responsible party is dead.

Jack

The candle nearly went out, then surged back, leaping at its wick. The legs of the console table writhed above her. Sweat sprang from her pores like a thousand pinpricks. Drops formed at her hairline and trickled down her cheek.

Outside, a tomcat screamed.

She rubbed the letter between her fingers. The paper was rough and dry. Pulling the candlestick toward her, she touched the page to the flame. It was wondrous, how it was destroyed in a few seconds, reduced to nothing from a white square defiled by her father's black ink. In seconds the fire burned every pen stroke, every fiber of what had once been a tree, then a vat of pulp, then a flat white page.

Another. She didn't bother to take this one from the envelope, but held it to the flame at the red-yellow tip where it burned the hottest. Briefly, smoke curled from the paper as if the letter held back, trying to save itself. Then in one thrilling exhalation, it burst into flame and was gone.

Abby felt a surge of joy. She burned another letter. Smoke stung her eyes, and feathers of burned paper drifted in the air.

She was a fallen girl with no baby to touch after nine months. She had no lover, no husband, not any hope of one.

They had taken it all, her baby, her lover, her dreams. Revenge belonged to her, she knew it as surely as she knew the whorls on her fingertips.

She ignited another letter and let it drift upward. From far away, Alice began to cry. Ah, my little one, she thought, there was justice. But it wasn't Jack's bloodthirsty Highland revenge. Nor was it her mother's theft of Alice as recompense for her own lost babies.

The fire caught the curtain fringe. It danced, sending up smoke, then tongues of purifying flame. Justice would come. She knew all at once why saints chose to die at the stake. They were purified and made whole.

Her memories came to her with extraordinary clarity now, those few times when it had been only she and Seamus. The two of them singing bravely as the snow beat in their faces on the trip to Tully. Their fight over the china doll at Dr.Cuthbert's. The slow luminous minutes in Seamus's office, where she'd sat in his lap and they'd kissed.

The entry was completely ablaze. The thin wood of the console crackled; fire ate at the curtains and curled upward like a serpent. Smoke tore at her throat and lungs, and heat scraped the skin of her face. She heard Emmett yelling. He tucked his head to his chest and lunged this way, that way, struggling to reach her. As the fire ate its way into the living room, it drove him back step by step. She didn't move. With a cry, he abandoned his rescue and went to save the others.

None of it, the terrible scarcity of air, the heat that seared her skin and sucked the fluid from her eyes, nothing was real. She remembered only his heat, his fiery tongue on her lip, the hot, sweet fold in his neck, the fever of his hand moving on her breast.

If there was justice, she thought at the very last, they'd be together. "Ahh, Tiger Stripes," he'd say.

43

Cora
April 2000

Mimi drove west on Route 20, skirting the tips of the Skaneateles and Owasco lakes. She pointed out this and that landmark, talked about the Seneca and Cayuga. There was little traffic, and the Mercedes dominated the road. The sun dropped low in the sky. The deep gray valley dusk enveloped them, punctured by occasional bursts of brilliant light when they mounted the crest of a hill. Cora was conscious of an overwhelming arrhythmia, both inside and outside her body: the car's uneven sway; the slight tire screech and the lurch of recovery as the car rounded the curves on the descent; the bump of her ribs against the door; the troublesome engine knock as they climbed; the sudden radiance that made her cringe.

Mimi was in a dark mood and made no further reference to her purchase of the store property. Questions rubbed at Cora, but she was too tired to press for answers. The fire had robbed her of some insight about her mother. Alice was as elusive as she'd always been.

Outside Seneca Falls, Mimi lightened her foot on the accelerator as they passed roadside markers for the Women's Rights National Historic Park. The town entrance was marked by a phallic water tower painted turquoise. Cora raised her eyebrows. "That tower says, you girls can have your little park, but the power of the penis still rules."

"Oh, yes," Mimi said.

The historic center of Seneca Falls was preserved, appearing much as it had been at the time of the First Women's Rights Convention in 1848. Eighteenth-century saltbox houses, clapboard Federal-style houses, and turreted brick Victorians lined the streets. They were painted wheat and celery green, trimmed in brick red, black, and cream. The historic town was charming, but there was something wrong about the buffed, self-satisfied houses. They reminded Cora of the beautifully painted Sutter Street Victorian in San Francisco where the murder-suicide had occurred. There had been beatings and broken bones behind the shuttered bay windows in California, and probably behind some of these in Seneca Falls, too.

The windows in Cora's childhood home had been covered with venetian blinds. Alice had tugged the cord to close them every afternoon at five o'clock, before Roy Brooks came home from work. Cora had a vivid memory of one particular afternoon when the light crept through the slats to paint bars on her mother's gold-red hair. No one had known about the sounds of fists and breath forced from compressed lungs, her mother's slow, careful movements the next day, her arms pressed close to her body.

How could Cora not have known? Wasn't six old enough to be aware? Even at that age, a playground combatant had given her a black eye when she'd interfered to break up a fight. Why had it been outside her comprehension that her mother could be hurt, or her father beat someone?

The road swooped toward the business district. Mimi turned right on Fall Street and cruised slowly past a brick shell of a building.

"That's the Wesleyan Chapel," she said, "site of the First Women's Rights Convention. Elizabeth Cady Stanton and Lucretia Mott organized the meeting. Part of its Declaration of Sentiments was, 'All men *and women* are created equal'."

Only the walls remained, giving it the appearance of a ruin from Pompeii or Greece. Mimi accelerated past the memorial and crossed the Cayuga-Seneca Canal. The last of the sun seeped through the trees. Mimi parked in front of a one-story brick building with a sign in front, Utica Acres Skilled Nursing. She didn't get out right away. Her nails plucked at the leather on the steering wheel cover. A low fog rose from the damp ground, and the air seemed thick, difficult to breathe.

"Are you going to tell me what we're doing?" Cora cursed her snap decision to ride along on Mimi's excursion.

Mimi shook her head. She removed a briefcase from the back seat and locked the car. They walked beneath two rows of locust trees, crushing a few pods under their feet. At the entrance, Cora noticed the windows were clean, but paint on the sashes peeled in small bits, exposing the bare wood. Weeds grew between the crocuses in the garden.

When they stepped inside, she was hit by the urine smell that clung to the walls and carpet fibers. It was the odor of alleys and bridge undercrossings and other shelters for the world's dispossessed, helpless, and forgotten.

"We're visitors to Room 117," Mimi told the attendant.

He sat behind the counter with a half-eaten Big Mac on the desk. A large bead of ketchup clung to the front of his green medical smock. Although she was nauseated by the mixed odors of incontinence and fried meat, she couldn't avert her eyes from the red droplet.

"East wing. Third on the left." He didn't raise his eyes from his dinner.

Cora swallowed to calm her stomach. She followed Mimi through the reception area and down a hallway lit with strips of fluorescent tubing. They passed a common room crowded with wheelchairs and walkers arranged in a semicircle around a huge TV. On the wide screen, silver-haired actors with perfect teeth and no wrinkles advertised Lipitor while they played golf and danced. The residents' backs were bent, their heads drooped; some slept with their mouths open.

The noise from the television faded as they turned left into the easternmost wing. Mimi disappeared into a room. A step or two from the threshold, Cora heard a bleating, animal cry. Three minutes, she promised herself, and she was out of here. Inside, a woman lay in the bed. One swollen, arthritic hand rested on a coverlet as blank and white as an empty page. Her blue eyes were open, but they didn't move.

"Alice," Mimi said. "Alice. Cora is here."

———

It was not, it wasn't her, it couldn't be.

Roy Brooks had stood in front of Cora, shifting his weight from one leg to the other, black printer's ink forming dirty rinds under his fingernails. He hadn't looked at her, Cora remembered, but let his eyes wander to the venetian blinds, half closed at the windows, to the ceiling, but nowhere in the room where Alice might have sat, where she might have stepped on the flowered carpet, dusted the coffee table, flicked on the lamp.

"She's dead, chickie. The bastard she ran away with, he got a child on her, and she died when it came out." His thumb rubbed the corner of his mouth as if a bit of food or swipe of ketchup lodged there, but there was nothing.

Cora had collapsed on the couch and felt, suddenly, the plastic upholstery flood with moisture. She'd wet her pants. Cora had walked to her room, fourteen steps, aware only of the sodden squelch of her shoes and socks. She'd made sure the bedroom door latch caught in the strike plate. She'd dragged the chair out from her wooden study table and slid it exactly between the table's two legs, hearing the sound of the chair leg dragging on the floor. She didn't change her wet underpants and skirt or her shoes and socks. Instead, she inserted her number two pencil into the sharpener, twirled the handle, and watched the shavings drop into the container. She wanted to push the sharp tip into her arm. She held the pencil close to the blue thread of a vein in her wrist, but pulled back at the last second. Instead, she wrote each of her spelling words ten times: *Say, great, where, help, told, fold*

… The smell of the pink eraser and the movement of her fingers filled an empty place inside her where no light shone, not a single flicker.

The woman lay on her side, facing the door. Her face held no curves, only sharp wedges of cheekbone and a nose beaked with cartilage. A white scrim clouded her eyes. Soft hairs sprouted from her chin. Cora tried to overlay the old snapshot of her mother on this woman. It was hopeless, comparing a young woman's smooth, round cheek and unlined skin with the pouches under this woman's eyes and her coarse, enlarged nose. Cora strained to remember details of her mother's face. The nose, yes, but lots of people had a bump on the bridge of their noses. Did Alice have a mole? Crooked teeth? Cora couldn't remember. What she did recall about Alice was a feeling, the overwhelming sense of her mother's vast restlessness, which never allowed her to settle.

"You don't recognize her?" Mimi said.

"Not one particle."

"It is Alice Brooks, so you might as well stop denying it."

Cora turned. Her teeth rolled back from her lips.

Mimi took a step backward.

"What an ugly way to amuse yourself," Cora said. "You must have people taking numbers to spit on your carcass when you die."

A tremendous struggle of will rippled the muscles in Mimi's face, making her earring jerk. "She is who I say she is: Alice Macpherson. Born February 1, 1918. Ask the nurse."

"How did she get here? Who found her? Who provided the information?" Cora swayed a little on her feet. She felt dizzy.

The patient spoke, a loud, despairing collection of vowels and consonants that filled the room. Her clouded eyes flicked back and forth.

"My mother's dead," Cora said. "She died in 1962. The bastard got a child on her, and she died when it came out." *Say, great, where, help, told, fold* … The spelling words came back to steady her.

"Did you ever see a death certificate?"

"I was seven years old." The room tipped, and she clung with both hands to the footboard of the bed.

"And in all this time, you never looked it up, never checked?"

"She left me, she had a baby, she died. I didn't want to know."

"But you do now, want to know, don't you?"

"Who are you? Someone I met for the first time last week when I was drunk." She squeezed her eyes shut for a second.

Someone tapped on the door. An attendant, hair bundled on the crown of her head with a clip, padded quietly to the bed on her rubber-soled shoes. "Is everything all right?" She lowered the metal railing with a clatter, and tossed back the sheet. The patient's hospital gown had crept above her waist. Cora wanted to shove the attendant aside to cover up the wrinkled abdomen and white, bony thighs.

"We're good, Sandy. Alice had a little moment," Mimi said.

"I'll check her while we're here." Sandy worked her fingers into a latex glove from a box on the bedside stand. She peered down the back of the old woman's diaper. "You're dry today, sweetheart." After making a note on a chart, Sandy tugged with both hands on the sheepskin pad underneath the woman, rolling her onto her back. The old woman's mouth fell open.

"Say, great, where," Cora whispered.

The attendant straightened the old woman's legs, pulled down her nightgown, and belled the bedclothes over her. "She's one of my favorites," Sandy said, raising the side rail.

Cora cleared her throat. "What's the matter with her?"

"She's in late-stage Alzheimer's."

"Her memory is gone?"

"Shot. She'll groan or call out sometimes."

"And you know her as Alice Macpherson Brooks?"

"I don't know about the Macpherson. I'd have to look up her records, but this woman here is Alice Brooks."

"Her Medicare records say that?"

"Honey, we don't bill Medicare for phantom patients. It's against the law."

"But you have documentation that she's actually Alice Brooks."

"Her conservator, appointed by the judge," Sandy inclined her head toward Mimi, "says so."

Cora turned slowly. "You have your fingers in everything, don't you?"

"If you have a problem," Sandy said, "you can take it up with our administrator. He's here from nine to five, weekdays." She was about to add something, but a pager attached to her waistband buzzed. She tilted it to read the numbers. "I have to answer a call."

As she left, she brushed the patient's hair off her forehead, exposing deep furrows. This was a woman who had suffered serious illness, poverty, or unfulfilled dreams. Cora circled the bed, holding tightly to the cold metal railing. Why was Mimi trying to foist this woman on her?

"It is Alice," Mimi insisted. "I have her birth certificate and social security card." She sat in the visitor's chair, flipped the catch on her briefcase, and removed a sheaf of documents.

Cora snatched them from her hand. "Where'd you get these?"

"Her trailer."

"The trailer you can see from the road? That's where she lives?" Cora rocked unsteadily on her feet.

"It was until a couple of years ago."

Cora had trouble moving her lips to form the words. "Where was she? Before?"

"Can't say. I tried to get to know her, but she wasn't friendly, although we're distant cousins. When Sean O'Brien saw her wandering in the road at night, he called me. I went through her papers, but many records, such as work history, seem to be missing." Mimi removed a photocopy from the pile. "Here's her Social Security card. That's how I got her on Medicare."

Cora felt as though she might fall, so she lowered the railing and crouched at the foot of the bed near the old woman's feet. Springs creaked under her weight. She studied the card. Alice M. Brooks. Cora knew the numbers on each Social Security card were carefully structured to indicate the area of the country where it was issued, and included certain sentinel numbers to alert officials to a fraudulent document. It was an arcane code, revealing facts about a particular person, a sort of bureaucratic DNA. What did the code say about this woman?

Her hand trembled as she scrabbled in her rucksack for a pen to jot down the number. Perhaps it could provide a key to Alice's secrets, Mimi's secrets, the secrets of this woman who wasn't her mother. Then she picked up the birth certificate. She ran her thumb over the small nodules in the corner where a registrar had pressed his seal. The certificate was folded in half, and she slipped her fingers between the halves. There it was: Alice Leah Macpherson; father, Jack Macpherson; mother, Ruth Elaine Miller; born February 1, 1918. The certificate was written with a fine, narrow nib, the pen lightly held, the letters delicately curved, the tail of the *J* in Jack dropped with a mere breath of ink.

San Francisco. No wonder New York didn't have a record of her birth. Although Alice had been raised in New York, she'd been born in San Francisco. Within miles of where Cora herself was born, perhaps in the same hospital. Cora's head throbbed.

Something. Some crisis had launched Jack and Ruth Macpherson on such a journey, dangerous during her pregnancy. She imagined how it might have been: Ruth and Jack on the train for nearly a week of slow, rattling days to San Francisco. Ruth's shoes tight over her swollen feet. Her belly like a suitcase in her lap.

Cora rubbed the corner of the certificate and a flake of the thick paper fell away like old skin. "You knew that night at Debbie's."

"When I saw the picture."

"But you didn't say anything."

"You were strange. Said you were here to research family history, but were actually poking into the O'Brien case. I couldn't figure out what were you after. Was it a news story or a roots tour? I'm still not clear," Mimi said.

"Cora Brooks and Alice Brooks, connected by Macpherson's General Store. It wasn't much of a stretch, yet you kept quiet."

"You might be trying to take advantage," Mimi said.

"Of what? Her great wealth? The old woman owns that rust-bucket trailer and a collection of second-hand junk." Cora immediately regretted what she'd said. The woman's possessions might have great meaning for her. This was her life, and she deserved to be spoken of with dignity. On the other hand, she might be a thief. Otherwise, how had documents belonging to Alice Macpherson, whom Roy Brooks said was dead, come into the old woman's possession? Unless Mimi had foisted Alice's identity on her when she was incompetent.

"You might have been after the property, not that it's worth a whole lot." Mimi stroked the drops on her earrings as if confirm that everything about her attire was exactly in place. It was a smug little motion, her touch on the silver, a confident move that telegraphed she knew something Cora didn't.

Cora's heart beat so fast it strained against her chest. This can't be Alice. *She's gone*, her father had said; *she's not coming back. Don't look for her*, her father had said. His eyes had roved over the ceiling, out the window. *Say, great …*

Cora could barely hold her head upright against the weight inside her skull. She touched the skin between her ear and eye and flinched at the pain. A sorrowful tumor must be growing there. Wouldn't it be strange, she thought, if an X-ray could see it?

The white bedspread moved as the old woman's feet twitched wildly. Her eyes flew open. "Curly." The old woman's voice was loud and uncontrolled. "Curly."

Mimi jabbed the call button twice with her gleaming, painted fingernail.

Cora clutched the woman's foot to quiet the tremor. This wasn't Alice, not this poor broken, mindless thing. Light shone on the old woman's thin silver hair, and she continued the same strange cry, the tendons in her neck swelling, her voice cracking, all her body's remaining energy concentrated in her vocal chords. A fine line of blood appeared in the split skin of her lower lip.

"Cora Lee," the old woman called. Her voice was clear this time, the way one's mind suddenly clears before dying. Cora pressed the heels of her hands against her temples. The pain was so terrible it stopped her breath. She couldn't remember any of the spelling words.

44

ALICE
July 1937

Alice Macpherson swore she wouldn't spend her life behind the store counter. There had been nights in the prior summer after her high school graduation when she feared her overwhelming desperation would swallow her. All day, she waited on customers, sold stamps, ordered stock, and paid bills. Her mother, Ruth Macpherson, was nearly blind with cataracts and couldn't be relied on to make change or do the books.

She saw the same people she'd seen all her life: Uncle Will and his sons, Peter and Henry; Aunt Flo Miller; their nearest neighbor, Leland O'Brien; the familiar lecher, George Wright; her older twin cousins, Emily and Edna, Emily who was married, and Edna who was a spinster, and both of them poor, with bad teeth and ill-fitting, homemade clothes. At night Alice left her bedroom window open like an unfastened cage door. How she'd escape, she had no vision. She wanted more from life: a great revelation, some blinding insight or deep comfort.

On this particular Saturday night she drove her father's Model A roadster north on Otisco Valley Road after an afternoon dancing the swing and drinking gin at the Owego Hotel in Preble. At one time Jack Macpherson had distilled bootleg whiskey somewhere close to the store. She knew, by what means she couldn't say, that he hadn't operated his still for many years.

She was rather drunk, and repeatedly squeezed her eyes shut and then opened them wide to clear her vision. Her father had told Alice always to keep two hands on the wheel, but tonight she ignored his warning. Using both hands seemed closed, timid. With one hand on the wheel and the other propped on the open window, she let the car accelerate on the downgrade just past Uncle Will's farm. There was a blind curve at the bottom, and instead of braking she stepped on the gas. Wind rushed over her arm. Strands of hair whipped her cheek. Terror settled between her legs with a strangely sexual stirring; another car might be approaching on the narrow turn. The Model A skidded around the bend. There was no car lunging toward her, only trees lining the road and the gray light of evening touching their tips. She let out a long sigh, mulling over whether she were happy or sad that there had been no collision.

While she was preoccupied, a large buck burst from the trees and raced across the road in front of her. Frantically, she spun the steering wheel. Tires squealed on the pavement, the car's rear skidded, and the wheel recoiled in her hands. When the car stopped, the right rear was mired fender-deep in a ditch muddied by this afternoon's rain. The air stank of overheated rubber. She spun the tires to extricate the car, but they failed to gain traction.

The Model A was tilted backward, and her arms trembled with the effort of shoving open the heavy door. She scrambled down from the slanted running board, dirty and wet with sweat. On the ground, her high heels dug into the wet leaves.

She dreaded another of her father's lectures. Although home was less than two miles away, she walked a half mile and turned left on Plato Crossroad. Maybe she could sweet-talk Leland O'Brien into pulling her out with his Model A truck. Grass was chest high along the road's shoulder. Frogs croaked in the ditches, and the sound seemed very close, as though by some trick of the dusk they were underfoot. This was the first summer since she was nine that she hadn't gone with her father and cousins Peter and Henry to spear frogs in the marsh grasses along the lake. Summer was nearly over, and in two weeks she'd pack her suitcases for Syracuse University. Peter and Henry were upperclassmen there, but she didn't want to go. Her schedule would be class at 8 a.m., lunch in the boardinghouse at 12:10, biology lab from 2 to 5, library after dinner, curfew at 9. It was like being skewered on the point of a frogging spear. For the first time, she felt sorry for the heaving, trembling frogs.

As she walked, one shoe rubbed against her heel. She pulled them both off and dangled them from her fingers. Rocks poked her tender arches. When she reached the farm, she didn't see any lights at first, but then she spotted a lantern in the barn's central corridor and a dim glow in the kitchen of the two-story white clapboard house. She heard from the back stoop a radio playing Benny Goodman's arrangement of "King Porter Stomp."

She knocked on the screen door's wood frame. Volume abruptly dropped, and the door flew open. Leland's green eyes widened. "Little late for you, Al."

"Don't call me that, old man." She hated being called Al. It was so masculine, as if he were saying something unflattering about her.

Leland wasn't actually that old, thirty-five or forty. His nose was sunburned, and his hair was a sandy color, as if even at his age, his hair hadn't given up the struggle to be red. He certainly wasn't good looking, but there was some attraction in his searching eyes, which looked at her more closely than anyone's she knew.

He hesitated, then held open the screen. A single bulb lit the cavernous kitchen, creating a gradation of shadows from yellow-gray to sooty black around the elephantine wood stove. The windows were open, but the humid, motionless air didn't stir the smoke rising from a lighted cigarette in an ashtray on the table.

She approached the solitaire game laid out beside the ashtray and quickly moved several lines of cards.

"You're here to mess with my game?" He hooked his thumbs in the belt loops of his dungarees.

She laughed. "No, I need your truck—and you. Dad's car is in the ditch just south of the intersection."

"Go get your father."

"He'd just come down and ask you."

"And this way, you don't have to let him smell the liquor on your breath."

"Come on, Leland. No lectures." She batted her eyes at him, like she did most men, but with Leland, something was different. She had a hard time looking away from him. His stare made her fcel as though she was about to discover something.

They were silent a minute, the only sound the drip from the sink faucet. He was first to glance away.

"Okay." He stubbed out his cigarette and lifted his truck keys from a nail by the door. On the stoop he slipped into a pair of leather boots from a lineup of muddy footwear. He threw a chain in the truck bed and held the passenger door for her. Inside, cigarette odor oozed from the upholstery. His scabbed knuckles brushed her rayon skirt as he maneuvered the floor-mounted shift lever.

"Jack and Ruth know about your visit to the Owego Hotel?" he said.

"Of course not, and don't you tell, Leland." She thought about her father, his hands so thin she could see the light through them, and Ruth's clouded pupils.

"I'm not, I'm not," he said irritably.

At the accident scene, his headlights caught the car, tilted like a sinking ship. He climbed out. The chain's heavy rattle made her think of captives imprisoned in medieval dungeons. She stood barefoot in the wet grass on the road's shoulder while Leland attached the chain to the Model A's front bumper. He cursed under his breath.

"Can I help?"

"Just stay out of the way."

"Sorry."

"I don't want you to get tangled in the chain and lose and arm or a leg." He turned the truck around so its rear bumper faced the roadster, secured the chain's loose end, and started the truck. For a few seconds the truck's wheels spun. Then the two vehicles lurched forward like a drunken couple struggling to stay upright. Alice slipped behind the wheel of the car and waited until he unfastened the chain. Instead of continuing north on Otisco Valley Road, she followed him to the farm. When she stopped in the gravel turnaround, Leland was already parked. Her headlights caught him about to head up the brick path to the house.

She switched off the engine. The crescent moon was so fragile she could have broken it between her fingers. "Do you have a beer?" she called out the car window. Her voice was weak and girlish.

The frogs continued their intermittent croaking and a mockingbird sang from some dark-leafed tree.

"Go home, Al. It's late. I start milking at 4:30." His eyes flared briefly in a gleam of light from the barn.

"You're going to have one before bed, aren't you, to go with your last cigarette of the day?"

"What if I do? You're too young. Eighteen is barely out of diapers." He slid his hands into the back pockets of his dungarees, as if it were the only place he could think of to put them.

Alice went up the walk and entered the kitchen; the screen slammed behind her. She unlatched the icebox, found a bottle of homemade beer, and pried off the top.

"You need company," she said. Actually she was less interested in relieving his loneliness than in avoiding a confrontation with Jack Macpherson. Perhaps if it were late enough, her father would be asleep at the kitchen table with his chin resting on his chest.

Leland opened his own beer, leaned against the drain board. She felt his eyes on her as she wandered around the room; she touched a platter, a soup tureen probably left from when his mother was alive, and a set of wicked-looking German steel knives. His eyes were very green in the light from the overhead bulb, and his head was cocked to one side as if he were a hunting dog in search of a scent.

"Why aren't you married?" she said. "It's strange, a man living in this big house all alone."

"I'm used to it."

She perched on the edge of the table and let her bare feet dangle. The beer was cold, and its clean, spicy taste was better than the drinks at the hotel dance.

"Am I the first woman to visit you in a long time?" She was a little drunk, that must be why she prodded him like this.

"You're not a woman. You're a girl."

"I'm no girl, and you know it." More to incite his reaction than from sexual attraction, she inched the soft skirt of her rayon dress above her knees.

"That's enough. I'm calling Jack." His words were crisp, but he didn't sound angry.

"I would be fun." She moved her skirt up to her thighs.

He turned to look out the window, and then back at her as if he couldn't keep his eyes away. "I hear you're leaving."

"Syracuse." She breathed deeply to slow her heartbeat. "I'm going to college and never coming back."

"You don't like it here?"

Her body swayed as she leaned forward. She was definitely tipsy, she told herself. "This valley isn't my place. I've always felt as though I was dropped here by mistake. Do you ever feel like that?"

He shook his head.

"Don't misunderstand, I love my mother and father, but I'm nothing like them."

"You don't want to run the store?"

"Never. I want to find … something, I don't know what, but I have to begin looking."

A breeze fluttered through the screen door, making the incandescent bulb sway on its wire. Shadows danced on the walls. "That's extremely interesting, because I'm looking for something, too," He pulled out a chair and sat at the table, nearly touching her knee.

"A wife?"

"No, not right now."

"A girlfriend?" She felt a sympathetic stirring. Perhaps he also felt empty sometimes, scooped out, like a cave with the wind blowing through it. Drunken tears filled her eyes. She slid off the table, a little unsteady on her feet. Her hand on the back of his chair gave her balance, and she straddled his lap.

"This is a really bad idea." His legs moved under her thighs.

"Sometimes you have to do the bad things. You have to reach for what you want, go away and not come back." Her arms crept around his neck.

He dragged her hands away, but kept them clasped in his fists.

"We're both looking," she whispered. The beer taste was strong in her mouth.

He sat very still. A pulse beat in his neck just below his jaw line. Then he nodded as if he heard her for the first time. The air between them was warm with the smell of sweat. She stood, fumbled under her dress for her panties, and stepped out of them. It took her awhile to unbutton her dress, because her fingers worked the buttons clumsily, but while she did it, she watched him remove his shirt and lower his zipper.

When she straddled his lap, the coarse hair on his thighs prickled her skin. His tongue entered her mouth, wet and aggressive. She didn't close her eyes, because it made her dizzy. Instead, she looked down at his hands while he slipped her dress and brassiere off her shoulders. His fingers were scabbed and cracked and nails broken from farm work.

He moved to touch her between the legs, but she flinched at the thought of his rough hands. Instead, she shifted slightly and guided his penis inside her. Her face was above his, and as they moved, he lost the watchful look he always had when he glanced at her. His mouth slackened as though he were lost.

He climaxed too quickly for her. She moved restlessly against him, but couldn't come before he softened. The kitchen seemed sad and empty to her now, one plate and cup upside down on the drain board, no curtains, the bare table gouged with knife marks and burned by a hot kettle.

"I didn't tell you what I'm looking for." He kneaded her bare legs with his chapped hands.

She barely heard him, lost as she was in the desolation of the unhappy kitchen. "What?"

"What I'm looking for. Have you ever heard of the Irish gold?"

She pulled back. "Is this your idea of pillow talk? You don't wait for me, you come too fast, and now you want to talk about gold? What's the matter with you?"

His cheeks reddened with embarrassment, but he continued, clearly focused on this line of thought. "Did you know I once had a brother?"

"Of course. Everyone knows about him. He collected a fortune in gold for the Irish rebellion and disappeared with the treasure. It's like the story of the goat eating the food at the 1917 graduation picnic. Someone brings it up at every dance and fish fry."

"Well, no one knows whether it's true about the gold, but it's certain he disappeared. How did you hear about Seamus?" His gaze flicked here and there, on their shadows cast on the kitchen wall, and on her dress and underwear on the worn wooden floor, as if he didn't want her to read what was in his eyes.

"This is stupid. I don't want to talk about it anymore. I'm going home." She dismounted from his lap, but her legs wobbled when she tried to stand. One hand reached out to clutch the edge of the table to steady herself.

He rose abruptly, catching at his pants before they fell to his ankles.

"Do Jack and Ruth ever talk about your sister, Abby?" The snick of his zipper and clank of his belt buckle seemed loud in the high-ceilinged room.

"What is it with you? She died before I was born." She jammed her fists into the armholes of her dress, ignoring her panties and bra on the floor.

He grasped her hands to keep them from the buttons. "It's very possible my brother and Abby Macpherson were lovers."

"I don't believe it. You're making this up." The sweat on her hot skin cooled suddenly, and she shivered.

"Not only that. I think you are their child."

45

Cora
May 2000

Cora didn't want to get up. She imagined roots growing out of her skin, punching firmly through the sheets and mattress, digging through the tile floor into the dirt, spreading fingers in every direction so it was impossible to move. She was a plant with unbreakable roots, an oak tree, fixed, so she would never have to arise, see anyone, think about painful things. Others could urge her, doctors, psychiatrists, but it would be useless.

A paper cup of water on the night table was too difficult to lift. When the psychiatric technician insisted she eat, her head was drawn downward, too heavy for the weak stalk of her neck. Her back curved, her fingers couldn't maintain her intention of holding a fork, her eyes drooped closed.

Sometimes she remembered how she arrived here: Del had come to the nursing home after a call from Mimi. He'd found her curled at the foot of the old woman's bed, unable to sit or stand. He'd driven her to this psychiatric hospital and had her admitted on a temporary hold.

Dr. Laura Stern, who looked like a fourteen-year-old masquerading in a white coat, sat beside Cora's bed with the case file open on her lap. "You have a major rapid-onset depression. I'm prescribing Zoloft for you." Her straight brown hair was twisted into a knot at the top of her head and anchored with a spring clip.

"In a few days, you'll feel much better, but it may be as much as six weeks before it becomes fully effective."

Cora watched the ends of Dr. Stern's hair, which had popped free of her clip, jiggle like little beckoning fingers above her head. Cora didn't speak or move. She was certain the relentless weight that pinned her to the hard, plastic-covered mattress would last forever.

After Dr. Stern left, Cora rose from bed and peed, then lay down again with her arms curled against her chest. The ambient dust, pebbly ceiling, buzz of the fluorescent light fixture, and smell of her roommate's sweat and oily hair sucked her energy.

Brenda, the woman in the other bed, talked all day and night. Words flew out of Brenda's mouth and hovered like black crows. She paced in and out of the room. She opened and closed the door, flushed the toilet, ran the shower, ripped the sheets off the bed, dressed and undressed, accused the staff and other patients of theft, conspiracy, assault, rape, and sodomy. Cora lay on her side, squeezed her hands between her knees, and breathed only the shallowest of breaths.

The sun crept in during the morning and inched across the tile floor and up the bare wall, but Cora was awake only briefly to swallow a pill while the attendant watched. Her sleep was heavy, packed with a dense concentration of ferocious nightmares about the drug cartel cutting off her head.

When the world outside the window was dark, Cora's eyes bulged with wakefulness. Her thoughts attacked, stuffed her head, sucked away any joy in cleanliness and food, every impulse to walk or run, all desire to talk to anyone. If only, if only she'd told someone back then when she was a child that her mother was being beaten. Cora should have told Andrea Chan's mother why she fell asleep in the afternoon in front of her friend's TV: she got no sleep at night, crouched among the shoes and dirty underwear in her closet to hide from the noise of hitting.

If only she'd spoken to a teacher. If only she'd asked her mother about purple bruises that climbed out of her shirt collar like creeping mold, about a cut lip that puffed with injured flesh, and a fingernail ripped deep into the quick. If only she'd been more aware, that last afternoon and evening, she would have said, I love you. She should have said please and thank you. She should have picked up her muddy Keds from the living room rug; eaten all the salmon loaf Alice prepared for dinner, though Cora hated the little bones. There were other things she'd done: Stealing a dollar from Alice's wallet when she was five. Pulling up the bedspread over the rumpled sheet and blanket instead of making a proper bed. Failing to flush the toilet. Telling fibs.

Cora wasn't the only one awake at night. After lights out, there were sounds in the hall outside their room—a groan, a spate of sobbing. On this particular night, Brenda's voice ratcheted up and she gathered her anger around her like an overcoat. A male patient, she claimed, had masturbated, then shaken her hand without washing. Brenda slid closer to Cora's bed. "You should have taken care of this. Why is it you never take care of things? I could have AIDS. I could be pregnant. You should see to it he's castrated."

Cora heard Brenda's hoarse breath and pulled the blanket over her head. She smelled the corrupt odor of her own body. "I can't. I'm not a doctor," she said.

"We need a knife. You search for a scalpel."

Cora coiled her limbs more tightly against herself. "Go away." She began to cry loud, hoarse sobs.

Brenda's mouth opened in surprise.

Cora wrapped herself in sheets wet with tears and snot. Her heart beat in her throat and she wanted only to be alone, away from this crazy woman and doctor and the psychiatric technician and the drugs and toilet. All of it was exquisitely painful, like the most unbearable high, screaming tone.

"He'll be here again tomorrow," Brenda said. "He'll want to shake my hand. You said everything was going to be all right, but you lied. You're a liar. I can't believe a word you say."

Brenda snatched Cora's hand, and with her big blunt fingers, she twisted the pinkie. The snap was not loud, just neat. A small, tidy sound.

46

Alice
1937

"I never saw much of her," Mrs. Martha Nesbitt said. She'd been a distracted mother of four boys in 1917, living in San Francisco next door to Jack Macpherson's sister, Mary, and her husband, Emmett.

Alice watched Martha Nesbitt pour more tea for the two of them from a blue and white china teapot. With a quick glance at her guest, the old woman plucked a silver flask hidden behind the sofa cushion and topped off her cup with a generous splash of liquor.

"The war was on, and the dreadful Spanish flu made the city a mortuary. No one went out unless they had to. School was cancelled, and my boys were home all day, under foot and squabbling with each other.

"A few times that fall, I saw her walk toward the ocean in the afternoon. All bundled up. I would have thought she'd be used to cold, being from the East and all."

San Francisco was an upside-down city, Alice thought. It was late August now, but a chill fog huddled outside the windows. The oil-burning stove in the living room was lit to warm Martha Nesbitt's thin, white legs.

"I had my sons, and they kept me busy washing and ironing. Oh, my, the stew, and beans, and mashed potatoes I cooked. I wanted a girl, but I wasn't going to fill up the house with boys to get one. That girl, that Abby, had a pretty face and long blonde hair, I do recall that."

The night Alice had fucked Leland O'Brien and learned his secret had blasted her life to bits. She drove home in a drunken fury and shook her father, who dozed at the kitchen table. She screamed at him to tell her the truth, but he rubbed his cheek with his thick, yellowed fingernails and lied to her. A tidal wave of anger and outrage surged through her. She knew, oh yes, she was sure Leland's suspicions were true. Her fingers dug into Jack Macpherson's arms, and she rattled his fragile bones. Ruth stumbled from bed, and in the hours that followed Alice wrang the truth out of them like water from rags. Abby was not her sister but her mother.

A code of silence had been shattered, and a lifetime of small wounding incidents that had hollowed her out, gutted her of some vital organ, suddenly made sense: odd glances between Jack and Ruth, as if they looked at her but saw someone else; a puzzled wrinkle in Uncle Will's forehead when she played in a dress from an old trunk; odd, intense stares from her much older cousin Emily, one of Abby's closest friends. All these added up to some truth she only then began to see. What provided the explosive force of her screaming battle with her father was her certainty. Something was missing in her—had always been missing.

She aborted her matriculation to Syracuse University, packed her bags, and bought a train ticket for San Francisco. Ruth begged her forgiveness, pleaded with her to stay. To Alice, her words were babble. It was as though the story of Alice's birth, cloaked for nearly two decades, was so fragile it might dissipate if she waited too long.

She rode her anger not helplessly but with relentless energy to Syracuse, onto the transcontinental train, and across the country to Oakland. On the ferry to San Francisco, wind whipped her red-blonde hair as she sailed past the gigantic piers of the nearly completed Bay Bridge.

With an address on an old envelope given to her by Uncle Will, she found where she'd been born—a narrow city lot overgrown with weeds. The house had never been rebuilt after the fire. Broken concrete and burlap sacks full of rusted tin cans littered the site. A skinny black dog snuffled and clawed at a hole, searching for a rodent.

Alice's whole torso ached from the weight of her suitcase. She ground her teeth to contain her disappointment. What had she expected, that her real mother wasn't dead, but waited on the front step?

Next door, an old woman peered at her through the lace curtain. Alice climbed the steps of the narrow, white-painted Victorian, knocked, and used the story she'd invented during her train trip: she was an investigator trying to locate next of kin for award of a World War I pension.

Martha Nesbitt was somewhat senile and considerably drunk, or the ruse would never have worked. Inside, Alice caught the odor of old age she associated with Jack and Ruth—worn shoes, dry skin, and soft-boiled eggs.

"That girl with blonde hair and her mother, they mostly stayed inside, like they were hiding." Martha Nesbit gave Alice a sly glance.

Alice set her cup on the carved, curlicued table beside her chair. "Why do you think so?"

"I guessed it was because it wasn't the mother's baby, like they told everyone, but the blonde-haired girl's."

Alice nodded. At last, someone told the truth. "Did you ever see any sign of the father? He may have been a war veteran, that's why I've been asked to investigate," she lied.

"Not a whisker. I figured he was a doughboy who left a seed in the garden and then went to France. That's what you're looking for, isn't it? The father?" Martha's red-rimmed eyes opened in mock innocence.

"Yes. Next of kin are entitled to service benefits," Alice said, with no notion of whether it was true.

"Well, I can't help you there. Never saw any uniforms at Mary and Emmett's place. My boys were too young for military service. Four in five years, if you don't think that wasn't terrible."

"Do you know where the girl with the blonde hair is buried?"

Mrs. Nesbitt startled Alice by taking out her false upper teeth and placing them on the tea table. "My son Harold bought those for me, but they're not worth a darn. Never did fit right," she lisped.

The teeth gleamed whiter than anything in the room. Alice shivered. It reminded her that the only remnant of Abby was her bones and teeth.

"Terrible. A terrible way to die, burned to death," Martha Nesbitt said. "Emmett got Mary out, then went back and rescued the older woman, Ruth, and the baby. He was badly burned on his hands and face. Couldn't get to the girl. It wasn't until the next day, after the ashes had cooled enough, they found her."

"Were there—" Alice could hardly summon enough breath to speak. "Were there church services? A funeral?"

"I don't remember. Everything was higgledy-piggledy after the fire; our house was damaged, so we moved into a tent in the backyard and lived like gypsies. I cooked meals on a spirit stove and washed clothes by hand in a tub. No hot water. The boys, oh my, they ran wild." Martha Nesbitt unscrewed the top on the flask.

In a lightning move, Alice snatched it and held it out of the old woman's reach. She breathed quickly as if nearing the end of a race. "What happened to Mary and Emmett and the others?"

"You are a naughty, nasty girl. For sure you're no investigator." The old woman bared her toothless pink-white gums.

"Where did they go after the fire? What happened to them?"

Martha Nesbitt's eyes didn't waver from the flask held high above her head. "Friends from the church took them in. They lost everything, not a toothbrush or pair of underdrawers between them."

"There must have been a church service for the dead girl," Alice said.

"Not that I ever heard." When Alice scowled, she said hastily, "They had no money. She might have gone to a pauper's grave."

Alice's hand shook as she handed the flask back to the old woman. Since she was a child, she'd been aware of an interior hollowness. She'd stuffed herself with mashed potatoes and ice cream. Her body grew puffy for awhile, but the fat didn't make her feel better. She didn't lose weight until she discovered that liquor and danger eased the emptiness for a few moments, sometimes hours. But the feeling always came back. It was as if she were a skeleton, ribs cupping a dark empty space, her skull empty, her bones scraped of marrow.

She bent over her lap and cried until her skirt was soaked and her legs were wet. Days and years stretched before her without a promise of relief, and it seemed almost too much to bear. Adding insult to injury, it was humiliating to break down in front of this horrible woman. Alice could have released her misery in front of Ruth, but Alice had always recoiled from revealing herself to her grandmother. There had been so many times when she'd longed to throw off Ruth's arm from around her shoulders or duck away from her kiss. Surely she never would cry so helplessly when Ruth could hear her.

"You cried a lot when you were a baby," Martha Nesbitt said. "I could hear you when I got up at night to pee. When you have four boys, your bladder isn't very strong."

She picked up Alice's tea cup and poured a splash of liquor into it.

47

Cora
May 2000

Through the open window of Del's guest bedroom, Cora heard the frogs croaking in the marsh. The day had been warm, as though the weather gods were luring her to believe summer was nearly here, but she was still wary. Weather in New York could turn bad at any moment. She'd been at Del's nearly three weeks.

He'd spotted the metal splint taped to her finger when he arrived at the psychiatric hospital for visiting hours. "Assault, plain and simple, but the incident will never be prosecuted," he said in a low, dangerous voice to Dr. Stern. "The roommate is too mentally impaired to face charges. Where would the court recommend she be placed? Back in a psychiatric facility, where you people have inappropriately housed her with nonviolent patients."

Dr. Stern nodded at the same time she stared at a spot on the wall over his left shoulder. The conversation flew past Cora, too far above to touch her. The pain of her broken little finger was disproportionate to the thin twig of bone. It throbbed so intensely she cradled the hand close to her chest. If she admitted the truth, she welcomed the pain. It released her for awhile from the relentless grip of her anxiety.

Against Dr. Stern's advice, Del removed Cora from the hospital and established her in his spare room while he contacted other facilities. All the beds in the area were full, and by the time one opened up, Cora's layoff from the *Standard* had become effective. Del, despite help from Nathan as her next of kin, had been unable to reverse a decision by Cora's healthcare provider to terminate her coverage.

So she remained here, alone during the day while he worked, mostly sleeping, swallowing the pills he pressed into her hand along with a cup of water. The Zoloft prescribed by Dr. Stern seemed slow to take effect.

At night Del reclined in the leather chair he had hauled upstairs from the living room and positioned at an angle to her bed. During those dark hours she awoke but didn't move. Instead, she lay curled up and often cried in an odd, seamless way, tears wetting her face without any conscious onset of sadness. He pulled tissues from a stack of boxes on the bedside table and awkwardly wiped her cheeks, his big hand nearly covering her face.

Del had left early that morning for a two-day law enforcement conference in Buffalo, and Frieda had volunteered to sit with Cora. During the evening Cora heard her start the washer for a load of Del's laundry. Frieda will still act like a mother if she lives to be a hundred, Cora thought. She smiled, the first time in weeks, and drifted back to sleep.

About ten o'clock, Frieda set a cup of tea on the bedside table and settled into the chair. Drago, who slept on the bed at Cora's feet, raised his head protectively, then gave an enormous yawn. A breath of sweet spring air drifted in the window. Light from the reading lamp touched Frieda's curly white hair and turned it into spun sugar. She was so small in Del's big leather chair, her legs barely able to reach the footrest, that she had the look of a sympathetic fairy godmother, twinkling with inner light.

She studied Cora a moment, then leaned over to brush her damp, tangled bangs off her forehead. "I hear you found your mama."

Cora nodded. Frieda's hand against her forehead smelled old, like the pages of a favorite book. An annoying curtain of tears appeared on Cora's cheeks, and she wiped them away with the back of her hand.

"It's all right, sweetie," Frieda murmured.

Cora sat up and blew her nose on a tissue. Drago's front paws scratched at the bedspread.

Frieda rotated her gold wedding ring, held there permanently by her arthritic finger joint. "Awhile back, I told you I stopped at your grandparents' store once," she said finally, "but I never gave you the whole story."

"Not now." Cora tented her arms over her head to ward off Frieda's tale. With the help of drugs, she was beginning to disinter herself from her relentless thoughts.

"All right, but it's not a bad story."

"My brain is too busy. It can't take any more."

Frieda nodded. She picked up her cup and blew on the tea to cool it.

"Especially about my sick family." The sharp, lively scent of peppermint stirred the air. Cora flexed her fingers, stiff with disuse. She leaned over to scratch Drago behind the ears.

"It was strange, I'll say that about it," Frieda said.

Cora felt a tickle of interest. Her dreams during these weeks had been a jumble of dying cows, burning buildings, bloody Alice, and the mysterious third man.

"All right, I'll bite the hook," she said.

A smug look crossed Frieda's face. She settled herself more firmly into the chair and spread a crocheted afghan over her legs. "I remember it really clearly, for a reason you'll see in a little bit. It was the summer of 1941, a hot sticky day with no rain. Eddie called in the afternoon at my boarding house and invited me to the weekly fish fry and dance at Munger's Resort.

"I was sixteen, and we'd been dating four months. We saw each other once a week, sometimes twice, in those months before Pearl

Harbor. I wore a little sundress—I still remember it—a cute thing in a sunflower print that dipped low in the front."

Frieda was a good storyteller, with a nice eye for detail, Cora thought. In her mind, Cora began to embellish the reminiscence beyond the boundaries of Frieda's narrative: Eddie wore a pair of khaki pants and a short-sleeved striped shirt. His smooth-shaven cheeks smelled of Old Spice. As they drove along Otisco Valley Road, he and Frieda rolled down the car windows and held their arms out like children, inviting the air to tickle their arms and faces.

"Eddie was low on gas," Frieda said, "so we stopped at the store. He filled up from the pump out in front. A little gas spilled on his shoe—I remember the smell." They went inside to pay and buy two orange Nehis.

Cora felt the story unfold. At the same time she heard Frieda's narration, she was also reliving it in some fold of inherited memory. The bell jingled as they opened the screen door. The store was dim; low afternoon sun caught the edges of the lettering, Macpherson's General Store, on the front window.

"It was mostly empty," Frieda said. "Nobody had cleaned the winter ashes from the potbellied stove, and the only things on the shelves were motor oil and beat-up cans of Dinty Moore beef stew. We put nickels in the soft drink cooler and fetched out two sodas."

She stopped. Her face seemed transformed for a moment and Cora saw the young woman Frieda had been—observant, eager, in the first flush of her sexuality. Cora saw Eddie as he popped the caps, handed Frieda one, took a long swallow, and deliberately nestled one of the cool, sweaty bottles between her breasts. There was a slight sound, perhaps the scrape of a shoe on the plank floor, and the two of them jumped apart.

"Eddie called out to raise someone so he could pay for the gas, but nobody answered. We wandered to the back. I remember it smelled bad, like spoiled meat or rotten fruit. All of a sudden, out of nowhere, someone appeared behind the counter."

Frieda sipped her tea. Drago jumped down off the bed and trotted over to stand beside her chair arm.

"He was very, very old," Frieda said, stroking Drago's head. "Even now, when I'm old myself, he still seems ancient in my mind. His hair was white, of course, but his skin, every little bit of it, looked like shoe leather. He badly needed some Mary Kay products, but it was too late, of course. The damage was done."

The old man sold Eddie a pack of cigarettes and rang up the cigarettes and gasoline on a huge cash register with brass keys. Something flickered in the corner of Frieda's eye, and she saw a woman sitting in a straight-backed chair behind the counter.

"It was a woman, blind or demented. She tipped her head back at a strange angle and swung it from side to side, as if she weren't human, but an animal, sniffing the air.

"And here's the interesting part," Frieda said. "She spoke in a kind of raspy voice like she hadn't used it for a long time. The old woman said. 'Alice, is that you?'"

"I only saw them that once," Frieda said. "After we arrived at Munger's, I forgot about them."

Her story, told in the quiet room, seemed fresh now, steaming like today's dinner. "That was the first night, the first time. Do you know what I mean, Cora?"

Cora understood. Frieda's generation didn't speak easily about sex, but Cora wrote their story vividly in her mind. Very late, after they'd eaten fried fish and cole slaw, after they watched the reflection of the moon on the lake's surface, after they danced on the dock and rubbed their bodies slowly against one another, they drove to Eddie's apartment and made love on his narrow bed. He fell immediately asleep, making small huffing sounds, but she lay awake. Her skin glistened with sweat.

Frieda pressed her fingers against her mouth as if she'd said too much.

"It's okay. I'm not shocked," Cora said.

"It wasn't the same back then as it is now. I was sixteen, and all my life I'd been taught that girls waited for a wedding. As I lay there, I thought about the old couple again, and realized it was guilt, what I felt in the store. I prayed it wouldn't happen to us, that huge lump of guilt."

Frieda continued to talk, but Cora no longer listened. After Alice had disappeared, Roy began taking Cora to work with him on the Saturday shift, because there was no one to look after her. She'd sat in the foreman's dingy office while her father and the other printers hoisted huge rolls of newsprint onto huge rotors and launched the press with buttons on an electric controller box.

As she sat in the foreman's ink-smeared swivel chair, she felt the pound of the press in her buttocks. Her homework was fanned out in front of her, but she paid it scant attention. Instead, she fished the *Star* from a stack of tabloids. She savored the pictures with gluttonous pleasure: Elvis sightings, movie stars disfigured by botched surgeries, mutant babies, women abducted by aliens. Every hour or so, her father popped in. A blue jump suit covered his clothes, and a disposable paper cap perched on his head.

"You bored yet?" he said.

"I've got plenty to do."

He tossed her a bag of potato chips from the lunchroom vending machine. "You're not reading the *Star*, are you?"

"Nope." She used her toe to slide the bundle of tabloids under the desk.

"Sorry this is taking so long, Chickie."

"It's great, Pop."

It wasn't great, and they both knew it, but the Saturday beat of the presses compressed the two of them into a unit. The rhythm and noise disguised their guilt. What her father had done, she sensed only in the vaguest way. It had to do with her mother, something Cora had nearly forgotten, and when she tried to recall it, she vomited. She knew he was guilty, though, because she saw the shame in his face day after day until his guilt was as familiar as his crooked nose.

Cora had felt that same arrangement of her own features. Sometimes she traced those lines of guilt with her thumb. Over her cheekbones and nostrils. Around her mouth. As the presses beat in her ears, she remembered her mother's hairbrush still on her parents' dresser after she left. Red-gold hairs were trapped in the bristles. She remembered a single bedroom slipper in the dust under her parents' bed. Once, when she remembered the small blood spatters in the hall, it led to another recollection, the terrible odor of a blood-soaked rag lying in the garbage can.

By the time each shift was over, her father's face was gray. His eyes bulged as if they were about to explode, and she felt it, too, an excruciating expansion of her guilt-swollen chest. When she was eleven, she stopped going to the plant with her father on Saturdays. She was old enough to stay home alone, she told him. Still, she knew what she'd done—forged a dark and slippery pact with her father to forget who Alice was, and how she'd disappeared.

A year later, after her father told her Alice had died having another man's baby, he never spoke of her again. The two of them agreed to scrub her from their past. Roy came home and washed printer's ink from his hands with Lava soap until they bled. Cora sometimes distrusted his version of her mother's death, but she hid her discomfort. She turned thirteen; her hips curved and her breasts swelled. The new flesh surrounded her childhood guilt until it was imbedded in her like a grain of sand.

If she hadn't conspired with her father, she might have found Alice waiting tables or cleaning motel rooms or washing berries in a cannery, before her memory was wiped away. Cora might have asked her why, screamed at her: why had she taken her purse but not her little girl? Why, in all those years, hadn't Alice written a birthday card or dialed her telephone number?

Cora wanted to say to this woman she hadn't recognized, who was old and frail and not the person she'd been, she wanted to say, did you ever wonder who went with me to buy my first bra, how old I was when I kissed my first boy, whether I passed algebra, if I was married, did I have children? Didn't you wonder, Alice Brooks, when you saw a curly-haired woman in a restaurant eating pizza, if she looked like me?

A hot flash brought heat to Cora's chest and neck. She buried her face in the pillow and smelled the sweat on her temples. In the lamplight she saw Frieda had fallen asleep, her cheek rumpled against her shoulder like a yellowed page.

Slowly, like the cold ooze of river mud, Cora realized it was useless, all these thoughts and questions. Time had crept past the point where there would be answers. She'd refused to think about Alice, and somewhere along the way, she'd lost the opportunity to understand her.

It occurred to her that the losses of her childhood were the result of decisions made, not just by her or her father or Alice, but by others over generations. Her father's brutality and her mother's disappearance expressed the accumulation of thousands of incidents that had scoured their lives and those of their forebears like pulverized rock carried by the glaciers that had carved the Finger Lakes. Each tiny pebble in those lives—a careless tuberculin cough, a mother's momentary distraction, a heat spell, a snow storm, a letter written in blue ink, a touch, a kiss, a few moments of sexual heat, a shovelful of dirt, a predawn finger of whiskey—had moved Roy and Alice to the night they parted and beyond.

48

Alice
August 1942

Alice flipped her welding mask down over her face with a sharp nod of her head. The mask's shaded lens left her in darkness, but she'd positioned her welding stick just an inch from the steel seam. She tapped the stick against the metal surface and a green flame leaped between the wand and the pipe. In a second, the metal glowed red hot.

"Closer, closer," she whispered to herself. She pressed the electrode against the round, glowing pool of molten metal just as she'd been taught.

Everything in the world was dark except the intense green flame. Her hand guided the welder slowly, smoothly along the joint until the flux-coated stick had melted to the length of a cigarette butt.

She jerked her chin to toss the mask up to her forehead. Carefully she hung the electrical conduit over a peg. The back of her leather glove dabbed at her sweaty forehead. It was two a.m. on the night shift, but the noise in Bethlehem Steel's San Francisco shipyard that pressed against her temples was as binding as the strap that secured her clumsy welder's mask.

Huge fans rattled as they sucked up the smoke and chemicals that hovered over the deck of the freighter. Acetylene saws keened as they sliced openings in steel plates. Engines on the huge gantries and cranes roared. An army of hammers pounded slag off the welds. A whistle screamed lunch hour.

It was October 1942, and this old freighter was being renovated in the Bethlehem shipway for duty as a military supply ship, as Japan's naval power marched from one Pacific island to another, headed for California.

After Alice had settled in San Francisco in 1937, she'd worked as a hotel maid, cigarette girl, waitress, movie theater usherette, and, when the war started, a milkman. But her real life during that time was lived on Sundays, when she tramped the rows of tombstones in dozens of Bay Area cemeteries. She traveled miles by bus, streetcar, and ferry to pore over brittle yellow records, wade through weed-strewn graveyards, and use a wire brush to scrub the lichen from granite stones, but she found no grace of Abby's grave.

Her efforts to trace Seamus O'Brien were equally frustrating. She was stubborn enough never to contact Leland again, but through dozens of letters, she determined that the man Leland suspected was her father hadn't appeared in any U.S. or British army records, or lists of dead Irish independence activists.

The restlessness she'd always felt was still with her, that reamed-out hollowness that pushed her to look for another job, a different apartment, a new man. And there were as many new men as new jobs, men she slept with once or twice before she saw how small they were, not strong and confident, not comforting, but sometimes unsure, confused, muddled. Once she divined their weakness, she was frantic in her haste to get rid of them.

For awhile after she started a new job or met a man, she felt complete, but the emptiness always returned, like water draining from a sieve. Now, she thought perhaps the gnawing hollowness was behind her. She loved welding. This job in the shipyards was different; the physical demands filled her up like a holiday meal. Her small womb-like workspace on this particular part of the ship was inside an eight-foot diameter pipe lying horizontally on the upper deck.

Tonight she worked with her boss, Simon Hardcastle, because her usual partner, Ellen Small, hadn't reported for work. Alice and Hardcastle worked back-to-back on parallel seams that joined two half-pipes, one that curved over their heads and one under their feet. The two halves resembled an eight-foot-wide metal tunnel. When their weld was complete, the seam would be tougher than the original steel. Other sections exactly like theirs would eventually be tilted upright by a huge crane, and lowered to the deck for the final welds to form the ship's exhaust stack.

Alice felt the power she had under her control—a dangerous electrode that burned so fiercely it could damage her vision if she even glanced at it without the smoked lens shielding her eyes. The heavy welder's mask challenged the muscles in her neck and chest. The energy it took to brace her arms and feet in the eight-foot steel tube, hold the apparatus, sometimes at odd angles, and create a smooth bead of molten metal along the seam of the weld gathered every scrap of her attention. The world was as distant as a speck on the horizon, at last unthreatening and neutral.

With the sound of the dinner whistle, the thick slurry of noise in the shipyard faded. Voices and laughter floated on the stiff night wind that blew in off the Pacific. Gulls flew so close she heard the leathery flap of their wings.

"It needs another pass," Hardcastle said.

"It's dinner time, and you need a nap."

"I could fire your uppity ass." He looked critically at their welds, still too hot to touch with an ungloved hand. He was a short man, bald except for a gray fringe over his ears. His chin receded, and Alice might have dismissed him as insignificant, but for the hard, knotty lumps on his hairless head that gave him an air of toughness and tenacity. He headed a crew of ten women, and handled their quarrels and inexperience with a fairness Alice hadn't expected.

Alice took off her mask, stuffed her gloves into the pocket of her jacket, and retrieved her black metal lunch pail from a storage chest on the deck. She dragged a wooden crate along the deck into a circle of women hunkered down, each on her own makeshift seat.

Looking south, five more shipways marched along the west side of San Francisco Bay, aligned like pencils on a desk. Seven-story scaffolds cradled the ships' immense hulls while gantries moved whole prefabricated decks and wheelhouses into place. The moon paled under the intensity of thousands of mercury vapor lights.

The welders propped their elbows on their denim-clad thighs, feet planted mannishly in their heavy leather boots. They'd unscrewed the caps of their thermoses, and wisps of steam rose from their hot coffee. When a spate of deep, uneven laughter rose from the other end of the deck, the women turned to stare at the huddle of men who refused to join them during breaks. Men performed the toughest jobs—overhead welding, tungsten arc welding of aluminum and brass, delicate cuts with the torch—and held themselves apart.

"Girls, you've gotta know this," said Sharon Brown. She was a black woman, nearly fifty, which cast her as the mother figure for the other women. "Ellen got word today. Joe's missing on Guadalcanal." Sharon was a close friend of Ellen, Alice's work partner. "I seen her this afternoon. She's staying with her mother on Potrero Hill," Sharon said. "I don' understand her. Not a tear, her face so white, white as cotton. A girl like that, she need to scream and cry."

Alice froze with her Spam and lettuce sandwich halfway to her mouth. The smell of her food, which she'd looked forward to during the long night of cold and physical exertion, nauseated her now. She threw it back into her lunch pail and closed the lid. Ellen had married Joe in January, two days before he boarded a ship for Pacific. Both eighteen years old, they had been sweethearts at Berkeley High School.

Alice lit a cigarette. The smoke stung her throat, numbing it after a few drags. Ellen had shown her their wedding photo, kept in a little leather folder in her dungaree pocket. The couple stood outside under a canopy of trees. The baby-fine blonde hair that Alice usually saw tied up in a blue bandana flew around the girl's head like a halo. Ellen was taller than Joe by a couple of inches in her pumps, but he stood up very straight with his arm stretched awkwardly around her shoulder. Despite the strained pose, his face was wreathed with a smile, and sunlight slanted toward them in such a way that his eyes were shining.

Alice sucked angrily on her cigarette. Abby and Seamus had been robbed of their chance, too. If the first war hadn't come, they might have married and settled here in San Francisco.

Alice found it strange to think she was nearly twice as old now as Abby had been when she was born. Alice had seen pictures of Abby snapped at about that time. Her favorite was a portrait of Abby wearing a cotton summer dress that showed the shadowy outline of her arms through gauzy sleeves. Her hair was tied back, and her face, although young and fresh, seemed infused with experience, as if some adult perspective had settled firmly upon her.

The whistle shrilled to signal the end of the meal break. As the women gathered their lunch buckets and ground their cigarettes under their boot heels, Hardcastle joined them.

"Ladies, you've undoubtedly heard that one of our own group— Ellen—has lost her husband in the Pacific. She'll be gone a week, and I'll have a replacement filling in for her beginning tomorrow. As you go back to work, remember this tragic death is exactly why we're here. We're building ships that'll help our boys drive those dirty Japs back to their lousy little islands. So we've got to work hard, work fast, and work careful."

His voice was unemotional, but his eyes scanned the circle carefully, looking directly at each them, as if they deserved his respect and unflinching resolve. Alice felt her anger dissolve a little. Hardcastle was one of the few men in the shipyard who appreciated what they were doing. The clothing and equipment were heavy, designed for men, and the physical demands of welding were more difficult for women, who didn't have the muscle mass to hold the awkward positions. The chemicals released during the welding process affected women's lungs more than men's.

Alice first met Hardcastle in January, when she'd taken over a predawn milk route for a creamery delivery man who'd enlisted in the navy. Fog had gathered close to the ground, as it often did just before dawn, and she heard the engine chug of a pickup, which slid into a driveway. The door slammed with a tinny thump.

"You like this job?" His hair was plastered to his scalp—from his welding mask, she learned later. The empty milk bottles clattered in her wire carrier, sounding loud on the quiet street.

"It pays the rent," she said.

"Come to work for me at Bethlehem. I'm recruiting women welders for my crew. Good pay, and you'd be doing your part for the war effort."

Alice laughed. "A welder? Why not a machinist or a pipefitter?" It seemed impossible a woman could work as a welder.

"I'm not looking for them. Only welders." He rubbed his palm over his cheek, whiskery after his all-night shift. She looked at the neat white milk truck, thought about the immense, sprawling ships, and said yes.

Now, the knot of women began to dissolve. They rebuttoned their leather jackets and pulled on their gloves. It was 3:30 a.m., and they were scheduled to work until 6. Alice and Hardcastle walked back toward the steel tunnel they were welding, careful not to trip over the electrical conduit from compressors used to operate the welding equipment and metal saws.

Hardcastle spoke to her in a low voice. "I got word a few minutes ago the Merchant Marine captain and some of his officers are making a surprise visit tonight to check on progress."

"Is there some problem with the refitting?"

"I don't think so. The big guy is probably anxious to leave port behind and get out to sea."

They began a second pass over the seams in the stack. Sweat dripped from under her mask; the smell of burning flux filled her nostrils; blackened slag crunched under her feet. The next time she flipped up her mask to reach for a new stick, he was talking to three men, two dressed in blue gabardine uniforms with gold braid on their hats, and one in khaki and a garrison cap. These must be the merchant marine inspectors.

"Tomorrow night we should be ready to put the stack together," Hardcastle was telling them. One seemed to be the captain, because he had more gold on his hat, a short man with exceedingly small feet encased in his spit-shined black shoes. His uniform jacket cupped a basketball-sized belly. The second man, she thought, might be the first mate, since he wore narrower gold braid and displayed fewer ribbons. The third stood several paces behind the others. He was dowdy in his khaki pants, short-sleeved shirt, and flat cap, yet he seemed the most alive of the three. He leaned forward slightly, balanced on the balls of his feet, as if he were prepared to fight. His eyes, under thick blond eyebrows, roved over the weld and narrowed as he watched a gantry lower a bulkhead assembly slowly to the deck.

He looked at her and frowned. What was he staring at? She selected another stick, fitted it into the electrode's clamp and climbed back inside the pipe. He still was watching as she flipped her mask over her face.

When Alice finished for the night, she arched her back to ease a cramp. The shift had been difficult, working directly under Hardcastle's scrutiny, afraid she'd make an error while he was watching. Not only that, the two of them had pushed to complete the section so the next shift could begin preparations for assembly of the four large pieces.

"You'll get used to it after a year or so," Hardcastle said. "You'll have muscles like a regular Charles Atlas."

"Charlene Atlas," she told him. She walked among the crowd of other workers out of the shipway to the supply depot building. There she changed out of her dungarees, boots, and leather jacket to slacks and a wool coat.

Alice stopped outside the gate just past the sentry shack to light a cigarette. It was nearly dawn, but the fog seemed to clutch at the darkness. Streetcars lined up at the curb to deliver A-Shift workers, then lumbered along to the boarding area to wait for C-Shift.

She felt small and lost, as if some inner support had been jerked away. She thought of the ships buttressed by scaffolding as the keel was laid, as the decks were built, one atop the other, how this supporting structure was removed, and the ship was forced out into the Bay with another ready to take its place within hours. Tears stung her eyes. She was tired, she told herself. Sleep should be her priority, go to bed before the fog lifted, the sun came out, and she felt lost in the vast expanse of light.

The touch of the cigarette on her fingertips soothed her. She shielded the lighter flame with a cupped hand and inhaled. From a few feet away, through the thin smoke, she watched the roly-poly captain and his first mate climb into the back seat of a navy vehicle driven by an enlisted man. The dowdy underling in khaki carefully closed the car door and stepped back respectfully as the vehicle crawled slowly through the crowd of off-duty workers and accelerated into the street.

"You're not good enough to ride with them?" Alice asked.

He wheeled around. Alice thought perhaps he didn't recognize her without the mask on her forehead and bandana covering her head. "The stack. I was welding on the stack," she said, her eyes bold and unwavering.

"I remember. Green eyes," he said. "And I begged off on the ride. Three hours with the brass is two hours and fifty-nine minutes too long."

"You won't be promoted to captain with that attitude."

"Chief engineer is as far as I want to go. I plan to make chief after the next trip."

His close, hot gaze fixed on her like a tight sweater that pressed intimately against her skin. Even though she was exhausted, she was suddenly reluctant to catch the trolley to her boarding house.

"Let's go somewhere for breakfast," she said. "There's a diner about two blocks from here that has good ham and good fried eggs."

"Even better, let's go to a place where I can get a good Jack Daniel's." Before she could form a reply, his fingers encircled the back of her neck, pressing on wiry tendons sore from the weight of her welding mask. He urged her toward a trolley whose bell clanged for departure. His shoulder muscled the accordion doors, and he braced them open with a hard, meaty hand. She would remember that right hand later, the two long scars across the back and the twisted nail on his ring finger. Today, however, she barely noticed them. They leaped aboard and slipped laughing into a slatted wooden seat.

They were silent on the ride. Up in front, an off-duty driver in a blue wool uniform, coat unbuttoned, talked through a green fabric partition to his unseen friend at the wheel. A waitress in white uniform and thick-soled shoes read a paperback novel. Alice couldn't think of anything to say to him, and didn't try too hard. If he wanted to talk, let him make conversation. He was partially turned away from her, to allow long legs to extend into the aisle rather than bump the seat in front of them. When the trolley rounded the corners, their shoulders brushed each other as if they were dancing. Their bodies approached and retreated, each pull away making the air between them sharp with electricity.

His scent—a faintly medicinal soap and warm skin—blotted out the smells of moth balls and damp socks and ingrained dirt she'd become accustomed to on the trolley. Her nostrils spread to snatch more of it.

When the trolley arrived in the Lower Mission district, he arose and seized her hand. They jumped to the curb on the same foot, with the perfectly matched rhythm of Fred Astaire and Ginger Rogers. The beveled mirror in the Black and White Tavern reflected the two of them darkly as they entered, almost in silhouette above the bank of liquor bottles. The customers, all men, turned on their stools to stare as they passed. She caught the smell of onions and potatoes frying in the kitchen.

The booth was narrow and she slid in across from him and fumbled in her purse for a cigarette.

He stacked his hands one atop the other. "I'm Roy."

She glanced up at him quickly, realizing she'd ridden all the way to a downtown bar with a man whose name she didn't know. Why hadn't she asked?

"Like Roy Rogers?" she said, to cover her confusion.

"Exactly, except no palomino, no white hat. Your name isn't Dale Evans, by any chance?"

"What if it were?" She leaned over to cup the flame from the lighter in his hand.

"We'd be meant for each other, I guess."

"Well, my name's Alice."

"Too bad. What would you like to drink?"

"Scotch. Always Scotch."

He raised his eyebrows inquiringly.

"My father—that is, my grandfather—drank Scotch. In fact, he made it illegally in a little distillery in the hills of New York state." It surprised her she said anything about Jack Macpherson, especially a secret he'd never whispered a word of during all the years she'd lived with her grandparents. She'd only heard about his bootleg liquor from gossip among her school friends and oblique jokes during fish frys at Munger's.

They talked then, their heads nearly touching across the table into which dozens of lovers over the years had scratched their initials. The wood was sticky from many spilled drinks.

He picked up her left hand and ran his thumb over her third finger. She felt the roughness of a nearly healed blister on his skin. "I'm assuming you're not married," he said.

"I'm not, and I don't know if I ever will be. I don't think I'm cut out for it."

"Of course you'll marry. It's what all women want," he said fiercely, his cheekbones hatchet-sharp in the dim light, and at that moment, she believed him because he was so sure.

"You're not wearing a ring," she said.

"I won't marry until I'm absolutely sure." He talked about himself, about his father, who had died in France during the Great War, and his mother, who'd contracted tuberculosis when he was three. Although Irene Brooks had been managing to care for him with help from an elderly neighbor, a meddling public health worker had wrested him away, and he'd spent his boyhood years in Father Fitzpatrick's Catholic Boys Home in Oakland.

"I saw her again a few Sundays when I was ten, but by that time she was in the sanitarium. She died a few months later," he said. "The home wasn't a bad place. There were cooks and laundresses to feed us and wash our clothes; the brothers oversaw the dormitories and taught school classes, but they were just caretakers."

Alice felt a tremor, as though an iceberg was slowly breaking up. He, too, had lost a father during the World War, and had been separated from his mother by unfeeling people. His mother, too, had died young. He had been left alone to make his way in a hostile world. She and Roy were alike, she saw in that moment, and her heart contracted.

49

Cora
July 2000

Shower water trickled off Cora's hair, down her shoulders and over the ends of her fingertips. It was unremarkable, yet the patter of drops on the tile and the cloud of steam swirling against the glass door, these small details felt as if they'd been offered to her like candles on a birthday cake.

It had been eight weeks since she crawled onto her mother's bed at Utica Acres and five weeks since the night Frieda sat beside her. That evening had been a turning point. When Cora visited Dr. Stern, the psychiatrist was certain the Zoloft had finally kicked in. The ends of her hair had quivered in the spring hair clip as her stethoscope jiggled around her shoulders. Perhaps fourteen-year-old psychiatrists are occasionally right, Cora thought, but she knew privately that sharing the guilt with Jack and Ruth Macpherson had brought her back. Guilt had consumed them, perhaps over Alice's first disappearance, when she'd fled the East and headed for San Francisco.

Alice had disappeared not once, but twice. Perhaps more. She had fled Roy and Cora, and spent three decades somewhere. She might have moved from San Francisco to the South to the Midwest. Perhaps she'd lived in Los Angeles or Florida; some broken relationship had brought her back to the Otisco Valley, the road, the ruined store. Cora considered the lie she'd told Alice on the last night, her flannel pajamas soft against her back and legs, her hair wild around her head from the bathtub steam, not wanting the pool of toothpaste and saliva under her tongue. She'd wet the brush with water from the tap. "I did, Mama," she'd said, her eyes were open wide. Alice nodded, not listening closely, tilting her head to listen for Roy as if he were a wild animal about to leap out at her.

As a child, Cora had woven stories for her friends about children in dark caves, girls abducted by aliens, boys born with two heads. She'd spent her adult life with stories about violence rolling off her fingertips. Her father had never outlived his guilt. Neither, apparently, had Jack and Ruth.

Now she wanted to know how Ruth and Jack Macpherson fitted into her personal story. Why had Alice scrubbed them out of her life? Cora had never met them. They'd made no visits to San Francisco, and Cora had not once heard her mother talk about them. Was Cora's own story connected in some way to the death of Sean O'Brien? Why had the ruins of the store been set afire?

Since Frieda's visit, Cora had hobbled toward normalcy, one small moment after another. This week, she'd shampooed her hair without urging, walked three miles on shaky legs along the country road behind Del's place, and tossed a rubber ball for Drago. Each action returned a piece of her.

As she rubbed herself dry with a thick towel, she examined the wrinkles in her arms and calves where unused muscles had gone soft. She dressed and went downstairs to the kitchen, where Del sat at the table sipping coffee. She had a memory of him from last night in the recliner beside her bed, his reading glasses propped on his head.

He wore his uniform, and his belt and holster were draped over the back of a chair. A laptop stood open on the table. She wanted to put her fingertip on the chin fold where his necktie met his Adam's apple.

He looked up. His eyes widened, and his face had such a look of calm happiness that Cora felt sick. Dizzy and short of breath. She might slip back into craziness and disappoint him. Drago squirmed against her calves, trying to push her forward. She patted his head for a few seconds, and then slid two pieces of bread into the toaster.

Del sat on the edge of his chair as if it might at any moment be jerked out from under him. The metal filaments in the toaster popped as it warmed, and after a minute, he began to leaf through the *Syracuse Post-Standard.*

"What's the news?" she said.

His mouth quirked into a half-smile. Her inquiry was a milestone. When she'd been sick, the hour-by-hour record she'd kept in her head as a journalist—car crashes, fires, arrests, meetings, elections, scandals, new highways, ribbon cuttings, and murders—had been suspended. Her brain waves hadn't spent a second's electromagnetic vibration on news.

Del handed her the front section. "Bush is the nominee, apparently." He rubbed the side of his cup as if to anchor himself in the new reality of Cora at his breakfast table.

"Have I been asleep for twenty years?"

"He's no match for Gore, although he'll probably get good advice from his father," Del said.

"Did you pay attention to your father?" She sliced her toast into small pieces. It seemed more palatable that way.

"Not until I was about to graduate from college. By that time, he was sick, and he died a few months later."

She rolled a pill in her palm thoughtfully before she washed it down with a swallow of coffee. "How is she?"

"The same. She hasn't changed since Nathan was here a month ago."

"I remember now. He sat beside my bed and bit his nails. I wanted to tell him to stop it."

"It was a big meal for him to digest. You, I mean, not the fingernails."

"Only a depressive mother and a previously unknown, demented grandmother," she said.

Del's cell phone rang. He flipped it open and slid his laptop in front of him. "Yeah, I got it. I made a couple of changes, and I'm sending it back to you." He tapped the keyboard. "What?" His back straightened. "Damn, he's not going to go sideways on us, is he?"

He jotted down a number in the margin of the newspaper. "I'll call him as soon as I hang up."

Cora studied Del over the rim of her cup.

His fingers drummed the tabletop while he waited for the new party to pick up. "Onstad? Somer. I understand you had a question about the press conference."

Cora heard the faint pulsations of Onstad's rapid, scratchy voice.

Del's face twisted into a ferocious scowl as he listened, but when he spoke, his voice was calm. "There's no way it can come back to bite you. They were clearly involved in trafficking."

Toast caught in Cora's throat.

"I'm handing you the case tied in ribbon. You get the media coverage, and your stats will look good."

Her vision blurred. The pills she was taking must be scrambling her brain. He was turning over Judith and Tyler to the DEA? She reached across the table and clutched his arm, upsetting her coffee cup.

He held up a finger. "They aren't going to say a thing, because nobody will believe them," he said into the phone.

The spilled coffee spread across the table, running under Del's laptop. He tipped his chair back and ran his fingers through his hair in frustration. She jumped up to pull a fistful of paper towel from the roll.

"Maybe my department should go it alone. The county DA could file the case, rather than the federal prosecutor." He cradled the phone against his ear and lifted the laptop to allow Cora to blot the coffee.

Del nodded in agreement with whatever Onstad was saying. "This case will make you look very, very good. Yeah, okay. See you at nine-forty." He clicked off and breathed a noisy puff of air.

"You're arresting Tyler and Judith?"

A shadow of hurt crossed his face. "You believe I'd do that?

"I … didn't think so, but then you began talking about trafficking."

"We're going to do a show and tell with the recovered coke."

Her eyebrows shot up. "You found it?"

"Tyler told me where it was."

"You didn't beat it out of him did you? Just kidding," she said after looking at his face.

"I told him he needed to do it to protect his mother."

"He knew that all along. Why did he give it up now?"

"I told him he could come to live with me once he's out of rehab."

Tears flooded her eyes. It felt strange, to be such a Weepy Wanda. "That's good, Del. Really wonderful."

He swept the sodden newsprint into a pile and carried it to the wastebasket, careful to hold the dripping pages away from the perfectly pressed creases in his uniform pants. "I've got to go. The press conference is at the farm, and I need to stop at the office first."

"I want to come."

"No way." He wiped his hands and buckled his duty belt around his waist. "You haven't driven in nearly two months, and the shrink hasn't given her okay. I hate to think about you on the road."

"I walked three miles yesterday. I've called Nathan, and my checkbook is balanced. I'm better. Honest. Give me the keys to your truck."

"No."

"If you don't, I'll call Frieda and have her drive me."

"For God's sake, she's a menace on the highway."

"I won't be on the road long, half hour out, half hour back."

"This is a very bad idea."

"Please, Del. It's a big piece of the story, and I'm going crazy with nothing to do."

"Okay, okay. If you get out there and feel bad, let me know and I'll send a trooper to drive you back." In the mud room, he lifted a set of keys off the hook and tossed them to her. "You hurt my truck, I'll take it out of your hide."

———

Del's truck was one of those big-shouldered vehicles that rolled on huge tires and took a ladder to climb into the driver's seat.

With flabby legs and no hand up, Cora was sweating by the time she settled behind the wheel. Her hands trembled as she fastened her safety belt and started the engine.

Along the road, a fat, green hay crop rose in the fields, demanding to be cut. Trees seemed to rush at her, and light darted through the canopy of leaves like flashes of gunfire. She took a left at Plato Crossroad and surfed the low hills to the farm. Fields had been fertilized, and the smell of manure infected the air. At Sean's house, the shades were drawn. Boots that had lined the back step were scattered along the brick path.

She parked in the gravel-strewn turnaround, which was crowded with media vans, state police cars, and the DEA's black SUVs outfitted with black tinted windows. In the center sat one DEA vehicle with the hatch open and a stack of plastic-wrapped packages fanned out inside. Uniformed troopers and DEA agents stood alongside, ostensibly to protect the cargo, but mostly to make a good camera shot. Neville was in uniform, shoes spit shined and brass polished.

Del stood several paces away, near the derelict shed where the boar had been penned. He talked to a tall man in his forties that must be Onstad. The DEA supervisor wore a suit rather than a uniform. His shirt was blinding white in the sunlight. Both of them had their arms folded across their chests.

After a few minutes, Onstad stepped in front of the drug-laden SUV and adjusted his cuff links. Cora clicked on her mini-recorder and flipped open her notebook. Del stood to one side, clearly out of the TV shot. Officers from both organizations lined up behind them with their hands in the fig-leaf position.

"I'm pleased to announce that a joint task force of drug enforcement officers has interdicted a large shipment of cocaine and disrupted a major pipeline between Central America and the U.S.," Onstad said.

"The DEA, with assistance from the New York State Police," he nodded vaguely in Del's direction, "has located and arrested the individuals responsible. The cocaine, worth millions on the street, was transported by two individuals ostensibly working here under a guest worker program."

Onstad went on to outline how the two individuals, Rico Izarraras and Pedro Chacon, had held hostage the owner of the farm, only to flee when law enforcement moved in to arrest them. They later were captured in Miami on their way to Central America.

Del wore his law enforcement stance: jaw thrust forward, legs apart, hands folded over his crotch.

Cora thought about the press conferences she'd attended over the years, the piles of drugs hauled from secret vehicle compartments, guns confiscated from homes, stolen cars discovered in shipping containers at the Oakland docks. She'd always known that law enforcement's story was in some way shaped and manufactured, but this scenario was a masterpiece.

Her pen moved slowly. As she wrote, she glanced up now and then at the other reporters. They looked like chickens, bobbing their heads to peck up bits of news as Onstad talked. Didn't they notice how flat the story was? Why weren't they asking more questions? How had the drugs come to be left behind? Why hadn't word of the kidnapping emerged earlier? Had Mrs. O'Brien been under protection until the suspects were caught? Where was she now?

The reporters ignored the story's complexity—the whole river of circumstance that flowed beneath the carefully skewed facts. She thought of all the thirty-second television stories or five-inch and ten-inch print stories these journalists produced, flimsy pieces riddled with omissions if not outright lies fed them at press conferences. Not that she was blameless. She'd refused to delve into her mother's disappearance, and had been willing to let Del's version of the facts go unchallenged to spare Tyler. Those were her ten-inch stories.

Onstad wrapped up with some statistics about the increase in seizures in his jurisdiction during the last year and answered a couple of fluffy questions. Afterward, he did individual standups with the television reporters while holding one of the wrapped cocaine packages. He threw a bone to the *Cortland Standard* reporter about Troop C's valuable assistance.

The television reporters folded their tripods and hefted their cameras into the vans, which peeled away in a hail of popping gravel. Onstad was in the passenger seat of his SUV talking to his driver when he noticed Cora and rolled down the window.

"Anything I can help you with?" A breeze flipped his tie, and he smoothed it with his hand.

"I had a quick question for the major."

Onstad frowned in Del's direction, but the ring of his cell phone distracted him. The car rolled off. Two meadowlarks called from fence posts along the road. The pines around the house stirred. The quiet seemed to swarm with microscopic life.

"That was an amazing piece of manipulation," Cora said.

"Proactive law enforcement at work." Del unknotted his tie and took off his jacket. The uniform was too warm for the humid day, and he blotted his forehead with his handkerchief.

She touched his arm. "Where did Tyler hide it?"

"Guess. You're extremely familiar with the spot."

"Come on, Del. I'm weak and cranky."

He took her hand and walked inside the tumbledown shed where the O'Briens had kept the boar. He propped a boot on one of the planks around the pen.

Cora looked over the top rail. A large hole had been dug in the urine-soaked manure.

"Plastic-wrapped and sealed. What better place?" Del said.

50

Cora

July 2000

Cora slipped her notebook and mini-recorder into her jacket pocket. "I'm going to hang around awhile."

Del looked alarmed.

"Ten minutes. I promise." She pulled her shoulders back and tried to arrange her features to look normal. What was normal?

Once Del's car had turned onto the road, Cora sat down in the middle of the turnaround, hugging her knees to her chest. With the farm abandoned, grass grew between the pieces of gravel, flattened only by today's traffic.

The dust from Del's car settled slowly. Gravel dug into her skinny butt. No one had been here for weeks. Birds had taken over as the primary occupants of the farm, whipping from the eaves of the barn to the silo to the evergreens around the house. A male cardinal flashed past her with a scrap of cloth in his beak for a nest.

Rust had crept over the grain bins and tractors, the harrowers, hay mowers, and balers. At the rear of the property, the mud-spattered mobile home tilted precariously on its foundation. Once the drug-bust story had run its course, it would be as though Seamus and Leland, Judith, and Tyler, Sean, even Rico and Pedro had never lived here.

Clouds raced toward her from the south, and the play of light and dark set her heart beating erratically. She lowered her head and ground her knees into her eye sockets. Hopelessness licked at her, but she struggled against it. There was something she had to do; tell a true story. Dig up the truth about Sean's death.

She rose unsteadily to her feet and brushed the dust off the seat of her pants. Past the barns, milking shed, and grain bins, she stepped onto the porch of the small, weathered building Sean and Judith had used for a farm office. A rotted plank gave way under her foot, and she jumped clear.

When she tried the door, she found it was unlocked. Hinges complained as she pushed it open.

Inside, a rough pine desk was stacked with file folders, unopened bills, advertising circulars, and two ledgers with torn covers. A swivel chair was pushed back as if someone had risen a moment earlier, and across the desk, a captain's chair was held together with baling wire. Cold ashes leaked from the pot-bellied stove in the corner. Their sour odor made her feel uneasy. Someone had leaned back in the swivel chair, toes touching the floor for balance. Someone had swung open the stove door and shoved in a thick chunk of wood, dipped a pen into an inkwell, stroked numbers into the ledger.

The green metal filing cabinet was of more recent vintage, a battered relic from a government office. The drawer screeched when she slid it open. It was empty except for a stack of yellowed newspapers and a box of rubber bands. On the desk, bills had red, overdue flags on them. She thumbed through the business cards. Livestock judges, feed suppliers, large animal veterinarians, and real estate agents, including Mimi Shafter.

A bookcase held decades of hard-cover ledger books. As she thumbed carefully through them, some of the brittle pages crumbled. In the book for 1916 and 1917, several ledger sheets had been cut out with a razor blade.

Cora lowered herself into the swivel chair and combed through the desk drawers. Pencils, ballpoint pens, a bottle of dried Elmer's glue, smudged envelopes. Dust coated her fingers as she ran them over the desk's surface. It was gouged and scarred from its hundred or so years. Once the farm was sold, it would be hauled to the dump.

Her hands covered her face. An eyelid quivered. She felt dizzy, as if a plug had been pulled, and her will circled the drain. She longed, down to the soles of her feet, for the bed in Del's guest room. She imagined the scent of laundry soap on the pillowcase, the weight of the blanket on her shoulders.

A buzz in her ear, like the vibration of a power line. Was she sinking back into depression? She held her breath to eavesdrop on her own thoughts. Voices. Sean and Franklin and Tyler, every victim and perpetrator she'd written about in her twenty years as a journalist. They flowed by in a parade, not saints, not demons. Secretive, noble, conniving, selfless, flawed. Human. She'd write the story although everything was against her. There was nowhere to print it, she was still recovering, Sean and Franklin were dead, and not many people cared.

She cocked her head. The door of the pot-bellied stove was half-open. When she lifted the latch and stooped to peer inside, she saw a half-burned sheaf of papers. Only the blackened corners remained, curling delicately upward. She poked at them with a yellow pencil, and when the lead point touched them, they collapsed. She was about to fasten the door when she spied a flash of white at the back of the combustion box. She brushed the debris aside and plucked it out.

It was the top half of a page, all but one corner darkened to the color of toast. She set it carefully on the desk and pulled up the chair. A thin coat of oily soot covered the fragment, a real estate agreement dated August 6, 1999. It agreed to a ninety-day listing for the house, buildings, and three hundred acres of Maple Leaf Farm. Sean O'Brien was listed as owner, and the listing agency was Sentinel Realty.

Cora pawed through the pile of business cards. Here it was. Sentinel Realty. Mimi Shafter, owner/broker. Mimi had told Cora she barely knew Sean, yet her firm had listed his property last summer when he was desperate for money to reimburse the cartel.

Sean must have called Mimi and asked her to list the farm, either because he'd been referred to her or knew her from her family roots in the valley. They'd signed papers for the listing, perhaps at this very desk, and agreed on Mimi's fee. Presumably she'd shown the property and then met with him, or at least talked, when the listing expired. Yet Mimi had lied about knowing him. And someone had destroyed the paperwork documenting the listing.

It hadn't been Sean. Smoke had been drifting out the rooftop flue of the office on the day Judith had first greeted Cora in the farmyard. Sean had already been dead five weeks, and any residue in the stove would have been consumed. Judith might have burned the documents before she moved to Syracuse, but why? It wasn't a secret Sean had been trying to sell. For some reason, Mimi wanted to keep her acquaintance with Sean a secret.

Cora held the paper fragment to her nose and sniffed its sour charcoal scent. Franklin had confessed in his suicide note that a third person had joined their clandestine search for the gold. She slipped the scrap into one of the scruffy gray envelopes from the desk drawer. On her way out, she closed the stove and shut the office door behind her.

51

Alice
1961

Before sunup, the sky was clear, rare for San Francisco in June, when the fog often hovered near the ground like a clingy child. The pillow was cold against her cheek, and she grunted as she shifted to look out the window. Her ribs hurt. To distract herself from thinking about the pain, she focused on the patch of yellow-blue over the neighbor's roof. A jet's contrail inched across empty space. What must it be like, she thought, to pilot a plane, balanced so precariously on the lip between safety and death?

The shower sputtered in the bathroom, and she heard the slide of the curtain on the metal rod. She scrambled out of bed, alarmed she'd slept so late. In fifteen minutes, Roy's breakfast had to be on the table. The sleeves of her chenille robe were twisted, and the pain of forcing her arms into the sleeves made her stagger. Without bothering to comb her tangled hair, she limped past Cora's closed bedroom door to the kitchen, ran water into a pan and slid it on the stove.

As she measured oatmeal into a Pyrex cup, she spilled some onto the linoleum. She looked at her trembling hand, with the ragged, dirty nails. Pain overtook her as she knelt to clean the mess. She couldn't risk making him angry. It had taken her a week to gather her courage to ask him, and today she needed to have an answer.

He was there, suddenly; with his catlike movements, he'd startled her. She noticed he'd missed some spots when he shaved under his jawline. The small clumps of whiskers grew there like weeds. He carefully poured cream from a small earthenware pitcher around the edge of his bowl of hot oatmeal. The red plastic clock ticked on the kitchen wall. His silence was thick and immensely heavy. She remembered a magazine picture of an African woman bent double under a huge bundle of firewood. Alice could feel the woman's back, which bent and bent until she had no independent will left except to bear this burden.

"Simon Hardcastle called," she said. "He's left Bethlehem to start his own sheet metal company."

"He's too old to go out on his own. What does he know about running a company?"

"His son was a business major; they'll be partners." She sat across from him and propped her elbows on the tabletop with a cup of coffee between her palms.

"There's something wrong with this." He sniffed the cream in the pitcher.

"The milkman brought it yesterday."

"Then you left it in the milk box outside too long."

She removed the oatmeal bowl from his plate and set it in the sink. It was useless to argue with him, and whatever she said would fuel his anger. She thought of all the small accommodations she made, dozens every day: served meals at exactly five-thirty, ironed his boxer shorts, vacuumed twice a day, stopped wearing her favorite perfume, didn't talk to the neighbors or answer the door, hid her bruises.

He spread strawberry jam on his toast without looking at her. When had his eyes begun skewing away from her, a little to the left of her head, just above her face? At the time they first met during the war, while she was working at the shipyard, he said looking at her was better than the taste of JD rocks to a thirsty man.

Maybe it was after he beat a seaman, breaking his jaw and cheekbone, and the merchant marine discharged him. He was skilled with machinery, and the job at the *Standard* had seemed like a good fit, but he missed the prestige of being engine room chief of a huge freighter. He felt demeaned as just another shift worker in the pressroom.

She heard Cora's bedroom door open. Small feet padded down the hall to the bathroom and the door closed. Alice didn't have much time.

"He wants me to come to work for him."

"Who?"

"Simon. He wants me to come back to welding."

"That's a laugh."

"No, I'm serious. He said by the time the war ended, I was the best of anyone on his crew, man or woman. I'd have regular hours like the men, and he'd sponsor me in the union. The pay is good, enough so we could start a college fund for Cora. I know I'm rusty, but I can get it back, I know I can. He said I was a natural, and I think I was. It was hard work, but I did it as well as anybody."

Her words seemed to bounce off him. She imagined them like popcorn puffs, lying white and fragile at his feet.

He took a long swallow of coffee. Printer's ink formed a black crust in the creases of his fingers. "Is my lunch ready?"

"Roy, listen." She was breathing quickly. "I need to do this. I need to get out; sometimes I think if I don't ... don't have something to fill the empty time, all the empty space, I'll go crazy."

His mouth slackened for a second, as if he were afraid, as if he were still the boy who was torn away from his mother, who insisted he was treated well in the boys' home. He blinked and the child was gone. His lips tightened against his teeth.

So softly she barely heard it, the cup went back on the table. She braced herself.

"Mama, I don't want oatmeal. I want a doughnut." Cora's hair was tangled in the back, and her pajama top was half-caught in the pants' elastic waistband. Her eyes flicked back and forth between them.

"Hey, kiddo." He wiggled her ear lobe. "I've gotta go." He snatched his lunchbox off the shelf and slammed the back door. In a moment, the car roared out of the garage.

Alice's knees trembled and her ribs hurt again. What had her life come to, when she didn't run or hide to avoid a beating, but cowered like a craven fool? She despised herself.

Cora crept close and leaned her head against Alice's hip as if to hide in the solid flesh.

Alice knew she should gather her daughter fully against her, rock her, stroke her sweet-smelling hair, sing in her ear, but she couldn't. Instead, she felt lost in her emptiness. It was as though she'd been scooped out like a squash, all the rich golden meat dug away until only the thin, pliable shell remained.

She needed the job Simon Hardcastle offered. Going back to work, using her arm muscles, bracing her back and legs, guiding the melting flux along the seam, seeing the two heavy steel sheets bond through her efforts and her skill—she wanted it. She desired it so passionately it was almost sexual. She needed to be herself, apart from his fists and shoes, away from his silences and shouts.

She was ashamed she even wanted to be away from her girl, the only child she would ever have. Alice knew she should be a better mother, but there was a connection missing. A cord was unplugged from the lamp of her caring. She'd tried to mend the separation. Once, she and Cora had written poems to each other. Another time they took the bus to the beach. It was cold, and the wind slapped their faces and crept between the folds of their clothes, but Cora remembered the trip and begged to go again.

To Alice, she and her daughter seemed as distant as two planets.

Cora hardly moved, as if Alice were a skittish woodland creature who might bolt at any second. Alice's heart slowed. Her icy hands warmed.

"No doughnuts this morning. Bacon and eggs." She opened the refrigerator, leaving Cora in her rumpled pajamas like a small island surrounded by dangerous seas.

———

The slam of the front door announced Cora's arrival from school. "Mama, where are you?"

Alice sighed. The question came each time Cora returned, whether five minutes or five hours had passed. Her books tumbled onto the coffee table, where they sat until homework time after dinner. By that hour, Roy would be into his third JD. At the kitchen table, Alice refilled her coral Bakelite pen from a bottle of ink. Everyone used ballpoints now, but she enjoyed the ritual of filling the pen's barrel.

She continued to fill out the application for the job with Hardcastle and Son. She had ridden the bus to the company's office that morning, requested the application forms from Simon's secretary, and tucked them in her purse. She needed her Social Security number, her doctor's telephone number, and other information from home to complete the forms.

"Mama, who are you writing to?" Cora ran her hand over Alice's arm, and she jumped.

"An old friend."

"Will we get to visit her?"

"No. He lives far away, in Maryland." Alice thought that would be a vague enough fib to divert her, but Cora persisted.

"Is that as far away as China?" Cora burrowed her way under Alice's arm. She smelled Cora's school-girl odor, ironed clothes, sweaty socks, and warm skin. It seemed to slice its way between her ribs toward her heart.

Alice jerked away. A fine line of blood appeared on Cora's cheek, where Alice's ragged fingernail had scratched her. "No, it's not," she said, more sharply than she'd intended. To heal Cora's hurt look, she pulled a piece of the stationery from her writing box. "Here. Sit next to me. You can write a letter."

"To your friend?"

Alice's pen hovered over the space labeled "next of kin."

"No. Why don't you write a letter to your daddy?" Tonight after Cora was in bed, she'd ask Roy again.

52

Cora

July 2000

Cora propped Mimi's business card on the dash of Del's truck. Her eyelids felt heavy, and her foot didn't keep enough pressure on the accelerator. The pickup's windshield grayed, and the engine vibration scrambled her nerves. She veered off the road into a turnout. The truck noise modulated to a mournful hum as she shifted into Park. She'd settled into the corner of the driver's seat and rested her head against the door when her cell phone rang.

"How'd it go?" Frieda asked. "I couldn't reach Del, His phone's on voice mail."

Cora rubbed her eyes with her fist. "Tyler is out of it."

"Thank goodness. Where are you? You sound strange."

"Parked along the road."

"Stay right there. I'll come get you." Frieda could sound very commanding when she wanted to.

Cora cleared her throat. A lump seemed to have settled there. "It's okay, Frieda. I'm on my way to Mimi Shafter's office."

"No, you're sitting on the side of the road."

"For a minute."

"Go home instead of going to Mimi's. She's an odd one, if you don't mind my saying so, the two of you being related and all. Not that you're anything alike."

Cora smiled, feeling a little better. "Thanks for that."

"No, really. You have a kind heart."

"Frieda, you're the only one who thinks so, and you may have taken a fever."

"Nonsense. That's why you report."

Cora didn't think she was kind. She wrote about murders for a living, after all. Described in some detail terrible atrocities that were committed on vulnerable flesh and bone. Mothers and fathers read those words, sisters and brothers, sons. Daughters. But in her own defense, she tried to do something more. Tell the story. Assemble the facts into a narrative that made some sense. What personal history, what internal forces had led the murderer, the victim, and the bystanders into this nexus? Without an organized narrative, families and friends remained suspended in a purgatory of recollection and denial and recrimination.

She started the truck. With the window open, the engine noise filled the cab. The narrative for this story wasn't evident yet. The truck pulled out onto the road, and the accelerator crept up. She had a moment of disorientation before a hot flash began to smolder under her skin. Her hands on the wheel were red, and her face burned. In the visor mirror, she looked sunburned. Mimi had befriended Alice, not to help her cope with her past or with old age, but to take advantage of her. For reasons that still didn't make sense.

Mimi had lied about her relationship with Sean and Franklin. Mimi was almost certainly the third leg of the stool in their search for the gold. Mimi had insinuated herself into Alice's life and became her conservator. Mimi had appeared on the valley road while the ashes from the store were still smoldering. Mimi. Mimi.

Perspiration dripped down the back of Cora's shirt. The truck rolled to the outskirts of Cortland, and she slowed. On Main Street, she passed the Downtowner, where she and Del had eaten dinner the night they first made love. Mimi and her husband had stopped by.

Cora drove down the block past the restaurant. She spotted Sentinel Realty sandwiched between a tattoo parlor and an auto parts shop. Mimi's dented Mercedes sat diagonally at the curb. The office windows were partially obscured by two large placards displaying Polaroids of "three-bedroom country cuties" and "historic townhomes." A red-lettered sign posted on the door was turned to the Closed side, but a light inside emitted a blue glow.

Rain began to fall, not tentative drops but a torrent that skipped the overture. When she jumped out of the truck, vengeful sheets of water flowed over the curb and invaded the seams of her boots. At the rattling of the office door, Mimi appeared behind the glass, and, after scrutinizing Cora a moment, used a key on the inside deadbolt. Once Cora stepped inside, Mimi clicked the lock behind her.

53

Cora
July 2000

Cora's nerve endings jumped. Mimi loomed over her; her large feet and hands intruded into Cora's space, stiletto earrings swung much too close. Mimi's eyes were magnified behind a pair of rimless glasses.

"Why are you closed?" Cora said. A persistent sound from the office's fluorescent lights made the air buzz with unrest. She thought again about the fine round shape of a pill in her hand. She longed to sit in a corner where it was dark and quiet.

"I'm writing a counter-offer that was supposed to be sent to a client hours ago." Mimi's keys clashed as she laid them on her desk. She straightened her gold-lettered name plate. "I'm surprised you're up and about. Last time I saw you, you looked like you were headed for long-term treatment."

"I'm better, thanks to psychotropic drugs. No credit to you, by the way, with your little 'surprise.'"

Cora plucked a dead leaf off the drooping philodendron on the receptionist's desk and crushed it between her fingers. The office had the claustrophobic feel of a family forced to downsize from a dream home to an apartment. Mimi and Dick Shafter's desks, constructed of rich, pricey-looking mahogany, were slumming in this small space, squeezed side by side, with barely enough room for a single client chair. Dick's matching name plate peeped out from stacks of manila files, multiple listing books, and a cardboard box filled with decades-old plaques naming him a gold award sales agent.

Mimi opened her laptop. Perhaps as an antidote to her husband, she was ferociously organized, each folder standing at attention in a desk organizer, pencils and pens marching parallel, a bright metal letter opener next to the in-basket, the telephone console squarely aligned.

"I suppose you're here about your mother." Mimi regarded her without blinking, her black pupils large behind her glasses.

"For starters, I'm filing a petition to have you removed as conservator." Until that moment, Cora hadn't given any consideration to assuming control of Alice's care. During the weeks she'd been sick, she'd accepted that her mother was lost to her. Years had passed, every cell in her mother's body had been replaced, and all the beloved landmarks that were Cora's map of her mother had disappeared. Not only the physical woman, but the essence of her—preference, passion, memory, the amalgam that made her Alice Macpherson Brooks—was gone. The woman with swollen knuckles resting on the white sheet was just one poor old thing among millions of sick, demented old people. But Cora's impulsive decision to assume control of Alice's affairs gave her a surge of energy.

Mimi shrugged. "Her case was consuming too much time, anyway."

A slowly accelerating hot flash surged to burn Cora's neck. "I'm sure. One or two hours a week. A trip to Seneca Falls every six."

"There's a lot involved, as you'll soon find out. I doubt you can handle it from the West Coast."

"I'm thinking about relocating here, actually."

Mimi's laptop snapped closed.

"My job in San Francisco has been eliminated," Cora said, "and my son is living in Boston. It's time for a change."

"Winters here are hell. You wouldn't like it."

"My family lived here for generations. I think the climate is in my DNA." Jabs at Mimi were enjoyable, but did Cora really intend to move? The idea was too radical to consider seriously.

Tap, tap. Mimi's long fingernails drummed on the desktop. "There's nothing here for you. A rural community with one little rag of a newspaper."

Cora propped herself against the edge of Dick's desk, dislodging a couple of folders. "If I sell my house in San Francisco, I'll have enough money to buy a place here. With acreage."

"Vineyard around Cayuga Lake, maybe." Mimi waved her hand in the general direction.

"Closer. I was thinking about Maple Leaf Farm." Another stack from Dick's desk shifted as Cora settled more comfortably.

Mimi snatched the armful of files before they fell and tossed them in the safe, whose thick metal door stood open at the rear of the office. "You don't want that farm," she said over her shoulder.

"I think I do, and you're the person to represent me in the sale. Given your history with the property."

"I barely knew the O'Briens."

"Oh, really? With my mother's trailer only half a mile away? And with property you own located just across the road? And here's something else." Cora drew from her jacket pocket the envelope she'd taken from the farm office. She opened the flap and held the charred fragment between her thumb and forefinger.

"Does this look familiar?" Cora asked. "It's a real estate contract. A piece of the one Sean O'Brien signed when he listed the farm with Sentinel Realty."

Rain and wind drummed on the window.

"You little bitch."

"Bitch is good. Thief, not so good. When did you break into the farm office?"

Mimi's breathing was audible in the small space. "I didn't burglarize anybody's office, but what about you? Judith must have locked the place up before she left."

Cora slipped the fragment back in the envelope. "This confirms you were there. Who else would select this particular document? It's of interest to no one—a contract listing property that never sold. This paper could have gone in the shredder without a second's thought on anyone's part."

"I'm not talking."

"You were paranoid about those papers. You wanted them destroyed—or maybe you were looking for something else and came across them."

Mimi picked up the pointed letter opener from the desk.

Cora felt triumphant in a silly, dangerous way. "You're going to stab me? Hardly. That would be so foolish."

The blade tapped Mimi's palm. "You're mentally ill. You attacked me, and I defended myself."

Cora raised an eyebrow. "You think Del is going to buy that story?"

"This is the city. Out of his jurisdiction."

"Put that down. You're not going to do anything." Cora deliberately turned her back, ignoring her heart beating against her breastbone. Mimi had been on the attack since their first meeting at Seneca House. Mimi had befriended Alice as her mother's memory was disappearing into the storm of old age. It seemed likely Mimi had set fire to the remnants of the store to prod a reaction from Cora.

Cora studied the map hanging on the office wall, through which Highway 81 ran from north to south like a thick red artery. In the north, the map seemed to pulse with events and people. Every black vein of road and dot of village swarmed with stories connected to her. Her mother's feet had touched the road right here, where Cora had stood only a few weeks ago. Her grandparents had slept and eaten within the store walls there, just a fingernail from the county line, where soot from the fire had clung to Cora's shoes. Sometime during the last hundred years, her grandparents might have sat in the office visitor chair at the farm.

Cora spoke without turning. "You're still looking for the gold, aren't you? You thought you might be able to pick up some clues in the O'Briens' office."

"The gold is a fairy tale."

"You keep saying that, but you're in trouble. Your business is tanking, and you're ready to grasp at anything." Cora's anger stirred again, and the heat lubricated her thoughts.

"That's what you wanted from Alice—a fact or a clue? You were going to pry something out of her, a poor, daffy woman who lived in a rusty trailer. But she didn't help you, did she?"

Someone thumped on the door glass, and Cora swung around to see Dick, his cheeks screwed up against trickles of rain on his glasses. Mimi let him in. Her face held a look of distaste as Dick shook himself like a muddy Labrador. She relocked the door.

"Sorry I'm late. I waited at the Oak Ave house for three-quarters of an hour, but Renfro didn't show." Water drops scattered as he shook his umbrella and tossed his raincoat on the single visitor chair.

Mimi's keys clattered on the desk. She picked up a fountain pen and scratched a note to herself. "I'll call. See what happened."

Dick dried his glasses with a crumpled tissue and settled them back on his nose. "Hello again, Ms. Brooks." His eyes flicked back and forth between Cora and Mimi, aware, all at once, of the tension.

"I was telling your wife I'm looking for property in the area," Cora said.

"You've come to the right agents. City or rural?"

"Acreage, I think. What about Maple Leaf Farm?"

The lines in Dick's forehead smoothed out. "It would be a fantastic buy. I hear Mrs. O'Brien is motivated."

Cora narrowed her eyes and looked directly at Mimi. "I suppose there's a lockbox, since it's listed."

Dick nodded. "I can take you out now for a look."

"Ms. Brooks is already familiar with the property. She's not a serious prospect." Mimi slammed the safe door, twirled the dial, and switched off the fluorescent lights.

The dim light seemed to blur the couple's outlines, as if they faded into a gray dusk. She felt the weight of the story seep upward from the arches of her feet to her fingers, the tendons in her neck, and the bruised, terrifying places in her brain. She needed to know. The whole thing, Sean, Judith, Mimi and Dick, the Santerra family, Len Crutcher. Her mother. Life depended on it. She couldn't go on, love Nathan or Del or Frieda if she didn't solve it.

She reached across Mimi's desk and snatched the keys. They were ice in her burning fingers. Pressing them tightly into her palm, she rocked on the balls of her feet. "We're not done yet."

Mimi lunged for the keys, but Cora danced between the desks.

"Dick, get them!" Mimi screamed, but he stood rooted to the spot with his jaw dropped in stupefaction.

Cora slipped in a puddle from the umbrella and knocked over a stack of cardboard file boxes. Mimi's hand snapped again for the keys. Cora held them just out of reach. The office was so small, she couldn't stay out of Mimi's way for long.

Cora backed up. Air from the building's air conditioning system blew on her foot. In one quick motion she stuffed the keys through the grate. They rattled down the pipe with the golden sound of rare coins.

No one moved. A gust of wind sent bullets of rain hammering the roof. The smell of Dick's wet blazer grew in the damp, constricted space, and Cora heard the ragged rhythm of Mimi's breathing.

Cora's muscles began to twitch. Sweat popped out on her forehead and upper lip.

Mimi shouted, not at Cora, but at her husband. "For God's sake, your keys."

He tilted his head and surveyed the stains on the composition ceiling. "I ... ah, don't have them."

"You stupid, useless prick." Mimi snatched a heavy paperweight and hurled it past his ear.

"It was raining." Under her bullying, his voice thickened with emotion. "I was trying to get my umbrella up and locked them in the car. That's why I knocked."

"Excellent." Cora smiled, surprised at the unfamiliar feeling in her facial muscles. How long since she'd smiled?

She swept aside a pile of clutter and sat on the dusty surface of the receptionist's desk. "Tell me. All of it."

Mimi twirled her Rolodex and punched a number into the telephone keypad. "Jasper, it's Mimi Shafter. I'm locked inside my office without the key to the deadbolt. How soon can you come?"

Forty-five minutes, probably, before the locksmith arrived. "When did you meet my mother?" Cora asked.

"Go fuck yourself."

"I'm going to petition the court to audit your conservatorship. Find any irregularities."

"I report once a year. They say everything's fine." Mimi twirled her pen between her fingers, and it winked in the light, a coral Bakelite fountain pen with a gold clip on the cap. Cora watched her closely, thinking of the letter opener and the paperweight. All at once, her head seemed too heavy for her neck.

She shrank, become a child again, standing beside the kitchen table, one foot stacked on the other. The table's surface was high, about the level of her chin. Alice bent over her letter, a leg hitched up under her on the chair as if she were ready to leap up at any moment. Her fingers pumped as she moved the coral-colored pen. The gold clip winked in the light. The nib made perfect loops and circles like a song across the page.

"You wormed your way in," Cora said,

Behind the magnified lenses of Mimi's glasses, loathing swam in her eyes. "I introduced myself, learned she was related to Jack and Ruth. Let her know we were shirttail cousins."

"You did more." Cora saw it now. Mimi had stopped by the old blue trailer with a bottle of Cutty Sark, poured it into a couple of mismatched glasses, ignored the smells, dust and mold and unwashed sheets and old clothes, not dirty but saturated with the scent of old skin.

Cora imagined how Mimi must have settled herself carefully into a sagging couch cushion shaggy with pulled threads. Mimi probably leaned forward while Alice talked about her stock of semi-antiques and collectibles in the barn. Mimi offered to recommend Alice's business to her real estate clients while she swirled her liquor and tried to ignore the smears on the glass. And Mimi prodded as skillfully as a surgeon to learn why Alice had returned after sixty years to the place she'd left at eighteen and hadn't visited since. Mimi exploited the last years of Alice's empty life.

But Alice was tough. She'd endured Roy's fists and kept her bruises and broken bones a secret from everyone. After the last terrible beating, shoulders hunched over a broken rib, she'd swept a few items from her desk top into her purse and slid out the back door into the alley. The pen settled in the bottom of her purse among the crumbs and stray pennies.

"You searched her place," Cora said. "At some point, maybe after you were named conservator, you pawed through her things. For some reason, you assumed she knew something about the location of the gold. It had been a legend in the valley for years, when Alice was growing up."

Dick wheeled away from the window, where he was watching cars throw up curtains of rainwater from under their tires. "It was the letters. They started her on the whole stupid search," he said.

"Dick." Mimi's voice was a warning shot.

"We were rehabbing the old house—the Spellman place in the valley—that once belonged to Mimi's grandmother. Thirty years of deferred maintenance before Mimi's dad passed away. Terrible loss of value," Dick said. "Anyway, we were stripping the wallpaper."

"You botched that job, just like everything else."

"The plaster had gotten damp. It fell apart the minute I started peeling the paper."

"I had to pay hundreds, hundreds, to the drywall man. If you'd just waited until the weather got hot," Mimi said.

"You know everything, of course."

"The letters." Cora said. "What about the letters?"

Dick blinked. "Oh. Yes. I was working in one of the bedrooms when I found a packet of old letters hidden behind a loose section of wallpaper."

"Shut up." Mimi's hand trembled as she set the pen on the desk.

"They were in bad condition. Mice had eaten the corners, and it took awhile to read them, what with the faded ink and fancy penmanship."

"You can't resist, spilling it all, can you?" Mimi said.

Dick's face paled, and his skin gleamed with sweat. "It turned out to be correspondence between Mimi's grandmother and another girl in 1917 and 1918."

"Not my mother. She was born in 1918," Cora said.

"It was the two grandmothers," he said. "Your grandmother and Mimi's. They wrote each other when a girl named Abby Macpherson was sent away to California to have a bastard child."

54

Cora
July 2000

Cora heard the story, not from Dick as he told it over the pounding rain, but in her own head. She listened to the thud of a shovel in the damp earth, saw the gleam of gold ingots in the lantern light. She heard Abby Macpherson and Seamus O'Brien whisper and moan, felt mosquitoes pierce their skin, let the dark, liquid song of the nightingale wash over her.

Cora swayed across country in a Pullman car with Abby, who had lost her lover. Cora watched Abby's stomach swell and shook with labor pains. Cora nearly groaned aloud as Abby gave up her baby to be raised by her parents, Jack and Ruth Macpherson.

Dick, of course, slid quickly over the part about Abby's pregnancy and Alice's birth. He stirred the story of the gold like a pile of dog shit.

"Mimi didn't tell me, but I knew. It was the letters that started it. She became secretive. Obsessed with the gold after reading the letters," he said.

Cora squeezed her lids shut. She felt as though she were watching the elliptical orbits of planets as they revolved and intersected. Sometime, probably in her twenties, Alice had traveled west, searching perhaps for Abby Macpherson, her lost mother. And now, in her forties, Cora had traveled east in search of hers.

Cora opened her eyes and slid to the edge of the desk, which dug into her butt. "What happened to Abby Macpherson?"

"She died on the coast. But not before she wrote to Emily Spellman, Mimi's grandmother, the location of the gold. Part of it was still buried under a huge elm tree," Dick said.

Mimi tapped the pen against her cheek. Cora tensed, torn between Dick's story and the sight of her mother's pen between Mimi's pointed fingernails. Dick continued his spiteful monologue.

"Mimi didn't cook, didn't clean, hardly talked. She studied maps. Got thick with that posturing fool, Sean O'Brien." Sweat stained the back of his shirt.

Cora jumped as a knock rattled the front window.

"Jasper! Thank goodness." Mimi tossed the pen on the desk and hurried to the locked door.

Dick didn't turn. "But Mimi, our Mimi who knows every boring little wrinkle of county history, overlooked something."

Jasper spread out his lock picks and coaxed a series of clicks from the deadbolt. The door swung open. Jasper tucked the folded bills Mimi handed him into his wallet.

"I'm turning the pages, Mr. Shafter. Don't stop now," Cora said. "What did she overlook?"

"History. The valley has changed since World War I." He shoved his arms into the balky sleeves of his wet raincoat.

"Farmers began using tractors rather than horses and mules, but the hills were too steep for them. A couple men were crushed when their top-heavy tractors overturned, so farmers stopped growing hay on the hillsides. "

Jasper worked on the lock of Mimi's Mercedes and drove away in his truck. Mimi flicked on her headlamps, which shot narrow beams of light through the office windows. The room abruptly went dark as she backed out of her parking space.

"Small farmers couldn't grow enough hay to feed their cows, and buying hay was too expensive. Mimi's dad was one victim. He sold his milking herd and got a job in town as a janitor. Mimi had to wear hand-me-downs from her cousin."

Cora's fingers flexed. She wanted to be at the keyboard to record every word.

Dick brushed the moisture off his umbrella. "The trees grew back on the hills again, and covered all the hollows. Erased the landmarks. Mimi couldn't find it. She couldn't find the big tree that Abby Macpherson wrote about in her letters."

He patted his pockets. Jasper had left without unlocking his car. "It was as if the land was laughing at her." He sounded full of satisfaction. "As if the hills were saying, 'eat splinters.' Good luck finding what you're looking for."

Evening traffic whipped by; water gushed over the curb and across the sidewalk. Tires tossed up waves of oily, trash-filled water. Thunder shook the roof overhead. Cora was jangled and unsatisfied, as if she'd stopped making love just short of an orgasm. "That's it? Even with the letters, she couldn't find it because the landscape had changed? What about Sean? He was excited the night he died, as if he'd found the location."

Dick didn't answer. He dialed the telephone and waited. "Jasper, it's Dick. Call me back, ASAP. I need to get into my car."

Cora plucked the keys to Del's truck from her backpack. "I'll give you a ride. In exchange for copies of the letters."

He smiled, an ugly display of teeth that lacked any trace of humor. "I'll give you the originals. I can't stand to have them in the house."

Before she left, Cora picked up the pen off Mimi's desk, wrapped it in a tissue, and laid it gently in the front pocket of her rucksack.

55

Cora
July 2000

Cora tripped both locks of Del's pickup, but Dick couldn't seem to open the passenger door. He tapped insistently on the window. Once inside herself, she leaned across the passenger seat to release the latch.

"I tried, but it wouldn't open." He slipped into the seat with a fussy twitching of his coat and umbrella. He seemed completely ineffective at the ordinary tasks of life, and it probably drove his neatnik wife crazy. Cora had written about murders committed with less motive.

The rain spat a few final drops on the windshield, and a streak of yellow light struggled out from a mass of steely cloud. Night was a few minutes away. The radio station, Del's selection, not hers, played a howling lament.

She wondered if Dick had left the office unlocked. He probably should have waited until Jasper arrived to open his car and liberate his key ring. Del's truck inched backward from the parking place, and the stream of headlights on the street scrambled her thoughts for a few seconds. She wanted the letters, letters in her hand. She'd slip them under the pillow in Del's guest bedroom and sleep with them.

The handle of Dick's umbrella clicked nervously against the dashboard. A car honked. The truck lurched as she straightened the wheel. He directed her right, two lefts, then a right, always waiting until the last possible moment to indicate the turn.

"Here," he said. "Pull up in the driveway." He motioned toward a 1970s-era one-story house with two large maples in front. The sidewalk was torn up and a trench split the yard from house to street. "Tree roots invaded the sewer line," he said.

No light showed from the windows. Mimi hadn't come home. "So, what now?" Cora said. She was tired to her toenails. A pill. Its contours would fit so nicely in the palm of her hand. The momentary tightness as it went down her throat would be welcome.

"I'll see if there's an open window." His voice sounded different, and Cora tried to figure out what it was. Deeper perhaps, absorbing complexity from the darkness.

He walked along the side of the house in the dim beam of her parking lights and disappeared around the corner. Two cats sprang from the bushes, racing after him on stiff legs. A red gleam from the sunset was reflected in the large front window.

One of the cats yowled at the back of the house, a long, childlike cry. A shiver rippled through Cora, and suddenly she wanted Del. He didn't answer his cell, so she left a message. "I'm at the Shafter's. Dick is locked out. See ya."

Her wait stretched on. She was rolling down the window to yell to Dick that she was taking him back to town when the porch light snapped on. The front door opened.

"Watch the construction, Ms. Brooks." Dick leaned out the doorway.

Wet dark mud, piled along the gash in the lawn, glistened in the light. Cora wrinkled her nose at the smell. She sidestepped a construction barrier and two shovels to climb the front steps.

Inside, the house was dark except for a glow from the back, in the direction of the kitchen. Dick seemed unaware of the dimness as he stooped to pick up mail scattered under the mail slot and squinted at the envelopes.

"The letters?" Cora said.

He appeared confused, looking at the mail in his hand. "What?

Oh, yes." He motioned her left through an archway into what was once the dining room but now had become a larger version of his desk at the office. A vase of plastic flowers tilted precariously in the center of the table, surrounded by piles of books and magazines, cardboard boxes of business flyers, and three laptops surrounded by a tangle of cords.

He turned on the light, a chandelier with only one of the four flame-shaped bulbs working. The six dining chairs were also full, and he swept an armload from one.

"Can I get you a cup of tea?"

"No. Just the letters."

"Yes, yes. I'll look for them."

Cora eyed the mess on the table and hoped Mimi, rather than Dick, had stored the letters away. He disappeared toward the back, and a thick silence settled over the house. In the dim light, she tiptoed across the main hallway to the living room. It was clearly Mimi's realm, the glass coffee table and two lamp tables clear of litter, couch pillows neatly arranged, vacuum cleaner marks still imprinted on the carpet. Dick's shoeprints disrupted the pattern. Cora returned to the dining room and sank into a chair. No sound from Dick. Maybe he'd gone to bed.

She was about to call out when a cat trotted in and began rubbing its side against the leg of her chair. Cora leaned down to scratch its head. It was a Maine coon cat, short-haired, with orange fur and darker stripes. The cat crouched on its haunches and launched itself into her lap. Cora tried to push it off, but it dug its claws into her slacks. After a couple of turns, it curled onto her thighs, and Cora felt the vibration of its purrs.

She'd never owned a cat. Nathan had a black lab when he was growing up, but it had died about the time Stephen left. As she stroked the cat, fine hairs clung to her fingers and drifted into the air.

Cora's eyes itched, and she rubbed them with the back of her hand. A paroxysm of sneezing seized her, sending the cat to the floor, and Cora scrabbling in her pockets for a tissue.

She was surreptitiously using the edge of the dusty tablecloth when Dick appeared carrying a shoebox under his arm.

"Here they are."

Another sneezing bout struck her. She leaned over her cupped hands.

"There's a powder room just down the hall on the left." Dick put the shoebox on the table.

She switched on the bathroom light, still sneezing, and grabbed a fistful of tissues from the counter. She'd finished wiping her nose when she felt something rub the hem of her slacks. It was the orange cat. With a shake of its head, the feline laid a gift on the floor.

A dead rat, its long, hairless tail curved obscenely on the white tile an inch from her foot.

It was silly to scream. She wouldn't lower herself to such weak, little-girl shit. She looked at the rat's dark whiskers and leathery feet tipped with long claws. A clump of blood had congealed in the fur next to its ear. Laughter rose like vomit in her throat and echoed off the cold white tile and the hard white porcelain sink and toilet.

Dick was there suddenly, more quickly than she'd imagined he could move. With a strong grip on her arm, he led her back to the dining room and set her in the chair.

"Don't move. I'll get you some tea."

Her sides hurt and her face was sopping with tears before the painful heave of laughter subsided. Her hands lay half-closed in her lap, and she flexed her fingers but didn't have enough strength to rub her sleeve across her cheeks.

She felt the same burden of sensory overload as she had at the nursing home: thousands of bits of paper on Dick's table pressed on her, the smell of dust and cat urine lodged in her nose, the beep of the microwave in the kitchen and the yowl of the cat stabbed her ear, salt abraded her eyelids, all of it made her brain swell. Pain throbbed against the bony curve of her skull. Her head drooped with the weight. She rested her cheek on a pile of magazines. Her eyes had nearly closed when Dick returned with two mugs of tea. He set one at her elbow.

"It's good for you. Chinese herbal."

Steam rose from the cup, spicy and faintly medicinal. The ceramic mug had a thin crack in the handle and was decorated with a Santa Claus and Christmas tree. Its heat stung her palm.

He tipped a load of newspapers off another chair and settled himself across the table. "I'm very sorry about the ..." he lowered his voice, "rat incident, but it wasn't my fault. It was the rain. The weatherman forecast rain, and I left the cat door open."

He clasped his hands earnestly in front of him. "We rescued the two of them from the shelter last fall with the idea of taking them to the farm, but we never got around to it. Now we've got nine kittens. The male is probably the one that brought in the rat."

Cora blew on her tea. She remembered the swarm of cats that roamed Santerra Farms, in and out of the shadows around the barns and feed bins. Her hand began to shake, splashing hot liquid on her wrist.

"It's draining, really." As Dick sipped from his mug, he rattled on about their country property. "I try to run a business and keep up with two places. My plan was to improve the farm and sell it as a rural estate. Appeal to the people from Syracuse who want city wages and country lifestyle. But the market's slow. There are no buyers, and we don't have enough money to fix it up the way we want."

Squeezing the mug between her palms, she set it carefully in the center of a magazine pile. "I'm done here, Mr. Shafter."

"No, no." He half-rose, then sank back into his chair. "You're not well enough to drive. That's understandable, considering your recent illness. Plus the incident. Unfortunate. Cats like to show off their prey. Make a gift of it, so to speak."

"It was the cat. The cat and the rat," Cora said.

She reached for the shoe box, which had once held a pair of Ferragamos, and lifted the lid. The smell of a granny-era perfume, sweet like rose or gardenia, made her nostrils twitch.

How few letters were in the box, only eight or ten. She slipped the slim stack of envelopes into her rucksack. Her fantasy of hundreds of juicy letters laying bare the Macpherson family history was left unfulfilled. She riffled through them. The edges had been gnawed by rodents. One was half eaten.

She pressed her forefinger against her lip to keep it still. Small bites. Rodent teeth had ripped words her grandmother wrote and chewed the strip of flap moistened with her grandmother's tongue. She ought to go home to Del now, give him a kiss and tell him everything, but a deep anger welled up. It swept her along, and there was no stopping it.

"I think the night Sean died, Mimi was at her family's farm at the lake," she said. "She and Sean went there a lot, to compare notes, maybe to fuck. It was only a couple of miles from his place, and that night he drove over despite the snowstorm, very excited. Told Mimi he'd discovered some old ledgers containing a diary of Leland's speculations about the gold.

"People had begun to whisper about Sean and Mimi," she continued. "You noticed she was receiving gifts. You searched the Spellman farm and found a small stash of recreational cocaine."

Dick nodded and picked at a sore on his face. "It was that, but she'd done coke before, when business was good. It was more—a smell, a different odor in the laundry basket and on the sheets at the farm. On her underwear. "

Cora watched his hand, the movement on his cheek of fingernails bitten down to the flesh. She forced herself to keep alert, let the story move.

"You'd gotten used to having the cats around the house here in town," she said, "so rather than taking them to the farm to kill the rodents, you bought a commercial rat poison. When you realized what was going on between Sean and Mimi, you reached for the container of strychnine-based poison to cut the coke in Mimi's stash. The stuff she hid at the farm for her and Sean to use."

Cora rose, the rucksack clutched to her chest. "Why Sean? Why not your wife? Did you do it out of jealousy?"

"Jealous? Of that pretentious twit?" Dick stood up, and his tea cup overturned, sending the last of the liquid running over the mess on the table. "Killing Sean was a mistake. Mimi had a cold that night, and her nose was stopped up, so she didn't snort any coke. He used it instead. Mimi lucked out of her own death."

56

Cora
July 2000

Dick stood in the living room doorway between his side of the house and Mimi's. His was dim, filthy, and cluttered. Mimi's was flawless, as though it had been staged for an open house—pillows plumped, dessert tray laid with painted plaster petit fours, rug stiff with parallel vacuum tracks.

"She didn't come home that night. I sat by the window and watched the snow fall. I could hardly wait for morning, when it would be clean and pure, no footprints, no tire tracks, just white, fluffy snow.

"She'd called that night to say she was going to sleep at the Spellman place, but I didn't find out O'Brien was dead until later." He dug at one of the perfect parallel vacuum strokes with his toe. "O'Brien's dead, and he's rotting in his coffin by now. I hope the worms are boring into his flash. But she's still here. I have to listen to her. Hours, days, she talks, yammers, blah, blah, the expert on everything. It's the world according to Mimi, she tells you about how things are in this city, this county, how things have always been."

A confession. Murderers can't help it, a police detective had told Cora once, and over the years, she'd learned he was right. Murderers always told someone. A drinking companion in a deserted bar or a lover in a bed sticky with sex. A crazy reporter in a house stinking of cat piss.

Murderers confess because of the nature of their crime, Cora thought. The snatching of a life—like the birthing of one—is so cataclysmic that even the most amoral and despicable can't stop themselves from spilling it all. Like when she was pregnant with Nathan, and women dumped their childbirth stories on her, despite her efforts to cut them off.

Dick's story tumbled out like a grade schooler's at show and tell. "I made up several bindles. Wrapped them in foil. Meant for her, of course. Stashed them in a Wheaties box at the farm. I knew she hid it there, in the lower right cupboard. Mixed right, the bindles were close by, ready for her. All I had to do was wait."

He rubbed at the vacuum track with his toe, probably the same short angry strokes he used to scrape dog shit off his sole. Pressing the rucksack to her side, Cora inched closer. Dick's upper lip was wet and a drop of perspiration clung to the hair above his ear.

"You can't do it," she whispered.

He didn't answer, but pawed at the carpet, his head lowered between his shoulders. The intensity of the rhythm caught her, his hoarse breath, the beat of laces against his shoe tops.

"If you worked for an hour. Even two, you couldn't rub her out." She was trembling suddenly. The rucksack with the letters tucked inside seemed too big for her hand.

They were nothing alike. Dick Shafter was soft, belly loose over his belt, nails bitten on his white accountant's fingers. He wore suits, starched shirts, a tight necktie squared under his Adam's apple. Her father's arms were muscled from moving huge rolls of paper and repairing the press. At work he wore a pair of navy blue coveralls with a zipper up the front. Roy Brooks's hands were scraped and torn from his daily struggles with machinery. No matter how much he scrubbed, a line of black ink stayed under his thumbnails.

Yet they both were vicious men. Men who'd tried to kill their wives.

She remembered how tense she'd been as a little girl, always searching her father's face for hints of anger. When he told a joke, she responded with wild laughter, trying to delay the moment when he changed. She knew the signs, not bared teeth or clenched fists, but more subtle, a knot of muscle in his cheek, a pinpoint of light in his pupil that hid something terrifying. Alice knew it was coming, too, and she shut Cora in her room.

Pathetic men. Dick, who had endured a thousand verbal jabs from Mimi. He didn't walk away but, like a battered pugilist, stayed while he absorbed a thousand more. Her father, a blue-collar pressman baffled by his wife, with her long, thin fingers and lavender-scented hair. He had greedy longing for all her attention, this Alice who instead bent over her desk writing in her clear, careful hand with a gold-trimmed coral pen.

There was a similarity, she saw it now, Dick peering from behind his glasses, a pinpoint of yellow in the center of his eye magnified in the thick dusty light, his head slung between his stooped shoulders, still digging at the carpet with his hard leather sole.

She heard the blow again as she crouched in the dark childhood closet, the thud of a fist against flesh, a sound so full of degradation and shame it was too much to remember. The blue carpet in the Shafter's living room darkened with the movement of the nap until it was almost black. She swayed and brushed her hair from her eyes.

"I'm leaving, Mr. Shafter." Backing up a foot at a time, she held her breath.

He stopped.

She groped behind her for the cold metal doorknob. A tug didn't budge it. Dick approached, his breathing loud in his throat. She whirled and wrenched the door open.

The porch light was out. Dick's dark form in the doorway blocked the trickle of illumination from the house. She plunged down the steps toward the driveway and Del's truck. She slipped sideways on the wet bricks, dropped her rucksack, and had nearly scooped it up when a fist hit her between the shoulder blades.

She cried aloud. Her feet slid on the mud, and a second hard blow sent her headlong into the sewer trench. Her head smacked against the steep, hard side. Colors flashed behind her eyelids. It was black down there, as dark as a closet with the door closed. As she tried to move a finger or an eyelid, she felt dirt falling. One shovelful after another, onto her face.

57

Del

July 2000

Del checked his cell phone when he got home from work, and listened to Cora's message. It had been hours since the press conference, her first day out of the house. Rain had flooded the streets in some places, delaying evening traffic, and now she was at Dick Shafter's. Why hadn't she driven straight back to his house? What did she want with that flabby little man?

Del clipped his phone back on his belt. He opened a new sack of dog food and poured some into the bowl. Drago didn't eat, but circled Del, stepping on his feet.

From the back window Del saw a lightning flash as the departing storm rolled toward the northeast. He counted the seconds until the thunder came. He touched the weapon holstered under his arm and headed for the car.

He drove fast, but didn't activate his forward reds. Cora might be fine, not in some trouble. His pulse was beating fast as he swung into the Shafters' driveway. There was his own truck, illuminated by his patrol car's headlights, but no silhouette of Cora in the cab. He stepped deliberately from the car, peered through the truck windows. It was empty.

He saw Shafter's gray outline past the circle of headlights. Del rounded the hood of his car, beams catching his pants like a wash of water. He noticed how slowly his eyes adjusted to the dark beyond the lights. Over fifty was shit.

"Evening, Shafter."

"Del."

The air swam with moisture and stank with the odor of sewage. Mosquitoes buzzed around his head, and he waved them away. Damp rhododendron leaves under the front windows shone in a faint glow from the house.

"Rain's stopped." Del edged closer to Shafter's dark silhouette. When his pupils adjusted, Del could see that a trench split the yard from the house to the street. Along the edge, mounds of earth gleamed a fecal brown.

"Quite a storm." Shafter stood on the sidewalk close to the porch. Under his thin hair, his scalp shone like bleached bone.

"Where's Cora?" Del said. The front door stood open, and the contractor had left a shovel lying near the excavation. A power saw, an auger, and a pickaxe were propped against the porch railing under the eaves.

"I was just about to go looking for her. She was here. Drank a cup of tea, but took off running, about ten, fifteen minutes ago. She didn't look too well, if you know what I mean." Shafter's breathing was raspy.

"Which way?" A makeshift bridge of slimy wooden planks creaked under Del's weight as he crossed the ditch. He noticed a section of the trench closest to the house had partially caved in.

Shafter blinked, as if trying to comprehend.

"Which direction?" Del moved impatiently, brushing against wet bushes, which spewed a shower of drops on his pants cuff. When he glanced down, he saw a rucksack with a padded strap lying half-hidden in the foliage.

"Oh, yes. Toward Union."

Del rotated his head slowly from side to side. In addition to the smell from the sewer, there was something else, sharp and acid. His eyes narrowed. Shafter's shirt was soaked with sweat. Mud caked his shoes. The wet earth in the cave-in glistened as if it had been recently expelled from the earth's troubled bowels. A cave-in.

In one swift motion, Del whipped his gun from its holster and slammed the butt on Shafter's head, just over his left ear. The stocky man collapsed like a sack of cement dropped from a truck.

Del raced to his car. He snatched the radio microphone and screamed his location to dispatch. His feet slipped on the mud as he crashed back across the plank bridge, grabbed the castoff shovel, and leaped down into the narrow trench. It was deep, more than eight feet, and the muddy walls arched over his head to trap him.

He hacked at the dirt, his arms pumping, his heart swollen until it threatened to rip open his chest. He tore the skin off his knuckles trying to work in the narrow tunnel. After a minute he threw the tool aside and clawed with his hands at the wet, stinking mass.

His shoulders barely fit between the sides, and mud oozed into his shoes. Perspiration dripped into his right eye, and he rubbed it with the point of his shoulder to clear his vision.

Five minutes. How long could she last without air? How long had he stood there talking to that asshole? How long had he been tearing at the wet, gluey dirt? A part of his brain was counting the seconds as he cursed, scrabbled, threw mud over his shoulder.

Not after all this time. Not like this, not in this shithole, not because he took a walk on the O'Brien investigation, not when she's just found herself, when she's found her mother, please. His prayer filled his brain, seeped into his bloodstream at the same time the clock ticked down.

He didn't hear the sirens, didn't see the lightening of the narrow vein of sky overhead, didn't see faces peering over the edge, just grabbed the scrap of cloth under his fingers and hauled with every fiber of muscle and bone. She popped loose with a suck of wet earth.

———

"I should've run," Del said. "That first day, when I spotted you in the lobby, I should've sprinted out the door." He paused in drying himself to snap his towel at her.

"It's only twice since you've known me that I've been covered in stinking, filthy shit. Not such a big deal." Cora lay on his bed, a raw, angry scrape on her forehead and her skin so pale it made him hurt.

"My car's full of dirt. Upholstery's a mess. Again." The odor of soap and moist air from the shower followed him.

"Don't tell me a little pig shit or some sewer mud is the worst that's ever touched your precious upholstery. What about drunks puking in the back seat?"

"I'm the boss. I don't do drunks."

She shook her long, wet hair, and a few cool drops landed on his face. "You should be thanking me."

"Why?"

"A lot of men dream of a dirty woman in their car."

"There's that." Del tossed his towel on the chair and sank down beside her on the sheets. She was naked, her thighs and butt flaccid from lost weight, her breasts smaller. He touched the wrinkled skin of her upper arm and rubbed it slowly. He remembered comforting Tyler this way when the boy was seven or eight and had woken up with growing pains.

She pushed a second pillow behind her shoulders. Her fingers relaxed and curved over her palms. Her lips drooped as if her jaw were too tired to close. Her eyes moved quickly under half-closed lids.

"What about Dick?" Her voice slowed as the pill took effect.

"Booked on suspicion of attempted murder. It's the city's case, but since I know the chief and the DA, it'll probably be turned over to another agency to prevent conflict of interest."

She smiled. "Good decision on the city's part."

"I hope the case doesn't get screwed up. I want Shafter convicted, sent to prison, and double-celled with a three-hundred-pound, body-building pervert."

He climbed off the bed, unable to relax. His cock was half-erect, and his skin prickled with outrage. The hospital had examined

Shafter and released him to Cortland police with a slight concussion. Damn weakass swing. He should've caved in that fucker's skull.

When he'd pulled her out, she wasn't breathing. She'd been buried under five feet of stinking mud, mud in her mouth, mud in her nostrils, mud sucking at the soft substance of her eyes.

He'd lifted her out—sweat dripping off his face, his clothes soaked, his shoes caked—up to EMT's who gave her CPR and restored her breathing almost immediately. When they tried to slip the oxygen mask over her face, she was seized with claustrophobia and struck it away.

Once she was on the gurney, he stumbled. His legs buckled, and he sank onto the steps. Flashing emergency lights filled his eyes with bloody red. Sewer gas saturated the air, and the staccato squawks of police and ambulance radios made him flinch. She was released after a thorough checkup and X-rays at the emergency room.

"Relax. I'm only slightly brain damaged." Cora turned her head to watch him pace.

The bedroom was hot, and he felt as though he, too, were suffocating. He breathed fast, trying to get more air. Once she was safe, he saw the steps he'd taken that led to the stinking trench: his cowardly investigation of O'Brien's death, his failure to treat the O'Brien house as a crime scene, his subtle hints to Neville to declare it a suicide, his tardy follow-up on Santerra's autopsy, his lapse in not investigating the Shafters, not checking his cell phone earlier, and not speeding to their house Code 3.

"I should've put it together quicker. Now it's probably too late to charge Shafter with first-degree murder for O'Brien death. Too much evidence lost."

"True."

To get some air, he tried to open the window wider, but it was stuck.

"You never should have gone to the press conference," he said. "It was too soon after your breakdown. I told you, but you didn't listen."

"If I hadn't gone, we might never have known."

"I'd have figured it out, damn it." He whacked the sash's underside with his fist. The window jerked upward with a crackling of dried paint.

"I'm not blaming you," Cora said.

"You should."

"I'm done with blaming. You did what you had to."

"If I'd only pushed the investigation, there might have been evidence. Mimi's drug dealer, maybe, or some remnants of the coke at the Spellman place, or fingerprints on the baggie Shafter wrapped it in. A receipt for the rat poison."

Cora turned onto her side, her body curved toward him. "Forget it. Think about the three-hundred-pound pervert. That, and the story I'm going to write."

He sat beside her. "We can't use his confession to you. It's hearsay."

She took his hand in hers and held it away from her, surveying the damaged fingers. He hunched his shoulders as if a blow were coming. Instead, she kissed each finger, touching them with her tongue, licking the scars and rough stumps.

He bowed his head with the pleasure and forgiveness of that touch, and some of his guilt eased away. She kissed his palm. He traced the thin blue skin on her eyelids, the small lines around her mouth, the softening under her chin. Lamplight highlighted the fine gold strands in her hair.

When her legs opened he moved over her. She raised her hips and he slid inside. They moved awkwardly, bumping noses and clashing elbows, all the residue of fear, tension, and remorse coming between them. They looked at each other for a moment in surprise, remembering the last time, when they had seemed to anticipate the other's rhythm in their muscles and tissues.

She laughed. He laced his fingers into her hair, cupped her head between his hands, and moved more leisurely now, small frictions, slow delvings, long kisses with lots of tongue, and they sank into each other, melting under a concentrated fire. Her hair glittered around her head and as he came he thought of gold, his treasure here under his hands.

———

When he awoke, he knew it was late. The sun had stopped creeping around the window shades and had made its way south. He reached for Cora, but her side of the bed was empty. Water ran in the bathroom sink, and after a few minutes Cora came out, wearing a pair of white cotton panties.

"Come back to bed." He shifted to ease his morning hard-on and turned down the sheet.

"Not this morning. I've got work to do."

"Give it a rest."

She reached behind her back to fasten her bra. "This is going to be a great story. *The New Yorker*, I think. That's where I'm going to pitch it."

"You can't publish a story without a guilty plea or jury verdict. You might get sued."

"Not a chance," she said.

"What, you're immune?"

"Better than that. I've got the evidence."

"Shafter's confession? He'll deny he ever said it."

She looked at him out of the corner of her eye.

"What?" he asked.

"After the press conference, I stashed my mini recorder in my jacket pocket. When he started talking, I clicked it on. I've got the whole thing on tape."

58

Cora
July 2000

They sat at the kitchen table for awhile. Out the window, shredded leaves and broken branches littered Del's yard, ripped from the trees by yesterday's storm. The damage, plus news reports of downed power lines and a freeway pileup, reminded Cora of the aftermath of a war. Perhaps it was. She ached from Shafter's stunning blow on her back, and she was covered with gestating bruises on her arms and legs that tomorrow would look like bad meat.

She should have been depressed by the destructive nature of weather and humans, but instead she was oddly energized. Bits of Dick's confession exploded in her brain like bursts of light, and she felt the story in her fingertips. It was going to be a winner.

Del called a handyman to come out with a truck and chain saw; then he scrambled three eggs and forked them absently from his plate while he read the front page story in the *Cortland Standard*, "Local Broker Arrested in Attack."

"Good. They didn't mention me." He turned to the jump page.

"Too bad. 'Somer Saves Journalist' might win you a promotion."

"A headline like that would likely cost me my career. The department loves to hate journalists."

Cora pushed aside her coffee cup. She flipped open her laptop and got out her mini-recorder. "What'll you do when charges are filed in the O'Brien case? The publicity is going to be bad, especially after the Troop C scandal—that's going to come back, you know."

He folded the newspaper carefully. His hands were scratched and nails torn from the previous night's rescue. "If I get lucky, he'll plead guilty. If it goes to trial, I'll take my lumps. I deserve it, and I'm not going to blame the screwup on someone else, like Neville."

Del looked beautiful in that moment: his cheeks were firm and smooth from the razor, his gray hair crisply trimmed above his collar, his torso solid and safe. He gazed steadily at her across his eggy plate and the mugs of cold coffee. He knew Tyler was safe, and now he'd take responsibility for his failings in the O'Brien investigation. She felt a movement inside her. It was as though a story were gathering momentum, creating an opening for something new.

The cerulean glaze on the coffee mugs, the clean wash of light through the window blinds, the comfortable groan of the house as it warmed in the sun, Drago's soft whining at the back door, all seemed so fresh and full of possibility. Maybe she could do this love thing.

She reached out and ran her fingertip across the back of his hand. His shirt rose and fell with the slow movement of his breathing. After a moment, he encircled that one finger with his hand and shook it gently, as if he were introducing himself.

He sighed. "I've got to go to work."

He put the truck keys on the kitchen table. "You going out? Should I put troopers on alert?"

She laughed, then winced at the soreness in her ribs. "Nothing's going to happen. I'm spending the day transcribing the tape."

"Why am I not reassured?" Del scratched Drago under the chin and picked up his briefcase. "You've got to turn over the tape to police, you know."

"Tomorrow. You forgot your hat."

"I'm going low profile today."

"And your gun."

"Jesus. I'll get popped on the way to work." He threaded his arms through the shoulder harness.

Through the window, she saw his car weave a serpentine path down the driveway to avoid the debris. When he reached the road, the engine's throb deepened, and she knew he'd be over the speed limit within a quarter of a mile.

She pushed the dishes away to clear space and clicked the recorder on. The voices unreeled, slightly distorted, but recognizable. Dick's had always sounded meek and submissive, but now she caught a dark, hot undercurrent. Why hadn't she noticed it earlier? She tapped a few sentences into the laptop, but every word contained a typo. Her fingers were keying in some other story.

Traffic noise from the road rose and ebbed, and the ceiling fan blew air in her face. After a few minutes, she snapped off the recorder. She opened the rucksack police had fished out from under the Shafter's rhododendrons and withdrew the letters.

The yellowed, brittle envelopes were smeared with mud. Eight letters. Mailed when it was still the U.S. Post Office, not the Postal Service. The one-cent stamps were imprinted with a bewigged George Washington. She arranged them by postmark, the dates and times still dark and legible. The first was mailed August 29, 1917, the last, February 27, 1918.

She spread the sides of the first envelope along the slit in the top. The scent of old perfume that had clung to the paper last night was gone. Inside were two letters, both folded into thirds. Her heart beat fast and the aches in her back and neck disappeared. She unfolded one, but the paper closed again along the old, old creases, reluctant to divulge its secrets. With the heel of her hand, she flattened it on the table. "My Dearest Cousin Emily," it began.

When she was finished reading all of them, her face was sticky with tears. As she scrubbed them away with the back of her hand, her cell phone rang.

"Hello," she said unsteadily.

"Del called me this morning so I wouldn't read it in the paper. You sound terrible," Frieda said.

"I'm sore and bruised, Frieda. It hurts, but I'll heal." Cora searched unsuccessfully for a tissue, and settled for one of Del's cloth napkins.

"You've been crying."

"I've been spilling quite a few tears lately. Last time I saw you, as a matter of fact. "

"Well, salt water is a great remedy—used for centuries to heal burns and wounds."

Good old Frieda, the Band-Aid. Cora smiled. It felt pleasant. She reminded herself to try it again soon.

"I'm baking pies tomorrow for the bishop's visit to the church," Frieda said. "I could teach you how to make strawberry rhubarb."

"Is rhubarb as disgusting as it looks?"

"Just you wait, Miss Smarty. I defy you to stop at one piece."

———

Utica Acres hadn't changed since her last, dimly remembered visit. Why hadn't adult diapers eliminated nursing home stench? She breathed shallowly as she passed the common room. A couple of residents were propped in front of the wide-screen TV.

She pushed open the door to Alice's room, where the odor was underlain by a vigorous whiff of Lysol. Get over it, she told herself. This was her mother, who had probably changed Cora's wet diapers five thousand times when she was an infant.

The bed rail clattered as she leaned across it. Alice's physical presence seemed to have receded since Cora's last visit. Her eyes were deeper in their sockets, and her lips shrank back against her teeth. Light filtered through the blinds. The imitation leather armchair, the brown wheeled tray table, and the flower print on the wall were insubstantial. Beyond the closed door, the lunch trays rattled softly as they were stacked on the cart. There was no tray at her mother's beside. A glucose drip passed through a needle taped to the back of her hand.

"I have a secret to tell you." Cora found herself whispering.

Alice's breath trembled through her open mouth.

"Over eighty years ago, there was a girl who lived in the Otisco Valley, barely into her teens, who was in love with her neighbor. He was a handsome man, a bit of a swaggerer perhaps, with red hair and an Irish brogue. This was during World War I, when Ireland was struggling to free itself from England. The Irish farmer was part of a group secretly gathering gold in the U.S. to fund the rebels."

A strange bedtime story, but with all the right elements: prince and princess, treasure, weakness, forces of darkness. The sun illuminated the room with brief flashes when the elm's branches moved restlessly outside the window. Alice's eyes were fixed on balls of dust that fluttered from the air conditioning vent high on the wall.

"Our girl discovered the plot, and the Irish laddie seduced her, partly to keep her quiet, and who knows, perhaps because he cared for her a little bit. No matter, he was a fornicator and statutory rapist and today he'd be jailed. She got knocked up, but refused to name him as the father."

Cora leaned closer, a foot or so from her mother's ear. "Here's the interesting part. The girl was sent away with her mother to San Francisco to have the baby secretly. The child was born, and the teenager relinquished her little girl to her own mother to be passed off as her parents' baby.

"The teenager named her baby Alice."

Alice seemed to make a decision at the end of each breath whether to take another. Her lips were dry and chapped. Cora plucked a tube of ChapStick from her purse, rubbed some on her fingers, and stroked it on Alice's mouth. A prickle ran up her arm. It wasn't that she recognized anything about her mother. Age had long ago stolen the shape of her face, her chin, the set of her eyes, any physical clues that might have created a thread of connection. But this touch was familiar, and Cora had a brief recollection of Nathan putting a baby finger on her lips, fascinated by the movement of her mouth.

"And then ..." Cora was interrupted by louder voices and footsteps from the hall. She peered over her shoulder to see Mimi.

The real estate agent's porcupine hairdo had lost its spike and clung greasily to her head. Her ear lobes looked stretched and fleshy without her trademark earrings. A wrinkled blouse was misbuttoned.

A sour taste arose in Cora's mouth. "You're the last person I expected to see."

"I knew you'd be here, after you got your hands on the letters." Mimi's hand trembled on the doorknob.

Alice, who hadn't made a sound while Cora was speaking, gave a soft cry at the sound of Mimi's voice.

"Thirteen million, that's what it would be today. Thirteen million would solve everything—pay Dick's lawyer and give me the cash for a new life. Florida, maybe, where real estate is good."

"You want to pay a lawyer to defend your husband for killing your lover?"

Mimi's eyes shifted, coming to rest on the fake leather chair. "We never had an affair. That was one of Dick's twisted imaginings. He's a very sick man."

There's only a finite amount of gold on earth, Cora thought, as opposed to bullshit, of which there is an unlimited supply.

"When you read the letters, did you see anything? A hint, a secret message? If we find it, we could split whatever we get."

"I think my grandmother was good at secrets," Cora said. "The baby's father, the whiskey still. She kept both."

"It wasn't much of a secret. Everyone drank Jack Macpherson's whiskey. Even today, the old-timers talk about it."

Her mother uttered a small grunt.

Mimi glanced at Alice, whose mouth was open and eyes closed. "If that ever happens to me, I'm putting a bullet in my ear."

"I'm curious," Cora said. "Was it you that burned the remains of the store?"

Mimi ran her tongue over her teeth. "It was my property. I purchased it for back taxes after I became Alice's conservator. She hadn't paid the county anything for years."

"But why set the place on fire? It could have burned the neighboring house."

"I'm not saying I did."

Cora raised the hem of her shirt to expose her midriff. "No hidden recording devices. What would a person gain by torching the pile of debris?"

"A new, unknown quantity might have appeared on the scene. A person might want to stir things up. See what the reaction might be."

"You didn't get much, did you?"

Mimi shrugged. "Well, Cousin, if you have any unexpected insights, my offer holds." Her flip-flops slapped against her dirty heels as she went down the hall.

Cousin. Wouldn't you know. She had lived her whole adult life with no relatives except Nathan, who wanted only to be with his pierced girlfriend, only to discover her poor, dying, brainless mother and a cousin who was a liar, a thief, and an adulteress. The four of them: Cora, Nathan, Alice, and Mimi. Their double helixes, their purposeful strands of DNA, were so closely related that scientists could trace them back for thousands of generations. Is there any thread, she wondered, other than a brew of chemicals, that binds families from one generation to another? She could conjure up a visual resemblance, but it was all in her imagination, a twitch of the eyebrow or curve of the cheekbone that proved this was her mother. She had no legacy from her mother: no skill at needlework or musical talent, not a single Scottish story or recipe for bannock, whatever that was.

While she was rolling these thoughts around, someone came in, not Mimi, but a nurse aide smelling of cigarettes and wearing a scrubs-type uniform and rubber-soled shoes. Cora recalled dimly this was Sandy, the employee who'd been a witness to her brainiac meltdown.

"How's my old gal?" Sandy's voice was loud enough to reach Alice seven feet under. She took Alice's blood pressure, attached a new bag of glucose, and measured the urine in her catheter bag.

"The daughter, right?" Sandy stopped with her pen in midair over a chart.

Cora nodded. As simple as a bob of the head, and Alice was hers. It had taken a nod and an "I do" to marry Stephen, that adulterous bastard, and this was less. Less, and so much more.

"She's not excreting much fluid," Sandy said. "Makes me wonder how her kidneys are doing."

"Very little time, then."

Sandy turned Alice over and rearranged a pair of sheepskin booties over her heels. "Probably, but you never know. Bye, Alice. See you later."

Alice lay on her side, the bedclothes tucked neatly around her shoulder. A hush settled over Utica Acres, and Cora heard the rumbling engine and undulation of a train somewhere nearby. How far their search had taken the two of them, her and Alice. Her mother had felt the emptiness early. Something missing, an ulcerous need, chewed at her gut. When had she learned Abby was her real mother? As a teen, perhaps. Alice rode the train west, unknowingly or knowingly tracing the path Abby had taken twenty years earlier. Alice had married a man who failed to fill her emptiness.

Neither had Stephen filled Cora's.

She pulled a chair up to the bedside and reached through the bars of the railing to smooth Alice's hair back from her forehead. "We might not get another chance, so listen up."

Abby's last letter was written on the same brittle paper as the others, but the *r*s were cramped and *y*s were inked at painful angles. Cora swallowed.

February 27, 1918

Dearest Emily,

My little girl was born Feb. 19, five weeks early. She is a tiny thing, hardly as heavy as a bag of sugar, with a head full of soft hair. I secretly cut a few strands and I'm enclosing them in this letter. See how they shine in the lamplight? She smelled so sweet, like a warm bed on a winter night. When she lay against my bosom, she was completely limp, as if this place against me was her favorite on earth.

Too soon, I had to give my Precious One to Mama, who has assumed her complete care. I have named her Alice, a light, pretty name, like translucent silk.

I know now how mistaken I was to give her over to Mama. She is not thriving, crying day and night. Each sob is a stab of love in my heart. I could stop her cries, but I promised Mama I would not interfere.

The future looks very dark. Food tastes bad. My skin is so sensitive I can hardly wash myself. Her cries fill me, and all I can see is Mama, Mama, everywhere I look, in every corner, beside my plate, beneath the coverlet at night. I know as well as I know every stone between my house and yours that Alice yearns for me, as well. She also may ache for Seamus, her own True Papa, but she doesn't long for him as I do, in my lips and breasts and privates.

Does this shock you? I apologize, but I am so alone, I must share with someone what is in my body and mind.

You are very far from me now, my dearest friend, three thousand miles by land, and an eon in brutal experience, but still close in my heart until I leave this earth.

My deepest love and friendship,
Abby

Cora's salty tears flowed. She dampened her fingers in them and stroked her mother's face.

———

Later, her eyes filled again as she spooned cheese and onions on a serving of Del's chili. He and Frieda already had eaten, and he rinsed their empty bowls.

"I brought you something," Frieda set a pink plastic bag on the tabletop. "Guaranteed to repair years of neglect to your skin."

"Good luck," Cora said between bites.

It was ten o'clock. Del had ridden his mower over the lawn, and scent of evening and cut grass drifted through the open windows like the first sweet beginnings of a story, when the idea trembled at the edge of her mind. She gulped some ice water while Frieda continued to harangue her about moisturizing. Drago lay hot and panting on her feet, and Del sat down beside her and draped his arm across her shoulder. Tyler was being released in a couple of days. She imagined him across from her, gobbling huge portions and drinking gallons of milk. He'd have that sullen look that sixteen-year-olds have, which in two years turns to geniality, almost a sly flirtatiousness. She imagined Nathan, too, down for the weekend, his big feet planted wide apart and his beard dark on his cheeks. Shanley, perhaps. No, not Shanley.

"But that wasn't the interesting part." Del was saying. "The fascinating thing was, the storm uprooted a huge old tree about a mile from Plato Crossroad. Hammond Wright owns the property— used to be an old wood lot decades ago."

Frieda nodded. "The Macphersons owned it at one time."

Del raised his eyebrows. "Anyway, Wright called our investigator. An old shed had been smashed to kindling by the tree, and a huge hole opened up where the tree roots had ripped out of the soil."

Cora sopped up the last of the chili with a piece of bread. "Please tell me you discovered the thirteen million in gold."

"Nope. It was a skeleton, flesh decomposed, some shreds of clothing. Strands of hair."

———

Author's Note

In 1994, *New York Times* reporter Lindsey Gruson wrote a story about the apparent suicides of two prominent cattle breeders, one in Maryland and one in rural New York's Finger Lakes region. They were puzzling deaths, Gruson wrote, possibly linked to insurance fraud, but suicide seemed an exaggerated response for relatively minor offenses. If there were hidden truths, they eluded Gruson and law enforcement investigators.

Gruson's story gave me a gift: the inspiration for *Thread of Gold*. My great-grandparents owned farms in Finger Lakes' Otisco Valley in the 1800s; my grandmother taught school there at the beginning of the twentieth centry; and together she and my grandfather ran a country store that sold everything from pickles to pickaxes.

Thread of Gold is a work of fiction. I've taken some liberties with the geography, but I hope the text reflects my love for the rich history, steep green hills, and fascinating people of the Otisco Valley.

Acknowledgements

I am grateful to all those who helped and encouraged me over the years as I wrote *Thread of Gold*. Daniel and Lois Casale gave me a comprehensive tour of their dairy farm in Denair, California. John Wilson, then an officer with the California Highway Patrol's Drug Recognition Evaluation Program, helped me understand the effects of various drugs. Dr. Bob LaPerriere, curator of the Sierra Sacramento Valley Medical Society's Museum of Medical History showed me around his fascinating facility and educated me on medical practice in 1917. The Cortland County Historical Society told me about Ft. Dix. The late Thomas Constantine shared his deep knowledge of the New York State Police. Jay Schaefer's input inspired me to put Alice to work in the shipyards. Eagle-eyed editor Dorine Jennette worked her magic on the text and boosted my morale. The cover is the work of designer and fellow writing retreat attendee Karen Phillips. CSU, Sacramento Professor Doug Rice advised me on a chapter about Abby. I can't say enough good things about my tough and loving writing companions in Nevada City, Sacramento, and Davis, California, especially Donna Hanelin, Virginia Kidd, Barbara Link, Dorothy Place, and the amazingly generous Scott Evans. My mother, Jean MacDonald Seitz, and aunt, Clara MacDonald Mowitz, provided dozens of lovely details about their childhood in the Otisco Valley. Thanks and love go to early readers Joan Seitz and Carol Mowitz, to my children, Brad, Patrick and Rebecca, and always, to Tony.